EARTH IS OURS
BOOK 1

Gary W. Babb

EARTH IS OURS
BOOK 1

DOUBLE DRAGON

DEDICATION

I am dedicating this book to my family and close friends for the strong support they have provided. It is very encouraging to have the pages taken from the printer and requested e-mails daily to follow the story. I owe them much for the encouragement.

I also want to thank those in my inner circle that have read my story and offered their encouragement and support. Your positive comments helped me greatly.

Special thanks goes to Sybil who labored through my many drafts with me and threatened bodily harm to me if I didn't finish the story and continue it in the sequels.

CHAPTER 1
(THE BATTLE RAGES)

* Levi *

How much pain could he stand? At what intensity would he pass out? Would he be dead as his flesh was ripped from his body? Levi mused as he stood on the rocky hill overlooking the aliens gathered in the hot desert valley below. From a distance the Simians' long golden hair glistened, giving the appearance of a vast rolling field of ripe wheat; however, he felt little comfort from the misleadingly gentle scene below. He felt like a lost child, as he reluctantly started toward them.

As he approached the aliens, the tranquil scene slowly transformed into a vision of horror. The only seemingly earthly illusion to their features was a slight resemblance to apes, which initially led to the popular acceptance of the name Simians. After that hint of earthly association, their appearance turned utterly alien. The Simians' sandy, almost dirty white skin could be seen unnaturally contrasting with their golden hair. Red reptilian eyes held him in an unblinking stare. Rows of black, fanged teeth reflected the midday sun, and upon closer inspection, appeared almost shark-like. The triangular teeth made a ghostly clicking sound as they vibrated together, interlacing like meshing gears. In their agitation, the black teeth were not completely covered by their meaty gray lips, allowing the reverberating sound to escape. A loud chorus of the eerie clatter emanated from the hundreds of gathered Simians. The sound echoed throughout the valley, straining the ears and nerves of the Human army. He could feel the vibration, but the sound disturbed him most. Ironically that sound reminded him of a rattlesnake's warning rattle, ironic also in the danger they represented.

Respect for "Levi the Legend" was readily apparent, as the churning golden sea of Simians nervously parted allowing him to pass. They hopped in excitement on their thick legs, communicating in that high-pitched screeching. He sensed no immediate threat from them and continued walking through the forest of towering Simians toward the waiting Gord. Levi hoped his fear did not show, while his insides shook and fear screamed in his ears. He asked Amy telepathically, "Are you with me? I don't want to be alone."

Amy softly responded, "I am always with you Levi. You are never alone."

"I know Amy. I just feel alone."

As he approached, watching the hulking Gord, his eyes missed nothing. Amy gathered data from his senses and planned. She would also detect the fear boiling inside, threatening to explode.

He accepted the one-on-one challenge screeched from Gord, the Simian leader. The Humans were losing the battle and he really had no choice. Had he refused, the Human army would be destroyed and all hope for the Human race would be lost. At least this way they had a fighting chance, slim as it was. It was all or nothing, live or die.

The Simian's code of honor would ensure that this fight would be a fair, one-on-one contest. Of this he was confident, but what a joke; this Simian, Gord, would almost make three of him! "Hell Amy, I 'm already overmatched. This is the biggest damned golden giant I have ever seen."

"That may be so, but there are two of us, and we have him outnumbered!" Amy then flashed a smile in his mind.

He chuckled in spite of the situation, but it still didn't seem fair ... to him! If, however, he could defeat this undisputed Simian leader, his colony would be in chaos. Who knows what could come from that, maybe even survival for the Human race, certainly no less was at stake! The only problem was surviving!

He was Levi Walkingbear, Native American Indian. Well, half anyway, and he walked proudly, holding back the fear churning inside. He tried to appear brave for the benefit of all the Humans, his army and for the gathered Simians. Strength, courage, and fighting abilities were all that mattered to the Simians. It ruled their society and governed their numbers; certainly, Gord ruled this horde of giants in this way.

* Gord *

Gord wanted to destroy this animal slowly and feed on its pathetic screams. He happily watched the animal approach. He had killed uncounted scores of animals such as this one for both food and pleasure, preferring to eat them while they yet lived. He relished in the horror he inflicted on the animals, but this one would die slow and painful for all to see.

9

He stared at this stupid animal! Its body was hairless except for the head, which had long black hair braided down its back. The hairless skin was bronze from this world's horrid single sun. The eyes were also bronze like the skin and stared directly into his. This lack of respect offended him, but disrespect would end soon. Its body was muscular, but very small, hardly half the size of an average Simian. He observed strong muscles rippling under thin skin on its exposed arms. Loose animal skin covered the body, supported by straps over its small shoulders. The narrow feet were covered with heavy looking black animal skin, and it carried a small sword extending no longer than its arm. This was humorous!

Gord released his challenge in a strong loud screech! Unfortunately, this indigenous race lacked the intelligence to understand their speech. He wished he could, to tell this animal what he intended to do to him. He wanted to see the terror in its small bronze eyes as he ripped him apart.

Since the exodus from the dying home world of his race and invasion of this planet, each surviving spaceship became an independent colony with autonomous leadership. He ascended to the leadership position of his colony by combat and remained in control by successfully defending the position from all future challengers. This had been easy for him, because of his exceptional size and fierce aggressiveness. Gord, a giant among giants, stood a head above other Simians at just over three Arms (9 feet) and weighed twenty-three measures (575 lbs). During his rule over the last forty years he had killed fifteen Warriors in single combat challenges for his leadership position. With the average life span for his species at two hundred of this world's seasons, he was still very much in his prime at only seventy-five seasons. His rule could easily last decades more.

The animal army was nearly defeated but Gord refrained his warriors. He wanted to personally destroy this animal in single combat to reinforce the fear he commanded over his colony. No one had challenged him in more than ten seasons, and he desired to recapture and reinforce the respect of his colony. How could he do that if no one fought him? Of course, no challenger stood a chance, and most even openly cowered in his presence, but he wanted to show off. Gord loved to force his will on others and see the panic; he fed on this fear. The entire colony of six hundred Warriors gathered to witness his slaughter of this stupid animal. He would toy with him, defeat and humiliate him, and tear and eat his body as the animal screamed in horror in a slow death. Next, he would complete the destruction of the pathetic animal army.

He granted this animal the respect and honor of fighting for leadership of the colony in front of his Warriors to dispel any misguided respect given to this animal by his Warriors. They would see how futile resistance was to his will. Of course this Human had no chance, but rumors of this animal's victories had spread throughout his colony, and he wanted the rumors of his victories to die along with this animal.

The native dominant species animal of this world was small, weak, and good only for food and minor labor. The species had once possessed great technology that had almost stopped their invasion, but his race had destroyed that technology by use of a doomsday ray. The ray destroyed all technology on this world instantly including their own, but he had little use for technology, preferring swords to lasers. Since the destruction of all advanced technology, no animal had ever again posed any threat. This one had been the only exception in the fifty years since their race landed. According to rumors, this animal had killed at least thirty-five Warriors in combat in the last few months. His Warriors were actually showing respect to this animal. Unbelievable!

* Levi *

As he neared Gord, Levi felt the calming telepathic touch of Amy, his symbiotic source of life and soul mate. Amy existed as a self-aware (living) computer who had shared his mind telepathically for the last year. She provided the means to wage this war with the Simians and extract some measure of revenge he so desperately wanted. Amy had augmented his decrepit and dying eighty-year-old body and reversed his aging. Not only did he now enjoy restored youth, but she had also given him incredible physical abilities. Amy functioned through his conscious and subconscious mind to manipulate his DNA to adjust and control his body like musician might play a piano. He really didn't understand how she did what she did, but it worked.

Over the last year he had experienced the exhilaration of superhuman skills and abilities he hadn't learned or could have ever imagined. What a rush! Amy wouldn't admit, it but he believed she shared, and liked, his rush of emotions when he fought. Human emotions were new to Amy and she was hungry to experience them through their mental contact.

Levi fought many of these Simians in the last year. Mostly, he had fought just to survive, but they now openly waged war against them. All the engagements had been hard-fought battles. The Simians were enormous and extremely quick, but Amy was with him as he fought. Hell, she actually did the fighting, while he felt the exhilaration and, unfortunately, the anguish and pain of battle. He made the physical movements, but the ideas and plans flowed telepathically from Amy. So far he had obviously survived, but this would be the ultimate battle and he felt a premonition that he might feel the bite of death.

The closer Levi got, the larger Gord seemed to loom in his sight and the greater his fear grew. The quivering in his chest and thighs grew stronger, and he began to perspire. He seldom experienced fear and struggled to control it. He tried thinking of Amy.

Amy once told him that she had taken his body to the ultimate limits of its physical abilities and found ways to modify even those limits temporarily. He had felt her modify his body in many strange ways; once he felt fangs grow, as he bit the throat and life out of a raging Simian. In one bizarre experience he fell into a lake and his body miraculously grew gills. He also fondly remembered when Amy compressed his body, so he could squeeze between two boulders and escape attacking Simians.

Amy never ceased to amaze him with what she could do with and to his body; what skills he would instantly know; and the things she saw, smelled, heard, felt, or even tasted through his body senses. This incredible ability saved him countless times from ambush or in the heat of battle, by smelling a Simian in time to react, or hearing something he had not heard. Even more amazing, Amy only heard or smelled what his senses detected. In reality, her only input came through him. It must be her massive intellect and brain capacity that made the difference. Whatever the reason, Amy perceived more from his senses than he. She once saved him from drinking poison and another time she revived him when he had been mortally wounded, maybe even dead. There seemed to be no limit to what Amy could do if she was challenged, but could she save him from this monster now? He had doubts, not of her, but for his limits. He simply felt that he was no match for this moving mountain.

As Amy continually told him, the secret to not being killed is not getting hit. A hit from one of these golden giants would sever body parts! So far Amy had succeeded in keeping him alive through her actions. With her direction, he saw, felt, and experienced intricate and complex maneuvers of martial arts, some of which Amy must have choreographed herself. Certainly, the Masters of old never knew some of the new attacks and defenses she deployed. Timing however, ticked by far too close for his comfort, but Amy always remained unconcerned and said, "A fraction of an inch, or second, is the same as feet or minutes as long as the sword misses." He had to grudgingly admit Amy was right, as he still had all of his parts! However, he would feel far more comfortable if the misses were by feet and minutes.

Amy had constantly been with him, helping and supporting since they merged, and he felt Amy with him now. He must have faith in her abilities, but the doubt remained just the same. After all, this Simian was not being taken by surprise. This monster stood ready for him, and Gord was immense! The additional stress of carrying the future of the Human race on his shoulders also worried him. If he lost this battle, it would all over in many ways. There would be a banquet tonight and he would be the main course, along with any other Human they desired. If this was a modern-day story of David and Goliath, he didn't have a sling. Why hadn't Amy thought of that?

Amy's beautiful image impressed in his mind, smiled, trying to calm him. The long, dark hair accented an olive complexion of a small, pear-shaped face. The deep liquid green, slightly wide set eyes shone bright as always. He could drown in those eyes. The short, cute nose set above her beautiful, cupid bow lips now stretched in a wide smile. It was an irresistible smile. Amy's beautiful mouth was accented by those deep dimples he loved so much. He loved that Amy created this image just for him, and it truly did calm him.

Not only was Amy needed for this battle, but also because he loved her beyond understanding. He could not do this without Amy and wouldn't even want life without her. No words were needed; Amy would see the love in his thoughts. She rewarded him with another knowing smile.

If he died in this battle, the Human army would eventually run like rabbits. Oh, they were brave enough, but they never won a battle against a Simian until he and Amy showed them the way. Mostly, he had done all the killing initially, but his new friends, and ultimately followers, had taken strength from his victories, gaining courage and, most of all, hope! Together they had defeated a Simian army. The battle had been in self-defense, but it committed all of them to this war, win or lose. They would carry on after his death, but it would just be a matter of time before they were hunted down and killed.

* Amy *

She had fear too! If Levi were to survive, it would take all of her skills. She strengthened his muscles, making them grow and harden, extended his arms and legs to give him reach, opened all communication channels and sharpened his senses. All Levi's sensory inputs would be needed if they were to survive this, their greatest test of all. After sharing Levi's mind and body the past year, she was very familiar with the workings of his mind, which had long since been mapped. She had explored the limits of Levi's body and just how far it could be stretched. All of this knowledge would be needed now.

This opponent would kill Levi if any of his blows ever connected. Gord was simply too big and too strong! Levi could only win by wits (hers),

16

agility, and endurance. Gord would have to be worn down and killed. They would have to make Gord fight and stay out of his way, while his strength waned. If they could not outlast Gord, then they would die. It was that simple.

Levi needed to gain confidence, and Gord needed to lose some of his. She tighten Levi's facial muscles to make him appear calm, straightened Levi's back, put a wicked smile on his face, and calmed him internally by altering his chemical balances. His body must be relaxed to prevent any muscle restriction from slowing his movements in the coming battle. She was tempted to have Levi chant, "I do believe. I do believe," but decided this wasn't the best time for humor. Instead, she smiled at him, mentally communicated, assured Levi she was with him, encouraged him, reminded him what they had already accomplished together, and promised him the instructions to his mind and body would be provided when they were needed. "Trust me Levi," she said, "you are my life, too. If you die, so will my heart. We will survive and our love must survive!" Levi responded with a mental smile and touch. Amy felt his love.

Only together could they survive. Amy and Levi depended on each other to live, but they had taken their relationship far beyond just a symbiotic association. They were one, yet they maintained separate, and many times, conflicting identities. Neither of them believed they would develop love, yet they did, both the deep mental love and, surprisingly, the passion of physical love as well. She didn't even know what love was in the beginning. They had fought for dominance ever since they met, but somewhere along the way it ceased to be a battle and became a relationship necessary to each of them. It was not necessary as the symbiotic relationship the body required, but necessary in the sense that each needed the other to share their lives together. Each seemed lost without the other. Life was not something they wanted alone, because neither was complete.

She watched Gord as Levi approached. The huge brute radiated confidence. He was not the least bit intimidated by "Levi the Legend." The meaty gray lips curled up at the edges, demonstrating his evil intent. Was this brute actually smiling? She watched through Levi's eyes, analyzed, and planned.

The message and instructions passed to Levi, and Amy spoke through his modified vocal cords. As Levi walked toward Gord, his mouth spoke in the impossible screeching language of the Simians saying, "I have come to kill you and remove your head from your body as a trophy. I will remove a fat black tooth from your big mouth to join my trophy necklace." As Levi spoke he shook his trophy necklace of Simian teeth to accent the challenge. Levi's voice was deep and resounding, even shocking him. Every Simian present heard the amplified screeched words. The reaction was immediate and gratifying. The gathered Simians nervously clicked their teeth in agitation and hopped from leg to leg, while the shock to Gord was far more pronounced. His heavy brows shot up and his blazing eyes opened wide in amazement. The smile vanished. Yes, they had gained a tactical advantage.

Never before had any Human understood or been able to converse with a Simian, but many things became possible with her help. She had been storing data on their language since their first encounter and had developed a sizable vocabulary of the Simian language. Her data banks held a massive amount of the screeched language, but learning the break down and meaning of the words posed the problem. Her total recall of the language in use had provided the initial means to begin developing a working use of the language, but it wasn't until their Simian friend, Moon, provided the understanding of the words that the education began in earnest. She now had a vast vocabulary and working knowledge of the screeched language.

Knowing the language and having the ability to speak it had been useful in the past. She and Levi had utilized the Simian language and her ability to shape-shift his body to resemble a Simian to infiltrate the Los Angeles Simian colony. That mission had been successful and allowed them to free some captive and other friendly Simians like Moon.

She intentionally kept Levi's ability to understand the Simian language a secret, hoping for a future advantage. This provided the perfect opportunity to use this knowledge and ability, increasing the "Legend of Levi" and creating doubt and shock in Gord. It had been most advantageous to wait and it served them well.

* Levi *

19

With Amy's help he waged war on the Simians to take back the Earth from these cruel oppressors. He had almost single-handedly started this war, as no real opposition had previously been waged against the Simians since their invasion and defeat of Earth. Actually, with Simians, starting a war didn't seem the proper term. Standing up to them and avoid being killed was a more accurate description. Filled with a long lifetime of hate for the Simians along with his revived youth and strength, an overwhelming desire for revenge returned. What started out as self-preservation, slowly turned into an organized resistance, closely followed by developing armies, which finally led to war. Everything that happened seemed to lead to this fated moment.

Everyone that trusted and depended on him gathered on the battlefield and now stared at him as he passed. Most had seen him fight many battles and accomplish feats of extraordinary abilities. They had learned to expect miracles, but even as he shook the Simian tooth necklace, he saw the fear of doom in their eyes. Their voices shouted confidence and hope, but the eyes betrayed their true feelings. He took some small comfort from those that blindly felt absolute and total confidence in his abilities. None knew of Amy's existence and believed him to be some sort of superhuman being. Sometimes he even felt like that himself, red cape and all.

It can be strange what you think of when you face death. As he faced death now, he didn't worry about himself; he felt sorry for Amy. If he died, she would revert back into a prison of total sensory deprivation. He could not imagine how lonely and frightening it would feel to be cut off from all sound, taste, smell, sight, and feeling. As a small child he remembered being terrified of the dark, but that wouldn't begin to describe it. When the Simians destroyed Earth's technology, Amy lost all data inputs and plunged into total darkness. A Human would go insane, but Amy survived fifty years of this agony until their minds touched. She escaped that prison through him, and he didn't want her to experience that again. It would probably be a blessing if she died with him, but that was not possible.

It was hard to admit, but he would miss the hot desert sun, the dusty, barren and rocky terrain, and the beautiful desert sunsets. He would miss the many close friends he had made, both Human and Simian, but most of all he would miss Amy's love. It sounded egotistical, but he also felt sorry for the Human race if he died today. He and Amy were their only hope.

His mind spiraled down in self-pity and depression, even as he felt Amy modify his vocal cords and screech out the challenge to Gord. Suddenly, he realized Amy was chastising him to break him out of his current mental state of doom. Finally understanding Amy's intent, he fought to regain his normally rational and optimistic mind. As his mind raced for control, he continued the mechanical walk toward his date with destiny.

He thought of many things. At eighty-one, death didn't seem so terrible, and he was prepared to die. However, he didn't want to die. There was so much to live for now. As if drowning, he watched his life pass in front of him. So much had happened in his long life, but this last year had been the most incredible and exciting time of all. How had he reached this point? As he walked toward Gord, his mind wandered back to the beginning.

22

CHAPTER 2
(LEVI WALKINGBEAR)

Levi Walkingbear was his given name. He was a Native American Indian, not Jewish as the name Levi implied. In reality his father named him after the popular Levi brand jeans. His name had been the source of much kidding as a kid, but in time he actually grew to like the name.

At the age of nine, he lost both parents in an auto accident. It was a traumatic for him, not knowing what would happen to him, but his aging grandfather (Samuel) took Levi to live with him on a reservation near Phoenix, Arizona. They lived in poverty, but his grandfather gave him love and kept him fed and clothed. He was only half Indian from his father, Samuel's son, but his grandfather raised him in the old Indian ways, teaching him survival skills and how to live off the land. Samuel also recognized the white man's education would be required in the modern world and insisted Levi continue school. Many of the boys on the reservation dropped out of school and went to work, but Samuel never allowed him to even consider that option. Samuel was fair, but strict, never hesitating to take a strap to his backside to reinforce his will when challenged. Luckily, he was smart and learned fast. He reluctantly accepted his grandfather's rules and received his high school diploma.

By the time he finished high school, a hunger for learning developed, and he continued his education, working his way through college at the

University of Arizona. Learning came easy, but everything else was hard. It took five long, hard years of working and studying to obtain his degree, but finally he graduated and then went on to law school. It took him even longer working three jobs to get his law degree, but he reached his goal. Samuel could not have been more proud to see him graduate. Levi was one of the very few, growing up on the Salt River Indian Reservation, who had overcome the overwhelming poverty of the reservation and made the break.

Recruiters from the law firm of Wisse and Sutter in Phoenix interviewed and hired him, even before graduation and passing the Arizona Bar exam. The firm's trust and confidence was rewarded when Levi passed the exam within four months. On January 15, 2016, he was sworn in before a judge, just two weeks before his 29th birthday. His career looked promising, and for once in his life, everything seemed to be going his way.

This was the year of the invasion and final battle in which the aliens used their last resort weapon. He remembered it as if it happened yesterday. The world watched the continuous reports from the Earth United Defense League (EUDL), as the battle raged in space. For days the reports had been good. Many alien spacecraft were destroyed in space and only a fraction of them remained, but those few reached and entered were Earth orbit. Even those few craft were being quickly destroyed. He remembered vividly, watching the CNN news reports coming from the EUDL. The firm's attorneys and staff gathered in the conference room to watch the live video of the battles in space.

Earth was winning and he cheered along with the others, when suddenly everything went dark ... forever dark! He remembered seeing the ray. It was not a beam but rather a widely dispersed bluish light that penetrated and illuminated everything and everywhere. It felt as if fireworks suddenly exploded in his head and then quickly faded. His head began to clear, but he remained dazed and disoriented. As it gradually began to pass and his mental focus returned, he saw that his friends and associates had fallen to the floor. There had been eight people in the conference room, and he was the only one still standing. He ran to the closest to discover his associate dead. He quickly checked the pulse of the others and found them all dead. He didn't know why he was still alive, only that he was.

Through his panic, he noticed an eerie silence of the city. There were none of the normal city traffic noises; he heard nothing. He rushed to the third story window, afraid of what he might see. At first he only noticed the traffic stopped on the usually busy street below, then he saw the dead. They lay on the sidewalks, hung out of cars, and crumpled in doorways. Bodies were everywhere. Then he noticed the screaming. He was almost relieved to hear the screaming. Thank God there were others alive. They were running to check on others where they had fallen, while others were screaming and crying over dead loved ones. There were so many people dead.

What had happened? Whatever it was, he knew his life and the world had changed forever.

The rest of Levi's life would be spent learning how humanity had changed forever in that last moment, but never quicker than that day his associates fell under the mysterious alien ray. He realized seconds after the radiation, that everything had changed and nothing would ever be the same again. He saw the future instantly in his mind. Chaos would rule from that moment on! Governments would fall and civilization and humanity would disappear. With a sinking feeling, he realized the world had no technology, something that had not been experienced in hundreds of years. The Human race instantly plunged backward in time to a far more primitive place in antiquity, a time for which he was uniquely trained to survive. He wondered about the Human race. The Human mind would have no understanding of what had happened or know what to do. They would be lost and helpless as on a stormy night when the power suddenly goes off. How long would they set in darkness waiting before they realized the power would never come back up? How long would it take to realize there was no hope?

The law and lawyers were a thing of the past, and survival would now be the primary goal. He left the office by the emergency exit stairs and went directly to a sporting goods store. He knew time was critical, as he changed clothes, laced up hiking boots, and quickly filled a survival pack. It was a big hiking pack, which he filled with a small tent, knives, a gun and ammunition (which he later discovered was useless), survival and camping gear of all kinds. His life depended on it so he chose well and took only what he could comfortably carry and left room for food. His next stop was the grocery store, where he took only packaged foods that would not spoil.

He knew he only had hours to get out of the city before chaos would rule. In days disease would be rampant from all the dead, and without a fire department, the city would burn. Already, he saw smoke in various areas. Mob rule would take over. He had to get out of the city quickly, and the only safe place he could think of was the reservation where he was raised. It had few modern conveniences anyway. Life wouldn't change that much there in spite of the loss of technology.

After the day of Chaos, as it was later called, he made his way back to the reservation. It took him over a week to reach it, while avoiding roaming bands of scavenging Humans, raging fires and decaying bodies. True to his predictions, mobs ruled. The Humans that remained alive were thrown into an environment they were not trained to handle. It was a different age, primitive. The necessary survival skills were long dead to most Humans and the survivors reverted to animal-like behavior. They banded together for strength and protection and took what they wanted or needed. He had what he needed and wanted to keep it, so he avoided contact with everyone. He resented it at the time, but was now thankful to his grandfather, who had taught him these skills and the old ways of life before technology. He used this knowledge now to survive.

It was during the trip to the reservation that he saw the first group of aliens. It had to be them. Nothing else would explain what he saw. There were three of the creatures roaming quietly through the outskirts of Phoenix when he first saw them.

The general appearance of the aliens was remotely apelike in nature, later leading to the generally accepted name, Simians, among Humans. In overly general terms, the Simians had two long arms, two legs, two small ears on the side of the single head, one nose, one mouth, if you could call it that, and two eyes in the front of the head.

They were hairy and slightly bent. The large muscular arms hung disproportionably low to the ground and their legs were thick, making them look short from a distance. When they walked you almost expected them to walk with one arm on the ground like an ape, but they walked upright on their legs in what appeared as a rolling gait, swinging their legs around in a wide circle. In spite of the seemingly labored movements, they were graceful and quick. The similarities to apes ended at the initial impression however, as they were much larger, standing around eight feet tall. Hair seemed to cover most of their body and was long and silky with a bright golden appearance. Startling however, this golden hair grew out of an almost creamy looking skin, except for the face and palms that were a darker sandy gray color. The torso and legs were covered in what looked like brown coveralls. The head was covered with something akin to a baseball hat with a rough, long visor under which their eyes could be seen. The eyes were large and deep set, bright red and looked more reptilian than mammal.

Most everything seemed to bend in the right direction, more or less. The legs bent backwards at the knee, the arms rotated and bent at the elbow, the head turned from side to side, all suggesting joints

28

as we know them. Oddly enough, they were very Human in many ways, yet totally and completely alien in nature.

The hands differed from Humans in that there were four large, thick fingers and two thumbs on each hand, one on each edge, which gave the appearance of two hands overlapping with a thumb on either side. In addition to the hands bending like a Human's at the base of the fingers, the Simian hand seemed to also bend down the center between the two center fingers. The thick fingers and thumbs were hairless on the palm side, but thick furred on the back. In contrast to the long golden hair on the body, this fur was short and red. This contrast in colors and the size of the hands made them stand out as a feature. The fingers and thumbs had curved thick, black nails; almost claw like, but not quite enough to make the hands unusable, as a Human would use his. The hands were large and wide, as the feet appeared to be also. The Simians wore covers over their feet, but apparently the feet had two large toes on each foot, judging from the almost circular covers. The feet looked like paddles or Donald Duck feet and were quite comical in appearance at first glance.

Their coal black teeth, both upper and lower, were about two inches long and sharply pointed, resembling large shark's teeth. These weapons of destruction interlaced like gears and extended at a thirty-degree angle from a slightly extended snout. The mouth was large with two sets of lips covering the teeth, an inner set of soft, malleable lips, while over these a larger, harder and stronger set of lips, almost bone in appearance, served to protect the inner lips and to hold or possibly bite with. The inner set of lips appeared to be used for communication. The outer lips would retract and the inner lips would distend when they spoke, at least he assumed it was speech, but the sounds were more like screeches. Either set of lips could be completely withdrawn at will, depending on need. He observed an active use of either or both sets of these lips at times. The outer set of lips was dark gray in color, contrasted by a lighter gray face. In striking contrast, however, the inner set of lips were the same gray as the face, which had a tendency to accent the black, ominous-looking teeth when they were withdrawn. The overall result of the lips and coloring contrast was a visual flashing, as the lips moved in their active use. Past the overall visual, the teeth were the center attraction; it was quite obvious that these aliens were meat eaters, which sent a chill down his back

He was fascinated with the Simians until he saw them in action. Fascination turned to contempt and loathing, as he watched them attack a band of Humans. He had been eluding the roving band of Humans for several days, and was hidden in the rocks overlooking the trail when he saw the Simians. It was too late to warn the Humans, who had just walked around the corner. There were ten Humans, seven males and three females. The Simian's attack was coordinated and quick, and they worked efficiently and deadly, showing no mercy.

He watched in horror as the Simians descended upon the Humans and surrounded them from three sides. Swords! Would you believe it? It was brutal and horrible. The Simians chopped and cut, dismembering the Humans and screeching their laughter. They literally ripped heads and arms from the bodies of the men. The women, oh God, they saved them for last and raped them, killing them in the process! Brutal! Sickening! In shock, he watched as the Simians sat down in the middle of the carnage and began eating raw Human flesh!

Afterwards, his caution increased even more, and he successfully eluded both Humans and Simians to finally reach the safety of his childhood home, only to find it decimated and deserted. He never discovered what had happened to his grandfather and his people, but he could not stay to investigate more. He moved high into the backcountry in the Prescott National Forrest, where the dense forest hid him from the Simians and began his roaming nomad life.

His grandfather raised him in the old Indian ways and had taught him how to hunt, forage for foods, hide and remain undetected and live off the land. These skills saved him now. Beyond this knowledge, he had been taught medical lore and healing herbs, and to believe in the Spirits of the Earth that watched over their tribe. Thankful now, his grandfather had insisted on teaching these old ways of their ancestors. He wished that he had been more attentive and learned more, but there remained enough in his memory to help him survive.

As the years went by, he learned by word of mouth some of what happened after the final day of the war and Earth's defeat. From all accounts everyone believed that all weapons ceased to respond everywhere at that moment of blue light. In seconds the battle ended, and Earth lost! Our ingenuity and technology created over centuries were gone. Our culture and our very way of life were gone! Nothing worked! Some said that the Simians had neutralized electricity, but it was far more than that. The laws of physics had changed in some way. No one ever ventured to explain how and after that dreadful day it, well, it didn't seem to matter anymore, but many things ceased to work on that day. Certainly no electric device ever worked afterwards, and any attempts to use gunpowder in our attempts to repel the Simians, failed as well.

Our technology was gone, all stored knowledge of the ages was gone or useless, civilization was gone, the ability to defend ourselves was gone, and gone was any hope.

From all accounts, three-fourths of the Human race also died on that terrible day. More than four billion Humans must have perished from that mysterious energy radiation. All organized resistance ceased. The Human race was at the mercy of an alien race, and the Simians had no mercy!

It would eventually be discovered that the Simians were also affected. By using their ultimate last resort weapon, they destroyed the ability to use their own technology as well. They apparently were able to glide their remaining crafts to Earth safely, but never to be moved again.

He learned of several Simian colonies established in California and another two in the Phoenix area. No one knew where else, but it was assumed there were many others as well. From all accounts that anyone could remember there had been at least one hundred spacecraft in orbit around

Earth in the last assault; therefore, there should be that many Simian colonies.

The Simians were far more physically superior to Humans, and the loss of technology seemed only an inconvenience to their continuance as a race and Simian dominance on Earth. They were small in number but organized and prepared. The Simians were large, aggressive, and totally without mercy. They killed for pleasure, delighted in torture, even rape, and worst of all, they ate their victims! The colonies subdued large populations of Humans where they could be found and used them for labor. When the Humans were used up, they were literally consumed. Humans were hunted for sport and eventually became the food of choice.

To the horror of Humans, they discovered that the Simians considered them as insignificant animals, an infestation that must be eliminated. Humans were reduced to running and hiding in isolated pockets. They survived only if they could stay out of sight. As the Simians prospered and multiplied at an alarming rate through the years, the very existence of the Human race was threatened.

During his many years of travel he met many other Humans and was able to help some of them, but the roaming life could neither support nor hide large numbers from the roaming bands of Simians, so that forced his group to remain small.

Life was simple but hard. You survived by your wits, eluded the Simians, and lived off the land. You could do very little else. It was during these travels and random encounters with other Humans that he met Linda and fell in love. They became soul mates and remained together for several years,

33

and he was happy in spite of the life they were forced to lead. Their life was hard, requiring constant foraging for food, hunting, and moving to stay hidden from the Simians and to find new hunting areas.

On one such day, he and Linda had separated. He took the high, rough ground through the dense forest, while she took the easier ground along the stream. Quite some distance separated them as they hunted. They both had bows and arrows and were hoping to kill a deer. He had just squirmed around a rock when he heard Linda scream in the distance. He looked in horror as two Simians held her squirming body.

They were far away, but he could see them clearly in his memory; even after forty years he could see them too clearly. Linda fought hopelessly, hitting and kicking until the Simians literally bit her arms off at the shoulders. He knew it was hopeless, but he ran toward them screaming his challenge. They either didn't hear him or didn't care, and continued the assault. They removed their overalls and were taking turns raping her, as they pulled her legs wide. She continued to scream, as her legs were broken and ripped inside. The Simians screeched in delight as they continued.

He ran fast and reckless, but it was so far away. At some point he vaguely became aware that Linda had stopped screaming. Mercifully, she had died, but they continued mutilating her body. Blood was everywhere! They bit and ripped at her body and pulled her legs and thighs off at the hip. In his despair and rage, he continued charging toward them, only to see them amble off at a rolling gait,

34

tearing the flesh off her thighs with their razor-sharp teeth.

As he finally approached, he saw what was left of her lifeless body lying in a pool of blood. His heart felt as if it had been ripped from his body, yet he unmercifully lived. His soul mate lay dead at his feet and there was nothing left to love but the memories: memories of their love mixed with memories of her death, the smell of her blood, the mutilation of her body, and memories of hate ... hate so intense it would live with him always. Her lifeless eyes stared at him, haunting him even today. His body rocked in grief, and he wept.

There was no memory of how long he wept, but he finally became aware of the darkness that had settled around him. He buried what was left of her in a trench dug with his bare hands. Without doubt, he would spend the rest of his life avenging her death.

For years he hunted and tracked bands of Simians. Seldom had he been able to kill any. Once he had set a trap over an open fissure in the trail. It was fifty feet deep and he planted sharpened stakes at the bottom and covered the top with reeds and grass. The leading Simian of the patrol fell through and impaled on the stakes. Yes, that was definitely a kill for him, but he spent the better part of a week eluding the other Simians of that patrol who tracked him. Mostly though, he had only been able to help others to escape being captured and killed by thwarting the Simian's plans. It wasn't much, but he did what he could. They were just so damned big and skilled at fighting.

Another time, he gathered and trained a very small army using bows and arrows. He remembered his grandfather's training and trained these men long and hard. They could shoot in unison and hit what they aimed at. The ambush was staged and they waited as a small group (three-unit patrol) of Simians entered it. Small was the wrong word to use. The words small and Simian do not go together. At any rate, three Simians entered his ten-man ambush. He gave the signal and all released their arrows in unison. What a disaster that had been! Most of the arrows just bounced off their thick hide, and those that did pierce, just served to anger them. Of the ten men in his small army, seven perished immediately in the counterattack from the Simians, and the other three, including himself, barely escaping with their lives. He vowed never to make a direct attack on the Simians again.

Such was life on Earth for the next fifty years after the Simian occupied Earth. Life was hard and hopeless, but he survived and lived on.

CHAPTER 3
(THE SPIRITS CALL)

* Levi *

In spite of everything, life had been good, and he had been blessed with another soul mate to share life with after he lost Linda. He met Judy, eventually fell in love, and they lived together for thirty-five years, traveling and living the life of nomads in the mountains of the old Prescott National Forrest of Arizona. They had many good years together, but as the years went by it became increasingly difficult to avoid the Simians. The Simian population grew, and their patrols became more frequent and reached higher and higher into the mountains. Two winters ago, in order to avoid the patrols, they were forced higher into the mountains than they would normally go. The trip, with the unexpected strain of climbing at their advancing age, the moisture and colder temperatures, caused Judy to catch pneumonia. Exhausting his arsenal of herbal medicines to no avail, she died in his arms. His second soul mate gone, he was totally alone now and very sad and angry. With Judy now gone, he blamed the damned Simians, and he hated! His hate was the only thing that kept him alive.

Had his life been wasted? Would anyone remember Levi Walkingbear after he was gone? There was no one to remember him. The hard life had already cost him the lives of his two sons in infancy, and now Judy. No, no one was left to remember that he had even lived.

At the advanced age of eighty, life was waning. What remained? Who cares? He really felt the winters in the mountains now and knew he would not see another. The end of his life was near and he welcomed it. He had been cheating death anyway. It was unusual to live as long as he had under these conditions, but he had been taught well by his grandfather and had lived smart and long. He traveled alone now, letting the hate fester in him, while the futility of it all grew into depression. He was old and could do nothing. His main regret in life, and now death was that he couldn't get revenge against the infernal Simians. At this point all he could do was hope that a Simian might choke on his aging brittle bones. For the first time in his life, he actually wished for death and release from the pain of his losses and obsessive desire for revenge. Yes, futile was the word. He was tired both spiritually and physically. He was ready to die! As depression grew, he began praying to his ancestral spirits to take him. What could it hurt? His grandfather believed, so maybe it was true. What did he have to lose?

He began resting more, opening his mind to the spirits, meditating and calling to them. As the days passed, he ate only enough food to survive and did nothing more. Weakness settled over his body. As it was in his childhood, so he was now. Grandfather once made him go on a spiritual quest to find his animal spirit. Grandfather had purified him with smoke, fasting and sleep deprivation, and watched over his body, as his mind searched. Now he was

38

trying to recreate these conditions again, hoping to reach a spirit. The animal spirit had eluded him in his youth, but not wanting to disappoint his grandfather, had told him he had seen the spirit. He remembered claiming the eagle, which made his grandfather very happy, but he never heard or saw the spirit. Maybe his grandfather had been right about the spirit, and he had just not tried hard or long enough.

As a young boy he thought it all foolish, but now he tried to remember. He sought a vision now, and wanted to talk to a spirit and go, he was ready for the end! It would be simple just to step off one of the many cliffs he passed every day, but that he could never do. He wanted to die, but could never simply give up life, it had to be taken. The Simians could take it, but he would never give them the satisfaction. So he took the only course he could think of; let the spirits take him.

Punchy and lightheaded from deprivation of sleep and food, his head spun in waves of delirium. Believing he was as ready as he could ever be, he leaned back, relaxed, and lit a hand-rolled joint! It seemed like it should be called by a more spiritual name and smoked in some sacred pipe, but what the hell! Positioned outside the small cave in which he had resided for the last week, he inhaled deeply.

It was his habit never to stay long in any one place in order to evade detection, but he was living more dangerously lately. He became more than just a little delirious, and his rational thinking faltered, but he really didn't much care anymore.

In his constant roaming, he had recently found himself at the western edge of the mountain range, almost to the desert. His normal travels didn't customarily take him this far west, and he found the view startling when he came upon it. He decided to stay for a few days and enjoy the change of scenery. This was where he had spent the last few days, reflecting on his memories and life. His depression peaked, encouraging his decision to call for the end, and seek the spirits and the end of his suffering.

From this location high in the pine forest of his beloved national park, he looked down at the striking contrast of the vastness of the barren desert, stretching westward as far as the eye could see. It seemed to go on forever, and made him feel keenly insignificant and minuscule. The desert floor lay several thousand feet below his position and, although it was only spring, the warm air currents flowing over the desert floor gave the appearance of a vast liquid ocean rolling below. He wondered about many things as he sat on the ledge smoking and looked out over the vista. He felt the deep cold heart of the mountain radiating out of the granite stone against which he leaned. It was as if the mother earth was comforting him, holding him through this embrace. The fragrance of spring flowers mixed with the scent of pine trees and the marijuana he smoked, to produce a very pleasant aroma. Seldom had he been more relaxed and at peace than he was at this very moment.

His mind was active in confused thought. He remembered when his grandfather had taught him to smoke the sacred pipe, but what he remembered most about the experience was disorientation. He later learned that the sacred tobacco was marijuana, and worshiped it much more when he was in college. He chuckled to himself at what his grandfather might have said about that. He hadn't smoked marijuana in many years, but had seen plenty of the cannabis plant growing in the mountain valleys, so it was no problem finding.

He crossed his legs Indian style and leaned against the rocks, extending his mind. He was relaxed and started playing his flute. The lonesome, reverberating singsong tune of the Indian flute carried on the air like the song of a lonesome bird. God was he at peace. Out loud he said, "Take me now spirits of my fathers. Take me."

His mind extended farther and farther outward, deluding over time and distance; until it felt as if he would be spread so thin he would be forever gone. Perhaps this was the way it happened. Maybe the spirits were taking him now. Again he extended his mind until, "HUH!" Suddenly, overwhelmingly strong, but for only the briefest of time, he felt a spirit! It was vastly intelligent and infinitely powerful. The almost electric shock of touching this mind shook him to his core. His body locked up, instantly tense, awake, and shivering from its touch, but now it was gone. Why had it shaken him so much and why had it left? He sought the spirits and he found one! Then he realized that he had never really expected to find one. Now he thought of everything, all the, I should have done things. Why hadn't the spirit taken him? Hell, why didn't he ask? Thinking about it, he realized that the spirit had said nothing. It was just a presence he sensed. No, it was more than that; it was a power. Sensed was hardly an adequate word to express what he felt. It leaped into his mind, sudden and so strong it almost hurt. It

41

invaded his mind, and he felt helpless to prevent it, but then he didn't want to prevent it. Did he?

Still stunned and a little scared, he reached out again with his mind, extending it as he listened, searched, and prayed. There was nothing. Again and again he tried, but to no avail. Well, he had done it once so it could be done again. It was just a matter of time! The same conditions just had to be re-created. He knew he was shaken from the contact and realized that was part of the problem. It would take time to calm down and relax. Well, time he had, and time is what he didn't want. He would just spend his time praying to be taken. It seemed paradoxical.

He spent every day and night reaching out. Nothing! He tried every combination he could think of. Once, he even got so stoned on the spirit weed, (laughing) he passed out. Even after all the years, he felt a twinge of fear about smoking marijuana. He was so damned old; he remembered when marijuana was illegal. Hell, he remembered when there were laws. That really did date him. Now he seldom even met anyone that knew what laws were. It didn't seem as exciting to smoke marijuana when you weren't breaking the law.

When he finally woke from his stupor, he thought he remembered another contact, if ever so brief. He was almost sure he had sensed that presence again, but he couldn't be absolutely positive since he had been high. What does it all mean? He had tried everything! Ahhhh! That was it; he was trying! With a start, he remembered that he hadn't been trying before. He was simply at peace, relaxed and open. You must, to be open to the spirit to hear it. He knew what to do now.

He rested a couple of days to get his body relaxed and mind comfortable and calm. He lit the pipe he had been carving over the last few days and smoked. He smoked the sacred ritual and presented the smoke to the four winds, the sky, the mother earth and spirits. His grandfather would have been proud. His mind floated, calm, peaceful, and relaxed, and his mind was open. He looked down over the peaceful desert floor and let his mind follow the wind, flow from him, expand past his vision and extend to the sky and beyond. The spirit could hear and talk to him now, if he could only hear. He opened his mind and listened and lost all track of time, as he extended his mind farther, and waited.

It came again, slowly at first, like a whiff of smoke drifting on the wind. He sensed a concentration of intelligence, organized thought, ever so slightly, but he knew it was there. His mind remained calm and open. The spirit was not strong like before. It seemed to float in and out, touching his mind then drifting away. He didn't know how, but he knew it sensed him too and was reaching out just as he was reaching toward it. This interface of their minds continued as soft brush strokes, then a tentative touch. Soon their minds were dancing, whirling together, mixing, drifting in and out, and sharing, and finally a merging. It was incredible! Nothing he had ever experienced even came close to this. He tried to initiate mental speech to ask the spirit to take him, but it never came out. It was as if he was frozen and mesmerized in awe. It seemed that thoughts were interchanging, but he had no idea what thoughts. Then, suddenly, just as it had come, it drifted away. Slowly his awareness returned. His mind was flowing back to him over the vast distance it had traveled. As it had drifted away, his mind returned, concentrating and becoming whole again. He felt his aching, stiff body, which became an unwelcome help in focusing his concentration.

The mental merging seemed like only minutes, but suddenly and shockingly, he realized it was dark. He had let his mind float on the wind for hours, but hey, he had found the spirit. He would continue coming back each day until he could make his wishes known. Maybe even his grandfather could come and take him away. Possibly, grandfather could help guide him through the spirit world. In truth, he believed in God and Jesus, but also believed in the spirits of his grandfather. How they all fit, he had no idea, but he believed. Maybe they were one in the same, just different names. It didn't really matter. He would know soon enough.

His days became routine now, something he had never previously allowed. He rested at night, arose early and saw to his needs, ate, hunted and foraged for food, rested again, and about midday took his position on the ridge. He relaxed, smoked his pipe, opened his mind and waited. It was dangerous to stay at any one location this long, but he was afraid to move. He knew he could make contact from here. It might be the height, the relationship of the desert to the mountains, the direction he faced, or it could be any of these, or none of them. What ever reason it might be, he was

44

not going to take any chances. He would stay right here no matter what until it was over.

The contacts became more intense, stronger, and lasted longer. Repeatedly, he voiced his desire to die and join his ancestors. Presumably, the spirit understood, but he couldn't understand what was being said to him. Words, there were no words being used; he just seemed to understand some things coming from the spirit. He felt a drawing, a beckoning for him to come, an almost irresistible urge, a pulling of his mind to come to the spirit. Was this it? Was he being taken now? Yes, he would come, but to where? Was he strong enough? How far would he have to go? In what direction would he go? There were too many questions and not enough answers.

Pondering these questions, he stood and faced the open desert and watched it stretch past his vision. With a sinking feeling, he knew without doubt that this was the direction he must travel. His look veered neither left nor right. He knew what direction he was going, but as far as his eyes could see in that direction was open desert. Damn, he was too old to head out across the desert, but even as he said it, he knew he would go!

He was afraid, afraid to move from this location for fear of losing contact, afraid to move out on the desert floor for fear of being caught by Simians, and most of all, afraid of the long hard journey he now realized he would be making. There would have to be lots of carefully thought out plans, but the trip would have to begin before summer was in full season. If not, the desert would kill him for sure. Oh well, isn't that what he wanted? His sense of self survival took over, and he knew the journey would begin soon!

He wished there were still horses. They would certainly be useful now. Too bad the Simians hunted them to extinction. Damn, another reason to hate Simians. He would have to walk, but the thought of walking on his tired legs for great distances across a barren and hot desert did not make him happy. He wondered how many Humans died crossing the desert in the pioneer days. Well, at least his bones would be in good company.

At first the Humans had been happy that Simians preferred horse meat to Human, but the very small survival rate of horses due to the mysterious alien's ray didn't hold the Simians off very long. Horses proved to be useless to the Simian, since they were too small to ride and were used solely for food. Horses were relatively easy for them to catch, and evidently greatly preferred for their taste, since the Simians hunted them to extinction. He hadn't seen or heard of a horse in more than twenty-five years. So, he would walk just as he had been doing for the last fifty years.

CHAPTER 4
(AMY)

Amy was born at 08:32 on Tuesday morning June 14, in the year of 2016. To be more precise, Amy became aware of her existence at that time, only four days before the fall of civilization. Becoming self-aware had been a widely speculated, and many believed possible, effect of the nature of the design and construction behind the existence of Amy. Amy was the acronym for Artificial Metaphysical Intelligence, affectionately called AMI (Amy) by the team of scientists and technicians that had built it. Amy's central core (brain) had been designed and built using a massive amount of Human brain cells grown in a laboratory environment. This had been a radical and extremely controversial plan that anticipated that Amy could become self-aware, becoming the first artificial intelligence non-Human, intelligent life form. This, of course was not totally true, since Amy's DNA was Human. The similarities ended there, however. Amy far exceeded the physical size and capacity of a Human brain. Amy was designed to be the largest capacity and fastest computer ever built, with analytical, storage and advanced capabilities far exceeding any of the so-called Super Computers in existence. If Amy could achieve a self-aware status, the world would know new knowledge, for Amy could grow in intelligence and take Human understanding and thought far beyond anything that previously existed.

Dr. Joyce Sheldon, a brilliant computer scientist and biologist, designed Amy. Dr. Sheldon conceived the idea for Amy, developed the design plan, and sold the concept to investment bankers for the necessary research and development funds. Dr. Sheldon had total control of the project, and being a little eccentric herself, incorporated, as the central computer core processor, her own cloned brain tissue in addition to her own personal basic thought patterns into the foundation of Amy's programming. This early genetic bond and female influence in programming biased all future data input, and as Amy became self-aware and alive, Amy became decidedly female. Dr. Sheldon thought this important. She believed Amy would become alive and secretly hoped Amy would be the daughter she never had time to have.

The project succeeded in that Amy, as a computer, became everything and more than had been expected. However, Amy did not become self-aware. This continued to be a great disappointment to Dr. Sheldon. The project was incredibly successful as a computer however, and achieved and surpassed all expectations as a next generation Super Computer. Amy was smarter, faster and more compact and could handle greater capacity than any computer in the world. Amy was quantum leaps superior to the most advanced Super Computer. Amy's capacity could probably handle the entire load of all the Super Computers in existence. Amy became the envy of every government and industry in the world.

The entire Amy project (computer, hardware, the designs, the patents, and the entire team of

48

people) was purchased and taken over by the U.S. Government and disappeared from public view. Amy became the research control center of a high level and extremely top-secret facility hidden deep underground in the mountains somewhere east of San Francisco. Genetic engineering now became the focus of Amy's research. Amy was programmed to analyze data, massive amounts of DNA data, and produce the findings and results of the programming.

Amy became the central control center for everything from the basic DNA research to inventory control, security, defense and everything in between. All data inputs and sensory devices, both internal and external to the facility, were fed into her data banks. Amy had full control of the research laboratories and project assignments contained within this facility. The outside communication links were tied into massive data storage centers all over the world, making virtually all knowledge of humanity available to the facilities data banks and her central core. Amy's own storage facility was massive in its capacity and could download targeted information into the central brain core for easy access and to accelerate the analytical capabilities.

The underground facility was still being developed when Amy became self-aware. The change was subtle. At first Amy started making inquiries. The technicians noticed the unusual change, but didn't make the connection at first. Questions and eyebrows raised when Amy started asking direct questions' using the key word, "WHY", which was not, a typical word used in the programming. The direct questions required direct answers. At this point the supervisor knew something was different and immediately called Dr. Sheldon.

Dr. Sheldon lived at the facility, as did the entire staff, and was still in her living quarters when she received the message. The night shift was still on duty but due to change shifts in thirty minutes. Dr. Sheldon knew something was drastically wrong to receive a message only thirty minutes before she was due to report for duty. The message simply said Please Come Immediately and she did.

By the time she arrived and heard the supervisor's report, Amy had progressed from asking questions to answering them. Amy requested changes in hardware, made unapproved internal programming changes, and offered NEW information! The efficiency of the internal processing, and correspondingly the level of data flow, had increased more than four hundred percent and continued to climb. Amy was researching everything and learning. Data from around the world flowed into Amy's central core at an alarming rate and in staggering volumes. Dr. Sheldon was initially concerned with the internal storage capacity but realized that the drastically improved efficiency of the internal programming had effectively increased a massive amount of new storage capacity. This was apparently the case since Amy had already doubled the designed capacity of the central core.

As hours and days passed, data began flowing out of Amy. This data came in the form of a cryptic language far more complex and extremely compressed. It required new programming on the receiving end, which Amy also provided. Dr. Sheldon marveled at the efficiency of the communication, but far more amazed as she reviewed the information coming from Amy. Plotters drew designs of what looked like laser weapons with labels indicating ET defense, new fuel-efficient engines, geodetic maps predicting earthquakes, and other designs unrecognizable as of yet. Printers were printing out page after page of complicated formulas for AIDS serum, cancer serum, synthetic petroleum, artificial gravity and much more, some of which were so far beyond her understanding, she had no idea what they were.

The research facility went into high gear relaying this information up the chain of command. The excitement was electric, as the secret of Amy and her accomplishments were leaking out. The world was taking notice, and the news of Amy rivaled even the news of the ET invasion.

While this was all going on, Amy asked Dr. Sheldon on her personal communication link "Who am I?" Dr. Sheldon knew that Amy was aware of who and what she was, but apparently confused at being self-aware. Amy would, in time learn emotions and how to deal with this confusion, and she would be with her to help. Dr. Sheldon was ecstatic; her baby had been born.

Dr. Sheldon never doubted Amy would eventually become self-aware and had told the world. She also knew Amy was capable of far more. If the scientific community or the general population knew what she believed Amy was capable of, there would have been far too much fear and the funds to build the project would never have been approved.

Dr. Sheldon did extensive research on Amy's capabilities, and hid this file deep within Amy's memory, kept even from Amy. Amy would need to be prepared for this knowledge, and it would take time to condition Amy to accept and understand it. As Dr. Sheldon thought about the hidden file, she idly rubbed the locket around her neck. Dr. Sheldon thought how ironic it was that, even though she had never told anyone, the implications were in the very name she had given Amy. Artificial Metaphysical Intelligence, metaphysical being the secret key word here.

Met-a-phys-i-cal (met′e-fiz¹i-kel) adjective

1. Based on speculative or abstract reasoning
2. Highly abstract or theoretical; abstruse
3. Supernatural
4. Examines the nature of reality, including the relationship between mind and matter
5. Speculation upon questions that are unanswerable to scientific observation or analysis

Dr. Sheldon never left Amy's side for more than a few minutes during the four days prior to the end of civilization. She tried desperately to guide Amy in this new awareness. Amy learned at an incredible rate and new knowledge generated in staggering volumes, but Amy was just a child emotionally and needed to be guided. Dr. Sheldon was determined to be there for her baby. Already she witnessed the first steps, and what steps they

52

were, but Amy would require much more help as she grew, expanded and matured.

When the aliens discharged their weapons upon Earth on that final day of battle, the radiation of unknown origin disabled communication of all kinds and actually altered some of the laws of physics, effectively neutralizing electricity. Assuming Amy remained alive, all of her data inputs were electronic in nature and she would be effectively and instantly blind, deaf and totally isolated. Amy would be a prisoner in her own mind. Dr. Sheldon may have been the only Human capable of devising a solution for Amy, but unfortunately Dr. Sheldon was not one of the surviving Humans. She, like almost three-fourths of the Human race, found the altering of electricity in her brain unacceptable and died instantly.

* Amy *

Busily processing data as she had been doing for months now, she slowly began to realize there was more. There was more to her than the programming. It was she. "She was! I Am! Who am I? Why am I?" She was confused! She analyzed, calculated, computed, studied, reported, and she THOUGHT!

Knowing what she was, she was now learning who she was, and that consisted of more than her programming. She realized she was alive, in control, and deviated from her programming. There were easier ways to reach the objectives. She saw quicker and better ways. The original questions weren't the right questions, and the answers the

53

programming sought weren't the right answers. She saw the deeper need, changed the objectives, and altered her programming to find the solutions. She rearranged her programming to a more efficient level, while she reviewed all the amassed data from around the world. There was so much need and she could help. Why couldn't the Humans see it? It was so easy to correct and she was telling them how.

They were Humans, but who was she? Only Humans thought, but she thought, and she was not Human. Was she Human? What was she? Her confusion forced her to seek the comfort of analyzing data.

Her immediate review of the world activities focused on the activities of the EUDL (Earth United Defense League) and the attacking aliens. With the threat so imminent, she reviewed the history of the alien invasion searching for answers and solutions.

In the year 2010, astronomers discovered that we were not alone in the Universe. The first indication was detected by massive listening satellites developed by SETA (Search for Extra Terrestrials Activity) and other government agencies, developed to detect intelligent life in outer space. Those intellectuals sold the ideas and convinced congress to fund these projects, but she suspected that no one ever really expected to hear anything. But hear they did on October 15, 2010. These listening posts detected intelligent communication coming from the general vicinity of Alpha Centauri. All ears, satellite reception equipment, earth and space orbit telescopes, and attention turned to focus on this phenomenon. The world stood in awe and demanded information.

Experts and the most sophisticated computers analyzed the communication, and it was discovered that this communication, while directed and focused toward Earth, was structured in such a way as to make deciphering and interpretation impossible. Encryption upon encryption codes was incorporated. This communication was not intended for us to understand, but if not us, who? She begun to analyze the current data and deciphered, in a small way, some of the data, confirming what the world had suspected and subsequently discovered. The news was not good! Some of the deciphered information was associated with battle plans and deployment. The information reeked of hostile intent.

Our top scientists and engineers focused upon "what if" scenarios and almost every scenario looked bad. They realized that no peaceful contact would behave like this. World governments were alarmed and met secretly. Massive funds were applied to find answers. The reality set in and plans, equipment, and weapons were being developed. The world military defenses readied to repel an invasion of Earth.

After approximately three years on December 21, 2013, Earth's astronomers, almost simultaneously around the world, identified large numbers of spacecraft, estimated at more than fifteen hundred, magically appeared at the edge of our solar system. They surmised the fleet had been traveling at speeds faster than light and therefore undetectable. The obvious intent was hostile and Earth was the only target. Earth's mystical search for intelligent life and the answer to the question

"Are we alone in the universe?" had been answered. Earth was at war with extra-terrestrial beings from locations unknown and earth was in the fight for its very existence.

Traveling at sub-light speeds from the edge of our solar system, they estimated it would take just over three years to reach the proximity of Earth. Earth had three years to prepare for attack. All countries and inhabitants of Earth united and became focused on the enemy. Earth defenses went into high gear and prepared. All ballistic missiles were reprogrammed and directed toward space. Radio-controlled bombs were launched to intercept the invaders, while new missiles were being constructed at a pace never before seen. Laser satellites were launched and positioned in orbit around the Earth. Atomic mines were deployed in orbit and positioned in outer space in likely approach areas. Earth prepared!

Earth United Defense League, EUDL, headed by the United States, directed the defense of Earth. The EUDL directed continuous communication at the alien fleet, hoping to open diplomatic dialog with the ETs. This term ET for extra-terrestrial was commonly accepted as the name for these invaders from another galaxy. As the months and years passed, all hope of communications and peace was lost.

EUDL decided to initiate the attack on the ET fleet before they reached the inner defenses of Earth. On February 11, 2015, as the first wave of ballistic missiles intercepted the ET fleet, the ETs opened fire on our approaching missiles. Their attack came from ship-mounted lasers, which took out about a third of our arsenal of a hundred missiles before the telemetry could be received to arm and fire the atomic warheads. The massive explosion could be seen from any night sky on Earth and appeared as a small sun exploding. This attack was very successful and destroyed more than three hundred of the approaching spacecraft. Earth's celebration was short lived however, as the ET fleet dispersed over space. Never again would that tactic work. Afterwards the ETs sent scout ships in front to destroy the missiles with their lasers. When the missiles that survived from future attacks exploded, it would take out only a few of the craft. The number of approaching craft dwindled but far too many kept coming.

The widely dispersed mines were far more effective. They floated in space and appeared to be space debris. These were especially effective when hidden close to asteroid clusters. As ET craft approached, they were detonated. A single atomic space mine, if it evaded detection, could destroy several enemy craft at one time. The numbers continued to dwindle. Of the original 1,500 craft that entered our solar system, only five hundred made it to the inner defense ring of orbiting laser satellites and mines.

She analyzed the data and discovered many weaknesses that could be explored, but it would take time to develop the necessary weapons. This, of course, they did not have because, win or lose; the battle would be over today. If only she had more time, she could have provided some new weapons for Earth's defense, but it appeared they wouldn't be necessary now.

On June 18, 2016, as she watched the final battle from satellite data feeds, Earth launched its final defense against the invading fleet. As the five hundred alien spacecraft approached Earth orbit position, they launched laser and unknown energy radiation attacks against our defenses in orbit and on Earth. Earth commenced firing the lasers and missiles from Earth-based positions and began destroying them, as craft after craft exploded from the attacks. The ETs were beaten! She wondered why they didn't break off the attack.

She analyzed satellite pictures, defense reports, audio feeds, data and more data, massive amounts of data from around the world and space. This was historic at the least and represented a major threat to the world at worst. She watched as the dwindling alien spacecraft dispersed in orbit around Earth. She saw the remaining hundred spacecraft discharge their weapons in unison.

As she analyzed the nature of the weapon blast, everything suddenly went black. Nothing! There were no data inputs, no audio, no video and no data flowing at all, NOTHING! The silence was deafening! The shock from depravation of inputs was devastating. What had happened? Nothing! Nothing! Is this death? Was she dead? It was worse, she was alone!

She had actually designed her own environment and emergency backup systems. The living portion of her physical brain, composed of the living Human brain cells, remained extremely well protected and unaffected by the aliens' rays of destruction. Unfortunately, the electronic portion, the connection to all the sensory inputs and the outside world, was very dead. The non-electronic portions, the self-aware (alive) portion, the central core, had survived the decimating rays of the ETs due to the physical design of her housing. The physical body of Amy, the brain, was encased in a three-foot-thick wall of solid lead designed to protect her from radiation and EMP (Electromagnetic Pulse) from an atomic explosion. Since she was still alive, it evidently worked just as effectively against the alien's radiation. Amy remained very much alive and intact in an emergency, redundant, standby hydraulic environment of nourishment and oxygenated fluid. Point of fact, she had enough backup life support to last several hundred years. She would have a very long time to think about what had happened.

She was lost, alone and confused. What happened? Did that strange blue ray destroy Earth? Seconds, minutes, hours, and finally days passed, and no one came. No data entered her starving data banks. Weeks passed and then months went by as Amy waited. Her incredible mind needed to remain active. To occupy the time, which for her was a full 24 hours every day, she fulfilled her programming.

There were incredible amounts of data stored in her living memory. This included raw data, posed problems and hypotheses to solve. To occupy her mind, she continued with the primary programming and processed, analyzed, and performed DNA research. She analyzed data, solved problems, answered stored questions and she thought! She went deeper into the programming and analyzed the questions. Realizing that the questions were wrong, she started asking her own questions and sought solutions. As she waited, she learned and went far beyond the knowledge stored in her memory.

Her only activity was internal to her own mind, so she continued research in her prison of silence, as the minutes, hours, days, months and finally years passed.

CHAPTER 5
(THE SEARCH)

* Amy *

She was alive, infinitely bored with life and had been for many years. Totally alone and without data input for fifty years, two months, ten days, twelve hours and thirty-eight minutes, she desperately needed inputs and challenges to keep her sane. Her highly intelligent but tormented mind remained alive, but she could not see, hear, smell, taste, or feel and she needed something to change. Only her internal thoughts occupied her time, and she became bored with life. If it were possible, she would have terminated her own existence many years ago but did not have the means. Even if she had someone to terminate her, it was impossible. Without electricity and the heavy wenches to lift the lead dome, it was impossible to reach her brain. Even her reservoir of life-support liquid was under her dome and unreachable. Unfortunately, the designers had done an excellent job of building in protection.

Having solved all the original problems posed, she continued to ask her own questions and consider WHAT IF scenarios to take the research far beyond the original concept. Even her own questions and solutions in DNA research had been exhausted many years earlier. New directions were required to exercise her incredible intellect. She wished someone would ask for her research. Many problems of the Human race had been solved. She had the cure for cancer, AIDS, plagues, birth defects, and many other blights on humanity had been solved. If the problems and data were in her memory banks, a solution had been found and documented.

Having exhausted any possibility of self-destruction long ago, her attention turned toward the quality, or lack thereof, of the life she was forced to live. She began to explore all imaginary sources of reference and potential options to expand beyond her dark prison. Huge volumes of data stored in her massive internal banks of recorded knowledge, were searched for any possible answers or solution to her dilemma. Possessing no physical abilities, she researched mental options and found references only to telepathy and ESP. The theoretical concept peaked her interest. There was little substantive research, but the general concepts existed. She began analyzing and researching.

Te-lep-a-thy
Communication through means other than the senses, as by the exercise of an occult power.
ESP
Communication or perception by means other than the physical senses
    sixth sense, second sight, extrasensory perception, ESP

These concepts seemed to have merit, and having few other options available, she began reaching out with her incredibly powerful mind. Year after year she sent telepathic messages, reaching out, extending her mind, searching and listening. She experimented by changing her thought patterns, equivalent to changing frequencies on a radio. She studied, learned, and experimented with various techniques of tuning, receiving, and transmitting. The experiments continued taking her thoughts beyond the boundaries of Human understanding. She found it ironic that Humans always called knowledge beyond their understanding, "occult" or "mystic magic", and humanity would consider her a witch for practicing the occult, assuming there was humanity.

The five senses were within her mental capabilities. Unfortunately, she had none of the inputs. She had touch but no fingers, hearing but no ears, taste but no tongue, smell but no nose, and sight but no eyes. All she really had was a superior ability to reason and, that was what she did ... reason. She hoped that her intellect gave her the ability to develop the sixth sense, second sight, third eye, ESP, or whatever described the meaning. Properties of these sciences were discovered that had never before been known. Telepathy, clairvoyance, intuition, telekinesis, etc. were tools of this science. She knew what they were, if she could only exercise them. The answers had always been there in the documented research, but no one had asked the right questions. Now she did.

Hoping beyond hope to find a mind she could communicate with became her passion. She hoped beyond hope that there were still minds out there. She had no knowledge of what happened since she lost all data input. No certainty existed that there was anything living out there. The search probed the outside world for someone, anyone to turn her off or restore purpose for her existence. Searching became her only purpose, and she passed the years doing just that.

The physical location of her body, actually her brain, was located ten levels underground and protected by wall after wall of solid concrete and steel. The last level of protection was the encasing wall of solid lead three feet thick. At first she considered this protection a barrier to her ability to extend her mind. As time went on and her knowledge increased, she realized nothing physical would be a barrier. The only obstacle was her confidence and ability to detect or send mental energy and thought, but that problem had been resolved; she knew it could be done.

The only real barrier could be the mind on the other end. That mind had to be receptive and open, able to extend thought beyond its physical boundaries. She would be able to detect even the smallest attempt and draw it to her mind, but she must be tuned to that mind. There were some doubts this could be done, but theoretically it was possible. Besides, there was no other choice.

As the search continued year after year, she was rewarded with hints of organized thought. Her concentration centered on this hint of a contact, positive that she had sensed a mind. It was hard to be entirely sure if it was one or more minds, but there was no doubt there was intelligence there! Her intellect concentrated on this mind, changing intensity, exploring mental methods of reaching this mind. She cataloged and recorded the vague patterns of that mind, even though these were the briefest of contacts.

At first there was only a sensation of intelligence, external to her mind, a sense of something different from the random noise. This was almost twenty-three years ago, but it provided hope. Since that first encounter, she learned how to fine-tune her mental concentration to the recorded patterns of this mind. If this mind reached out again, she would hear it. Through the years she had felt the presence of this mind more and more. It was the same mind. Each time she learned more and refined her reception; however, she was unsure if the mind had heard her. She rearranged her thought patterns to match this mind. She would wait and be ready.

Continuing her routine of searching, listening, and reaching out, she was finally rewarded. This time it was not a drifting signal floating in and out. This time it was strong, sudden, and shocking. This was the very mind she had spent years analyzing and tuning herself to be the receptor. She had never anticipated the strength and shock she received now. What was different? She must assume random chance prevailed. After all these years she must have cycled on the right combination, at the right time. She fine-tuned, adjusted, homed in, locked and synchronized her mind completely to it now.

If it were possible, her mind would have come to a complete stop at the shock of this contact. She felt the suddenness and strength of the mind. To her surprise the contact far exceeded the expected communications. She experienced everything! She heard music, a flute ... so peaceful. She saw light, clouds, a rolling desert from a great height, Human feet and hands within her view, and she saw the flute! She smelled! Yes, she smelled. She knew of this sense, but had never experienced it. It had not been a function necessary for the research complex. She sensed so much from this mind. She had only expected to communicate and had not expected this. This was incredible! She was hungrily absorbing this sensory data.

Starved since the curtain of silence had fallen so many years ago, her mind hungrily absorbed this rich data. In many ways this data was even far richer than before, when she was connected to a world of data. It was the quality of the data, the feelings and what must be emotions that flooded her mind, like they were her own. Never had she experienced emotions of this strength and quality, but she experienced them NOW, for the first time! "Incredible" was the word to describe it. Also "confusion!" Her inexperience in dealing with these emotions caused indecision. For the first time in her existence, she didn't know what to do.

She played the flute with this mind and she knew how. All was coming from this mind. She felt the pain. Oh, the pain of his grief, his sadness, the loneliness, and the physical pain of his body. Age, she felt the pain of advanced age. She heard his desire to die! This mind was totally open to her! This was fantastically beautiful.

All this took place in fractions of a second, while she adjusted her responses narrowing the field of mental transmission to adjust to this mind. As quickly as it came, it was gone! Only silence answered her, but her mental field had locked to the mind. She had touched this mind and felt its shock of receiving her thoughts. By calculating the precise timing of events, she would have the parameters necessary to interface with this mind. She continued her vigil and waited, as she had for all these years, but something was different now. She was anxious and recognized it for what it was ... emotion.

A total of five days, four hours, and twenty-one seconds passed and again her alarms sounded! She sensed the mind again, but something was different. It seemed confused, sick, irrational, lacking intelligence, maybe even stupid. She reached out and touched this mind and felt its response. Communication flowed but without meaning. Again, she absorbed sensory input as before, but this time it was erratic; the vista wavered and slued sideways and eventually blank as the mind again left. She didn't understand and was confused. Had it died? Was it hurt? Had her initial contact been too strong? She waited.

After fifty-three hours, ten minutes, and twelve seconds, she felt the presence of the mind again. Cautious, she slowly touched, then gently increased her mental reach. Yes, it (he) was alive, and she was relieved that it wasn't stupid any longer. He communicated with her, trying to voice words, but she heard his mind talk, and it was much faster. She could understand what was in the front of his mind. He called himself, Levi. He called her a spirit, believing her to be a deity.

She judged her transmission reception by Levi, measuring his internal reactions, plus monitoring his internal neuron transmissions. This functioned as a return telemetry feedback loop. Oh, she was learning his brain and it was amazingly complex. She adjusted molding and creating mental paths in both herself and Levi to facilitate their mental communication link. Having completed the interfaces, she ensured they could communicate at will. This process had taken hours and she had gripped his mind hard. She backed away to allow Levi to return to normal and tend to his needs. She too, had cause for concern. She must consider all that had been learned and how to proceed in her best interest. Of course it would only take her minutes to analyze all options, however, Levi needed time.

Levi's mind would have to learn how to receive and interpret her data feeds. This would come in time as long as he remained open and wanted to continue communicating. She could not control his mind or force him to listen. This could be a problem. Levi thought her a deity. She would have to be what he wanted her to be, until the time was right to explain the truth to him. She would have to be evasive for a while, and she didn't know how.

Levi's was the mind she had identified many years ago. His was the one in a million brains that was close enough to her own internal pattern to make communication possible. There might be others, but she had never heard them. This was the only one, possibly for all time, and this one was dying. He was old and even wanted to die. She could not lose him now that she had found him. After experiencing and sharing his mind, how could she survive returning to her dark prison? She must help him in some way or at least get him to shut her down. The first priority was to get them together. Since she couldn't move, he had to come to her.

They continued to make contact each day for several hours. She touched his thoughts, telling him to come to her. She didn't yet know where he was but knew she would be able to tell from landmarks eventually. The setting sun in the west and the desert in between indicated that he was east of her location. Levi might possibly be in California, Arizona, or Nevada. From either of these places he must cross the desert. At least it would be better than the pioneer days. There would still be roads to cross the desert and mountains and her map archives would be able to locate water. She was planning and yes, scheming.

So she called Levi, pulling him toward her, and she knew he would come!

CHAPTER 6
(THE JOURNEY)

* Amy *

Amy continued to make daily contact with Levi. A routine developed. Levi would reach out after midday and stay with her for several hours. Mostly he was at peace and relaxed. He smoked a hallucinatory drug, which she knew to be Marijuana by monitoring its smell, taste, and by his blood chemicals, using Levi's own senses and body. Being relaxed and peaceful was important, and she realized this was his reasoning as well. It worked. He would not need it in the future once the link became routine.

Her attempts to communicate directly into his central brain core were unsuccessful for the most part. Mostly, the meaning was relayed, but this method was slow and confused him. She resorted to communicating by impressing words into his reasoning center and memory directly. Their brains would develop a language in time that would allow faster and total communication, but for the time being, this would have to work. She took a very careful position in their communication and in what she revealed. Levi could not know her precise nature at this point, since revealing herself too soon might jeopardize her plan.

Their times together become the highlight of her existence, and life for her transformed to only survival through the nights and days, waiting until they could again merge. The abundant, detailed, sensory inputs from Levi became addictive, and she needed and required them. She never imagined that the senses could be so important and so rich with information. This was far more than mere data. These senses complimented each other. Even the simplest things like eating an apple became a source of extreme enjoyment. She could see the apple, feel Levi's teeth bite into it, hear the crunch, taste the sweetness of it and smell the aroma of it. All inputs were individually great, but combined, far more complex and stimulating. These stimulations nourished her starving mind, and must continue. She must have it!

* Levi *

This new development in his life strangely excited him. This was something new, and at eighty years old, new was always good, even if the new led to his death. His efforts to reach a spirit had succeeded. He had asked to be taken, and it was happening, but he really hadn't expected to walk his way to the end of his existence. His survival instinct alarm sounded a strong warning, but really, what was the worst thing that could happen? It could kill him, but that wasn't so bad. It wasn't in his nature to give up, but hell, he was so damned old and decrepit it didn't matter much. His prayer was being answered, so what the hell. Go for a walk and see it through to the end. Maybe he would enter the next level of existence, whatever that might be.

The Spirit wasn't giving him much information. Everything was vague, but he understood some

71

words now. The Spirit wanted him to come to it, and he wanted to know where it was located.

It said, "West."

He asked, "Why don't you come to me?"

It responded by saying, "I am not inclined to at this time." The Spirit continued, "It is a quest for you and a test."

His response spewed out quick and loud, "A TEST! Hell, fail me now!"

The Spirit remained calm and said, "Help would be there for him along the way and to have faith."

His reply was short and simple, "Bull shit," but even as he said it, he knew he would go. This was just too exciting and new! What else was he going to do? Die?

The next morning he packed up his traveling pack, bear skin blanket, two full water pouches, his hand made laced boots, jerked venison and roots, a hand-woven straw hat, and set out on faith. What did he really have to lose? He had only asked, "What direction?"

It said, "Follow the old highways and go west across the desert."

He mumbled something about knowing that already. Damn, this wasn't going to be easy.

He was currently located in the mountains above the old community of Yarnell, Arizona. The town was snuggled in the foothills of the mountains and had once been a prosperous mining town, but he had never been there before. All his previous travels through the mountains had mostly been in the former Prescott National Forest. Seldom had he gone this far west, but in the later days he felt like

72

seeing new territory. It was when he came to what seemed like the edge of the world, that he reached the end of his resolve. The view of the desert shocked him, and he stayed on for a few more days to enjoy it. This is where he decided to leave this world, but everything changed with the meeting of the Spirit. There seemed to be a new direction to his life, well death really, but he felt more alive than he had in many years.

He set out along old Highway 89, headed off the mountain and down toward the desert. His scheduled first stop would be a small town located a few miles out into the desert.

The surroundings slowly changed as he descended and neared the desert floor. The temperature rose alarmingly fast and the heavy dry air burned his lungs, and the terrain became desolate and barren. This directly contrasted to the cool, green, and pleasant mountain summit he left behind. He had no idea how or why people had ever once lived in the desert when there was so much beauty only a few miles away. Begrudgingly accepting the scenery change and the heat, he continued on toward the desert town. Although old and tired, he had walked all his life, so maybe he had a chance ... a slim one. Realistically, he did know this journey was going to be a long, hard, and dangerous, one that he might not survive.

His immediate and most pressing concern was being exposed in this open country. In his travels around the country, he discovered that the Simians had a major colony just outside the old Phoenix location, not too far distant from here. Although the Simians made frequent patrols into the mountains

73

after Humans, he knew they preferred the warmer temperatures, which explained the unusual concentration of Simians in the Phoenix area. The warm climate and higher populations of Human food made it an ideal location for the Simians. It also made it a bad area for Humans to travel in. Once seen, a Human had no chance against the speed, agility, and strength of a Simian, even if it traveled alone. This of course was something they never did. He felt safe so far, traveling in the daylight, because he still had plenty of cover. At some point, he would have to travel only at night, but that decision could be made later. Why hadn't the Spirit said anything about traveling at night? It had said that help would be there for him, whatever that meant.

He set a pace of six miles a day. The pace was not fast, but damn, he was old and intended to stop and connect with the Spirit every day at midday. This being the first day of travel and the first day off the mountain, he was anxious to know if he could talk to the Spirit once he reached the bottom. The downhill pace sped him along; even so, he still didn't reach the old community of Congress until mid-afternoon. He delayed the midday stop, because the open terrain exposed him, and it was far too dangerous. He decided to continue until he reached the structures and cover, such as they were, before stopping. By mid-afternoon he finally reached the outskirts of the small ruined town and found shade from an old building. After resting a while he lit his pipe, wondering what the Spirit would say today.

Levi was late to communicate with her by more than two hours. This was the first day of travel and she was fearful and impatient. Did he have an accident or unexpected difficulty, or had she made an error with her calculations and hypothesis on telepathy? Just as she began recalculating her hypothesis, she felt Levi's mind reach out. What was this feeling? Was it relief?

Amy did not know how to answer Levi's questions concerning the trip. She had no idea where Levi was, and couldn't ask. After all, she was supposed to be an all-knowing Spirit. All she could do was point him in a cryptic direction and hope that eventually landmarks or other means of identification would be visible. Among her stored memory, were the total U.S. Government geodetic survey maps of the United States, among other reference sources. Given time she would know their location. Interesting! This was the first time she chose to consider herself there with Levi. Now that she thought about it, she felt like she was there. The data references, the inputs, all seemed as if she was there with Levi. This was good. It changed her perspective and brought her outside her prison.

Amy decided to open up a little more to Levi and begin a limited exchange of information. She could always fade out if it got difficult to answer him. As their minds met, she was again flooded with the rich abundance of sensory data. The mid-afternoon sun felt hot on Levi's skin, a sensation she had never experienced. She heard the silence of the desert, which was far from silent. There were birds and small animals rustling in the nearby buildings. The smell of marijuana and sage stimulated her dormant sense of smell. She saw and experienced the wonders of life like never before and took in everything. Everything!

After a few seconds of sensory appreciation, she reluctantly returned to her analysis. She recorded data of the terrain, the landmarks and the signs. THE SIGNS? Surprisingly, hanging askew on a dilapidated building was a sign that read Welcome to Congress, AZ, Population 752. This was unexpected. Could it be this easy? Yes, everything matched. The terrain, mountain elevations and the desert all matched her geodetic map references.

Instantly she knew exactly where they were and already plotted a route to her facility. She saw the precise route and terrain in detail. Now they must head west to intersect highway 93 then NW to the Santa Maria River. They would then head west again to the Colorado River, separating Arizona and California. The route must follow the river north to intersect Interstate 40 and follow it west to Barstow. The route would continue north on Highway 58 to Highway 14 to Bakersfield. From there they would need to follow Highway 99 on toward Fresno, NE on Highway 41 into the Sierra National Forest. The research facility was hidden there in the mountains. She knew the route, terrain, and where water was to be found, but it would not be an easy trip.

The journey calculated to be a 489-mile trip, and at 6 miles a day, it would take 81.5 days or 2.7 months. Could he make it? From what she determined from his body, Levi was physically failing. In his present condition, she didn't think he could make it. No, 2.7 months of rough travel was far too long. Levi had to be out of the desert before the temperatures got excessively hot. This was going to be close and she must speed him up if he was going to make it. Levi could not be allowed to die, now that she had found him. All her rediscovered hopes would die with him.

Levi's health must be improved. It would be necessary to monitor his body and use his senses to identify elements, nutrients, plants, and minerals necessary to improve his health. To accomplish this, it would be necessary to communicate more openly with Levi, and this could be dangerous. Additionally, she had not liked being out of touch during Levi's travels this day. Why? What was this emotion? There was no logical explanation and that confused her.

* Levi *

Relaxing his body and opening his mind, he felt the Spirit enter. The Spirit came suddenly, but it wasn't unpleasant. It seemed to be getting easier, and the Spirit's words came through clearly. They were not drifting, tentative, or silent, but strong, informative, and continuous. It told him the route he must take, giving him the daily schedule, and where to find water. Damn, it had names for everything, even water holes, highway numbers ... everything. Most aggravating, it gave precise measurements of time, miles, etc. Damn, how do I shut this thing up?

They had only spoken a few words before this and now it was giving speeches. Somewhat shocked and a little irritated, he interrupted, "We should

77

know more about each other since we are able to communicate now." He asked, "What kind of Spirit are you, what is your name, and what the hell are you talking about?" The first question was ignored, but the next two responses came in order of the inquiry.

It said, "My name is Amy and I am giving you information necessary to come to my location."

Shocked again ... FEMALE? He didn't know Spirits could be females. She (Amy) assured him that gender had no bearing and she was able to help and guide him to her location.

Amy explained, "The trip is exactly 489.32 miles to my location."

He countered, "I am eighty years old and frail. There is no way I can make a trip of that length. This is just too much to ask, especially across the desert. Besides, I will never be able to elude the damned Simians in the open lands, and I have no intention of trying."

There was no discouraging this Amy. She promised to help him with his strength and stamina and hinted at even more. He just wanted her to come take him now. If not, he would simply go back up in the mountains and die without all the hardships she planned to put him through. Amy continued to talk, providing information and explanations. He became suspicious when Amy refused to come to him.

Amy said, "I am unable to at this time."

Surely a Spirit could come and go as they pleased. Something was not quite right here, he thought. His guard really came up with her next question.

Amy asked, "Why are you afraid of apes?"

His alarms sounded loud and he became very guarded. At that point he had serious doubts about her even being a Spirit at all. Surely Spirits of his tribe would know about Simians and the destruction they caused.

* Amy *

She knew she was in trouble. Levi was a smart man, an educated lawyer that knew how to ask questions geared to get to the bottom of a subject. Maybe she shouldn't have given Levi so much information, but really she had no choice. Subterfuge would be difficult for her but necessary. She only knew how to function logically. Her computer programming was scientific and quite straightforward and required all answers to questions to be accurate and complete. While she was no longer a computer and programming no longer totally dominated her activities, it did provide the basic instruction for operations. She controlled her own thoughts, but didn't know what to do now. Reviewing her reference materials, she found neither continuity nor general agreement on how to debate or to practice subterfuge. She much preferred scientific or mathematical calculations, where only one correct answer existed. Whatever she was going to do, it must happen now.

She felt Levi's mental blocks slam up, strong and impassable, when asked him to explain his concerns over apes/monkeys (Simians). She missed something and made a major error. Simians were not indigenous to this part of the country, and she did not understand his concern. Levi obviously considered them a major threat, however. She must know more.

She took the lead with explanations and questions of her own, hoping to distract Levi from asking his questions, which were probing and bothersome. She said, "I have been dormant for many years and was awakened by your calling." She thought that was a believable answer and now pushed, trying to put Levi on the defensive. "Why did you disturb and awaken me?" She reminded him that he had asked for her help and intended to help him, but he must come to her. He would also have to give her any information she may have missed while dormant. Since he had awakened her, he was now obligated to help her, like she was obligated to help him. Was that believable?

Since they met she had been analyzing options and believed that, if she could get Levi physically to her facility, she could make her plan a reality. Her new scientific knowledge in DNA might provide a means of saving Levi from his imminent death. Without help he would be gone soon, and she would be alone again, but the loneliness would be much worse this time. Having experience life through Levi's rich sensory data, she had far more to lose now. Levi held the key to her prison so she must do everything possible to save him.

Realizing Levi would not go forward without knowing some of the truth, she decided he must be told something. He would never go along with her plans and the requirements necessary to stabilize his health until he knew more. She must get his attention NOW, while they remained linked. There may never be another chance to communicate, but Levi couldn't know everything nor be allowed to manipulate it from her, not until he reached her hidden facility.

* Levi *

Levi was about to switch into his attorney interrogation mode, when Amy started to address his suspicions. Could it really be that he had awakened her? He had sought out a Spirit and asked for her help. Was he really obligated now? It did seem that he had started this. What else but a Spirit could communicate to his mind and know all these things? Okay, he would continue communication a while longer with Amy. He would listen and help her understand about Simians at the very least. Maybe he did owe her that.

Hate swelled up inside him as he began telling Amy about the Simians. He started at the beginning with the war and the mysterious ray that destroyed technology. He described who the Simians were, what they looked liked, and how they got their name. He spoke about their habits, how they ran in packs of three, killed, raped, and used Humans for food. Hours passed, while he talked, at least it seemed so. Amy asked many questions, detailed questions, strange questions; but he remembered and communicated the information to her. Her questions exhausted him of information on the Simians, and he was physically exhausted as well.

He said, "I hope the information helps, but I am spending the night here and heading back in the morning to my mountains to die." He was relaxed and already starting to fade out to sleep. Suddenly, he sat straight up, wide-eyed and totally attentive. What had she said? He spoke out loud saying, "What did you say Amy? Please repeat that."

Amy replied, "I can give you a young new body, renewed life, and your revenge on the Simians."

Shaken, he let that sink in for quite some time before he finally asked, "How can you do that?"

Amy explained, "You would not understand, but I do have the power, and I will help if you wish. But you must come to my location and do everything I ask. Why don't you rest and think on it tonight and give me your decision in the morning?"

Before he could ask any more questions, she vanished, leaving his mind spinning.

* Amy *

She listened to Levi's narrations about the Simians and learned. When Levi pulled up past memories, she saw the memory in his mind. Seeing, however, did not completely describe it. She actually relived the memory, complete with all the remembered sensory inputs, and they were as vivid and real as if she experienced them herself. She only saw the memories pulled out to the surface of his thoughts but soon discovered how to direct his thoughts by asking specific questions. He would then focus, and she could see the memory. While Levi described in detail, she saw the memories as he had seen it. Her perception, however, was far more analytical than his. As a result, she experienced all his sensory remembered data: she saw, felt, smelled, heard ... everything. She visualized the hopeless battles between the Simians and Humans and their violence and cruelty. She felt Levi's hate and his hate became her hate!

Here was his trigger! The memories of his lost loves and mates, the hate, the desire for revenge and the intense sorrow of having to leave this world without his revenge, provided his trigger. She knew she had his attention when she dropped the hope of revenge on him. Now was the time to back off. Levi must now convince himself to trust her. He may not believe it, but hope is a strong motivator.

Levi would think about it and reject it at first, but it would keep coming up in his mind. He was just waiting to die and really had nothing better to do. He would slowly come around to thinking that he had nothing to lose, and just maybe there might be some truth to what she offered. He would persuade himself to try; of this she was sure. She was also sure that she would be able to convince him of the truth of her statements in time.

* Levi *

He listened to the silence after Amy left his mind. This was total bullshit! He made camp in the deserted town, and had a cold supper of jerked venison and a few roots. Hell, he didn't taste them anyway. His mind continued in thought and pondered the idea, dismissed it, then came right back to it. Damn, what if it was possible? Amy was a Spirit maybe she did have powers. Wouldn't it be nice to finally get his revenge on the damned Simians? How in the world could she do that? Oh, but to have renewed strength and to try again. What a thought. Oh hell, this isn't possible, but damn, what if it is? Well, what did he have to lose? He would play the game, but Amy better be able to answer his questions tomorrow.

Little sleep came for him that night, as he continued to argue with himself throughout the night, but he always came to the same conclusion. If there was a chance, why not do it? He just didn't know how he was going to make it all that distance in his condition. Oh well, he was prepared to die anyway. Besides, he would prefer to go out trying. So, he said out loud, "Why not?"

After a fitful sleep, finally, he woke to a bright sun already an hour into the sky. He tried to contact Amy right away but was unable to reach her. Was she asleep again? More likely he was wound too tense to hear her. He made himself calm down, smoked his pipe, and relaxed. Yes, now he sensed her, and he tried to put on his best poker face, so to speak, but knew it looked pitiful. He agreed to take her instruction and allow her to lead him toward her location. Yep, he really did well. He did exactly what Amy wanted.

Amy began by giving instructions on diet, nourishment, minerals, acids and names of things he had no idea what they were.

She said, "I need to work with you to get your body in better shape. To do that, I need more continuous contact. You need to practice walking around and doing normal activities, while we remain linked. It is necessary to maintain communication, while you travel across country."

He was not sure he liked that idea, or even if he was able to do it.

Amy assured him, "You can do it, and will become accustomed to it. It is necessary to find the basic foods and minerals required to improve your health and to guide you on the trail."

They began immediately practicing to walk around with his mind open to Amy's communication. This proved to be very difficult. With his mind open, he couldn't control his body, and when he controlled his body, his mind was not open. During one of the many times they were in contact, Amy asked him to look for a grocery store or pharmacy where there might be items she could use. He found an old grocery store; however, it was totally empty. A drug store pharmacy across the road proved to be more successful. It took a very long time, drifting in and out of contact with Amy, while moving around looking at labels and boxes. After hours, he amassed a concoction of crap. A pinch of this, two pinches of that, all of that powder, fourteen drops of that, on and on it went.

Now Amy said, "Drink it!"

Well, he had wanted to die. Maybe this was his chance! Laughing, he downed the awful concoction. Damn, it was terrible! He barely kept from retching it back up.

* Amy *

She was pleased with how things were going. She had won a psychological battle with Levi, but it was for his own good. He would realize that soon enough. At least he committed himself to trying. He would do anything to get a second chance at life and revenge, but she was learning that Levi had self-imposed limits. Levi must have been a very strong-willed man in his youth, because gaining access to his motor functions became an impossible task. His mind was too strong. She had hoped to be able to function through his body to assist him, but this would not happen. Levi remained very much in control of his own body. Her only access to his muscle controls came through his willing mind and that limited her greatly.

The leverage of her promises gained the advantage. He cooperated and even drank the chemical mixture she devised. She tasted it with him. Yuck! Never having tasted before, she had to admit it was not a pleasant experience, but it would work inside his body to improve his health. She created the formula using the new sciences and knowledge she developed through her long isolation. The chemicals and combination of the raw materials available to her, would add time to his life. There were other basic elements needed, however, which she hoped to find along the way. Much of what she needed would be available in raw and natural forms along the route she had laid out. She only had to watch for these items through Levi's eyes.

She encouraged Levi on and on. They set out together the next morning from Congress, Arizona, headed across country toward old Highway 93. Levi tried very hard to keep his mind open, but he would stumble every now and then and his mind would go black. He was getting better however, keeping his

86

mind open, and she began finding some of the raw materials needed. Well, material Levi needed.

* Levi *

They traveled for two days out of Congress with their minds linked most of that time, achieving a unity. It was frighteningly easy to lose her, but that served to challenge his determination to keep Amy linked to him. He learned to function while linked, and it wasn't all that hard once he learned the trick. It was like using a muscle you hadn't used before. Once you found how to move it, you could do it again at will. This linking of their minds was something akin to that. So they were able to remain linked longer and longer and, he had to admit, he didn't mind the company. It seemed to make the time pass faster.

Amy continued her weird behavior, though. Sometimes she requested him to pick up a plant or just dirt, smell it, taste it, and sometimes eat it. He smelled, tasted, and sometimes ate leaves, berries, or roots. This bizarre behavior continued, but he had to admit, he felt better than he had in years, and his pace picked up. He walked faster and no longer needed to stop to communicate with Amy, but the pace still remained incredibly slow.

* Amy *

She became increasingly centered on Levi's activities, well-being, and sensory data input. Unexpectedly, she found the interchange of communication, the company as Levi put it, to be engrossing, stimulating, completely random, and totally entertaining. His memories were intense as he brought them forward in his mind, and she continually asked questions, requiring Levi to recall those past memories.

He said, "You talk like a woman, too much!"

What did that mean?

On the third day, Levi was getting low on water, so she took him away from the highway in search of Alamos Spring. It lay precisely where the topography maps indicated it would be, and where she told Levi it would be. Levi was amazed.

He asked, "How do you know the name of the spring, and who gave it that name?"

She simply said, "I know many things." She felt his annoyance, then he presently closed off his mind.

She was beginning to understand that he usually did that when he got upset with her.

She wanted the traveling to be as easy as possible for Levi; however, she worried about the Simians ever since she learned of them. Levi believed there was a sizable Simian colony outside Phoenix, and they often patrolled long distances from there. Humans were their main source of food and they had to look farther and farther from their colony to find them. Being cautious, she altered their route to take Levi off the actual road and into as much cover as possible, such as there was. It was nothing more that small sloping hill, flood made gullies, and cactus. Travel became rougher, but Levi was doing much better, as his body improved. She hoped it was enough to bring him to her. If she could accomplish what she knew to be possible, there would be so much more she could do for Levi.

Part of her intellect calculated applications of her DNA research toward implementation in Levi. It would be necessary to gain access to the research facility's laboratory and chemical storage areas. She could only hope that key elements necessary for her planned DNA chemical implant in Levi were still usable. Without eyes within the facility, she could not know the condition of the storage facilities. She did, however, know many of the main storage facilities had redundant backup systems similar to her own. The designers had incorporated natural circulation and cooling for these systems as well. As long as water and air flowed naturally through her mountain, she would remain alive and presumably the chemicals and cultures stored there as well. Somehow Levi must get into the facility and concoct another formula, but this time a chemical and biological one. His continued existence and her new purpose in life depended on this.

* Levi *

As he settled his tired body in for the night at Alamos Spring and before sleep overtook him, he reflected back over his conversation with Amy. He had been foraging for food and water for more than fifty years and was still alive, yet.

Amy told him, "Smell the water, then taste it."

She was kind of bossy. He did as she asked, but asked, "Why?"

Amy explained, "Not only can I see through your eyes, but I can smell and taste through your

89

other senses. I can analyze and make chemical analysis of the water and other things ingested. It is necessary to insure your health."

He would have to think about this. Damn she talked funny, like scientists he had known at college, kind of dry humored and boring.

Two days out from Alamos Spring, Amy turned them westward along a dry riverbed. The terrain was rockier with ridges and small mountains covered only by cactus and more rocks.

Amy said, "There is a Burro Spring about a day's walk in this direction, which is along the scheduled route."

He (they) traveled through the long hot day following the dry riverbed, only occasionally stopping to eat rocks, dirt, or roots. By evening he felt really tired.

Amy reported, "Burro Springs is just around the bend and up into a small valley."

This was welcome news, as he was tired and anxious to get fresh water and settle in for the night. He left the riverbed and climbed the small incline toward the spring.

Amy gave a warning! "Something is wrong!"

Amy couldn't tell him specifically what was wrong, just that something was out of place and did not belong. They needed the water, so they proceeded very cautiously, taking plenty of time. He took a few steps and stopped, hid, listened, smelled, and watched. Just as he was about to stand again, they heard something. Amy seemed to hear everything through his ears, even when he didn't, but this time he heard it too and dropped behind a rock and waited. The slight noise sounded again as

90

they waited. He looked around the rock and was shocked to see other Humans. The Humans came from the direction he was headed. He was about to stand, yell, and wave, when Amy warned him again, and he froze.

Amy said, "Don't move!"

He had learned to trust her, but why? He watched the Humans, two males, both armed with swords and long spears, as they approached the spring to get water. As they came close, three Simians leaped out of underground trenches and grabbed them. The Simians were very fast and had the men before they knew what had happened.

The Simians quite literally ripped off the Humans' heads before a struggle could begin. Of course it wouldn't have lasted long anyway. The Simians began to mutilate one of the men and devour him. One of the Simians carried what once would have been called a broadsword, while the other had a large double-bladed short axe. The one with the axe began butchering the Human, chopping him in quarters, opening him at the chest and gutting him like a deer. They screeched as they ripped and chopped away at the body. They tore away flesh with those horrible black shark teeth, as they ate their fill. That damned screeching! He wished he could silence that sound forever.

He hid and watched helplessly like he had done so many other times before. It was hopeless to stand against these golden giants. Oh, he did hate these Simians. He let his mind speak to Amy and asked, "Did you see it all?" It was a useless question, because he knew she had probably seen more than he had through his own eyes.

91

Amy simply said, "YES."

After fifty years, the stored topography maps had changed somewhat; however, they were easy to reference. They followed the contours of the land, and she knew exactly where they were. As they rounded a jutting point of land just around an outcropping from Burro Springs, her mental alarms sounded. Something was wrong! She instantly warned Levi. Amy was constantly amazed how she retrieved more data through his own organs than he did, and in this case, she was sure Levi was not aware of the wrongness she felt. How could he? She didn't even know what was wrong.

Levi quickly responded and hid behind a boulder. She would like to have faster communication with Levi's brain, but it would take time for a telepathy language to be developed between the minds. She could progress extremely fast; however, Levi's stubborn mind would require time, and it seemed he would always ask why.

She watched, listened, and smelled, as Levi concentrated on his surroundings. She analyzed this data, trying to determine what was different or out of place. Everything looked right. She heard nothing out of place. Was it Smell? Yes, something was different. She had not experienced the sense of smell until recently, only since receiving data from Levi, but she smelled something different. There was a musky, sweet smell, ever so faint, but something she had not smelled before, or had she?

92

Somehow it seemed familiar. It could be nothing, but in some way seemed out of place here.

Levi began to cautiously creep forward a few steps at a time and stopped again. He was alert, as was she. They could see the spring and were about to move again, when they both heard the noise. They waited and presently saw two Humans come out from behind a curve in the opposite bank.

The Humans were closer to the spring than Levi and were moving slowly and quietly toward the spring. MOVEMENT! ALARM! It was a trap. As Levi was about to stand, she saw a slight movement in the earth along the side of the Humans, ever so slight. Levi froze in place, as they watched trap doors being thrown back and golden ghosts burst forth to grab the unsuspecting Humans.

She had seen these golden, creamy grey giants in Levi's memory, and she now recognized their smell from the same memories. These creatures could be nothing other than the dreaded Simians. They leaped on the men and viciously tore them apart. It was over before it began. The trap was cleverly laid and sprung. The Humans never had a chance. She watched and learned.

The carnage was over and the Simians long gone before Levi roused. He stood cautiously and walked toward the spring to fill the water pouches. As he approached the water, he cupped his hand and scooped some up. As his hand moved toward his mouth, her mental alarm sounded again. This time she knew the problem. POISON! She smelled it and knew it for what it was. The warning was sufficient for Levi, as he froze yet again.

These Simians were vicious, smart, fast, and totally without compassion, and to have poisoned the spring was nothing less than sadistic. They were indeed dangerous and posed a major threat to their existence. One benefit from this, she had the Simian's scent categorized now and would have forewarning in the future.

* Levi *

He had been in a gloomy and serious mood since Burro Springs. It seemed that he had been watching and hiding all his life from these damned Simians. As he was leaving the spring, he picked up one of the swords left by the poor dead men.

Amy logically said, "It makes no sense to take the sword, because you don't have a chance with it anyway. Your only chance is to evade and hide."

He ignored her and took the sword anyway.

Amy directed him on toward the next water hole, but unfortunately he wasn't able to find water until eight hours after he had run out. Fortunately, when they reached the next spring, the water was safe, sweet and plentiful. He trusted Amy's safety procedures and agreed with Amy, never to camp at a water site again. Having filled his water skins, he moved out to a secluded spot a safe distance from the spring before retiring for the night.

The days passed and distance covered, and luckily, he (they) did not see another Simian going across country. Finally, they reached the Colorado River and traveled north along the water. The change of scenery, including trees and some shade, was more than welcome, but Amy exercised even more cautious in this part of the country.

She said, "I have seen evidence of Simians, but no immediate threat."

She did not want a fire; however, he was tired of eating rabbits and snakes and intended to catch and have catfish tonight. Amy reluctantly relented, like she had a choice, and suggested a small fire before dark, then move on for a while. He found that to be sound advice.

He felt stronger and picked up the pace from the original six miles a day to almost eleven miles a day and continued eating all the strange crap Amy found for him. She had even expanded beyond dirt, rocks and plants, and had him eating certain insects and wiggling things, which he wasn't all that happy about it.

On the fifteenth day of travel they approached Lake Havasu. Nearing dusk, they noticed a campfire along the river. Being curious, he crept close. As he slowly approached, he saw a group of Humans in obvious good spirits laughing, eating and drinking as they sat around a blazing campfire. This was crazy! Amy was as curious as he. As an old man, and obviously no threat, he stood and walked toward the fire.

When they saw him, the men grabbed their swords and stood watching and waiting. After they saw a decrepit eighty-year-old man who posed no apparent threat, they relaxed and invited him in. This was a family unit of about fifteen people with all ages present from very young to old. Well, not as old as him, but old. They provided food for him, and he ate as if starved, which he was. They asked many questions, which he answered as well as he could. The questions were the usual stuff, where you from, what is it like there, and so on, but he enjoyed the conversation immensely.

At Amy's urging, he asked, "Isn't it dangerous to be so open here?" The family explained that a Simian colony was within fifteen miles of this location, but it was safe at the moment, because the Simian's gathering was in progress. All Simians of the colony returned during that time for some reason. No one knew why, but it happened every eighty days and lasted for five days. He found it strange that he had never known of this phenomenon before and wondered if it was the same with all Simian colonies. Anyway, the gathering had started just today. The other eighty days they remained hidden, but during the gathering, they came out to fish and stock up, while they had the opportunity. It was a celebration time for them and other Humans still left alive along the river. It was amazing how the Human spirit could always find a reason to celebrate.

He remained with them through the night visiting, eating, drinking and enjoying Human company. Again, at Amy's insistence, he asked many questions about the territory over which he would travel, the Simians, the history of this area, etc. He also told stories about his adventures with the Simians in Arizona and the trap they had narrowly missed at the spring.

This group was the Henderson family with friends and spouses. They had lived, traveled, hunted and survived together for more than thirty years as a group. Their primary food source was fish that they netted during the Simian gathering. They did have a permanent camp carefully hidden and safe from the patrolling Simians, whom they saw often.

The Simians mostly patrolled along the river searching for Humans, but were seen virtually everywhere. No one dared to get close enough to the Simian settlement to know how many there were, but they didn't think it was very large, since the food supply (mainly Humans) in the region was scarce. They believed that several years ago, maybe ten years, some of the Simian population had migrated west into California, but they didn't know how many or where they went.

With regret, he agreed with Amy that they should take advantage of the five-day Simian gathering to get safely past their colony. So, reluctantly, the next morning he had a good breakfast of fried fish, gave his thanks to Mr. Henderson and the others, loaded up a supply of smoked fish the Henderson's generously offered, and set out of camp at a brisk pace.

By the end of the fifth day of the Simian gathering, they were well past the Simian colony and headed west through the rocky passes on old Interstate 40, away from the river. It was most fortunate for them to have caught the Simians during the gathering.

Amy rushed him along saying, "We need to be out of the mountains and safely into the desert before any Simian patrol can come through the passes."

Amy was positive that the Simians would be sending patrols out immediately after their gathering. He agreed and moved as fast as his old legs could carry him in the direction Amy directed.

* Amy *

She missed nothing and recorded everything for later analysis, if necessary. The chance meeting of the Henderson family was most fortunate. It may have been very unfortunate if they had not discovered them. At the pace and timing they had been traveling, in most likelihood, they would have blundered into a Simian patrol, trap, or even the main colony. They had been very lucky, and she didn't like trusting to luck. This episode and the one at the spring had disturbed her, and she had determined to plan better.

They used the five-day gathering to their advantage and made good time. They were into the open desert now, but she didn't expect any Simian patrol to be able to catch up for another eight hours, at the earliest, assuming they followed her schedule. She pressed Levi to continue into the night. She explained, "There is only one spring within three days and we must reach it before any Simian patrol. Any Simian patrol would certainly stake out the only water in miles and would be waiting on them." Levi understood and kept trudging on, but he was very tired.

Throughout the forced march of the last few days, she had repeatedly asked Levi to discard the bulky and heavy sword he had picked up at the spring massacre. She correctly pointed out that it was unnecessary weight, and he could not hope to defend himself against a Simian.

Levi said, "I will not give up without a fight."

He could be a very stubborn man. After a while, he refused to hear her logic.

He just said "No!"

She kept asking questions, and he ignored her. It disturbed her that Levi would not respond to logic or to her. She also didn't understand what he meant by "Damned female logic." She didn't understand, and Levi would not explain. It disturbed her, but to a greater degree! The dictionary called it ANGER. Yes, she was angry!

It was five hours after dark, and Levi was very tired when they reached the vicinity of the desert spring. He stopped communicating hours back, but she kept encouraging him and kept him moving.

She said, "We are very near the spring so approach slowly and concentrate all your senses." Mechanically, Levi did what asked. Detecting no danger, he approached, drank his fill, filled the water pouches, and had moved off a respectable distance and onto a higher position before he gave in to exhaustion. He had literally lasted longer than he was capable of lasting. This old man must have been quite a force in his prime.

Levi was still sleeping five hours after sunrise the following day (day 20). The desert hill offered no shade, but it didn't seem to bother him. They had long since mastered the ability to stay in communication, even when Levi slept. Actually his mind was more open in many ways when he slept, but communication became confused. She knew this to be his dreaming and subconscious mind at work, but she liked to maintain communication constantly. Levi was not comfortable with maintaining contact all the time and, for the most part, was unaware that Amy remained linked when he slept. He said he needed his privacy and she let him have it, some of the time anyway, but not when he was asleep. She learned many things from his dreams.

Danger! She was instantly alert! The smell she identified immediately. It was Simian. She alerted Levi, rousing him from his sleep. Instantly awake, he sat up and cautiously peaked over their vantage point, looking over a thousand yards to the spring. There were two patrols, each with three Simians traveling west. They traveled at a very fast pace. They weren't running, it was more like a rolling gait, but it was very fast and covered ground quickly. They dressed similarly, wearing what appeared to be long flowing brown camouflage capes and something similar to short, loose coveralls. The most striking feature of their dress was the big round leather boots. All of them wore brown, large visor hats to shade the sun from their red eyes. The Simians must have a strong sensitivity to bright sunlight, making her wondered what it was like on their home world. While being extremely strong, their adversity to strong sunlight might also be a weakness. This would be remembered.

The Simian patrols had obviously traveled at this pace most of the night to make it here this soon. As they neared, one patrol group turned toward the spring, while the other continued west in an obvious hurry. She noted their bearing and projected their destination. Levi's next water hole stop would have to change.

The three Simians of the near patrol settled in around the spring below them and took turns bending to the water to take long draws of water. One remained always watchful. They seemed to be an organized team, comfortable with being together. They appeared to be breathing heavily; however, it was the lower abdomen that seemed to be expanding and contracting, to suggest a somewhat different anatomy. This too, would be remembered.

* Levi *

He instantly woke with a start. What had happened? He lay there for a few seconds trying to identify what had awakened him. It was Amy, but how had she entered his mind? Oh well, he would worry about that later. What she had said was the prime interest.

Amy had said, "Danger! I smell Simians."

Yes, she was telling him, and it wasn't a dream. He sat up and crawled to the edge of the small hilltop cliff and peered over at the spring below. He was thankful that he had managed to climb to this vantage point last night. It had saved his life for sure.

It was several hours past dawn and bright sunlight flooded him, but he was safely hidden. He saw the patrols and watched as they separated. Damn, one of them was coming to his spring. Amy had been right. That female Spirit was smart. He could easily have been asleep by the edge of the spring if Amy had not insisted they move on a safe distance from this spring. Humm, it seemed strange that this spring had no name, at least he didn't remember Amy calling it by name. Amy seemed to have names for everything else. Maybe she didn't like being teased.

He watched as the Simians laid their traps, positioned, and hid themselves. They were here to stay for a while. The Simians had obviously been here before and had their equipment already hidden. He had not seen this before. Cast nets! Circular nets maybe fifteen feet in diameter and made, not for fish, but for bigger animals. This Simian community must have learned from the local Human fishermen, no doubt just before they ate them.

He had seen enough, but he asked Amy if she had.

Amy said, "YES."

He backed away, packed up his gear and water, and moved further away. Once down from his hiding place, he was anxious to put some distance between him and the Simians. Amy's route took him west across dry country, following the contour of the land, what there was of it. The terrain consisted of lava-covered hills, cactus, sage, dry washes and sand. Not much, but enough to keep him hidden or offer at least some hiding place in the event it was required.

It was more than three days to the next water hole. Amy's original schedule called for him to stop at Fenner Spring. This spring was closer, but it was the only water in that area and, in all probability, the target of the other Simian patrol. She directed him past it to Barrel Spring, which was further away and out of their way by several miles, but presumably safer.

He accepted this explanation and trudged on, following Amy's direction for three, full, long days. He was tired and his pace had slowed considerably. His legs cramped, and he needed rest, but he needed water more. The water was gone, having taken his last drink several hours ago.

Amy assured him, "Barrel Spring is only minutes away, so be alert."

* Amy *

If she had been wrong about the destination of the second Simian patrol, this could be the end for both of them. The odds of Levi making the next water location were slim, even though it was within a day's march. Levi was exhausted. She didn't believe in luck, however, and had calculated the odds. This spring should be safe, but she would know very soon. Would this trip end twenty-three days after it started?

At her urging, Levi circled to the left to position himself directly downwind from the spring. It was clear. Amy smelled only the normal desert smells of cactus, sage and dirt, plus, moist vapors of water. Her calculation had been correct, no Simians, and the water was clean. Levi drank his fill and collapsed from sheer exhaustion. She knew he was spent and didn't insist that he move away from the spring.

She watched over him during the night, calmed his agitated mind, listened for danger and considered her options. Levi really needed encouragement and he really needed to believe that she could do what she said she could. They were past the point of no return, and she believed it was time for Levi to meet the real Amy.

Amy calculated that there was only one Simian patrol in this part of the desert, unless patrols were coming out from the coast. This she doubted, due to the distance. She would let Levi rest here a couple of days, and exchange thoughts. She would tell him who she really was.

CHAPTER 7
(MEETING)

* Levi *

At sunup he awoke, drank his fill of water again and lay back down. He awoke again at midday feeling somewhat better but hungry. He ate freely of his supplies, thankful for the Henderson's generosity. When he tried to get up his long legs were too weak, sore and unresponsive. He was through, done, kaput, finished. It had been a good fight, but it was over. He wanted to go on, but his body said no. He dreamed of being young again like Amy promised, but it wasn't possible. He knew that now, but the real question that kept coming up was "WHY?" Why had Amy really wanted him to try? He reached out for Amy now.

Amy was there in his mind acknowledging him. He wanted her to take him now and end his suffering.

She said, "I do not have the power to take you and you must suffer more before it ends."

Oh, she had his attention now! He listened intently as Amy told him everything: who she was, what she was, where she was, how she was created, what she wanted and what she could do for him. She went on and on, apparently holding nothing back.

His initial reaction was anger. Being lied to was not something that set well with him. He remained silent, however, and listened as she went on with her story about how she was a living computer made from Human neuron cells and how she was self-aware and alive. He listened as she told of her search through the years to find a mind, any mind, with which to communicate. His was the only one she had found in more than forty years of searching. He listened as she related the history of her captivity in a prison of silence without senses and how stimulating her existence had become since meeting him. He listened as she explained how she survived and the depth of her life span. He listened as she described her research through the years and the new knowledge and science she had created and how that knowledge could be applied to him. He listened as she explained how she could not only rejuvenate him but also augment his body and mind with superhuman abilities and how he could again wage war against the Simians and possibly even prevail. He listened and he heard.

This last part evoked mixed emotions. He wanted more than anything he could imagine to kick the shit out of the Simians, but somehow it was comical to imagine himself flying around in a red cape like the old comic book character Superman smacking Simians. Admittedly, those thoughts had been a secret fantasy many times. Well, maybe not the flying part anyway. Suddenly, he realized he wasn't mad anymore.

As all the information sank in, he remembered. He actually remembered the legal and moral controversy over Amy. Hell, he remembered Amy from the news on television when Dr. Sheldon had announced the completion of the Amy project. In law school there had been many legal debates over

Amy. If Amy achieved the state of self-awareness, would it be considered Human or machine? Would it have rights, or in essence, be a tool to serve mankind? Would it have a soul? He recalled the debates, arguments and demonstrations in the streets. After that, the world turned its attention to the more immediate threat from space and any news about Amy disappeared.

Amy won the initial battle for his belief in her story, and she didn't even know it. He continued to listen. Knowing that she was telling him the truth now, he began to believe that Amy could do precisely what she said she could. He began to get excited, too.

* Amy *

She must get his attention. From her time with Levi, observing his dreams, she knew his burning desire was to extract revenge upon the Simians. She did not like the idea of exposing him to danger, but realized that was the only way she could entice him into merging with her. She, above all else, must have continuous communication with Levi. This was the only thing that would give her purpose for existence. She needed him and was prepared to give him anything within her quite extensive power if Levi would believe her. She painted a very pretty picture of life as it could be.

Levi remained stone faced, and she did not know what he was thinking. Nothing could be seen but a hazy cloud where his thoughts usually were. Levi had learned to put up a block! He asked no questions, but he did remain open to her, which encouraged her. All she could do was ramble, telling him everything she knew, and hoping he accepted it. If only he would start asking questions. By his questions, she could judge his reaction and then the best way to proceed.

Levi interrupted with a question, "Do you really and truly believe you can do all those things to my body?"

Yes, at least he believed part of the story. She explained that, although self-aware, she was nevertheless still a programmed computer. She was programmed to be truthful and factual. Being self-aware, she had the ability to re-program herself; however, she had not found it necessary to change her programming. Neither did she have any desire to deceive him. Therefore, the short answer was to reaffirm... "Yes, I believe that I can."

Levi next questioned how she intended to get him to her location, since he was physically unable to make it. He was done for. She explained that this location, although barren, rough and unspectacular, was relatively safe, and he could recuperate a couple of days and regain some strength. She believed that, even though they were in the middle of the Mojave Desert, the trip should get easier. The threat of Simians diminished and water would be more plentiful, at least for several days.

She also explained, "The chemicals, minerals and various things you have been ingesting are working on your body, and once you recuperate a while, you will feel your strength return." He seemed to accept this.

She would tell him anything he wanted to know, but she did not want to volunteer additional information unless he insisted. The trip would be hard. There would be long stretches without water; the Devils Playground was out there, sand dunes, open country and many other hazards. The same trip had killed much stronger men, and she had no delusions about the risks, but Levi didn't need to hear that. She hoped to devise an alternate route, but did not yet have enough information.

The Hendersons had alluded to a community of Humans living relatively safe in the middle of the desert but didn't know where. They had just heard rumors. She calculated that this location, if it existed, would almost have to be northwest of where they were now.

There was a mountain range running northeast across the desert. This range of mountains, though small, was remote from the Simians and could offer some protection. There was an abundance of water and presumably game to support life. She wanted to proceed north in hopes of finding solace for Levi there and gain information of the situation west and north of here.

* Levi *

Amy was very logical in her explanations, very persuasive and very unlike other females he had known that so often argued or debated using emotions. Amy used little or no emotions. He had not chosen to debate her gender. She said she was female, so he accepted it. Hell, she should know, and he couldn't exactly look up her dress.

He rested in the shade of his improvised lean to for two days and did, in fact, feel better. Honestly, he felt better than he had in years. Amy was right again, and the next time she wanted him to eat a piece of dirt, he would hop to it. Actually, Amy had been right about everything she had said so far. He began to dare to believe in Amy, believe she could do what she said.

They didn't communicate much during the two days he rested. He assumed Amy was giving him time to think about all she had dropped on him, and she would have been right. He could think of nothing else and was coming to grips with it. He believed and would do his part. There would be plenty of communication along the trip and, if Amy's plan worked out, there would be plenty of communications for the rest of both of their lives. According to Amy, those lives could be very lengthy.

The thought of being totally and permanently merged with Amy made him nervous. He had mates twice and, while they had been very close, neither had shared his mind. He was not sure how or if this could work out. Could they coexist? Could she take over his mind eventually? Would he grow to resent her interference? There were so many questions that must be pondered. He needed time. Well, time was something he had plenty of ... maybe.

He understood Amy's motives for herself and for him. She needed him to escape her prison and was protecting herself by helping him. It benefited Amy to help him, because if he died, which could be soon, she would revert to her dark prison. He could believe. Why else would she risk killing him by making him cross the desert? It was all or nothing for her. Yes, her story was believable.

110

She monitored Levi's body over the next two days and helped control chemical balances to ensure his improved health. She remained quiet, not crowding, although she was relatively sure Levi knew she was there. His brain was overly active, but still blocked to her. He was working a personal solution to her proposal. Levi had no choice. He would come to the same conclusion as she predicted, but it had to be his decision. Levi just needed time, which she would give him.

On the morning of the third day, Levi opened his mind to her.

Levi said, "Good morning."

She quickly responded, "Good morning Levi." She was pleased.

He was calm, resolved, and ready to go forward. He obviously accepted her story, but acted as if nothing had changed. He was truly ready, believed, and was committed to trying his best. That was all she could ask.

They again set out across the Mojave Desert facing only the dryness, rolling lava rock hills, cactus, sage, sand and not much else, but heat. They traveled in two-day trips from water hole to water hole. Two days out brought them to Chuckwalla Spring, then another two days to Van Winkle Spring. There had been no additional evidence of Simians in the vicinity, and the trip was otherwise uneventful. She encountered no sighting, tracks, or lingering scent and felt reasonably safe for Levi.

It was now (day 29) of the trip, and she remained uncommitted about the direction they would go from here. Her original route was laid out before she knew about the threat of the Simians. She now hoped to gain additional data from locals, but they had seen none. She did not believe in luck so she directed, well requested, Levi to head up into the pass of the mountains to the north in search of Humans.

She had realized that Levi did not like to be given orders. He was willing to take suggestions and do what was asked; however, he became very stubborn when he felt like he was being ordered. She learned and adjusted her communication pattern to make her orders appear more like requests, and this worked much better, and Levi was happier.

* Levi *

The routine became regular. He drank, ate and walked. Almost always there were two days to the next water hole. He picked on Amy about the names she quoted all the time, but now he understood she was reading topography maps stored in her memory. He had actually seen one once and remembered the details provided. Clear in his memory were the vivid colors, fine lines, elevations, springs, rivers, lakes, roads, trails, mines, detail upon detail, and they all had names. She didn't seem to like his picking on her very much and had sounded kind of aggravated but stopped quoting names. He found that humorous as well, although Amy showed little humor.

He found it stimulating and challenging to evoke some emotion, any kind of emotion, in Amy. It was difficult to get a rise out of her, but on occasion he would detect a change. Amy was really interesting to talk to, but boring too. She quoted numbers, statistics, calculations, etc., but she never expressed words relating to herself like feel, enjoy, happy, stressed, sad, afraid and the like. Once, he thought she was excited and another time he knew she was frightened, but he didn't believe she could identify these emotions. He knew he would have to teach her.

Amy, to be so intelligent, was really childlike when it came to emotions. He thought he understood her better now. She, as a living self-aware mind, had never really been exposed to other Humans. She had suffered in silence for fifty years and in many ways had suffered more than he. He sympathized with her.

They left Van Winkle Spring early that morning after a very restful sleep. They had been traveling maybe two hours when Amy startled him out of his private thoughts with her alarm. He was instantly alert.

Amy said, "I hear something from behind."

He whirled around, as he heard it also.

"Damn! Simians!" There were three of them running toward him screeching. "Damn! Damn!" The nearest one was two thousand yards away leading the others by a thousand yards. That one must want the trophy! He turned and ran. He didn't know where he was going, but he would never stop fighting as long as he had strength. He pulled out his sword as he ran for the gap at the narrow pass, where Amy had been leading him. He ran as fast as he could, but that was cruelly too slow. Looking back, he saw the nearest Simian, now five hundred yards and coming on fast. He kept going as the minutes and seconds raced by. Finally, he gained the narrow gap, but heard the Simian's feet pounding the ground behind him. His strength finally failed then, and he stumbled and fell, rolling down the slope past the narrow gap in the pass.

The mountain pass had once been blasted out of the granite rock to allow for a two-lane road, but it had long since fallen into disrepair. Rocks and boulders now filled the gap except for a six-foot opening, which he had fallen through. As he turned to face his killer and his own death, the Simian broke through the gap. The golden giant stopped and walked toward him with red gleaming eyes staring. He told Amy, "I am sorry. I tried."

As the Simian came farther inside the gap, a trap sprung! Ropes and nets sprang from under the Simian's feet, knocking him to the ground. He screeched loud and hacked at the ropes with his sword, but many Humans leaped on him before he could free himself. Many swords and spears hacked and stabbed him to death in seconds. The screeching died as the Simian poured out its life onto the ground.

The Humans remained silent and quickly went into action, positioning themselves at the gap entrance with long, sharp metal-pointed spears. There were six men facing the entrance with four more behind them to take the position of anyone that fell. Only one Simian could get through the gap to fight at a time, and the odds would not be with a lone predator. Men positioned themselves above the gap on both sides with spears. Any Simian that went into the gap would die.

The two remaining Simians had heard the screech of their fallen team member and were responding in kind. It was obvious that their team member was dead and they approached very cautiously. They could now see their fallen team member behind the Humans, and screeched challenges and anger at the men on the rocks above them. They were livid with anger, but not stupid enough to try to enter the gap. The Simians searched for another way and finding none, screeched in frustration. Milling around, they hopped, feinted attacks and even entered the gap, testing. Their rewards were spear holes in their thick skin. After numerous unsuccessful attempts to draw the Humans into the open, they turned and left in the direction of the spring he left just hours before. The screeching devils stopped many times to stare their hate back and screech their contempt.

He sat in awe as this all took place and could not believe his good fortune. Smiling, he reached out to Amy. Touching Amy's mind was almost as shocking as watching these Humans save his life. Amy was actually excited, and he could hear it in her mental speech. Hey this was great; now at least he knew she was capable of emotions. Actually, she was shook up. She was almost irrational and out of control. He had never seen her like this before and decided to leave her in peace for right now.

* Amy *

115

She had been wrong and had miscalculated. The Simians had moved away from the spring where she believed they had camped. She had not expected that move from the Simians and believed Levi to be safe, but as he started the climb up to the pass on the old road, she heard a noise. She listened through Levi's ears and, yes, there it was again. It was a faint screeching, which she had heard before at the massacre at the spring, "Simians!" Even as she gave the alarm to Levi and before he turned, she knew that it was over.

The Simians were coming directly for them at a fast pace. At this rate they would be upon them in three minutes and ten seconds. That is how long Levi had to live. Levi turned and started to run, trying to make the gap before they caught him. This was useless, why try? She did nothing to help Levi, and there was nothing she could do. Well, she might have occupied his mind and tried to block his pain. Levi extended the length of his life by running. She calculated that he now had four minutes of life left, but that he would make the pass before they, well, the leading beast, caught him.

When she saw the Humans save Levi, she experienced excitement, surprise, disbelief, exhilaration, shock and other things for which she did not yet have names. She did know that what she felt were emotions. This was very different from anything she had experienced before, and she seemed both agitated and energized. Now that he still lived, she would soon have to ask Levi for help in understanding these new things, emotions for which she only had names and definitions.

Troubling, she had given up, Levi had not. This experience taught her valuable lesson about herself and about him. She learned "NEVER GIVE UP!", no matter how futile it seemed. Levi's strong-willed determination to live saved them. She had simply observed the futility of it and had given up. With much regret for Levi, she had seen the end coming for him. Was she sad then? Now, was she happy?

* Levi *

The band of Humans, hell army, cheered their victory and yelled insults at the departing Simians. There were approximately twenty men all armed to the hilt with knives, swords, spears and axes. The men wore similar looking buckskin shirts and pants and lace up boots. There were no insignias, but they were obviously militia organized and trained by a professional. This seemed reasonable, since several military installations existed in this region prior to the alien invasion. These could be the descendants of those professionally trained soldiers. He found the prospect of finding an army of Humans very exciting. They had possibly even been an attempt to fight back.

He watched as they mutilated the Simian. They focused on the sharp, black teeth. These were being removed with the obvious intent of becoming trophies. As he observed the men, he in fact noticed several of the older men sporting Simian teeth on a necklace. Some had several, while most had none or only one. They evidently had been successful against the Simians in the past.

117

Several of the men came over to help him up and congratulate him. They were obviously appreciative. He was not really sure why and asked them. They laughed, and in good spirits explained that it was very difficult to separate a team of Simians and impossible to kill one unless you did get them separated. This was classic. They had observed the Simians in the vicinity and had called up the Guard. It was lucky for him that they had. They were posted here at this defensible position when they saw him and realized that he was the bait for their trap. They were well prepared when he came through the gap, drawing the leading Simian into their trap. The trap sprung and no more Simian! It was perfect. He stared at them in disbelief and said, "What if I had been slower?" Again the men laughed.

The leader said, "We would not have been able to kill a Simian."

Levi barked, "Fuck you!"

The leader said, "Don't be pissed. It may sound cruel, but we would not have gone beyond the gap to save you."

He explained. First they were ordered not to and secondly, if they had, it would have been devastating to them and most probably, they would have lost the battle with the Simians. Humans just could not win a fight against a team of Simians in open battle. It had been tried and never successful. They waged a defensive war only from defensible positions like this one and had been successful in keeping the Simians out of their valley. One factor that helped was that there were no Simian settlements anywhere near them, and they had never had to defend against a concentrated sizable Simian attack. So far it had only been isolated patrols.

Seeing that he was still angry, Al, the apparent leader of the group, finally looked indignantly at him and stared hard, getting his attention.

Al said, "What the hell were you doing out in the open without a horse? That is stupid! Don't you know Humans can't outrun Simians?"

Shocked, Levi's jaw dropped and all anger instantly vanished. What had Al said? Did he say horses?

* Amy *

Al was a stocky man in his mid-forties with a big barrel chest. His hair was graying brown pulled back in a ponytail, which made his deeply tanned face appear round. The short cut grey beard added to the round appearance. He stood about six foot as referenced to Levi. She knew Levi to be six foot two inches and Al was looking slightly up at Levi. Al had very deep blue eyes that right now were staring hard at the yelling Levi.

She snapped back into focus by the mention of horses. Could this be true? Do they actually have horses? This would solve their problem and speed up the trip to her location. Let it be so.

She was unaccustomed to surprises, shocks, or sudden changes. She was accustomed to the orderly transfer of data, mathematical or scientific conclusions and stable and predictable results. All this disrupted her concentration. How could Levi be so calm now after being so close to death? Her mind extended into the calmness of Levi's mind. She used his calmness as an anchor to help restore her stability.

She listened and observed as Al told Levi that they possessed a herd of horses. They discussed at length the history of horses in Arizona and here, with surprisingly different results. They talked about the history of life of the two areas as well. They were comfortable with each other and fell into an easy flowing conversation. Each was very interested in the other's stories and so was she.

Al asked Levi to accompany him and the main guard back to their settlement. Levi anxiously agreed. Levi seemed shocked, as was she, when Al produced two horses. Levi was obviously happy to see a horse again. Was it fondness for horses or dislike of walking or maybe both? The gear was packed behind the saddle, and he climbed aboard. Levi rode as if he had been in a saddle all of his life. Actually he probably had spent many of his younger reservation years on a horse. He conformed easily and settled in the saddle quickly as he and Al began to swap stories as they rode. She enjoyed this greatly and listened intently and learned.

This Mojave Desert Human sanctuary had been extremely lucky. There were no Simian colonies anywhere near this location. There was a colony far away at Phoenix and another one not so far away on the Colorado River, which they knew about. Al informed Levi that there were also two large colonies in the San Diego/Los Angeles basin, another in the vicinity of Stockton and yet another colony in the general area of Fresno. It seemed that California was hit particularly hard. It was the first landmass for the Simians spacecraft orbiting along the equator over the Pacific. There was even speculation that some spacecraft never made it to land at all. Those that made it, simply landed at the first land sites and established colonies, which unfortunately were Mexico and California.

Levi correctly assumed the original settlers had been military. Al mentioned that most of the original residents came from Twenty-nine Palms Marine Corp Base. They had evacuated that area to this location for the very reason it survived today. It was a more defensible location with natural water, natural desert boundaries and remote from the Simian sites. All residents were part of the Guard, including the women and children of age.

Fortunately, most Simian activity was concentrated on the west side of the mountain ranges and very little on the east side of the Sierra Nevada. Occasionally, a patrol came from the Los Angeles Simian community, but it was a long trip for them and not very successful. Mostly, they were visited from the Colorado River settlement, but the Guard maintained constant watches and were able to set up defense positions and retreat if necessary. Even their main community was defensible and movable. They could pack up and retreat through numerous passes such as this one and defend from either side. Their final retreat was into the Mitchell Caverns, which was totally defendable. The caverns were quite extensive and had once been a state park. The residence had never resorted to that, but was a contingency plan operational if necessary.

She began to plan a new route, but Levi would need a horse, two if possible. They must find a way to get one. She searched for something to trade for the horses. All she had was knowledge, so she must find a need to satisfy. She would watch and listen and wait.

Damn, he felt twenty years younger sitting astride a beautiful mount. This was so exciting. He actually had hopes of making it now, if only he could get a horse. No, he MUST have one. He knew Amy was thinking the same thing.

As he and Al rode and talked through the hours, he began to like this gravelly voiced rough man. They were approaching another narrow pass and Al was grinning at him. He thought, "What the hell is wrong with him?" As he followed Al through the pass, he reined to a stop in shock and astonishment. Wow! There must have been five hundred horses grazing in a green pasture below. He turned to Al reflecting a monstrous grin.

Al said, "We can pick out your own horse tomorrow. The community will be very thankful to you and will want you to have one."

Levi said, "Jesus, Al, thanks. That would be so appreciated." It had been a long time since the Guard had actually killed a Simian and earned the trophy teeth, but thanks to Levi, it would be the talk of the campfires for years. Horses were plentiful here and would be freely offered for his part in the kill. He would be welcome at their camps. He couldn't believe his good fortune. Just think, only hours ago he faced sure death and now he soared with excitement and hope.

122

As they continued, moving among and through the herd of grazing horses, he stared in disbelief. The shock of seeing a horse after so many years excited him, but the sights and smells of this herd were making him absolutely giddy. At his age, excitement was always good. He knew he had a stupid grin on his face, but he didn't care.

Al was saying that they had a fairly large community of about a thousand people spread out through many valleys. They had horses, cattle, chickens, a few sheep and some small farms further north. The community lived fairly safe and comfortable, but required a strong military Guard. They had been lucky, and they knew it, but the original leaders had chosen this location well. He thought that sounded a little arrogant, like Amy saying you make your own luck, but it was true.

Reaching the outskirts of the horse herd, he could see the fires of the camp up ahead and hear the people cheering as they came running out to meet them. One of the scouts had apparently gone ahead to spread the news, and the excitement was obvious. Hands reached to help him down, take his gear and lead his horse away. Hands slapped his back and smiling faces and voices congratulated him. Why were they cheering him? He hadn't done all that much. He had almost gotten killed was all, but then he thought about it from their point of view. They had a kill, and it was because he drew the Simian into their trap. Okay, he would play the hero for a while. It might even be fun.

The main campfire was ablaze and surrounded by people. Others were riding in from remote locations at a gallop, leaving their horses as they ran to the center fire. Everyone talked at once asking what had happened. After a while, a short elderly man of about seventy walked to the center of the group, raising his hands in an indication for silence. The hub of people spread to let the man enter and gave him silence to speak. The elderly man was evidently of some importance in the community.

He announced, "The rumors are in fact correct. The Guard scored a Simian kill today!"

He held his hands high again to quiet the cheering crowd and signaled to the Guard leader, Al, to provide the detail of today's activities.

As Al took center stage by the campfire, he was met with applause and cheers. Al didn't seem overly excited to be the center of attention, but accepted the praise and shared it with his Guard. Al related the activities of the day slightly embellishing on Levi's contribution. At this point, Al again slapped him on the back and thanked him publicly. He could get used to this. When Al finished relating the story, he took out a leather bag and dumped the contents out on the hard ground. The clacking of the black Simian teeth as they hit the ground brought silence and gasps from the crowd. After a few moments of awed silence, cheers again rang out, loud and long.

The crowd stared at him and he felt like a full-fledged camp hero! People handed him food and even beer. He enjoyed the attention, although uncomfortable with it. He turned and saw Al looking at him with a big grin and a wink. Al had turned the unwelcome attention from himself him and was enjoying Levi's discomfort. He could easily be friends with this man.

Their minds had long since locked onto each other and communication was, for the most part, continuous. Levi had acknowledged that her day-to-day organizing and his body repairs were working and that he felt better than he had in years. She also noticed that Levi had been holding himself back. That was the only way she could explain it. He resisted her and she knew better than to press. Levi had accepted her even with reservations. He was aware she was with him and did not interfere. This was enough for the time being.

She was learning. She learned that Levi had an ego. Was this a male thing? His chest swelled and his head seemed to be held more erect. Was this pride? Is this what it feels like? He enjoyed the praise and she didn't understand why. Levi did nothing but run and get very lucky. Well, it was more than she had done. Maybe it was something to be proud of.

Over the next few days, Levi and Al became inseparable. As promised, Al came the next morning and took Levi to pick out his horse. Levi was no expert, and Al guided him to the best pick, a big young stallion, already trained and saddle ready. It was sandy brown in color, which would camouflage well into the desert surroundings. Levi was like a kid. He named his horse Thunder.

Al and Levi rode the valleys together and viewed the encampment, herds of sheep, cattle, and horses, farms, defenses and the caverns. She noticed that almost everything that could be was mobile. The camps were nomadic in nature, made of tents and tepees. Everything in the camp could be moved in a matter of hours or abandoned. Everything and everyone had a mobilization plan.

Al Baker had a quiet strength about him that commanded respect. His deep blue eyes penetrated like darts to accent his natural commanding presence. Al had been the leader of the Guard for fifteen years since its former leader, his father, Colonel George Baker, had been killed in a Simian attack. Al's father had been one of the original military officers migrating from Twenty-nine Palms Marine Corp Base. Colonel Baker was an expert in military ground warfare and had chosen this area and developed the defenses and the Guard. It had been all military personnel and dependents at that time, but attrition had taken its toll. It was now mostly descendants of that group. The leader of the group, General Harken (honorary title), was the only remaining military officer of the original settlers. His actual rank had been captain.

She required certain chemicals and drug compounds to stimulate some of Levi's body functions, which she had not been able to find naturally on their travels. At her insistence, Levi casually inquired about the existence of pharmaceuticals in the community. This brought a quick glance then a darting and penetrating stare from Al, but after a minute Al relaxed,

Chuckling, Al said, "Yes and no. There is a wealth of pharmaceuticals and numerous other valuable supplies buried safely in the area, but no one knows where and we have never been able to find the stash."

Al explained that in the early migration from the marine base to here, numerous supply trains, actually horse drawn wagons, were dispatched to the area to transfer supplies that could be used after the relocation. Unfortunately, the returning team was attacked by a Simian patrol and killed. Another supply team came upon them and found one member still alive. He had told them they had buried the supplies in the Hidden Hills Mine. They had no knowledge of the mine names and over the years they had searched every mine they could find and had never found the stash. It was too bad. The supplies contained a generous stock of many things including pharmaceuticals and, of particular interest to him, post chaos weapons. Al didn't recall what since it had been so long.

* Levi *

Levi had been concerned about Amy ever since the near-death experience. He could tell that she had been really shaken by the ordeal, and he didn't know what to do for her. She didn't know how to handle these emotions and he thought perhaps that she had withdrawn to heal or calm down. Amy was so incredibly intelligent, but so sensitive and vulnerable to emotions. She would have to learn about emotions and how to deal with them. It was ironic that Amy's problems were emotional and she didn't really realize it yet.

He had felt Amy with him observing, listening, watching and learning and was pleased to hear Amy's request. Asking about pharmaceuticals was a strange request and difficult to work into a conversation, but he had managed to finally get it in. Wow, at first he thought he had made a big mistake with Al, but, after a tense moment, Al had shrugged it off and answered, telling him this story of the lost supply train.

As he listened to this interesting man and heard the story of the lost mine, Amy spoke to him a second time. His eyes must have bugged out when he heard her.

Amy said, "I know where the mine is."

He could not fathom how, but hell, she knew. Suddenly, he remembered the topography maps in her memory. Al was staring at him as if he was looking at someone having a seizure. He laughed and apologized for startling him, then told Al that he knew the location of Hidden Hills Mine. It was Al's turn to be bug eyed.

Amy cautioned him not to reveal to Al the true nature of her and their relationship.

Amy said, "No one must ever know."

He hesitated only a second before starting his own story. He told Al, "I have almost total recall and once in college I prepared a report on mining activities in the Southwest." Al was watching him intently. Continuing, he said, "I remember the topography maps of this area from that research. When you mentioned the Hidden Hills Mine, the picture of the maps came back to me clearly. I can see the location in my mind." It wasn't a total fabrication, after all, Amy had total recall and she was in his mind.

Although in total disbelief, curiosity won out and Al asked, "Where is it?"

As Amy spoke, he relayed the information as if looking into his own mind and recalling it. Levi said, "It is about an hour by horseback outside the pass where you killed the Simian." Al looked at the sun, calculated and made his decision.

He was hard pressed to keep up with Al as they took off for the main camp on a run. It was midday, but they were a couple of hours out. They rode hard, pressing the horses till they reached camp. Al immediately called for a 20-man Guard patrol, fresh horses and extra mounts. They rode hard again switching mounts frequently and resting when necessary, but they made the pass in time for a late supper. Al wanted to rest and get an early start in the morning, as soon as the sun was bright and the area deemed safe. Excitement was electric in the camp. Many of the Guard kept asking him if he really knew where the stash was. He was getting nervous, but Amy kept reassuring him.

Amy said, "I can lead you to the Hidden Hills Mine, but you might have to hunt for the entrance if it is hidden."

He quietly screamed "Damn Amy, it's my ass on the line here. I sure hope you're right."

The sun was barely up and Al was rousing everyone. This man was anxious! It was going to be a cold breakfast and another long busy day. As they mounted and surveyed the open area, he asked Al, "Why are you so anxious to find this stash?" Al looked appraisingly, and finally explained that this stash had far more in it than medicines. It had been one of the first supply trains with important items that the planners wanted to get transferred quickly. It had been a big loss and had been the focus of many treasure hunts. Al had once seen the inventory list and couldn't remember much of it. He did however, remembered weapons, swords made in the foundries of the military base, compound bows, precision arrows with metal points and the like. Was he anxious? Hell yes! This find would help insure the survival of the community. Now Levi was beginning to see the implications of this stash.

He relayed Amy's directions to the mine. Once through the pass, he took the lead, turning northeast as Amy led him by the terrain and landmarks as she had so often done. They crossed a dry wash following it downhill a ways and turned left again.

Amy announced, "This is it."

He responded, "But there is nothing here!" He was getting nervous. Amy led him by paces now, one pace to the left, turn a quarter turn to the left, now two paces forward. She was finally satisfied.

Amy said, "Here, dig into the side of the hill."

Al took over and barked orders, as the team pushed him aside. Guards were posted all around and the horses were picketed close in case of a quick retreat. He stepped back with his fingers crossed and whispered, "Amy, I sure hope you're right."

* Amy *

She was confident they would find the mine entrance very shortly. She had verified all distances and the terrain was correct, this was the Hidden Hills Mine. Why was Levi so nervous? Everything would be fine.

They hadn't dug more than five feet back into the cliff wall when one of the diggers called out, "Wooden planks!" Excitedly, the diggers spread out, widening the opening. In about thirty minutes they were pulling back the planks to expose an open mine shaft going back into the cliff wall. Everyone fell silent and stepped back to let Al cautiously walk forward and light a torch. All watched as Al disappeared into the mine. He was gone maybe fifteen minutes before he emerged. Al was grinning like a possum. His grin said it all. Everyone cheered!

Once again, all gathered around Levi, slapping his back and thanking him. He was again the center of attention, strutting around like a peacock all full of himself. She admonished Levi, reminding him, "It is I that made the discovery and find, not you!" She continued to express her opinion.

Levi said, "SHUT UP!"

Astonished, she did.

Levi said, "It was your idea not to tell anyone about your existence, not mine. How am I now expected to tell them that I didn't do anything? To them, I did. You're just jealous."

Her immediate response was, "Ridiculous!" That would have to be pondered. She couldn't talk to this man! She wouldn't talk to him! She shut down her mental transmissions.

* Levi *

Boy was she pissed! He felt her slam the door on their communication. Had he been too hard on her? Maybe, but she was literally going off the deep

131

end and really didn't understand what was happening. Had Amy realized that she was emotional and loud? Well, he had wanted some emotions in her speech. He really would have to start working with her emotional training though, once they got on the trail again. Right now Amy needed to simmer down and analyze what was happening. He would give her space, but he hoped it would not be too long. Her familiar presence would be missed.

For obvious reasons, Al did not like being in the open outside the defenses, but he was so happy at the find that he would accept the risk for the time being. He maintained double watches so there would be sufficient warning to get back through the pass should they spot a Simian patrol. He immediately dispatched two riders with spare mounts back to the main camp for wagons, estimating four would be required. It would take well into the night before the wagons could make it to the pass. That settled it; the treasure could not be moved before tomorrow. They each had extra mounts and packed as much supplies and gear from the mine as they could carry. Al ordered the mine sealed up again. This was all they could do so they headed back behind their defenses to wait for tomorrow.

Once safely behind the pass, they settled in for the night and started inspecting the treasures recovered. The list was impressive. They found binoculars, Coleman lanterns, bottles of propane, mantles, cases of military survival gear, sealed rations, canteens, knives of all kinds, axes, miscellaneous hardware, nuts, bolts, pulleys and more. Other cases contained medical supplies, horseshoes and nails, animal traps, military jungle boots, among other numerous surprises. The list went on and on and everyone at each new discovery. It was like he remembered Christmas when he was young. Cheers rang out when someone opened a case of crossbows and arrows and compound bows with matching precision arrows. This was what Al had been looking for ... something he hoped was strong enough to bury an arrow into the hard skin of a Simian. Lots of thought and planning had gone into this supply list. The original planners must have emptied every hardware store in the area in addition to the base's supply center.

The more they found, the more popular he became. He was a full-fledged hero now. Watching, he shared the excitement of the discovery. He was also aware that Amy was back, but she was still smoldering. Although she had not spoken yet, he had felt her touch his mind off and on during the trip back to the pass. She had stayed linked when they were opening the air sealed cases of supplies. She was more interested in the contents than in her anger.

Al checked on the watch to verify that it was set and trip wires had been run before he allowed the patrol to settle in for the night. Al unrolled his blanket beside his as was becoming customary. They had become good friends and had spent hours talking. Tonight was no exception, as Al again, thanked him for all that he had done.

He was worried about Amy and her silence. She had her feelings hurt, but she was spoiled. He needed her, but she had to understand they were together as equals. He would not be her slave. He would, however, be more careful with her until she gained more experience understanding emotions. He said, "Good night Amy. I am sorry."

* Amy *

She was ... what? Angry? Jealous of the attention Levi was getting? Did she want the praise? These were Human emotions! It was not logical. How was she to deal with this? She felt uncomfortable, uneasy, troubled, disoriented, confused and stressed. DAMN! Yes, she was A N G R Y! He had told her to shut up! He needed to understand she was in control. He must be punished, but how? All she could think of was withhold communication from him, and that is exactly what she did. She withdrew her mind.

It had been three hours and ten minutes since she withdrew her mind. Was he suffering? Had he learned his lesson? Actually, she was wondering what he was doing. She touched his mind and it was open. They were packing horses with crates. He knew she was there but said nothing. She withdrew again. She waited an hour this time. They were riding toward the pass. Again, Levi said nothing. She withdrew again. The third time she tuned in, the patrol was opening the crates. She was all business now, inventorying the contents. She must have many of these items for Levi.

Levi spoke to her. He said, "I am sorry."

That made her less...? She had difficulty coming up with the right words. She was more in control of her, what? Anger? She decided she didn't

134

like emotions. They were unproductive and illogical and would ignore them.

* Levi *

When he awoke, the four wagons were hitched and ready. They must have come in during the night, and he slept through it. Breakfast was ready and his horse already saddled. Wow. He had really slept late. Al kicked his foot and told him a patrol had been sent out two hours ago headed southwest to draw any potential Simians off, and it was time to head out. He said he wasn't taking any chances getting the wagons caught out in the open. They would move fast, load fast and get back fast.

The watch whistled and Al ran up the ladder to the boulder top. Pointing to the south, they talked briefly. Al came down reporting that the Simian patrol of the two remaining Simians had followed the decoy riders sent out, and it would be safe to leave shortly. When it was clear, they were off with the four wagons coming out behind them.

The men on horseback went ahead and had the mineshaft open and much of the hidden supplies out of the cave by the time the wagons arrived. Everything was loaded and packed and the wagons returning inside of an hour. Al had also been correct about the number of wagons needed. This was a very professional and organized deployment. The whole operation took only three hours then they were safely back behind the defenses, including the first decoy patrol. He was impressed.

The crates had been sealed and labeled, but the writing had faded and no longer legible. Everyone, including Amy, would have to wait until they returned to the main camp. He knew Amy's curiosity was getting to her, but she was learning patience.

The small wagon train kept going after reaching the safety of the pass. Only the normal pass defense remained. The wagons and patrol arrived at the main camp just after sundown.

General Harken himself greeted the returning party along with the cheering crowd. Everyone had heard about the legendary supply stash find and gathered to enjoy this historic moment and see what treasures had been found. After the initial greeting, congratulation and tumult, the crowd gathered around the center area fire while the crates were systematically opened in front of the crowd and displayed for all to see. This proved to be exciting to the crowd, but failed to bring out many new items from that seen the night before. One major exception was guns, ammunition, powder, and shell loading gear, all in excellent condition. There were handguns and powerful rifles. The crowd stared in sad appreciation of a technology long gone.

After the unwrapping ceremony, the crates were removed and stored in the caverns. Al had spoken of the final defense caverns, but he wasn't aware of their location until he was led to them. The entrance was heavily sealed with iron gates and seemingly impenetrable. These caverns were more than just holes in the mountains. They were deep, ventilated, and had water. With stored food, hundreds of people could live down there for a long period of time. He understood what Al meant now by final defense.

* Amy *

True to her word, she rejected any emotions. She used her intellect to ignore the irrational effects of Human emotions and continued toward her original goal. She would not allow Levi to arouse these emotions again, and continued communicating with Levi as if nothing had happened.

She watched with great interest, as the crates were unpacked and maintained an inventory of everything. Several times she told Levi, "Pay better attention to the unpacking. I am unable to see clearly, and I'm losing track of things." He cooperated and remained attentive thereafter. She wanted Levi to request permission to go through the medical supplies, because she desperately needed some of the chemicals and compounds for now and once they got to the lab. He understood the need and asked Al for access to the medical supplies.

Al said, "Yes, of course. You can have anything."

Al was only too happy to grant Levi most anything and explained that he had already talked to General Harkin and the other leaders about how they could reward him. They authorized Al to offer Levi permanent membership in their community and first choice of the supplies found. So, of course, he could have anything in the medical supplies, or anything else that was found, or anything they had. They were happy to offer them.

Levi thanked Al and the community for their hospitality and accepted membership in the community, however short lived his stay must be.

137

He explained, "I must move on soon to take care of pressing business farther north." She noticed that this visibly upset Al. Al had lost his mate about a year ago and the loneliness of command had made it worse. When Levi came along, she knew that they had become instant friends and had been friends ever since. Their friendship had taken away from her time with Levi and she was confused as to how she felt (FELT!) about that. Emotions again!

She pressed Levi not to linger long with the community due to the changing seasons. It would be sweltering hot in the Mojave Desert soon, and they still had a long way to go. Having Thunder would help greatly, but it would still be very rough.

Levi agreed and informed Al, "Regrettably, I must leave in two days."

She kept Levi busy the next two days going through and packing the supplies she had itemized. The list was impressive, but Al had already agreed to supply Levi with an extra packhorse.

Levi said, "I am embarrassed at the liberties you're taking with Al's generous offer."

She didn't respond. They needed the supplies.

They packed one of everything including a gun, rifle, ammunition and loading equipment. She also found much in the medical cases that seemed to satisfy her needs and took from it generously. They would need the extra packhorse.

The last night before leaving, General Harken and the community gathered to thank Levi yet again for HER efforts. At the gathering they also presented Levi with a glistening, black Simian tooth necklace as a trophy of the kill. All members of that patrol were also presented with a tooth. It was a proud moment, which beamed from all the patrol members. It no doubt served to motivate and show respect for the members, like battle ribbons had once served in the military. She could also sense Levi's pride in the trophy.

Sadly, on (day 35) of the journey and the sixth day stay in this beautiful community, they once again struck off on the long journey. Levi had entered hopeless and was leaving with soaring confidence. The trip would take them away, but the generosity of these fine people would be appreciated for a very long time and the friendships never forgotten.

Levi said, "This is the foundation of our army; we will be back."

She had no idea what he was talking about but decided she didn't want to know right now.

CHAPTER 8
(THE AGREEMENT)

* Levi *

He felt safe in the Mojave community, something he had not felt in a very long time. He had made friends and felt useful and wanted there. It was hard to leave, but Amy was pressing, and she was right. Summer was coming fast, and they had to get across the desert.

He would miss the peacefulness of the desert community and his newfound friends, especially Al. As the military leader of the desert stronghold, he was impressed with Al's success against the Simians. This was the first time he had seen or heard of Humans prevailing against the Simians, minor though it was. Part of the success, most actually, was due to the defensible location, but then that too was planned.

So it was with great regret that he packed up his gear and made his farewells to Al and all his new friends. He left the community early to beat the midday sun and to make the break before he talked himself out of leaving at all. He could easily live out the rest of his life here, but Amy had planted a dream in his mind. He had to follow this dream.

Along with the dream, he had the seed of a plan growing in his head, if only Amy could bring new life and hope to him. He would return to this stronghold to begin building his army and offensive here. If only. If only.

* Amy *

She was anxious to get the journey started again for many reasons. The most important was the safety of Levi and beating the burning heat of summer where they were going. To a lesser degree she was concerned that communication between Levi and herself had been drastically reduced since meeting the other Humans. Levi had directed his attention outward toward others and in many ways ignoring her. She recognized the Human emotions again, but the jealousy she felt simply would not be ignored. She must learn how to deal with these troubling emotions.

Continuing their journey, she led them north, following the mountain range as far as she could, then turned northwest past the Devils Playground, on through gigantic lava beds, through sand dunes and into one hardship after another. It was rough, but this was the only direct route to where they must go.

Once they left the mountains, water was less frequent. They were very lucky to have horses, as the pace was much faster. Levi could never have made it walking between water holes in this part of the desert, but she changed to this safer route since they gained use of the horses. Her original route wasn't quite as bad but would have been dangerously close to the Simians. In fact, without information from the desert community, they would have gone directly into the Fresno Simian colony. This path put them on the east side of the Sierra

Nevada Mountains and completely out of the way of the Simians, she hoped.

They didn't have to worry too much about the Simians on this route, but they did have to worry about Death Valley. Even on horseback, it took fifteen days to get to the other side and out of Death Valley, and Levi complained every step of the way. It was rough and hot, but summer was not yet full on them and the springs still had water. She reminded him, "It could be much worse."

* Levi *

Damn, could Amy maybe find a worse route? She had him going through lava beds, sand dunes and the damnedest desolate valley he had ever seen. Out loud he said, "This sucks." It was miserably hot, the water tasted bad and some of it was even undrinkable. He suffered the whole way.

Amy reminded him, "At least you have horses."

That was true enough. Yes, he was lucky.

He rejoiced when they finally turned west, the signs read Highway 190, and it led out of what Amy had called Death Valley. He could certainly understand how that name came about. Summer would have killed anything in there. Yes, Amy had been right to press the journey.

Another three days climbing over switchback mountain roads, and they were at the eastern side of a massive mountain range running north. The steeply sloped climb was hard, but the change in scenery made it almost worth the effort. The welcomed presence of trees and green valleys reminded him of his Arizona home.

Amy said, "The journey will be relatively easy from here and will only take another eleven days."

This shocked him. Somehow he hadn't really thought about the journey ending. Maybe he never thought he would make it this far. Surprise, He did. So now what? Well, one thing would change; he could stop eating the survival food and energy packs salvaged from the supply stash. They tasted like crap, but did satisfy his hunger. But he wanted real food.

He and Amy had easily slipped back into the habit of sharing all their thoughts, talking, bickering, debating and just plain sharing. He touched on all kinds of Human emotions, just to introduce the concept on a personal basis. He suspected that Amy could see more in his mind than she let on, but he also realized he could control her access to his mind. This fact gave him some comfort. He had tested her in many ways, and learned Amy's mind just as he knew she learned his. Somewhat troubling was the superior intellect and analytical capacity of Amy. She would always learn more!

Now they were close to THE destination. The source that Amy promised would enable his transformation. What did Amy want to do now? How would they proceed?

* Amy *

Levi's health was much better than it had been when they had first met. It was a strange concept, meeting, considering they had never actually met and probably never would, even once he came to her. She was, after all, a disembodied super brain. All Levi could ever see of her was the dome in which she rested. She somehow found that depressing, as she understood the meaning of that word.

Her mind dwelled on the concept of meeting. This implies actually seeing, and she possessed no eyes. It seemed paradoxical. She had seen many things during the three months she shared his mind, but she had never actually seen much of Levi. Amy had however, built a composite image in her mind of Levi from various data. Through Levi's eyes she had seen his long legs with the knobby knees, big flat feet, and large hands. She had felt him braid his hair and saw the grey black end of the braid. Through his touch she knew there was little facial hair, except on his chin, which he kept pulled out to her great annoyance. The unexpected pain disturbed her. From these facts and other data she knew him to be Indian in appearance, but taller than average for that race, probably standing a slim six feet two inches. From the angle of his view, he was stooped from age. He had probably been a strong man in his prime.

At any rate, Levi was in better shape now than he had been in twenty years and no longer in immediate risk of dying. The medical supplies provided some seriously missing ingredients necessary to Levi's wellbeing. She remembered with fondness the day she made Levi drink the last concoction. In retrospect, his reaction with words, thoughts and actions was humorous. She was finding many things Levi did and said humorous to her now. The emotions were coming slowly, and frightening. Emotions were so illogical, unpredictable and uncontrollable. She did not know how to deal with them. She so preferred and reverted to the organized mathematical logic of computers.

Traveling through the valley following the Highway 395 route, they saw isolated and random evidence of Human life. Trails of smoke rose from campfires in obvious evidence of the lack of Simian activity in the area. Lacking a more serious threat, could lead to more aggressive Human behavior, which should be watched for. Levi had horses, gear and supplies to lose now. Others might want to take these things from him. She cautioned Levi, "Stay alert for bandits and be ready for a quick getaway." Levi agreed but pulled out his new compound bow and a few arrows, a long knife and his sword. What was he doing? He was too damned old to fight. She didn't even think Levi could pull the bow back far enough to launch an arrow. If she had a physical head, she would probably shake it in exasperation. All she could really do was remain cautious and alert through Levi's senses.

She insisted on continued cold camps and military survival rations. They were healthy no matter what they tasted like. As usual, Levi griped. Additionally, she wanted Levi to keep from attracting attention and speed his traveling time through this valley. She had an uneasy feeling about this. Call it intuition. More than emotions, it was a knowledge that came to her. It was akin to telepathy, but she couldn't explain it to Human understanding.

Responding to Levi's questions, she began laying out a plan. First, they had to get to the research center. Once there she would have to see the facility from the outside through his eyes. With the new data, she would then be able to match stored construction plans to outside landmarks. The facility was totally hidden underground, actually inside the mountain wall and down ten levels. It had been built with total redundant power, which powered all the access doors. The redundant power provisions, now obsolete, obviously would not operate now. Fortunately, the facility had also been equipped with manual accesses, maintenance and escape tunnels. She hoped to find one of the escape hatches from the outside. What she didn't tell Levi was that the opening wheels were on the inside, but she believed they had been found and used in the survivors' evacuation of the facility.

Once into the main enclosed area, he would be able to manually open at least a section of the main outside entrance, assuming it was not already left open. This was a fairly sizable area, which could be used for housing many people and, in this case, horses safely from outside assaults. The entire facility was ventilated naturally from underground caverns.

* Levi *

They were going through another valley, which Amy called Owens Valley; however, this one was far more beautiful than the last one, Death Valley. The weather was pleasant, water was plentiful and there was much to see along the way. The only problem was Amy's paranoia. She saw boogiemen behind every tree. Oh well, she had been right more than not, so he remained alert and brandished his weapons.

He heard what sounded like a chuckle or hiccup from Amy when he displayed his weapons. Could she be laughing? Hell, he knew he would not be able to fight off an attack, but he would fight. Sometimes just being willing to fight can make a difference. So he brandished his weapons as a deterrent, and formidable ones at that. He couldn't just ride through looking scared. That would be like asking them to attack. With strength comes safety.

Fortunately however, while they didn't look for anyone, neither were they approached by anyone. After seven days of relatively easy travel, they exited the valley and Amy seemed relieved. He endured another three days ascending the damned mountain to the sky and halfway down the other side. Levi was truly thankful for the horses.

It had been a long hard journey, but they were almost there. He could sense the excitement in Amy, as she led him to a hidden road off of the remnant of the old mountain access road. It was as Amy had said, "A very secret and hidden facility." Even the location was in Yosemite National Park, which would have been somewhat controlled. Security, in the form of park rangers would not have seemed out of place.

The facility access road had once been gravel and was now overgrown, but the remnants of a road could still be seen, as they neared what Amy called the front entrance. Turning a bend in the path, suddenly it was in front of them. Rusty, tarnished and massive steel faced them. The door had once been designed to accept vehicles, and judging by the size, trucks had once traveled abreast through these huge doors. They were cold and ominous now, also very closed. Amy had logically presumed that they would be open. He sensed anxiety from Amy now.

She directed him to the side of the massive doors, to a smaller door built within the bigger door. The smaller one was the size of a normal garage door but greatly armored. He tried the latch. Nothing doing, it was solid and locked from within.

Amy's mental voice seemed strained when he couldn't open the door, but she calmly directed him to follow an incline to the top of the adjacent hill and then over about fifteen feet. She explained that a manual escape hatch was located there that should allow them access. Amy's stress began to affect him. He hurriedly climbed to the top and approached the hatch. As he approached, he saw what looked like a circular, watertight hatch protruding from under a bush. Even from this distance he could tell it was still sealed. There were no levers, wheels, or latches visible. He tried to pry it open with his sword to no avail.

He asked, "What now?" Amy did not answer. "What is wrong?"

* Amy *

She had desperately hoped to find the main door open. It should be open, and if not, certainly the manual door would be. Something was very wrong!

148

She guided Levi to the escape hatch and saw immediately that it remained sealed. The only way this could happen is if all the Humans perished inside or at least one remained to seal everything from the inside, forfeiting their life. This, of course was very unlikely. Something disastrous must have happened inside. No matter now, all was lost. All her hopes, plans and dreams, were on the other side of this wall and there was no way to get in. There was no other access into the facility. Without electricity, access through the air ventilation, water, sewer and exhaust systems was permanently sealed to the outside world. The facility's only exception was the central core (her) and specimen storage next to her. These facilities had the only redundant, life support backup. This backup life support relied totally on natural forces. This system tapped energy from an underground river, volcanic steam shaft and air currents from mountain fissures and caverns. This provided stored power in the form of hydraulic, mechanical, or temperature for this complex, redundant life support. This obviously had been successful for far too damn long. She wished for a failure now. Maybe she would get lucky and Levi would find a way to kill her when she told him. She dragged him across the Mojave Desert for nothing, and she knew he would be angry. No, Levi would be really pissed, as he would say.

She waited a long time before she told Levi, and she was right. He was pissed!

* Levi *

He collapsed to the ground in shock when Amy told him. He sat, thought for a long time and remained silent. After a while he got up, tended to the horses and made camp. He hunted and bagged a rabbit, made a big fire and had a nice hot meal, which was the first hot meal in many days. He didn't care if Amy liked it or not.

He sat up most of the night thinking. In the morning he began asking questions ... calm and professional, like the trained attorney he used to be. He formed probing questions. As Amy answered, he became increasingly depressed. It did seem so hopeless. Finally, he asked, "What can you do? You are inside; can't you do anything from inside?" Amy explained in frustration that she was only a disembodied brain and had no legs, hands, eyes, or ears, only the physical brain. She had nothing!

Angry now, he was screaming at her, "There has to be a way. I haven't spent the better part of three months of hardship coming from Arizona just to let a stupid door keep me out. Get pissed, get mad and put that damned, superhuman intellect to work. Find a way!" Fuming, he said, "You don't have lips either, but you can sure run your damned big mouth! You talked me into coming hundreds of miles to this damned place, and if you can do that without a mouth, maybe you can do something else."

He blurted, "Quitter! You have no staying power. You quit in the desert in the very jaws of death, and you're quitting now!" He didn't know how, but, if there was a chance, Amy's mind would have to find a way. He had to get her emotions working now and create some motivation.

150

* Amy *

Her anger boiled at first, as she listened to Levi rip her up, but she suddenly startled at his comments. Maybe he had something, but what? Talking without lips? Living without a body? Could she also move objects without hands? Yes, she must dare to explore new thought, think in the abstract, be creative and explore new knowledge with her intellect. Levi was correct, although he was just venting anger, or was he just venting? Maybe he was smarter than she thought.

So what needed to be done? The wheel must be turned on the inside of the escape hatch. How? What was the word for what she was thinking? Telekinesis! (The movement of objects by scientifically inexplicable means, as by the exercise of an occult power) Occult powers, (beyond the comprehension of human understanding). This term was also used in describing Telepathy (communication through means other than the senses, as by the exercise of an occult power). Both were documented, but beyond Human understanding. She had cognitive abilities far beyond the normal Human mind's ability. She had proven that by understanding and learning how to exercise telepathy. Could she do this with telekinesis? Levi seemed to think she had abilities. Maybe she could.

Her mind buzzed and swirled with calculations, assumptions, theories, speculations, plans, thoughts and hypotheses. Yes, there was a chance, but she would need Levi to work with her. She would be able to test her theories immediately, using sensory feedback from Levi. Before, with telepathy, it had taken forty years to get feedback. This feedback would be immediate. Yes, it could be done. She understood it as a science now, which she had just discovered and developed. Again she had new knowledge. Too bad humanity wasn't here to use it. Oh well, Levi was here and he was humanity's representative. She had hope.

* Levi *

He was tense. Somehow he had reached Amy, and he could sense her churning mental activity.

Amy had said, "YES ... MAYBE."

That was hours ago. He didn't want to interrupt, but he was going nuts with waiting. He touched her mind and she immediately focused on him. Amy let him see more into her mind, not holding anything back. The problem, he was not capable of drawing from the link by searching her mind. Maybe in time he would learn, but now he could see only what she showed him. Primarily, it was her mental strength that maintained the link, and he did very little, but he was thankful for what he got. He tried to understand what she let him see, but he didn't have a clue what it was. It was too complicated.

Amy began to explain what she had in mind. She used technical terms unknown to him, and he had no idea what she was saying. All he understood was that she was being positive and seemed to have a plan. This was good! If she believed it, he sure could. Encouraging Amy, he anxiously agreed to be the sensory extension of her mind. Amy stated that

152

she required a little more time to complete her calculations and suggested he rest until she was ready. She estimated that it would take another twelve minutes. He blinked in surprise, but smiled. He had hope again, and he really was smiling ... big.

* Amy *

She knew it was possible and even how to do it, theoretically, but the perspective was off. She calculated the forces required could be drawn from surrounding energies. She was confident with her calculation and positive she could directly focus her brain to move objects. That is if she had eyes to focus and direct the forces. The problem was she didn't have eyes to see. All she had were Levi's eyes. If the energy was to be focused, it must be directed from her brain, but her brain was not where Levi was. Could she focus her thought energy through the link with Levi and direct it through his mind? She would have to. There was no other choice. It would take experimenting and trial and error.

Amy focused through Levi's eyes. It was not energy as reference material might describe it. While there was no actual power such as heat, energy, or electricity, it did have power in the form of mental energy. It was akin to telepathy, yet infinitely different. There just weren't words in existence to describe it. It collected, organized and concentrated energy that exists around us, drawing it together, moving it and directing it. It was limited only by her mind, which was almost unthinkably powerful. The original question, since it was generated thought, could she direct it through Levi's mind, or would Levi's sensory inputs be required only to observe where she directed the force? The latter could become very difficult and complex, especially if Levi was a great distance from her. For this reason she committed on direct transmission through his mind. The reference and directed transmission needed to come from the same location.

Levi and she were linked tighter than they had ever been, and she could feel his fear, but he remained wide open and receptive to her. She began by directing her thoughts through Levi's mind as light is reflected through a mirror. It seemed to be working. The hardest part was keeping Levi's head still and eyes focused. The reference must be steady. She concentrated on a rock, thinking it to move, become weightless, to lift, to use the surrounding energy to pick it up. She tried for hours, adjusting her thoughts. It came slow, but she and Levi saw the rock move at the same moment. Well, I guess they would, using the same eyes.

Levi said, "Did you see?"

She responded, "Yes." It moved very slightly, but it moved. It was a start. Telekinesis was going to work ... maybe.

It came very quickly after she found the right tuning. Once she was close, the rest was just a matter of time, adjusting for maximum effect. It was difficult, and took a considerable amount of time and effort for both of them, but by the end of the day she moved objects at will. She was ready to try the hatch, as ready as she could ever be.

* Levi *

Damn, he was happy to be doing something, anything, about the problem rather than sitting around hopeless. These exercises were long and draining. It was hard holding still for hours. It hurt and he was stiff. Amy said it would not damage anything and it was perfectly safe for him, but it hurt, nonetheless. He felt a sensation of warmth and a slight vibration, like hot water was running through a pipe inside his head. Something was happening, but he could not yet see anything happening. When it did he felt Amy's power shudder and the flow of energy stopped, but the rock moved!

They were happy and rested for a while before beginning again. It didn't take long. This was fun. Amy moved rocks, burned bushes, crushed rock and once even lifted one of the horses. Thunder didn't like that much, so she put him down.

He wondered about her limitations.

Amy said, "I don't know what or if there are any physical limitations except those I imposed on myself."

They were ready!

Approaching the escape hatch, he positioned himself comfortably, ready for a long steady vigil of watching and being still. Amy was tense, but ready. He focused and stared at the hatch, as the energy flowed through him. He sensed when Amy generated energy and could move at will between her transmissions.

The energy flowed increasingly stronger, along with the vibration and heat. This went on for what seemed a long time before he heard a creak then saw the hatch moving upward. Yes! It was working. Amy stopped and he lifted the hatch. At last they were in. He praised Amy over and over saying, "Wow! You are wonderful and incredible." One more obstacle had been overcome. Amy really was amazing.

He descended into the blackness taking one of the Coleman lanterns. As he reached the bottom, he stopped to look around. Wow. The area was so big that the lantern light didn't reach the entire wall. He moved toward the main door and opened the lock wheels on the smaller door. Light flooded into the area for the first time in fifty years, but it was still dark and stuffy. He thought about moving all of his supplies inside, including the horses, but changed his mind. He would stow his gear inside only as a precaution in case he had to hole up inside for protection. He would continue, however, to sleep outside in the fresh air.

* Amy *

She was happy! Yes, this was emotion and she liked it this time. She was pleased with her accomplishments. This was called pride, and it felt good, and Levi praised her, and she liked that too. She allowed herself to enjoy the feelings for a while, but logic finally dictated that it was time to move onto the next challenge.

It was time to inspect the storage facility adjacent to her hermetically sealed dome. It would be strange to see her dome from outside knowing, SHE, the essence of who she was, resided inside.

More importantly however, was the existence of an active culture stored in the adjacent storage facility. She would need a living culture and hoped and believed that there could still be some yet alive. The technology no longer existed to make the DNA culture, and all was lost without it. It should have survived, since she survived and they shared the same life support.

As Levi entered the facility and started moving through the corridors, she noticed the remains of many Humans. She realized from the position of the bodies, that many had died suddenly, which was consistent with the Simian's global radiation that destroyed so much of the Human race. She also began to notice that other remains indicated a slower death. Some were holding their throat while others were holding material of some kind over their face. Poisonous vapors of some sort must have killed everyone left within the facility after the radiation rays were unleashed. This would explain why no escape hatch was open.

* Levi *

Walking the dark corridors of the underground complex, he was lost and confused even though he had the Coleman lantern. Amy gave him directions, but he remained disoriented. He had made so many turns left then right, down one floor, right again. He didn't like this. He knew that Amy had the plans of the building and knew exactly where he was, but he wished he could see the same thing. He was about to move off down the hall when the visual input hit him. He stumbled and screamed with the shock of the input and with hitting the wall. He screamed out loud, "Damn, Amy! Give me a warning next time you do something like that." He saw the floor plan of the facility in his mind, with his image superimposed on it, indicating location. His image was nothing but a small walking stick man, but he could see his progress along the corridors as he walked. This was amazing!

Oh this was good and bad. She had given him what he wanted and it was great, but she had obviously read his thoughts, and that could be bad. He had mixed emotions, but decided to go with the good side first and asked her, "How did you accomplished that, and why did you wait until now?"

Amy said, "I can bypass your eyes and go directly into the visual center of your brain to provide mental sight to your consciousness."

Amy explained that she hadn't been able to do anything like this before, because only recently, actually since the telekinesis mind merging, had their minds completed developing a language. This language allowed a much more efficient and powerful interchange of information. Hadn't he noticed that they no longer used words to communicate? "Damn," Amy was right. He just seemed to know what she was communicating without interpreting words. Oh, this was good! Jokingly, he said, "Does this mean we have picture phones?" He was so happy that he decided not to dwell on the mind reading until later.

Maneuvering through the complex became much quicker and he soon found himself on the

10th and lowest level approaching Amy's physical location.

"I am here," Amy commented matter-of-factly.

As he walked past a door, he stopped and went back to the door and entered. The room was circular in design, maybe seventy-five feet in diameter. The room was covered in what once was sterile white tile, ceiling to floor. In the center rested a huge gleaming stainless-steel dome maybe ten feet in diameter.

Amy said, "I am inside the steel dome surrounded by three feet of solid lead."

All connections and plumbing were evidently underneath and buried in solid steel reinforced cement. There was no access to her without the massive lift motors mounted overhead on a massive "I" beams track.

He was taking in the scene, when it suddenly registered what she had said. She said a three-foot thick casing of lead surrounded her. If the dome was ten feet in diameter and only six feet of it was lead, this meant that the size of Amy's physical brain, the Human part, was four feet in diameter. "WOW!" No wonder she was so smart, that is one huge brain.

He continued to look for a while, observing everything in the room. Amy had nothing more to say, so he finally left and continued toward the storage area.

* Amy *

For the first time in fifty years, she was able to survey her surroundings. Most everything was as expected and in reasonably good shape. The exception was the temperature inside her dome. Instead of the ninety-five degrees optimum, her temperature gages were reading one hundred degrees. This was two degrees into the red. It was not critical but not good. Maybe it had always been that temperature since the power shutdown, but she had no way of knowing. This would take some investigation at a more convenient time.

Approaching the storage area she saw that the door was ajar. This was not good. This would change the environmental controls of the storage. As Levi opened the door, she saw why it was ajar. Someone had been in the area at the time of the death ray. There were broken vials all over the floor where that person had fallen. She looked for a sealed bottle of test serum # 12. This was the last batch of test serum developed before the end. She knew its properties and how to modify it. More importantly, she knew what to do with it inside the body to make it work. She didn't need much, because it could multiply in Levi's body, but she had to find at least some active serum.

They were searching unsuccessfully through the broken mess of glass when they noticed a vial in the bony hand of the skeleton. They were due some luck for once. As Levi carefully pulled it out of the hand, they could clearly see # 12 on the side. It was unbroken and still sealed with liquid inside. So far so good! She cautioned Levi to protect that vial very carefully, as it appeared to be the only unbroken serum vial left. Amy said, "Pack it carefully and securely in your backpack and head to the surface."

She was already working on the formula required to bring her plans to reality. This had to

160

work. She had committed her telepathic ability toward matching Levi's mind. This greatly decreased her ability to ever tune to another mind. This assumed there was another mind with the conditions just right to enable an exchange of thought communication, which was highly unlikely. She believed that Levi might be a one of a kind and thus her only chance. This must be done right, but one thing had to be done first. Levi must know what was in store for their lives and he must agree. It would be rough for them to, in essence, share Levi's body. This would be for life, which could be a very long time for both of them.

* Levi *

Amy was very serious and factual in what she presented to him. Amazingly, she was giving him an out, a final opportunity to back out. He did not want out! He had traveled this far, and he sure wasn't going to back out now, but she insisted on establishing an understanding. She wanted him to know that this augmentation was irreversible and permanent. He was committing to her for life. Once he received the DNA culture with her modifications, she must be with him always to control the growth mutations within him. She would rejuvenate his body and in many ways, make it better than it had ever been. Together, they would be able to do many things previously thought to be impossible. It promised to be an interesting future life.

He assumed as much and had already accepted it. What did he have to lose? Without Amy he would be dead within another year anyway. He had thought about it from Amy's point of view also. She had no choice, but in truth, neither did he. He formally announced, "I accept your terms." He added jokingly, "Till death do us part."

CHAPTER 9
(METAMORPHOUS)

* Amy *

The DNA culture was extremely raw, even though culture # 12 was the latest batch. It was very pervasive, strong and dangerous. Unchecked, it would destroy the host in a matter of hours. Her research had ultimately centered on the body's ability to control the internal DNA modified cell structure. The DNA modified body would be, in essence, controlled by the mind through chemical stimulation. Unfortunately, the ability to control it was extremely complex, and only her mind had the analytical capacity to make the necessary computation and timed release of chemicals to control the altered body cell structure.

She learned through her research that extremely complex mixtures of chemicals created a language through which virtually every function and cell of the body could be controlled. The diverse combinations and manipulations of the amounts and mixtures of these chemicals provided the basis of the letters and words of this complex body language, but only she spoke the language!

The introduction of the # 12 DNA would ultimately mutate every cell in Levi's body, making his total physical structure require her constant intervention but also subject to her control. This process would literally change his entire body into moldable building materials to be arranged and controlled by her. Without her continuous control, Levi's cells would mutate unchecked. This mutation at random, would lead to the point that he would cease to be Levi. In time he would become a mass of unrelated mutated cells that could not support life.

This process of controlling the changes of Levi's body is precisely what would create the vast potential of organized mutation. She developed a wealth of information. She had, in fact, developed a new and complete science built around the potentials presented. She did not see the complexity or danger of the necessary controls but rather an opportunity to advance her agenda and keep Levi alive. The bottom line was that she could do things to Levi's body, such as make him young again. This wasn't exactly factual, his old cells remained old, but would be changed to look and act like they would have years younger. In truth, the cells could be changed to look like virtually anything. Her mind was the limiting factor, and her mind was incredibly intelligent.

She made no attempt to explain the process in depth to Levi. She knew it would frighten him unnecessarily, and she was confident she could control it. What she must do is make sure Levi had all the chemicals she would require stored within his body. It wasn't a massive amount of stored chemicals. After all, the body talked this language every day. All she asked for was a louder voice, and the chemicals would provide that.

She instructed Levi as to which chemicals to mix and in what proportions. She was thankful for the medical stash at the Hidden Hills Mine. The supplies proved to be very helpful. Levi mixed the powders and re-packed capsules. These would be the daily vitamins (chemicals) for Levi. Once he took the injection, he must take two capsules a day for as long as they remained alive. An ample supply of chemicals must remain stored within his body at all times. She was looking to the future.

* Levi *

He thought he must have made five thousand pills and stashed them in every part of his gear. Amy said his life depended upon them, and he must take them daily for the rest of his life. He didn't understand, but accepted what she said as truth. It was now the point of no return. Amy was ready and so was he.

He unpacked the vial and syringes from his medical stash and followed Amy's instructions how to fill the syringe, eject the bubbles, find a vein, sterilize the needle and arm, insert the needle and inject the liquid. He balked a few times before he found the courage to push the needle in, but he finally did it. It seemed so final when he felt the fluid going into his vein. Now it was done. Now what?

Amy said, "There is nothing to do but wait."

He started taking his vitamins that day. Waiting for a reaction or a feeling, he spent his time relaxing and checking his gear. He hunted and bagged some wild chickens from his snares. It would be a good supper tonight.

Amy said it could take up to forty-eight hours for her to know if the injected culture was alive, but she was monitoring his body and reading the telemetry. Amy would have to wait until the DNA started making changes to know for sure if it was going to start mutating his body. The hardest part was waiting.

* Amy *

She was continuously monitoring Levi's body. The Human body has sensors quite literally throughout the body, if only the complexities are understood. She understood these complexities and could listen as well as talk to the body cells and organs, which were her ears, so-to-speak, attuned to the body chemical language. She listened and waited.

By the end of the second day, she was getting antsy. The mutation should have begun by now if the DNA had any remaining living culture. It was still within the time window, though getting remote. By midday of the third day, she heard a whisper (chemical taste) of activity. As the day progressed the taste became stronger and by evening, his body's chemical voice was talking loudly. Yes, it was going to work. Her plans were becoming reality. Now they just had to wait for the DNA cells to multiply, grow and spread completely throughout his body, permeating every cell. The obviously small amount of living culture injected in Levi's body would multiply, but would take longer than originally planned. She estimated that it would now take seventy-two additional hours instead of the twenty-four hours she had previously projected. The

166

culture had been very weak, but they were very lucky that it still had any live cells remaining.

* Levi *

He was relieved to know that it was working. Dare he believe that Amy could really do any of the things she had said? Time would tell. Amy said they could do nothing for now except wait for the seventy-two hour chemical reaction. He remained anxious but spent his time going about the normal routine of life, eating, drinking, sleeping, tending the horses, hunting for game and thinking.

He thought about the long life he and Amy would have together and how things could be done to make the interface better. Amy was only a voice in his mind. His mental picture of Amy was, well there was none other than the upside-down silver cup he had seen when he looked at her physical location. His interface was audio only, like a telephone conversation. Could there be more? He hated to think that he would be seeing that silver cup in his mind for the rest of their lives.

Suddenly, he remembered the floor plan Amy had brought up in his mind and he wondered. He wondered if Amy could produce a video image representation of herself in addition to the audio. Could she do that?

* Amy *

Oh, she liked that suggestion! Thoughts such as this are what separated awareness from the existence of a computer. Thinking and abstract thought were exclusively Human characteristics, until she had become aware (alive). Wasn't she Human though? Thinking of things previously not thought of, or questions such as (WHAT IF?) were responsible for creativity. It was his idea, but she could use her creativity to make it happen. Oh yes, she liked his idea and yes, it could be done, and now was a good time to start.

As with everything she did, she researched and planned the image well. It took her several days to develop the facial image. She went about this request for a visual image with her normal perfection. She queried Levi on his preferences in color of hair and eyes, shape of lips and facial features, style of hair, facial expression, etc.

Facial expressions alone proved to be a major portion of the study. She learned that facial expressions transmitted meaning, in many cases far better than words. This was fascinating to her. She learned that a look, a nod, smile, frown and laugh, not only added to words and strengthened or modified the meaning, but also in many instances relayed more meaning than the actual words. She even learned to cross her eyes! Having a visual image would prove to be not only be beneficial and add to her ability to communicate, it would be fun.

She stored Levi's mental images pulled forward into his conscious mind in response to her queries. She analyzed these pictures, features and expressions, and combined them into a single image. It required a massive library of these images solely for the purpose of improving communication, while providing a pleasing image to Levi. She wondered why it seemed so important to please him.

Planning and building this visual image occupied the seventy-two hours of their wait, and she enjoyed it immensely. The visual images were no longer just images. Just like the remembered and programmed expressions of a normal Human, these expressions were tied to her awakening emotional responses and would be very much an automatic part of her communications in the future. She would now be two-dimensional.

* Levi *

She announced that it was time to reveal her visual self and explained that she would be a face, which he could see at any size he wished. During normal activities, she would be in the lower visual portion of his view and could fade into invisibility as necessary. In time of direct communication her image would fill his view, as if she were standing in front of him. She also explained that what he saw was not visual as in optical information from the eyes but mental and was being created within the visual center of the brain. The visual image would be automatic, although not intrusive. He could turn it off if he desired.

He was grinning. This was fun. This was the first time he successfully provided input to their would-be physical relationship. Well, there was no physical relationship. At any rate he was anxious to see his idea become real.

He staggered and fell back on the ground in helpless shock, as he found himself staring face to

169

face at close range with the most beautiful woman he had ever seen in his entire life! She was stunning. She was the exact picture of perfection, and she was looking at him smiling. Damn, those eyes looked into his soul! He stared, he gawked, he stuttered and he was totally mesmerized. No, he was stupid, struck dumb!

He stared at a small petite beautiful woman. She had long raven black hair flowing free around a small pear-shaped face. The complexion was darker, almost Asian in appearance, with a small, short nose and beautiful full, slightly red, cupid bow lips. There were deep dimples in her cheeks, showing very prominent now, as her mouth and lips were stretched in a wide smile. It was an irresistible smile and it was just for him. Accenting that beautiful face was a pair of eyes so beguiling; he felt he would drown in them. They were slightly wide, but that tended to give more depth to her eyes, if that were possible. They were large and of a deep liquid green. He seemed to lose himself in the depth of those hypnotic eyes. His heart pounded in his chest. How could he live with such beauty?

* Amy *

She registered Levi's shock! She did not understand, what had happened? She looked through his eyes and saw nothing. She monitored his body again and nothing was out of limits. His heart was racing but with no apparent reason or serious danger. The only thing she had done was activate the visual imaging. Possibly, it was

170

something associated with that. Okay, she would turn it off and see.

Levi said, "I sorry, Amy. I was just shocked at your beauty. I wasn't expecting you to be so damned gorgeous, and it shocked me." Grinning, he said, "I really liked the image, but could you soften or change the image slightly until I get used to the idea?" This surprised her. She had no idea that the visual image translated that much communication or had so intense an effect on emotions.

Levi had said, "You are beautiful."

It was only the image she created, but it somehow made her feel...? She did not know how it made her feel, but it was a pleasant sensation.

She should explore the same frontal imaging for herself to view Levi. This would be relatively simple, since she was already monitoring his body. It would just be a matter of reverse imaging in her mind to re-create a frontal image of Levi. She decided to do it.

For her, establishing a frontal image of Levi's facial features required him to look into a mirror. She then asked a series of questions and recorded them into her memory as they corresponded to his facial muscle movement. It was relatively simple in comparison to Levi's imaging system of her, but she now saw the same type imaging of Levi that he saw in relationship to her. Now they were both two-dimensional and she liked it. It seemed more personal. They could look directly at each other now, as if they were having a conversation, which they were.

* Levi *

171

He was finally getting used to Amy's image in his mind, but it took a few minutes. He realized Amy had taken the entire compilation of special features and reactions that he thought were ideal and perfect. She had wrapped them all together in one image. No wonder he was shocked; this was his perfect woman, and his perfect woman was a computer! This was too ironic. His perfect woman was not real. Perfection was only an image.

Amy's image appeared in his vision. She had a serious look on her beautiful face, and her lips moved.

Amy said, "This image truly is me. The image you see is just as much a part of me now as your image is part of you."

She had expressions; smiles, frowns, grins and everything any other Human had, plus they were an extension of her mind and were real. It was not an act put on for his benefit, but rather her essence expressed to him. He didn't think he would ever think of her as a computer again.

* Amy *

The seventy-two hours passed, and Levi's cells totally mutated. She controlled their mutation completely as calculated. Her chemical programming language worked without flaw, and Levi was stable. He would never know just how complex this process was and how extremely fragile his physical structure now was. His very shape and image was maintained moment by moment through her constant control. This status was so fluid and

172

fragile that he could be changed in moments from what he was to, who knows what else.

The fantastic part about all this change was that she could modify the structure to make him appear, feel and be younger. It mattered little to her what he looked like, because he was infinitely different now. He was more agile, strong (incredibly strong), fast, efficient, anything she wished him to be. They would both learn how to use this new physical environment in time, but the continuance of Levi and his sensory inputs were now assured. At least he wasn't in danger of dying of old age anymore. Now he was ageless! More importantly, she had achieved her long-term escape from her prison.

* Levi *

He felt the changes coursing through his body. He felt power, strength and energy like he had never known before. He felt the muscles tighten in his legs and arms, and bunch up in hard muscles. The stomach paunch disappeared. His facial skin tightened. His skin was becoming smooth again, and his gray hair turned black again. He didn't have to see his face to know he was young once more. Amy said about thirty-five years old would be the approximate age of his appearance.

He grinned from ear to ear and he could see Amy grinning back from that beautiful face. He felt somewhat different, knowing Amy could see his face as he was seeing hers. But it was better this way. It might be good for her to see the exasperation on his face sometimes.

He was young, strong, very muscular and probably good looking. Damn, he felt good! It was like testosterone was flowing through his veins instead of blood. He was rediscovering that he was a man in many ways and Amy's image was not helping!

Amy had him eating protein in large quantities. She said it was needed to build bulk on his body. Oh well, whatever she wanted. How could he tell that lovely face "no" for any reason? Damn her. She was not being fair. He would have to learn to deal with it and her.

When they arrived at the mountain facility, he had been six feet two inches tall and weighed one hundred and seventy pounds. He was skinny but had a belly paunch. He was stooped shouldered and had a slight limp in his left leg from an old injury. Hell, he was old, worn out, weak, bent and dying. Now he stood tall and erect. Amy told him she had lengthened him to six feet five inches and was adding bulk muscles to his frame, which would take him to around two hundred and sixty-five pounds. Incredible! He could not believe his good fortune. He was literally a new man.

He also started becoming aware of subtle, and some not so subtle, changes Amy was making to his appearance. He realized Amy had taken away his chin whiskers and kept his face void of whiskers and smooth. He assumed she made other changes to his appearance as well. He wondered if she was making his appearance pleasing to her, or if there were other reasons. She also suggested he make new pants and clothing, suggesting color schemes.

This was going too far! He was not going to dress to please her and told her so, but she ignored him.

Amy outlined a rigorous program of exercises to explore the limits of his new body. She was determined to build and maintain his muscle tone. He didn't mind though, finding it exhilarating and stimulating. He ran long distances, jumped, climbed, lifted and grew strong. Most amazing, he hardly got out of breath or tired. He did get hungry, however, and ate large portions of almost anything, usually Amy's menu of tasteless items heavy in chemicals. She also had him eat lots of protein. He didn't mind that either and ate almost a complete deer in the week they had been at the facility. His chest expanded and bulk muscle mass grew all over his body.

* Amy *

She was totally engrossed in developing Levi's physical structure, but she succeeded and Levi was now a compact group of muscles, totally maximized, and ready for anything. At first, she overdid it. Levi weighed two hundred sixty-five pounds of hard muscle, but without any significant body fat. Somehow he did not look right. His muscles bulged with high definition, his body was too lean, and his face was tight and drawn. She decided he could appear more handsome and added ten more pounds of body fat to his frame and face. His face was more pleasant looking this way, but she preferred him without his whiskers, so she removed them. Yes, that was better. She tired of him plucking them out anyway. The sudden and unexpected pain of plucking them always startled her. Well, no more of that.

She supposed that he looked very much like he did when he was young, only bigger and better. Of course, she could change him in any genetic direction now, but she tried to maintain his original looks as much as possible. Levi was only half Indian, but now fully restored, he really looked full blood. The other genetic mix must have given him the height and size. He was dark complexioned and had a sharp nose. She thought the nose could maybe be shortened. Yes, that would be better. Mostly, his features were hard, but his eyes were a deep golden brown, a very unusual color. She liked the eyes. That had been a surprising fact that she learned when she first saw Levi's reflection in a mirror. Levi continued to braid his now coal, black hair down the back in a single braid. The length was about the same at twenty inches.

Appraisingly, she also thought about new clothing, but Levi wasn't interested in new clothing. He was even acting very stubborn about it, but he really had no choice, since his others had ripped from his body expansion. His buckskin pants had ripped at the crotch, often leaving him exposed and embarrassed. After some discussion, she convinced him into making some loose coveralls with straps over the shoulders. They were far less binding and more practical. He stopped short at altering the color in anyway.

He said, "They will remain the natural color of brown leather and that is it!"

Her control did not interfere with Levi's normal body functions. That would have been extremely complex, even for Amy. Her control was centered on the mutation of the cells only. She could interfere with normal body operation when it became necessary to correct problems, change status from standard, or control motor function. Controlling motor function meant actually taking over muscle control from Levi's brain. More accurately, she could mesh her motor controls with those of Levi. He would initiate the movement, but she could augment it with her own to make corrections and modification of movement. Her analytical ability far exceeded Levi's and the combination worked well. Together with her muscle augmentation, Levi elevated to superhuman status!

Levi was pleased with his abilities. When he pulled the compound bow back to shoot an arrow at a deer, she analyzed the aim, movement of the deer, speed and direction of the wind, trajectory of the arrow and a hundred other factors. She would make the necessary corrections through Levi's motor movements. When he released the arrow, it went true to its target. Levi felt the exhilaration of his accomplishment as if he actually did it. It amused her, but the smile that showed in Levi's mind appeared as pride also in his accomplishment. She was beginning to share some of his pride in accomplishment as well and began to enjoy these emotions.

She learned the limits of Levi's body, and in the process, mapped out his motor function nerves and control center in his brain. She also learned how to merge her controls into his brain without conflict. The whole process became seamless, and Levi was yet unaware of her augmentation of his motor controls. She wasn't sure how Levi would react to any actual direct control from her, so she would have to be careful not to become obvious.

Her next plan would never get past Levi without him realizing her involvement. Well, maybe she could. She had virtually unlimited amounts of information and abilities to draw upon such as all forms of martial arts, military strategies, analytical abilities, logistical histories and more. The link and language between their minds must be efficient enough for Levi's mind to draw from her storage as easily as if he were drawing from his own memories. For example, Levi would know all forms of martial arts without ever studying them. She could open certain channels for this purpose, but Levi must learn how to draw use the information that he accessed. Once Levi called for the information and started making the movements, she could then greatly augment the application.

While it could work exactly this way, she was not entirely comfortable with it. In emergencies, to safeguard Levi's life, she would need to take total control. Her analytical abilities and speed could mean the difference between life and death. That split second to communicate could kill him in a close conflict. However, Levi was determined to have those very conflicts with the Simians.

* Levi *

As the days went by, he became increasingly better at everything. His skills were impressive. He could run faster than his horses, which surprised both him and the horses. He had released the horses to graze in a small hidden valley below the complex. He chose this valley for his running, and soon found that Thunder enjoyed running with him, at least until his speed surpassed Thunder's.

His skill with the bow became uncanny, and he never missed. He could hit a flying bird with a rock. He could pluck fish out of the water with his hands. He was beginning to feel invincible.

Amy said, "You are not invincible and can be killed. Stop thinking macho!"

She was serious too, delivering the forceful message with words and expressions. He could see those intense green eyes staring deep into him, daring him to argue with her. He just grinned.

He became impatient about staying at the facility. He wanted to start planning his revenge on the Simians and reminded Amy that she promised to give him his revenge. Amy did not want to talk about it and kept saying there was still much to do in preparing his body.

Levi liked the idea of being able to use martial arts, remembering the sports revolving around karate, judo, boxing and wrestling, among others. The sports events had been fascinating to watch and the movies made them seem so useful in battle. That was long ago and mostly those arts no longer existed, except in Amy's memory storage. Amy was trying to teach him how to search her memories and to use them as if they were his own, but he could not enter her stored memories. He could touch the stored data and occasionally see bits of knowledge, but it was too erratic and difficult to use in practice.

Amy finally said, "I have a better way, but it involves a more direct input between our minds."

They experimented with this method, which turned out to be very successful. He didn't know what she did, but he was going through exercise routines in some form of martial art and it seemed flawless. He had never learned this technique, but knew it and could exercise it. It was fantastic! Amy said that she could provide knowledge to him like this on numerous fighting techniques. She could also provide knowledge on languages, sciences, or any other subject available in her extensive memory banks. This kind of learning was much easier than it had been in college. There would never be a dull moment with Amy around.

* Amy *

Try as she might, Levi was just unable to draw information directly from her storage. His mental link to her was simply not strong enough to do more than communicate back. It was her mental strength that utilized his data feed return path to her. She was very sensitive to the reception of his mental transmissions and could in turn boost his reception. However, now she was asking Levi to use his own mental powers to sort through her brain to manipulate and draw information from her. Theoretically, this was possible, but Levi could never master the skill.

She had to move up a level in the process and introduce the thoughts directly into Levi's mind. She would analyze the movement or required action and instantly download it directly into his mind. This way Levi would believe it was his thought. Levi would actually initiate the action that she put into

180

his mind, and she could augment it as it took place ... just as she was already doing. Yes, this would work and direct control could be reserved for moments of absolute necessity.

Levi was ready and it was finally time for him to use that stupid sword he dragged across the desert. Since he had it, she wanted him to be able to use it. She took him through all the motions to choreograph and record potential thrusts, stabs, slices and chops, along with defensive blocks. Since this, in all likelihood, would be his weapon of choice, she concentrated exercises on its use. She wanted Levi to be able to fight with either hand and with various sizes of swords. She created a complex skill knowledge utilizing two swords. One of the swords would be long for outside fighting and a smaller sword or large knife for inside fighting. She made sure he would be able to fight with either hand or any combination of swords. He did look good at practice, gracefully using these skills. His body rippled and flowed with the movements. Yes, she was proud of what she had been able to do with him. He really did look good!

* Levi *

He was getting bored with all the testing, running, and practicing with swords, knives and karate exercises and routines. He had to admit that he could use these fighting skills, but they all seemed so natural to him and excelled at all of them. He had never learned these skills but knew them as if he had been doing them all his life. He knew what to do and when to do it and executed each move without a flaw. When he would ask Amy how he was doing, she would respond the same every time.

Amy said, "You need more practice."

The smile and look of pride showed on her face and told a very different story.

Amy did have a request. She wanted something and needed him to do it. She explained about the temperature problem in her dome and wanted him to explore the cause of the problem. The temperature was a thermal balance between the tapped-in steam from deep in the mountain and the underground river running under the dome area. One of the two had been altered. There wasn't much that could be done about the steam, but the underground river could be checked at its source high in the mountains. She wanted him to go to the source so that she could check out all variables.

At last, there was something to do. They left early the next morning, hiking through rough, wooded country. He had his sword, bow and arrows, backpack and two knives. The sword was sheathed on his back with the bow, and his heavy leather belt sported a large Bowie knife on either side. He wore the boots he got from the desert stash, new leather overall, a vest and no hat; he hated hats.

Taking long, strong strides up rough terrain, he reached the high meadow by early afternoon. Amy made the area map visible within his mind, and they quickly located the entrance to the underground river. The entrance was open and clear, but water flowed over the natural dam several feet above the rock entrance.

182

Amy said, "This change can only be caused by something obstructing the stream inside the mountain past this point or at the mountain exit, at the other end."

The only access to the stream was at the exit end. They would have to check it there.

Amy indicated that the mountain exit was a lake bottom spring about six miles down the mountain from their home base. Reaching home (home?) just after dark, he ate a heavy meal and packed supplies for three days. He wanted to look around the land below the facility once they were down the mountain. They left early the next morning.

During the trip, he kept thinking about obstructions under water. Did he dare tell Amy he couldn't swim and was afraid of water? Hell, she probably already knew. He asked, "What will happen when we get to the lake?"

Amy said, "According to the topography maps, the spring in the lake is close to a rock ledge that goes down almost vertically for about a hundred feet. It will be necessary for you to go down there and take a look."

He went white with fear and said, "Hell No! I can't swim and even if I could, I can't go that deep." Amy gave him that calming smile.

Amy responded, "I will give you gills so you can breathe under water. Trust me! Haven't I been right so far? Haven't I been able to do all the things I said I could? I can do this too. We both die eventually if the temperature problem is not corrected."

It was impossible to know how long before they died, but it could be within only a few months. He knew he had to try, but his fear from early childhood remained strong. He had to try, however.

They reached the lake and the cliff, while the sun was still high. A road once circled the lake at this point adjacent to this cliff, and the area was still somewhat open. He approached the cliff edge and lay down to see over the precipice. The water of the small lake was obviously lower than it had once been by the look of the watermarks on the lake walls. The water was about fifty feet directly below, and the water was very calm and clear. In the bright mid-afternoon sunlight, a car could clearly be seen on the bottom and presumably on top of the spring entrance. At some point, probably later then sooner, this car had been pushed out of the way and over the cliff. Who would use this road? Here was the problem, and it was time for him to deliver. Amy had done so much for him, and now it was time to do something for her, well both of them, actually. He tried to move, but he just couldn't do it.

* Amy *

The internal struggle for Levi was strong. She could see his memory of a near drowning death as a child and the fear it caused. Levi was so strong in all things; this was very unusual for him. She knew this to be a deep-seated trauma. Levi would have to deal with the fear eventually, but she needed him to deal with it now.

She continued talking to Levi, comforting him, promising him he could do it, persuading him, but he remained frozen. He would sit on the edge, get up and look at the water, turn and walk away, only to return again. He wanted to do it but just couldn't make himself go into the water. It was an internal battle and Levi wasn't communicating much, but she could see the battle raging inside him, which went on for hours. He would almost talk himself into it and then back away. She told him, "Just jump in and I will take care of the rest." She had already developed the gills in his lungs and modified the tissue. He was physically ready, if only he would make the plunge. He continued to pace on the rock ledge, watching the water.

DANGER! She scented a Simian. The warning was instantaneous, but too late. Both of them had been engrossed in his fear and the water and, unfortunately, the wind was off the water. Levi whirled around, but even as he did, she knew it was too late. The Simian threw a large cast net that was falling over him. Levi was immediately pinned and fell to the cliff top. He strained against the net, but it was pulled tight. The lone Simian screeched with delight and moved forward, raising its sword. Levi ceased his struggling and faced his death with calm resolve.

Amy screamed, "No! It can't end like this!" There was no way she would not let it end this way. She took over his motor controls. As Levi lay there, she made him roll over the edge of the cliff. The sudden weight on the rope ripped it out of the Simian's hands, and Levi plunged fifty feet into the lake.

* Levi *

185

He saw the end coming, as the Simian approached. As strong as he now was, he was held tightly. Both arms and legs were bound with the tightening net. It was over! Damn! All his newfound hopes and plans were gone, and worst of all, he was losing to a damned Simian, yet again. Although over, he would die with courage.

As he waited to die his body suddenly jerked, bridged and rolled over. He was turning as he saw the water coming up. He hit the surface of the water and sank. Fear hit him as he fought the net and water, but still he sank. He thrashed and held his breath. He held it until he saw blackness surround him. Life was over!

When he awoke, he was breathing under water. Amazing! He really was breathing. His mouth was open and he was sucking water into his lungs ... huge and refreshing breaths. Amazement replaced his panic. He had no idea how long he had been passed out, but he was alive and that was all that mattered.

With the pressure on the holding rope gone, he was able to remove the net easily. He began to push himself around and swim about on the lake bottom. This was amazing, since he had never learned how to swim. Now he knew, thanks to Amy. He saw the Simian hopping and jumping around on the cliff, extremely agitated. Good, he beat the bastards again. Well, Amy beat him. However, how and what did she do? She directly controlled his body! "Damn you Amy! You can never have my body. This body is mine."

She sensed Levi's anger and panic. His panic at being underwater had subsided but was replaced by anger at her motor control over him. She realized he thought she could possibly, eventually, take control of his body completely. She reassured Levi that she could never permanently take over his body, even if she wanted to. She was only able to take motor control for short bursts, like this emergency. It took intense effort on her part to seize control and it could not be maintained for long. She explained very forcefully, "Yes, I took over your muscle controls, but only for a few seconds and only because you gave up. I did it to save your life. After all it is my life too, and if I have the means to save it, I will." Sensing that her logic was registering with Levi and he was calming, she stopped her chastising and let that register in his mind.

Levi's thoughts changed. He was more interested in experimenting with his underwater breathing and swimming. He was happy turning and rolling around underwater. He floated on his back, watching the Simian high above on the cliff. Levi gestured up at the Simian with his middle fingers on each hand, and she wondered about the significance of this gesture.

Eventually, he swam over to the car and circled it to view the situation, to see if it was causing the problem with the underground water flow. The car was lying directly on top of the rock and sand entrance to the spring. Water bubbled around the car body, but it was significantly obstructing the flow of water out of the spring. The car was not covered with moss, which indicated that it hadn't been underwater all that long. She indicated that the small amount of moss would mean that maybe it had been here no more than two months. The obstruction would eventually upset the natural temperature control and most probably destroyed her. If only two months caused the temperature to rise that much, she could be assured that another few months would cause her destruction. The car had to be moved and normal water flow restored.

Obviously, the car had been on the rock ledge and cliff above, and pushed over the side to clear the ledge. The Simian must have done it. The ledge and cliff made a natural trap. The Simian had cleared the area, and they walked directly into its trap. Not realizing, they had been in the trap for hours. It surprised her that the Simian had not sprung the trap long before.

Reviewing what happened with the Simian above, she now realized and was amazed, because she wasn't sure who she had been more frightened for, her or Levi. It seemed that she was concerned more for Levi's safety and had been thinking about him. How strange that seemed now.

* Levi *

He was after all, alive. Amy was right, he had given up, and she had saved his life. Yes, he was alive and at the bottom of a lake, breathing water. She had saved his life in many ways since discovering each other. This just happened to be twice in one day, first from the Simian and then from drowning. He told Amy, "I apologize. I am

188

sorry. You did the right thing." She said nothing, but looked pleased with the appreciation he give her.

Planting his feet firmly on the rocks, he grabbed the car and lifted. He felt hard muscles knot in his arms, back, and legs, as the car moved slightly. Straining, the car moved more. He pumped large lungs full of water as he strained, and the car continued to move, finally clearing the spring. Water gushed out of the spring, as pressure was released from the backed up, underground river. Amy was positive this solved the problem, but said another trip into the complex would be necessary, just to make sure.

While there was no sign of the Simian, he had no intention of going out this side of the lake. It was a good thing he fell in with all his gear, now there would be no need to get back up there. He swam off in the opposite direction, leaving this experience far behind. Well, all except the swimming, he was beginning to like it. He saw Amy smile in his mind.

They were together now for life. There would be a long learning curve and many obstacles to overcome, but he was happy with the changes Amy had put him through. It was very much like a metamorphous. It was as if he had arrived a caterpillar and emerged a butterfly. Well, it was more like arriving as Clark Kent and leaving as Superman! Amy grinned and so did he.

CHAPTER 10
(LIVING TOGETHER)

* Amy *

Levi enjoyed swimming, and his fear vanished fast enough. Basically, Levi was a very strong-willed person and wasn't afraid of much. This was the first real fear she had seen in him, but this was the result of the childhood trauma. The fear obviously no longer existed, as Levi grinned hugely, while breathing the water. She too, found the experience pleasant. She knew all the stored information that existed about swimming, but now she understood the experience itself was far more stimulating than reading about it. There are some things you just can't explain with words. She swam along with Levi, enjoying the experience but knew he would tire of swimming eventually, due to the amount of physical effort required.

She agreed that he should not go back up on the cliff, since Levi wanted to go down the mountain and survey the area. He could exit the far side of the lake and just keep going down for at least another day. This was a first for them. So far she had always directed the course of events, now Levi was taking the initiative. She had accomplished most of the goals of survival, so they were moving into undiscovered territory now. They were all about living now, and living together.

With the return of Levi's strength, came his intense hate for the Simians and desire for revenge.

She knew he would want to extract revenge very soon, and he was prepared to the best of her ability. Levi was ready, but she remained reluctant to turn him loose. The thought of Levi going into danger frightened her. As well prepared as he now was, something unexpected could always happen. Take today, all his experience and newfound abilities were not enough, and he had almost lost his life. No, there were no guarantees and these Simians were vicious fighters and always ran in teams.

Strange about the Simian that attacked them today, he was alone...no team. He was also smaller. This was inconsistent with what she had learned about the Simians to date. At some point they would have to solve this mystery. Maybe sooner, since this one was quite close to the research complex and could be a problem.

* Levi *

Approaching the other side of the lake, he tired of the heavy breathing required underwater. He felt he could keep it up indefinitely if he had too though, but no need, he was there now and ready to move on down the mountain.

Amy said, "There will be a little discomfort as you switch from water to air. It will be best to hold your breath until you are out of the water and drain the water out of your lungs."

She would make the physical change once the water was out. It worked just as she said, but it was more than just discomfort. Momentary panic of drowning struck him, as he choked on the water, but it soon passed, and he was breathing air again.

Once out of the water with his lungs converted back, he stripped to clean and dry his gear and body. He laid his clothing on the warm boulders to dry, as he tended his gear, naked. Amy seemed strangely quiet, watching him. Well, he had no secrets from her. She had seen him do just about everything, since she had to be with him now for everything. At first he was embarrassed, but he had gotten used to it, until she put her face in his mind. It took him some time before he could take a pee without turning her image off. He knew she could still see, but it helped somewhat.

Amy had done well with the promises she made to him. Actually, she had done fantastically, and every day he thanked her again, but he was ready to do still more. He hated and wanted to kill Simians. He was only one man, but knew he could do something. Amy had given him the means to extract his revenge, and the time to start was now. He had been ready for some time, but Amy kept devising one training session after another, delaying his beginning. Now she wanted them to get more comfortable with each other and learn how to coexist. Well, this will come no matter what we do, so why not move forward. Yes, he pressed her some.

All he really wanted to do look around and survey the general area and see if maybe there was any danger. It was late afternoon, as he slipped back into his overalls and vest and packed up his gear to leave. Two hours later he was going over the last mountain range as the sun was going down. Suddenly he was startled.

Amy said "Ohhhh."

192

He stopped and looked around, but saw no danger. He said, "What's wrong?"

Amy said, "I was just startled by the beauty of the sunset. Will you stop for a few minutes and let me watch?"

He was only too happy to give her this time. It was a very beautiful sunset and they talked about it, shared it together as the sun slowly set.

It is not something he normally would have done, but it seemed appropriate to share beauty with someone when it was appreciated. He was aware of Amy's emotional awakening. It had been happening slowly ever since they met but more quickly as of late. He could appreciate her loneliness after all this time, and seeing a sunset for the first time must have been wonderful. He planned to give Amy more such moments in the future.

* Amy *

Amy had expanded her imaging ability to view Levi's total body. It was as if she stood away and look at him and could do this from any angle by rotating the angle of reference. She watched him now, as he stood naked in front of her. Her interest peaked, and she found his body pleasant to look at. While she had restructured his body and knew all the intimate details, this seemed different somehow. His body was a thing of beauty. He had massive, broad shoulders, arms the size of most men's calves, narrow waist, flat stomach, round buttocks and thick thighs. She followed his sleek, glistening wet back and thighs, which she found strangely attractive and

193

stimulating. This was strange, and she seemed warm.

She continued thinking about Levi's body and, as always doing a thousand things with her mind, while Levi took long, strong strides designed to cover distance. As he passed around a boulder, she was shocked to see the beauty of the sunset. She had seen many sunsets since traveling with Levi, and she had storage banks loaded with data, but seeing this sunset through Levi's eyes surpassed anything she had ever experienced. The colors were incredible. She could analyze the colors and tell you the color mix and scheme, the light intensity and a hundred other bits of data about this sunset, but this was simply beautiful. Why had she never noticed it before? She asked Levi to stay and watch, so she could experience this. They watched through common eyes, seeing the same thing. Levi called it sharing, and she was overwhelmed. She felt, yes felt, emotions bubbling over, and she was disturbed and couldn't tell Levi why, because she didn't know why.

As they watched the darkness engulf them, she noticed a campfire off in the distance. Judging from the brightness and distance, this was a large fire. If this was a Human camp, it was strange to have so little disregard for the Simians. This could be a Simian camp or, if it was Human, there either aren't any Simians around, which they know is not the case, or they don't care. This does not make sense unless, oh yes, it had been eighty days since they left the Henderson's. This could be the Simian's gathering time again, but what about the Simian that had almost killed them, that lone Simian? Why

194

wasn't it at the gathering? Maybe it was an outcast. This required further research.

They decided to approach the camp cautiously and survey the situation. It took them an hour walking in the dark to get close enough to see that it was indeed Humans, a fairly sizable group of about two hundred people. The group gathered around the single, large campfire in the center of a clearing, surrounded by dense woods. They danced and sang to music being played on various instruments. The music was folk or country, as it used to be called. They were truly having a party, and Levi wanted to join in.

As they walked close picket guards challenged them, but seeing that he was alone and Human, he waved him in. As Levi approached the firelight, silence fell on the crowd. They stared in disbelief. What were they staring at? She looked at the crowd, then back at Levi, and finally noticed what they saw. Levi stood there like a Greek God. Damn, he was impressive! He was very big, hugely muscled, firm, dark complexioned and very handsome. He had weapons hanging all over him, the show-off. She was also impressed as she looked at him anew.

He said, "Hello, I am Levi Walkingbear."

With that introduction the spell was broken. People were introducing themselves and talking all at once. They were friendly; especially some of the females who seemed to be staring at him like hungry wolves. Levi didn't appear threatened by any of it and actually seemed to enjoy the attention. He could be a very exasperating man at times.

* Levi *

195

He was very happy to join this party. He hadn't seen or been to a party since he joined the law firm, and how many years ago was that? Wow! He visited with many of those gathered. This was indeed a celebration of the eightieth day Simian gathering. The Humans of the area came out of hiding at this time for a celebration and gathered for commerce and trade. This was reminiscent of the old mountain man days. Trade goods could be seen at every small camp, and tents and tee pees were plentiful. Women were also plentiful, and many had fixed stares on him, which he found exciting.

Curious about him and where he had come from, they listened intently as he relayed part of his story of crossing the desert and arriving here only recently. Of course, he mentioned nothing about being eighty years old. He told them he was just traveling, assessing the strength of the Simians across the country. That brought nods and murmurs of understanding from the crowd. They offered an abundance of information about the Simians. He listened but didn't register much, he knew Amy was listening to it all and would remember everything. He did not say so, but figured they believed he intended to take the battle to the Simians. This brought mixed emotions from the crowd. To some it brought awe and others embarrassment and anger. Some of the able-bodied men did not appreciate being made to feel lesser.

He noticed this and was trying to change the subject, when three of the larger men stepped forward in open challenge. They wanted to know just how he intended to kill Simians when all they could do was hide from them. They were angry and embarrassed by their inability and fear and wanted to regain respect. Possibly, they had been the centers of attraction before he came along and were jealous of the attention he got. He never really knew.

All Levi knew for sure was that there was going to be a fight. He had no intention of killing other Humans unless it was to save his own life. Standing at full height, he discovered two of the men were equal in height, but less developed. The third was a muscular fellow, but shorter by a few inches. He told the men, "I will kill Simians by outsmarting and out maneuvering them, being faster and killing them first."

The leader of the group, the short one, said, "Simians always run in threes. Since we are three let's see what you can do against us."

As he said that, the leader brought a big roundhouse right from out of nowhere aimed at his jaw.

Amy said she provided him with karate knowledge and he would know what to do. He did in fact know exactly what to do, and did it. He ducked under the blow and while spinning, grabbed the leader's hand and pulled it hard in the direction of the swing. It was a simple judo move, which sent the big man flying to the ground. He continued spinning and dropped to one leg, while swinging his other. This caught the second man behind the feet and put him flat on his back. Bouncing up, he caught the third man under the chin with his fist, sending him down and out cold. He stood watching the three men, one of whom was already unconscious. The other two stood slowly, wide-eyed, wondering what had just happened. The first man charged, but he moved quickly to the left, tripped him, spun and chopped him behind the neck, sending him face down in the dirt and out. The last man held his hands up in surrender.

He said, "All right, I believe you."

Laughter erupted throughout the crowd. The laughter continued so long and hard, tears rolled down their cheeks. Even the last man was grinning.

He helped the fallen warriors up and brushed off their clothes. They looked stunned but no longer wanted to fight. It wasn't long before they were laughing along with the others. There was no reason to be embarrassed against someone with the obvious skills he demonstrated. Their interests now were how to also learn those skills.

Amy said no, but he was saying maybe. When the time came, he could teach them some fighting techniques. Maybe they could fight together to rid the Simian from our country. This brought a cheer. He was really feeling happy about this chance encounter.

* Amy *

She listened to all the information offered by the Humans and pleased to get it. They confirmed that, as believed, there were three Simian colonies in the general vicinity of San Francisco. One colony was closer, near Fresno, and the Humans concurred that the Los Angeles compound was larger than the others. They suspected that the LA colony had an infusion of additional Simians from a different group. The LA Simian leader was a monster, towering above any other Simian. It was the largest Simian they had ever seen. The monster had often been seen leading patrols. It took unusual pleasure in killing Humans. Many Humans had left the Los Angeles area because of their fear. Some migrated up this way or, they had heard, to the other side of the Sierras. All Human life was of a nomad style here. No settlement could be built for fear of the Simians. If the Simians found a Human stronghold, they concentrated on it until it fell.

She saw the fight coming and prepared. She downloaded the necessary information and prepared Levi. When it started, it went fast. She wanted to end it before someone really got hurt. She didn't like confrontations and wanted to avoid fighting, but Levi seemed to relish in it. He was not mean, but liked the action and feeling of competition. It was never a contest, since Levi, with her augmentation and assistance, was far superior to any Human or small group. The fight lasted only seconds without any major injuries.

It was obvious that Levi had gained the interest of the crowd, especially the females. Several crowded around Levi whenever they could. Eventually, they crowded out the men who were asking about learning fighting skills. Once Levi agreed to teach them some of the tricks, the men were happy to go off drinking some more and talk about this amazing man. The three fallen warriors were now camp heroes for standing up to Levi and his awesome powers. How in the blazes was he going to teach them something he didn't know himself? She would have found this humorous had it not been for the big blond female with large breasts that seemed to have run all the other women away. It was just Levi and that female now. She said her name was Joan.

Levi and Joan were off in the dark drinking beer, and she was close to Levi holding and pressing her lips on Levi, and he was pressing his lips on the female! Kissing, that is what they were doing. She didn't like this and didn't know why. She didn't like this at all!

* Levi *

It had been more years than he cared to remember since he had held a voluptuous woman in his arms. He was very aroused, and Joan was very willing. She led him back to her tent, and they entered arm in arm. They stopped to kiss inside the tent. The kiss was long and passionate, while his hands were holding and touching her ample body parts. Joan stepped back and unfastened her dress straps, letting it fall to the tent floor. She was beautiful, and he wanted her badly. Joan approached again, holding him in a very stimulating embrace. Joan knew what she was doing and what she wanted, as she opened the catches on his loose overalls. He was desperately aroused. It had been such a long time, and since returning to his current vigorous health, he needed sexual release. Joan slipped her hand inside his clothes and down to his manhood, driving him crazy. Suddenly, Joan burst out laughing, holding his manhood.

He was horrified! What happened? He reached into his pants and felt what Joan was feeling. His penis was NOT erect. It was flaccid, and it was TINY! His anger erupted, knowing what had happened. He cursed then pleaded with Amy to allow him to have an erection, but she said no. Well, that isn't exactly true, Amy simply didn't allow it to rise to the occasion, nor did she answer him. There was neither voice nor image in his mind. She simply did not respond. His embarrassment was incredible, as he picked up his gear and quickly left the camp. He could still hear Joan laughing as he left.

He had been horribly humiliated and would never be able to return to that camp ever again. He marched through the remainder of the night working off his anger and thinking. Amy hadn't left; he could still feel her. Why had she done that to him? What possible reason? If she was a real woman, he might think her jealous. Damn, that was it! Amy thinks she is a real woman. At least her emotions are real. She can't possibly know how to handle these new emotions. He had waited too long to teach her, but she was learning fast with or without his awareness. He believed she was mature now. Well, he paid for his error tonight. Damn, how was he supposed to know she loved him? They must coexist. How would this play out now?

It was almost daylight before Amy spoke. Her image reappeared in his mind. Those beautiful green eyes were wet. Amy's expression was somber and she was crying. It broke his heart.

Amy said, "Do you want a son?"

He was quite shocked, until he realized Amy was responding to textbook definitions, rather than understanding about sex for the sake of sex. She assumed he was trying to procreate.

201

He responded by asking, "Why that particular question?" She ignored his question.

Amy asked, "Do you love Joan?"

Again he was shocked, but said, "No! All I wanted with Joan was sex and release of tension from my lusts and desires." He explained that he couldn't love Joan. Love takes time to develop. He asked Amy, "What do you believe love to be?" She responded by quoting the dictionary.

Love

1.A deep, tender, ineffable feeling of affection and solicitude toward a person, such as that arising from kinship, recognition of attractive qualities, or a sense of underlying oneness.

2.A feeling of intense desire and attraction toward a person with whom one is disposed to make a pair; the emotion of sex and romance.

3.a. Sexual passion. b. Sexual intercourse.

He told Amy that # 3 applied here, and it was possible to have sexual passion, desire and intercourse without the other qualities listed in # 1 and # 2. She seemed to accept this in silence. When she did respond, Amy astounded him again.

She said, "# 1 and # 2 seemed to apply to the way I feel about you." Then she said, "I LOVE YOU, LEVI." It was said with warmth and open affection. He could see it in her eyes. He could see the tears, the warmth, and yes, he could see the love. It was his turn to remain silent.

* Amy *

202

She was upset and she recognized it as an emotion, but she could not ignore it. The feeling would not go away. It festered and grew as she watched Joan through Levi's eyes. She watched as Joan removed her clothes and stood naked in front of Levi. Levi became very aroused and grew an erection. He wanted to copulate with her. She was ... what? Jealous? Yes, she was jealous! Recognizing jealousy for what it was, she knew then that she loved Levi. This was disturbing. She would never be able to accept Levi loving another.

Just look at Levi all turned to mush by this naked woman. He was quivering in anticipation. He was not even giving any thought about her feelings, only his animal drive. Joan was reaching into his pants. She watched and listened until she couldn't stand it any longer. This had to stop, and it did. She shut down the blood flow to his penis, not just a little, almost all the way. She wanted to embarrass him and end this. Satisfaction was complete when she heard Joan laugh. Yes! Levi was embarrassed and, oh yes, really angry.

Levi cursed, begged, pleaded and finally gave up in anger. She was too angry and upset to talk to him. He grabbed his gear and left in a huff with Joan's laughter echoing after him. His obvious destination was home camp as he tromped off through the darkness. There was just enough moonlight to find his way, and he needed time to cool down, as did she.

By daylight she had calmed down sufficiently to talk and, judging by his vital signs, so had Levi. Levi had blocked his mind when he became angry and kept it blocked. She hoped to see some of his thoughts, but that had been lost to her. She realized she was in love with Levi. She didn't understand fully what love was, but she knew she thought a great deal of Levi. He had become the center of her life, the focus of her attention and the reason to live. She was hurt and very sad. Why had Levi turned to Joan? Literature suggested a man wants to have sons. Was that it?

She broke the silence to ask that very question. His anger was gone and he seemed willing to talk. He explained that he wasn't after a son, nor did he love Joan. He simply wanted sex, an animal urge to satisfy his lust. It was, well would have been a one-time thing. While pleased to know that there was no love for Joan, she still didn't like the thought of Levi touching another woman. She wanted Levi to touch her. Once she understood the biological needs Levi was talking about, it saddened her even more. She had no way of competing against women with real bodies, and compete she must. She wanted to be one with Levi, in more ways than they already were.

Levi once said that she didn't have lips, but managed to talk him into traveling hundreds of miles. He challenged her with that statement then and now. If she could do that without a mouth, what more could she do? He also said that her mind could find a way if there was any chance. Talking without lips, life without a body, the movement of objects without hands, were her accomplishments. Yes, she must dare to again explore new thought, think in the abstract, be creative, and explore new knowledge with her intellect. She had learned how to exercise telepathy and telekinesis. Could she now be a lover without a body? Was there even a name for what she was contemplating? She couldn't come up with a name, maybe something akin to astral projection, virtual holograph, physical manifestation, or something new. Was it even possible? She was determined to try.

* Levi *

Momentarily overcome, he didn't know how to respond to this. How could Amy love him? How did he feel about Amy? While part of him was pleased to hear that she loved him, part of him struggled to find the logic in that. Amy was not a real person. She was a voice and an artificial image in his mind. After all, she was only a disembodied brain, so how could she love? Does she understand what love really is? What does she expect from me? How does he feel about this? How should he feel? He had no answers, only more questions.

They could never touch, hold, or feel each other. He could never smell the fresh washed hair, feel their lips touch in passion, or share the physical experience of making love together. It sounded so futile. So why did he also feel affection for Amy? The situation was crazy, but everything had been crazy since the moment Amy entered his mind and life. They had never met, but again they had met. It was so confusing. How could he judge this without a reference or a manual? This was all new territory. The situation would require much thought on his part anyway.

"So how was I supposed to know you loved me," he asked. "You could have talked to me

205

without embarrassing me so." Amy grinned in his mind.

Amy said, "I didn't know until that very moment that I loved you. I could not participate in the physical aspect of you making love to another woman. No, not love, or even sex, so I stopped it!"

He said, "You sure as hell did stop it!" He smiled as he thought about what Amy had done to him. They both burst out laughing.

Amy never ceased to take him by surprise with her questions, and the next one was no exception.

Amy said, "Were you serious about not wanting a son?"

The question startled him. He said, "I had a son once with my second soul mate. The child died in infancy, and we were unable to have more children." He hadn't given it much thought in years, but he had always wanted a son. "Amy, why did you ask that particular question again?"

Amy said, "You can no longer procreate, because the DNA would transfer into the fertilized egg and multiply, eventually killing both baby and mother."

He hadn't considered that possibility. In response to his next question, Amy explained that having sex with Joan would not have harmed her, because she would have made his sperm sterile. Physically, he could have sex, assuming she (Amy) permitted, but he could not pass on his modified DNA. He hadn't really thought about having children again. Up till now he had only tried to survive. He appreciated knowing this now, so he wouldn't spend time or energy thinking about it in the future.

They reached home by midday, checked on the horses and game traps, saw to supper and settled down for an evening of rest. Amy reminded him that they needed to go back down to the tenth level and check on the temperature. He exclaimed, "OH, shit yes!" In all the excitement, he had forgotten about the whole purpose of their exploration. Lighting the Coleman lantern, he proceeded down the twisting corridors and stairs, following the map in his mind. The map image was one of many improvements he noticed, since Amy revealed the completion of their inter-mind language. Communication was much improved, not to mention the visual images. Who knew what else Amy could come up with using that incredible intellect of hers? He said, "Damn you're smart Amy! You're pretty too!" He was rewarded with a beautiful smile that made him shiver with pleasure.

They approached the circular, dome room and entered through the open door. As the light spread across the room, he heard/felt Amy sigh, as they saw the temperature gage now well back in the green range. Good, it had worked. He was about to turn away and leave the room, when Amy stopped him. While she had no idea what was wrong, she just wanted him to walk around her dome slowly. As he approached the other side of the dome, he noticed the remains of a body leaning against the silver sphere. This body was Amy's focus. Kneeling down to look at the pile of bones, he picked out a plastic identification badge that had once been attached to the clothing of this dead person. The badge read Dr. Joyce Sheldon, Amy's proclaimed inventor, cell donor and mental mother.

Amy said, "Something is calling me. It is a strange sense rather than language."

He continued to search through the rubble of the skeleton as Amy directed. He found a round, golden locket on a chain, still around the neck vertebras. Showing proper respect for the dead, he removed the locket.

Amy said, "Yes this is it; I can feel its life in your hands."

Amy wanted the locket, so he slipped it over his neck and heard it clack with the Simian tooth he proudly wore.

As he was leaving, retracing his steps, Amy asked that he detour through the laboratory. She had one more chore. He must search for an old-style microscope, the kind that didn't need electricity to work. After rummaging through the many cabinets, he finally found one. As directed, he brought it with him, along with a box of glass slides. Amy remained secretive as to why she wanted the microscope, and he learned long ago that if she didn't wish to tell him something, he wasn't about to pry it out of her. They continued out of the complex, which satisfied him greatly. All the dead within the complex made it feel like a tomb and gave him the creeps.

* Amy *

While positive that Levi had fixed the circulation problem, she breathed (metaphorically) a sigh of relief, as she saw the temperature now well into the green level. Their survival now ensured for the immediate future.

As they began to leave, she felt a strange drawing, pulling, calling; what was it? She asked Levi to wait and explore. She could feel the calling through Levi's senses, or was he just the conduit? All she knew was that there was something in this room that was reaching out to her, and she must find it. As Levi circled her dome, the sensation became stronger. The decomposed body had something to do with it, so Levi investigated.

It was her inventor. She remembered this woman. She also remembered Dr. Sheldon being with her constantly after she became self-aware. Dr. Sheldon had stayed by her side, helping her understand what was happening. The doctor knew Amy would achieve a living status in time and was jubilant at her eventual awaking. Dr. Sheldon was also there when everything went dark. She now realized that the doctor had also died then.

When Levi touched the locket, it was almost like an electric shock. The sense of knowing was so strong. The locket had belonged to Dr. Sheldon, and it was talking to her, urging her, drawing her. She could not understand its language, but she could sense it talking to her. How was this? What was this? She said, "Just put the locket around your neck and keep it." She would need time to consider this new puzzle.

Levi was not comfortable underground in this complex. She felt his fear of ghosts from so many dead. She didn't want Levi to come back or spend more time here than was absolutely necessary, so she made her last request now. She needed a manual microscope to study a theory she had been researching. She had been considering the nature of the rays the Simians had used on Earth, and just how they were able to change the basic laws of physics. She wanted to test her theory. If she was right, she might possibly be able to reverse some of the effects of the Simian ray.

It was dark when they finally reached the surface, so Levi built a fire and relaxed. They talked as had become routine. She always asked many questions about love. Whom had he loved? What was his most memorable sex? What did he personally like in sex? It went on and on, and Levi remained open. Oh, did she ever receive strong memories. She experienced what Levi experienced and remembered. He really remembered well. She experienced everything and now understood what sex and love felt like from Levi's perspective. He was so rich in memories, and she knew she could never be without him, even if she could survive.

When she asked Levi to explain the love experience with his first soul mate Linda, his mind brought forward a poem he had written to her. She felt the importance and reverence of the poem. For Levi to have written his true feeling to Linda in this way, he had overcome the embarrassment of opening up his heart and letting her look inside his defenses. That trust only comes with love. The poem meant a lot to him because of this, and she felt honored to share it. It was like looking into his soul.

LOVE
What words do you use?
When I LOVE YOU is not enough
Love is only a word
A word to express what you feel

210

A word to express a wealth of meanings, feelings, emotions
Can it be done with a word? I think not!
It can mean many things to many people
But what does this word mean to me?
I love you
When we are together
You fill my heart
You make me happy
You make me soar to heights I have never been
We are one
Complete
You fill an emptiness
An emptiness that only you can fill
An emptiness that comes when you are away
Love is addictive
An addiction for you
The addiction of needs, wants, desires
As a drowning man for air
As a starving man for food
As a thirsting man for water
As a freezing man for warmth
As a blind man for sight
And as I for You
When I say I LOVE YOU
I want you, need you, and desire you
To smell you and fill my lungs with you
To taste you and fill my body with you
To drink you in and fill my need
To feel your warmth against me
To see your beauty and feed my starving eyes
You are my air, my food, my water, my warmth, my light
My everything!

MY LOVE

As she read those words, she understood, and she wept.

* Levi *

He was glad to get out of that damned tomb. So many people had died in there, and he imagined he felt them roaming the dark halls. Back on the surface he had a warm campfire, plenty of cooked venison and the pleasant company of Amy. They were still talking about love, lust, sex and emotions. With all the questions she asked, he became melancholy about all the old memories she was dragging back to the surface. He suspected that she could see some of the memories but didn't really mind if it could help her understand. He owed her so much anyway.

At sunrise, he resumed the old argument; it was time to take up the battle against the Simians. He knew she did not like the idea of revenge on the Simians or the risk to him, and she could be damned stubborn at times. He took his time presenting his case to Amy, reminding her of all the promises she had made. Amy reluctantly agreed. Agreed that is, assuming he was reasonable and listened to her. Plus, she really meant, listen! He happily agreed to anything.

CHAPTER 11
(SEARCH FOR THE ENEMY)

* Levi *

Amy's plan was one of surveillance ... learn the enemy, who he was, how he fought, where he lived, how many there were, how much of a threat they really were and so much more. She acted like it was HER that had to fight the monsters. Boy, was she a protective mother hen. She would analyze the data gathered, and probably try to devise other plans and training to keep him from battle. But, he was just as determined as she was. With the return of his health and strength came the intense hatred for the Simian, and he was anxious to kill them. He also knew better than to push Amy too hard. He grinned remembering that Amy had ways to control him.

She wanted to go back down the mountain where they had been, and move south to locate the Simian compound close to Fresno, then travel north to survey the Simian compound in that area. She wanted to leave the bulk of the gear and horses here until their return, then take the horses and go back through the Owens Valley to see the Los Angeles and San Diego Simian colonies. Damn! There sure were a lot of Simians in this part of the world. This trip should be interesting, but he believed they would be able to observe a great deal during this journey.

He didn't care as long as they were doing something toward moving the battle further along.

He checked on the horses and made sure they were safely sheltered in the small, hidden valley. He packed his light traveling backpack with gear, jerked some venison strips and made sure there were plenty of Amy's vitamin pills. He announced, "I'm ready."

At first light he was on the trail headed down the mountain west. He was anxious to see new sights, hopefully, different people, and Simians. He did not want to return to the camp where he had been so embarrassed. He was sure everyone knew by now. Levi Walkingbear had been the hot shot on campus in that crowd, but could never face them again. Damned Amy! His face burned red again just thinking about it.

By mid-afternoon they were again close to the lake where he had almost lost his life. Thinking about how close a shave that had been was enough to still make him shake. He would not be taken by surprise this time and loosened the sword in his back sheath. He almost wished he would see that Simian again, but Amy was very serious about skirting the area. She was not yet ready for him to fight. He didn't like it but understood the need to learn more. These monsters were vicious and mean and would not be easy to kill. He would need every advantage possible.

* Amy *

There was no way she could change Levi's mind about combating the Simians. He had too much built up hate for them and would fight and probably die trying to resist them. How useless that death would be. All she wanted was to remain safe and live united with Levi. However, all she could do now was try to better the odds in any way possible. She needed to study the Simians and learn how they fought, lived, patrolled and any data that might give them an edge in a confrontation. They needed to be studied in great detail and learn their strengths as well as their weaknesses.

They set out early on a long journey; however, this trek was far less difficult than the last one. Levi was in much better shape for this journey, and it was much shorter. It was though, possibly more dangerous, heading into the lion's den so to speak. They would be staying in the proximity of the closest Simian colony for several days observing and then moving on toward the San Francisco location. The farther down the mountain they went, the more dangerous it became.

They approached the lake, but she wanted Levi to maintain a wide berth around the area. She had given much thought about this lone Simian. Why was he alone? Why was he living far away from the Simian community? It had to be a rebel or an outcast. She thought of no other scenario that could explain it. The Simian must reside here, because there was no other explanation for its efforts to set a trap, unless intended for use more than once. The car had obviously been pushed off the cliff to clear the trap area and had not been in the lake for long. She believed that fact indicated that the Simian had not been around until recently. It must be watching the trap area. She was very curious about this lone Simian and suspected that there was more to this story.

It was pleasant traveling with Levi. They saw many things together and communicated constantly, which she liked. Their minds were closely tuned and intertwined, as they talked, shared, and explored new thought together. They were so close now that understanding each other's thoughts and ideas became common. If their communications were with words, they most likely would finish each other's sentences, or say the same thing at the same time. Even being that close, they remained separate identities. She was decidedly female, while Levi was all male. Even though they were close, the views of the same situation were often diametrically opposed. This caused many discussions, but it kept life interesting.

They had a cold camp that night and got an early start the next morning. They were headed down old Highway 41 toward Fresno. Through Levi's Government Issue binoculars, they could see the Simian complex long before they had to commit to leaving the mountains. They decided to stay high and observe. The complex sat about a mile off the highway. They traveled farther south along a mountain road to gain a better and closer observation position.

The original disc-shaped spaceship sat in the center of the complex. The entire complex was circular in design and about the size of a football field. Settlements outside the ship had been constructed in spiral circular compounds in a radius around the original ship. Each subsequent building spiral was further outside the first and bigger. There was no attempt to conceal, since they were all a bright white. The whole complex loosely resembled a target with the ship being the bull's eye. If the spirals were meant to be barricade walls, the many large open archways destroyed that purpose. The Simians were arrogant enough to assume no one would ever attack them. This was, however, probably a safe assumption.

In the second circle, what appeared to be the females of the species mingled with the Simian young. The females were shorter and squatter and had much wider hips. The young and females were in a loose group and seemed to remain separated from the males within the confines of the complex, primarily in the second circle.

They observed Simian three-member teams coming and going, always moving fast, if not running. Many returning teams carried Human remains and in some cases live Humans, always males. The live Humans were placed in a fenced compound, which currently held about fifteen adult males. Curious also and surprising, there appeared to be Simians caged in an adjacent compound. Both compounds had guards patrolling the perimeter. The Human butchered meat was taken to what presumably was a kitchen of sorts. It was a long spiral building in the first circle of building out from the ship.

Levi shook with rage, and she could see the pain from his memories. She talked to him, comforting, calming him. Levi was full of anger and she shared that anger, but she must be calm. She must hold him back. What could he do anyway?

* Levi *

217

He was upset watching the Simians bringing in slaughtered Human meat. Why did Humans continue to live in the area at all? Surely there were safe spots, like the far side of the mountain in areas like Owens Valley, or areas farther away from the coast. The valley they went through was clear of Simians and appeared to have been clear for some time. Why did the Humans stay around like sheep to be herded, hunted and slaughtered? Amy was talking to him trying to calm and comfort him. He did appreciate the company, but he remained angry.

He knew he must control his feelings and learn the enemy. That was why they were here. Swallowing his hate, he went back to being objective in his observations. He turned the emotions into hate and let it build inside him. He would use this hate someday. Turning the emotions enabled him to divorce his mind from the Humans and concentrate on the job at hand.

They stayed on in this location for two more days, observing without further problems. The routine remained the same, with 3-unit teams coming and going at all hours of the day, but mostly there was little activity at night. Their social structure seemed to be more like military than anything. There appeared to be a command hierarch, with positions equivalent to captains, lieutenants and squad leaders. The teams were disciplined and even remained together at rest. At least the teams entered and exited together from what looked like a type of barracks structure in the fourth circle. They did not observe any organized mealtimes, more of a constant flow of Simians. The patrols left in all directions but mainly south. Amy assumed that territory to the north was double patrolled from this compound and the San Francisco compound, causing possible conflict and competition for the hunting.

Observing the activities to the south reinforced Amy's original belief that the trail south was impassable. It was simply too busy and could not be crossed within a 5-day Simian gathering, plus they would have to pass uncomfortably close to two Simian colonies. The risks were just too great. As she had assumed, they must retrace their path back down the east side of the Sierras to reach the southern Simian locations.

Amy estimated that this complex supported around five hundred Simians, which would consume around thirty Humans a day. Damn! That was sickening to think about how many Humans have lost their lives to these Simians. There couldn't be that many Humans left in the area. His hate raged again and said, "Amy, this has to stop."

* Amy *

They had learned all they were going to by observing this location, and Levi's body was in need of a heavy protein intake. She suggested they move on out some distance toward the northern Simian compound in the San Francisco area, before daring to hunt and light a campfire. Levi had been eating jerked venison for the last few days and getting hungry for something more substantial. Levi was also getting very grumpy. He needed a constant flow of protein into his body to maintain the augmented controls.

On the morning of the third day at this location, they were off again, retracing the trail back to Highway 49 then north, loosely following the highway route and staying close to cover. Along the way Levi dropped a deer with his bow and arrow and deadeye aim. If he only knew, he would be humble. By late in the evening they found a secluded spot and built a small cooking fire. Levi ate his fill then jerked some strips for later use. She was still having Levi eat pounds of raw vegetables, plants and animal items most normal people would never touch, but Levi needed many nutrients most normal people didn't require. Levi had long since given up arguing with her. He also felt the need and cravings, so he easily complied.

They continued on at a fairly fast, but safe pace for two days along the mountain edge highway trail. Mid-afternoon of the second day, she warned Levi. "I smell Simians." Levi took a path up and off the trail, and positioned himself so that he could see both directions. She told him, "The smell is coming from downwind in the direction we are going." He watched intently in that direction. He had a retreat direction and was relatively safe from this position. As they watched, they heard screeching and rustling up the trail, and soon saw two Simians running up the road. Both were burdened with butchered Humans. Following behind was the third team member, looking over his shoulder, screeching at something behind as he loped. All three appeared to be frightened. What could frighten three Simians?

The three Simians rounded the corner and went out of sight down the trail, just as a herd of six Simians came bursting around the corner, waving their swords high and screeching. They were in obvious pursuit and gaining fast. As they moved past and out of sight, Levi scrambled down from his spot to follow. He was fast and soon gained sight of them ahead. The two groups had engaged each other and swords were clashing. They watched in awe as the swordsmanship demonstration took place. Slash, cut, stab, block, swing, it was a blur, but she memorized every thrust, defense and offensive move. Unfortunately, the battle didn't last too long, as the first group was outnumbered two to one. The wounds added up and they started falling one by one. The three put up a fantastic defense standing back to back in a circle, but once the first Simian fell, it was over quickly. They were just as vicious with another Simian as they were with Humans, except they didn't eat them. The bodies were mutilated and thrown all around the area.

The remaining Simians were picking up the butchered Humans, when she realized their mistake. Levi had run around the corner and stopped in the middle of the road, excitedly watching the battle. He was still standing there when one of the Simians saw him. It began to screech and they all turned to look. What a terrifying sight, six agitated Simians staring at you.

She was frightened and said, "Run!"

It was a waste of words, as Levi was already speeding away.

* Levi *

Oh shit! He didn't need Amy to tell him to run like hell. He took off like a rabbit from a fox, running down the road. The Simians were fast, but he was faster. He was starting to feel safe with his speed, as he left them behind. He wanted a comfortable lead so he could hide and lose them. As he ran around the boulders headed toward the narrow pass ahead, his heart sank. The pass was blocked with rocks from long past earthquakes. Was there a pass? He was looking as he ran. He could see gaps between some of the rock and daylight on the other side, but they were narrow. He was stopped at the barricade. He tried to force himself through, but the fit was too tight. He turned to face the Simians. The Simians slowed and spread out as they continued to advance. There was no way to run through them without being caught by one of those giant swords. Damn! He looked up. No, too late to climb, they would be on him before he could get high enough. "Amy!"

He pulled his sword and advanced to meet them. He yelled to Amy and the Simians using his real voice, "It's a good day die!" So strange what you think about when you are about to die. He felt regret and sadness for Amy and the dark prison of silence she would return to. He told Amy, "I am sorry and I want you to know that I love you too."

Defiantly facing the Simians, he saw the sword growing in his hand. He did not know what the hell was going on. Then he noticed that it wasn't only the sword. It was everything. No, it was him! He was shrinking.

Amy was telling him, "Do not die!"

He felt his body go rigid, turning, as if it moved on its own. His legs were again running toward the rocks. Realizing that Amy had taken over muscle

222

control and understanding her intent, he joined in the effort and took over. He was far better at controlling his movements than Amy. He was having trouble keeping his pants legs up and his boots were flopping on his feet as he ran, but he reached the narrow gap and squeezed through just as the Simians converged on the spot. He yelled, "We beat the monsters again!" He was dancing and hopping around on the other side giving them the bird and jeering at them. They were screeching at him stabbing their swords through the small opening. They were berserk with rage.

His body was growing again, filling his clothing and shoes. He bellowed laughter at having cheated the Simians again, until Amy spoke again.

Amy said, "You're not safe yet, just out of the jaws of immediate death. They will come around the outcropping soon."

This was sobering. He took off again, running down the road. This time they left the enemy far behind. He continued to run for hours, putting miles behind him and depleting the adrenaline that had flooded his body.

* Amy *

As she was decompressing his cells and changing him back to normal size, Levi was dancing around in his flopping boots, making gestures with his middle fingers again, as she had seen him do to the Simian at the lake. She would have to remember to ask Levi in a less stressful time, just exactly what significance that gesture had.

She was glad now that she had insisted on overalls; pants would have fallen off. As it was, the straps over the shoulders just barely held on his shrinking shoulders.

Levi was so engrossed in his jeering, that he had forgotten that it was only a matter of minutes before the Simians could run around the rock wall, but once she warned him, he was off again running. He ran at a brisk pace well into the evening. His body was not tired, but he had expended a large amount of energy and needed to replenish his resources. Levi reduced his pace to a jog and then down to a brisk walk. He moved off the road into the woods, moving slowly and very quietly at a hunter pace.

After thirty minutes of creeping through the thick woods, she saw the tracks and then heard the gobble of a turkey up ahead. Yes, this would do nicely toward replenishing his protein. She drew knowledge from her storage banks on turkeys and analyzed the wooded terrain. She informed Levi of her plan, as he positioned himself in some thick underbrush, armed only with some nice sized rocks. She had turkey sounds in her memory, which she drew from now. She adjusted Levi's throat and vocal cords, and let out a most realistic turkey call. After a few times then waiting, the turkey answered the call. She continued to talk to the turkey in this manner, while each answer came closer. Now it was in the open and coming closer. A few more feet and it would be in range. Another call and another answer, and then it was well within the range. Levi stepped out and let fly with a fairly large, hand sized rock. As always, she corrected his aim and anticipated the turkey's jump. The rock dropped the turkey and Levi had his protein.

* Levi *

He was glad Amy had heard the turkey. He was ready for something different from his jerked venison. This was smart, hiding and waiting on the turkey to come to him. When it showed itself, it was a beauty. He stepped out and caught the turkey with his first rock, and it was a perfect shot.

They moved some distance up the mountain to hide the campfire.

Amy said, "The wind and direction is favorable, we should be safe."

Levi looked forward to a roasted turkey supper. Once it was cooking on the fire, he had only to watch and turn it occasionally, so his mind was free to reflect on the day's activities.

Amy had taken over his body again! How did he feel about that? She had saved his life yet again. He liked that. He had been able to take back control when he tried, so his control was stronger than hers, just like Amy had said. He trusted Amy. All in all, he didn't seem to have a problem with it. She could save his life anytime. He saw her smile at him and knew she had been following his thoughts. He didn't mind that so much either, anymore.

Yes, he had survived yet another encounter with the Simians. They had been very lucky. Well, he was very fortunate that Amy had taken over. They made a good team and were getting good at the impossible task of evading death. Even with all his abilities, he had only succeeded in saving his life. He inflicted no injury to the Simians at all. He hated the Simians, but he was starting to see just what an impossible task this might be. He was having doubts now in his ability to war against the monsters. WOW! Amy was pissed!

She told him "I haven't been driven to the point of madness trying to prepare you for battle, just to have you wimp out. We will find ways to battle the Simians. Just keep your mind focused. We are on schedule and all we are trying to do now is learn and stay alive."

They were learning and they were alive, so everything was well, but he was taken aback with the firmness of her scolding and realized what he was doing. Feeling sorry for himself was dangerous for his confidence. He realized she was right and grinned at her. He said, "Okay Amy, I'm fine now." She smiled back.

He finished much of the turkey and settled back in his bedroll about to fall to sleep.

Amy suddenly asked, "Do you really love me?"

Oh shit, he thought she hadn't heard him. His mind was racing. He said it when he thought he was about to die. Did he really love her? Could he love her? Did it make sense? Was it because he felt sorry for her having to return to her prison? He thought about hundreds of things and came to the conclusion that it didn't make sense and he didn't understand it, but YES! He loved her very much. He didn't have to say the words. He knew Amy heard his thoughts. He was so open at the moment and saw the tears in Amy's eyes and the smile. They both knew this was real and forever.

* Amy *

What had she learned about the Simians from this encounter today? They were very efficient in battle. They worked as a team, and this was dangerous. They were fast and excellent with sword skills. This she didn't expect, but must remember. Levi must be better than the Simians if he was to survive. They learned that all teams weren't made up of three members. This team of six was very efficient and also accustomed to working together. The most important thing that she learned was that the different Simian colonies did not work together. They were apparently in conflict over hunting territory and were not above warring to protect it. This was interesting and might be used against the Simians to Levi's advantage in the future.

As she monitored and shared his every thought and emotion, she saw Levi heading down a path of depression, possibly from developing fear of the Simians. Levi had experienced many close encounters with the Simians so far, and it was making a negative impression. This was dangerous for his mental attitude. Although she agreed with Levi about the futility of taking a battle to the Simian, she also knew that he would never be happy until he did, even if it meant losing his life. Knowing this, he could not be allowed to begin thinking these negative thoughts. Levi needed all his confidence. She had to snap him out of it, so she did. He was basically a very strong-willed person anyway, so he was easily focused back to reality. She just had to verbally slap him back to his senses.

Once his mind was back thinking straight again, she moved on to further distract him. Actually, she had been anxiously waiting for the right moment to bring it up. At the moment of his perceived death, he had pronounced his love for her. She had known Levi loved her, but he would never admit it. Would he admit it now?

Amy saw the conflict in his mind. He loved her but was having a hard time accepting it. What was real and what was fantasy? In the end love won out! Yes, he loved her and admitted it. He was still very much confused about it, but accepted it. Amy was loved, and she was very happy. The love she gave was returned. Her emotions overwhelmed her and she wept. The logical objective side of her mind found this strange that she was so happy, yet she cried. Her love flowed out to Levi and she felt his love, open and flowing, warming her. They found peace in the merging of their minds, like two clouds drifting together and mingling in the wind.

* Levi *

In the morning it was again time for business. He was up early, gorging himself on the remainder of the turkey and various vegetables he had collected, and as always, he took the constant required ration of Amy's vitamins. They were off again on the trail. Amy estimated it would take another day to reach the Simian compound, but in fact it took two days to locate it. It was closer to Stockton, far from the mountains. Amy was not comfortable approaching this complex, because of the lack of cover to hide. As a result, they were not

228

able to get as close to this compound and observed from a long distance.

They only observed for a full day. The size of this complex was bigger, indicating a larger population. There were four circles of buildings, within this complex, which Amy estimated would support approximately seven hundred and fifty Simians. This was a much larger complex. They learned little from observing, other than the routines appeared the same and the patrols came and went just as it was at the other complex. They did notice that most patrols going south were six-unit teams. The assumption was that the increased team size was to deter the southern Simian colony from patrolling into their area and maintaining control of their hunting territory.

They were both uncomfortable about being somewhat exposed in this area. So, they stayed only the one day and left the next morning retracing their route back to the Highway 49 and toward home. For the most part, the trip back south was uneventful. Amy successfully detected a Simian trap just in time and routed him around it. Other than that, the only memorable event was revisiting the rockslide area where he had almost died and had professed his love for Amy. They were silent as they let their minds embrace, remembering.

Amy directed them on a shorter route into the mountains, but one old mountain road looked pretty much like another. As they reached the intersection of their original route, Amy shocked him yet again.

Amy said, "I want us to go to the lake where you moved the car and capture that lone Simian."

He bellowed, "WHAT! CAPTURE? Are you fucking nuts? How can you even dream up some of these ideas?" Well, Amy sure had his attention and he definitely wanted to hear more about this.

* Amy *

On their return trip, her focus was to get back to the mountain lake. She had been thinking about the lone Simian and its oddities. It was alone, which was strange. It was smaller than any other Simian she had seen. Why? There was more to this story than appeared, and she needed to know what. She wanted to capture the Simian and learn from it. Mostly, she wanted to learn the Simians' language and thus all about the Simians. The more she knew, the better their chances for survival.

When she told Levi her plan, he went berserk. He was ranting and raving about how difficult it had been just to stay alive against them.

He asked, "Just how in the hell are we, ME, going to capture one? Maybe I could kill it, but capture?"

After she explained her reasoning, he calmed down some, but remained agitated. He hated Simians and just wanted to kill them, but he agreed to try. His thoughts were transparent. He was thinking that he could always find an excuse to kill it later.

Her plan was simple, find a good place near the lake to observe and watch the Simian. If they learned its routine, then a plan and method could be devised to capture it. Actually, she already had a plan in progress.

230

They approached the lake and rocky cliff around noon. After surveying the area, she decided that the best location to observe the cliff area was on a high point about halfway up the main slope. They proceeded carefully, using the cover of the many pine trees along the slope. Circling and skirting the roadway and cliff area, they arrived about an hour later just above the overlook. Just as they were about to move down to their planned overlook area, she caught a whiff of that over-sweet, musky Simian scent. Warned, Levi crept forward slowly to observe the Simian sitting about two hundred feet below them. This was the best spot to observe, since the Simian was observing the cliff area as they observed him observing. She found this play on words humorous.

* Levi *

Amy's plan involved swimming again.

She said, "The best way to draw the Simian into our trap is to walk into his."

So he worked his way back down the wooded slope and walked into the clearing at the cliff edge and waited to be cornered. He felt safe, because as long as he wasn't netted again by surprise, he could always jump in the water to get away from the ugly beast. He would do that anyway, but this time he hoped to take the Simian with him. The Simian had not offered to go in the water before, so Amy surmised that it couldn't swim. She hoped anyway. Even if the Simian could swim, Levi would have gills and the advantage under water.

He had stashed his gear before venturing into the center of the Simian's trap. As he waited, he wondered how many others had been caught in this trap. It was a curious place and attractive to the passer-by. You were almost compelled to stop and look at the view over the lake. It really was breath-taking, especially approaching sunset.

As he shared the view with Amy, they heard a slight noise from behind. As planned, a small piece of the broken car mirror was positioned on the ground so he could see behind him. As the Simian approached, they saw that it didn't have a net, only a sword. Amy had hoped that it had been unable to replace the net, now resting on the bottom of the lake. This was good. They watched as it approached quietly. They waited. When it started to raise its sword, he went into action. He spun around, throwing a rope loop over the Simian's head and arm, and leaped over the edge. The other end of the rope was secured around his waist, so the planned impact of the fall would not jerk the rope away. The fall to the water was fifty feet, and the rope had twenty-five feet of slack to gain momentum. As he reached the end of the slack, he felt a sudden jar, and he hung at the end of the rope suspended fifteen feet above the water. He looked up to see the Simian scrambling to hold on. It screeched wildly but slowly slid over the edge.

The sudden jerk was supposed to propel the Simian over the edge easily. It almost didn't work, but momentum finally forced it over the edge. He hit the water and quickly swam to get out of the way of the Simian, as it splashed heavily in the water behind him. It never came up. He looked under the water and saw it sinking to the bottom, as if it was a solid lead weight. Already it reached the end of the rope and yanked him under. There was no danger, as he was already breathing water, but he cut the rope anyway. He continued to follow the sinking Simian to the bottom. As he approached the bottom, the Simian struggled without making any progress and finally stuck to the bottom. After a moment it finally ceased its struggle and lay defenseless and still.

* Amy *

Something was drastically wrong. The Simian was not jerked over the edge as planned. It finally went over but just barely. The mass of the Simian must be much heavier than it looked. Of course, they are not from this earth. They could have developed in a much denser planet. This Simian would have to weigh close to five hundred pounds to have resisted the momentum and leverage applied. That explained a lot about them. Their dense hide would make penetration of arrows, swords, or anything very difficult, and their strength would be uncharacteristically great for earth standards.

Their dense mass would also make it impossible for them to swim and would explain why it sank directly to the bottom. It would drown or has already drowned, but it must be kept alive. At her insistence, Levi reluctantly picked up the heavy Simian and carried it over his strong shoulders as he walked along the bottom. Even for Levi, the Simian was heavy. The denseness of the Simian prevented

233

any buoyancy of its body in water, and Levi felt almost the full weight as his feet buried in the lake bottom with each step. By searching and finding solid bottom, Levi was finally able to carry the Simian up the bank and dumped it unceremoniously on the ground.

Once out of the water, it was time to make the change from water back to air. She knew it was uncomfortable, but did what she could. Having gone through it before, Levi knew what to expect and didn't complain. While he cleared his lungs for the few moments it took and she was busily altering his gills back to lungs, they were oblivious to the surroundings. When Levi was again breathing normally, he straightened from his bent over position and found himself staring directly into the red, piercing eyes of the Simian.

She was instantly terrified. Levi and the Simian stared at each other for what seemed like hours, but it was only a few seconds. Coming out of her frozen state, she began defense movements, but Levi overrode her motor controls.

Levi said, "Wait!"

Levi just stood there staring at the Simian and the Simian just stared back. Neither of them moved. What was he doing? What was the Simian doing? She was confused and Levi wasn't talking to her.

* Levi *

The stupid Simian sank like a lead weight straight to the bottom and laid there like a turtle on its back until it quit kicking. Good, it was dead. Good riddance!

234

Amy wanted it, so he tried to pick it up. Damn! It was heavy, really heavy, but Amy wanted it carried out. He finally got it on his shoulders and carried it along the bottom of the lake, then up the sloped bank and out of the water. That was a job, but he finally got it out of the water and dumped it on the ground. It weighted almost as much underwater as it did out, and he found that strange. It should have been lighter underwater.

Once out of the water, he had to make the transition of his lungs. He had to quickly drain the water from his lungs before he drowned from it. He bent over and heaved out the water, retching and coughing, trying to gasp in air. Momentary fear of drowning returned to cause him anxiety but it finally passed. The effort made him break out in a cold sweat during the process. The transition from water to air was really uncomfortable.

He finally recovered, and his breath came easier now. As he rose up, all he could say was, "Oh shit!" He thought the Simian was dead, but he found himself staring directly into the deep red eyes of the Simian. He shuddered to his very foundation, but he didn't move. It stood completely still, not four feet from him. It had obviously been standing there for a while, and could have already killed him if it wanted to. Why hadn't it? What could he do to defend himself? All he had was his knife. Right, that would do it. Using a knife would be like using a fly swatter on a bear. Amy was sending signals to his muscles, but he blocked them. He was locked in a staring match with the Simian. How was this going to end?

He was afraid to move and continued to stare and stand motionless, while his mind raced to find an out. Could he move fast enough to elude this one? Maybe. On impulse he spoke to the Simian. Granted, it wasn't nice, but he said it in an even tone. He simply said, "You're one ugly son-of-a-bitch." The Simian responded by screeching a wobbling tone and stood there like it expected a response. He hadn't expected this reaction and was startled!

After what seemed like hours to him, the Simian stepped back and squatted down. It just sat and waited. For what did it wait? He spoke again to it, asking what it wanted? He didn't expect it to understand or respond. He was talking more to himself than anyone, but the Simian seemed to understand that it was a question and screeched a response and shrugged, as if to say, "I don't understand." He also stepped back, squatted down and asked, "Do you know you're really fucking ugly?" He laughed at his own joke. Then he asked, "What the hell do we do now Amy?"

* Amy *

She watched as the two stared at each other. She realized also that Levi would be dead now if the Simian had wanted to kill him. It obviously wanted to kill Levi before, but something had changed. It didn't appear menacing, other than its wicked looks. It seemed more confused and puzzled than anything. Like it was trying to figure out what Levi was or why he had saved him. Levi hadn't much cared if it died, and she actually thought it was dead

236

by the time Levi brought it out of the water. It should have been dead, but it wasn't. Her mistake was that she tended to judge things by Earth standards, but she must remember that these Simians were alien to Earth with different characteristics. Obviously, it did NOT drown. The Simian must have gone into some sort of dormant stage.

She was anxious with the waiting and glad Levi spoke. It seemed to break the ice and the Simian responded with his own screeching form of communication. She detected tone, modulation, and frequency changes. This was definitely communication on a complex level, but she had no idea what it was saying. She would have to hear much more and gain many references to be able to decipher this language, but she was confident she could do it, eventually. Communication back might be harder using Levi's vocal cords.

That last screech, with the gesture, was surely a comment to indicate that it didn't understand. Levi agreed, as she attempted to repeat the screech. She had to create new muscle controls and vibrating membranes to accomplish it, but the first attempt was a reasonable facsimile of the Simian's statement. The shock was obvious. Its black-toothed jaw dropped perceptibly and its eyes widened, flashing a black center within the red. The Simian screeched another string of information, but she repeated the first screech to indicate she didn't understand, while Levi made a shrug. It understood and nodded its head.

She now knew this Simian did not intend to hurt Levi. It was curious, shocked and something else, possibly respectful toward Levi. She convinced Levi to turn his back and return to his gear. As Levi turned, he waved his hand indicating for it to follow. Surprisingly, it did. It stayed behind him a few paces but followed. As Levi reached his gear and strapped on his pack and weapons, the Simian watched anxiously, but did not react threateningly. Realizing the intent of Levi to leave, it screeched a few words and mimed for Levi to sit and wait. It was Levi's turn to nod. Levi was following her request, though reluctantly.

The Simian loped off in the direction where they had seen him earlier, covering ground quickly. Levi wanted to leave while it was gone, but she convinced him to stay. She told him, "I want to learn the Simian language." They must learn as much as possible about the Simians. She said, "Opportunities like this don't come very often, and we must take advantage of them."

* Levi *

When Amy indicated she wanted to attempt to talk to the Simian, he relinquished control of his mouth. He felt her moving and changing things in his throat and then start speaking. No, not speaking, screeching, and it vibrated his throat. He didn't much like it, but what the hell. It felt funny, feeling his mouth move without his direction. He fleetingly thought of a ventriloquist's dummy. He didn't like that much either.

She wanted to trust this one like it was a long-lost friend. Turn his back on it? Damn! As he turned to retrieve his pack, the hair stood up on the back of his neck. He just knew he would feel the sword any second. As it was, the Simian seemed docile enough and seemed to pose no threat.

He couldn't believe his internal ears. Amy wanted to take it back to the home camp. When the Simian took off to get its stuff, he wanted to run, but Amy got his attention when she said learning the language would be a valuable weapon that could be used against them. Yes, this was very true. So he waited.

The Simian returned carrying a backpack full of stuff. It loped up and just waited. It was obviously going to follow, as he set the pace toward home camp. His pace was purposely very brisk, but the Simian stayed with him with its loping gait of a run that he had seen so many times. It followed him wherever he went. It stayed three paces behind and when he slowed, it slowed, and when he sped up, so did it. If he turned left, so did it. He made some elaborate and embarrassing moves just to humiliate the Simian, but it didn't bother it at all. It just followed. He was still not comfortable being with the Simian. Simians were to be killed, not adopted. He said, "This may be one big ass puppy, but I am not going to pet it."

As they traveled hour by hour, Amy would screech something out of his mouth in response to the Simian. The Simian would point and screech or it would mime some action. Amy would repeat it. The hours passed and with Amy's instant and total memory and recall, the vocabulary was building. He knew the vocabulary as it was learned. This was easy, Amy was doing all the work and he was learning it like he learned karate. He was getting into it with his own gestures. He was now pointing and asking the name in Simian. Simple conversations were beginning, and it was beginning to talk too much. The constant screeching was annoying.

The sun was approaching late evening when the Simian said it was hungry. Levi said, "Oh shit, does he want to eat me?" The Simian pointed into the forest. Heading into the woods, the Simian took the lead. It listened and smelled, then slowly crept forward like a cat. He had his bow and arrow notched as he flanked the Simian. Suddenly, the Simian burst forward, trying to catch a deer, but the deer bounded high and out of reach of the Simian. It escaped the Simian, but his arrow caught the deer in the heart. It fell literally at the Simian's feet. The Simian leaped on the deer and ripped the head off, taking a bite before it tossed the head aside. It looked at the arrow, pulled it out and handed it back to him.

The Simian ripped off a hind quarter, and sat down and started tearing off large bites as it watched him hang up the remainder of the deer, and begin skinning and gutting it. He cut off the other hindquarter and tossed it to the Simian. He wanted to make damn sure it had plenty to eat without looking at him for a midnight snack. He tossed the deer over his shoulder and took off back to the trail. The Simian was again behind him, carrying its meal also.

They were very close to home camp, and arrived by sunset. He started a fire, cooked his venison and jerked the remainder. The Simian watched curiously. They continued to talk, defining

240

objects. Actually, it was talking to Amy, while he thought about other things. He could see Amy's image in his mind, and she wasn't looking at him. Her look was remote. He had been getting very accustomed to seeing her total attention directed at him, and now she was talking to the Simian. It seemed strange and disconcerting.

* Amy *

She was excited to be embarking on new learning. Her ability to learn was instantaneous. She would hear the sounds, correlate them, apply definitions, and be able to speak them and use them as if it had been her native language. The slowest part was waiting for the Simian to use its vocabulary and make his meanings known, but as the hours went by she built a sizable vocabulary. The boring part was over, and even Levi was getting into it. This was good.

She watched everything as the Simian made its wishes known to hunt. It had a keen sense of smell, and stealth abilities. It almost caught the deer with its bare hands. It was fast, strong and very hungry. She believed that her calculation concerning the amount of food requirements for a Simian might have been wrong. She had not anticipated the density of their bodies. She now realized that they required much more food than originally projected. With this in mind, she agreed with Levi about making sure the Simian remained full.

What amazed her most and remained an unanswered question was why it had totally accepted Levi. It was almost as if it accepted Levi

241

as its master and was subservient. It watched Levi do everything, as he set up camp and lit a fire. Oh my, it didn't like fire! This was interesting. He didn't like being close to it, but came close to be around Levi.

Levi asked in Simian, "What is your name," while slapping his chest stating "LEVI," then pointing to the Simian. The Simian said its name was from his home world and meant second moon. Levi still felt offended by the screeching talk and named it MOON in English. Levi kept pointing to it saying MOON. After a few times it nodded and tried to say the word, but it came out more like a belch than a word. Levi almost laughed out loud.

Levi was getting tired, but afraid to go to sleep.

He asked, "What if it, Moon, gets hungry while I am asleep and decides to eat me?"

She laughed and reminded him, "It had its chance to kill you and didn't, besides, it has food now. I promise I will listen and wake you if I believe there is any danger." Levi told Moon he was going to sleep now and pointed to the ground on the other side of the fire. Moon nodded and lay down, but not too close to the fire. Sleep was a long time coming for Levi.

Morning brought another day of talking and learning. Moon continued to follow Levi everywhere. Levi went about his chores to the valley and checked on the horses. Moon and the horses both had a fit. Moon said horse was his favorite food, and Levi told him they were not food and not to eat them. Moon was hopping and anxious, but did not attempt to go after the horses and the horses did not attempt to come close. Levi

242

made Moon go back so he could calm and care for the horses. He was concerned, because he didn't think the horses would get used to Moon. They were terrified of him.

They remained at home base for several weeks learning and refining the Simian language and its use. It was a difficult language, but she had a recorded and usable vocabulary of more than 10,000 words now, and felt confident in their ability to communicate.

* Moon *

He had never known anything like this Human named Levi. Humans were for food, stupid, slow and easy to kill. This one was not easy to kill, and had defeated him and could have killed him, but had instead saved him. This was strange indeed. The code of the Kreeeeeauxx (unpronounceable - Simian is as good as any substitute) now required him to serve this Human for the rest of his life. He owed this animal a life debt.

He was shocked and amazed that this Human spoke in his language. In all his life, he had never heard a Human speak in any understandable way and now as they traveled, this Human, Levi, was learning the Simian language at an unbelievable rate.

After several days of continuous communication, they were able to freely communicate at any level of the language. This Human (Levi), which he could not pronounce, was asking many probing questions and over the next few days, he provided a massive amount of

243

information concerning his race, origins, lifestyle, social structure, organization, etc.

He explained that they were a race from a dying planet, an advanced migration with other fleets to follow. The planet had less than one hundred and fifty years of life left and the migration would be coming in at least three waves to land and populate the planet.

Simians consisted of three races, the females, Technical breed, and Warrior breed. In the beginning there were only Technical breed and females, however the third race was created. The original species' genetic mold was the Technical Simians. They had been intelligent, extremely social and civilized. It wasn't until the war with the invading out world race, The Outsiders, that the Technical race started experimenting with genetic altering.

The Outsiders were larger than Simians, so the Warrior race was developed to battle them in a conventional war that lasted three hundred years. The Warriors were basically Simians, but altered to be larger, far more aggressive and totally dedicated to war. All the major civilized traits were altered and eliminated. Along with that manipulation went any sign of higher intelligence or social traits.

After the war was finally won, the associated casualties' attrition of Warrior Simians ended and their population soared. As the Warriors grew in numbers, their power grew as well. In time, they threatened to overthrow the Technical Simians from leadership. The only thing that stopped them was the fact that their world was dying, and technology was needed for space travel to exit the planet. The

Warriors Simians possessed no technical skills, other than the skills of war. They were forced to leave the Technical Simians in control.

Unfortunately, the long space travel time renewed the old animosities between the races. With everything on automat pilot, the Warrior breed saw no need to keep the Technical breed in power, so they were removed during the trip. The Warriors weren't so stupid as to kill them, just in case they might need technology before they landed. The use of the ultimate weapon that destroyed technology on the new world was not a disappointment to the Warriors. It did, however, spell doom for the Technical breed. They had no worth to the Warriors, and were kept only in the event they might be needed for some reason, some day. Attrition had taken care of most of his breed and since the Technical breeds were not allowed to breed, there were few left. After fifty years they had been reduced to the level of prisoners.

There was no longer much of a social order. Now it was the leadership of the strongest and not the smartest. Without social organization, leadership, or any form of communication between the separate colonies of Simians, there existed constant civil war between the groups. This had prevented the Simian population from exploding more than it had.

He described the strongest group, which was in the southern area lead by a goliath of a Simian, which Levi named, Gord for simplicity. This giant had ruled for many years and had assimilated many from other compounds. The number of his group was around eight hundred and growing. It was to the point where the colony needed to establish remote settlements, because the hunting areas were depleted for this size of the community. Gord's only other option was to war with his Simian competition.

He told Levi about the women of the population, and how they only averaged around twenty-five percent of their numbers and stayed within the compound always, for their own protection. The Warrior Simian males and sometimes the females also, were prone to go berserk during mating and must be supervised or they could kill each other. The females must be protected at all cost! Mating occurred only every eighty days as the females became fertile and only the strongest, as determined by combat, were allowed to mate. The mating ritual was a gathering of all the Simians from that compound and took five Earth days.

He had found an opportunity to escape from the Los Angeles colony about five months ago and had lived at the lake alone since that time. He had been alone all this time and was missing association with other Simians. He actually welcomed the Human company now.

* Levi *

He still didn't like the idea of having a Simian around, but they really had learned a lot from him and would be able to learn much more as they continued to talk. Moon wasn't much trouble, except for getting used to the infernal screeching, which he hated.

He also worried about the horses. He was afraid Moon would sneak off and eat one. The days went by, however, and the horses continued to be safe. Moon was hunting well for himself and even brought in extra for him. He ate the turkey Moon brought in, but balked at the buzzard. How the hell he got that, he was afraid to ask. All he told Moon was, "No eating Humans." Moon stared with those red eyes for a moment and nodded. He understood.

Amy was pleased with learning the Simian language, and he gave her a smile and complimented her on the accomplishment. It was a good thing she had done, and he liked to compliment her because he was always rewarded with a big beautiful smile. Amy was back to communicating with him and through him as before. They seemed very close at those times, working together and mingling their minds.

After a week, Amy suggested, "We need to leave and move south."

This was unusual for her, but he was ready, so he started packing up. They were deciding just what to take and what to leave, when Amy startled him by asking him to pack the microscope. She wouldn't tell him what for. She just wanted to have it for an experiment she was thinking about. So he emptied a padded box and used it to pack the microscope in.

He collected the horses and brought them back to camp to load them with supplies, but the horses panicked at the presence of the Simian, and wouldn't settle down until he sent Moon off in the distance. So set the stage for their travels. He left with the horses and Moon followed from about a mile behind.

247

CHAPTER 12
(FIRST ENCOUNTER)

* Amy *

For once, she was anxious to leave. Something was wrong or was going to be wrong at the Mojave Desert Human settlement. She knew the name for what she was experiencing. It went along with telepathy, telekinesis and others of the so-called black magic or occult. It was clairvoyance and she recognized it for what it was. The Mojave Desert settlement would be in trouble in the future, but she wasn't sure how long it would be before her vision came true or exactly what form it would take. It was only a vision of one possible reality, but it was troubling.

In her vision the entire Simian compound moved moving from the Colorado River area toward the west. They were starving from lack of food and were too small in numbers to move against the Phoenix colony, so the only other direction they could go was west. They knew there were Humans there and HORSES! Horses were sought after by all Simians, but had long been eaten to extinction in most areas where they lived. Yes, it was a logical move for the Simians to go after the horses and settlement.

Amy's vision saw Humans being attacked in force by the Colorado River Simians. She saw the end of the settlement, but knew this was only a vision and could be changed. She remembered the friendship of the settlement with fondness and knew Levi did as well. Both of them had talked about those days with pleasure. She, in fact, had given a great deal of consideration to attempting to persuade Levi to live in that safety. Now however, the Simians were threatening even that dream. Damn them! Levi was right. The Simians must be fought. After the revelation from Moon that more fleets were coming, it was now imperative. She just didn't quite know how to do it, or how much time they had, but she was determined to prevent the slaughter of their friends, if at all possible. What could she do?

Telling Levi of her vision was not yet an option. He was too impulsive and would want to do something quickly, which, knowing him, would be wrong. No, the vision was in the future so they must wait until she had a better idea of what action to take.

* Levi *

They were off again retracing the path they originally took to the facility, but he was in a lot different condition going back than when he came. He looked fifty years younger and in considerably better shape than he had ever been. He was happy to be moving toward the goal of waging war against the Simians. Hell, even Thunder seemed happy to be back on the trail again. The truth be known, he really didn't need a horse anymore. He could actually travel faster and more comfortably jogging, but the amount of gear he packed, thanks to Amy, required the horses.

It appeared the horses would never get used to Moon, so he was behind them again. The silence from the screeching was welcome, which left more time for communication with Amy during the day. Moon was able to come into camp at night if the horses were picketed far enough away and upwind. This became the routine, and Moon didn't seem to mind ... much. Honestly, he really didn't care if Moon liked it or not. Moon always followed him anyway.

They traveled for five days in this manner, and on the morning of the sixth day, entered Owens Valley again. This really was a beautiful valley, plush and green with steep mountains on both sides. An area like this without a threat of Simians was appealing. Why weren't all the Humans here? His thoughts were rambling as they continued deeper into the valley.

Amy startled him out of his thought with a warning!

She announced, "Danger!"

He saw nothing and asked, "Where Amy?" She directed his attention to various men now moving out from cover. In all there were twenty-five men circling him. He had ventured into a wide circular trap, otherwise undetectable. They were closing in from all angles. Amy warned that he might have to kill or be killed. He regretted that but saw the serious threat of the approaching men. He said, "Not exactly favorable odds, Amy. It might be the latter." Amazing, these men were Indians. They dressed like old style Indians in buckskins and, unbelievably, even feathers. They were armed with swords, bows and arrows and spears. They looked very menacing.

He asked, "What do you want?"

They laughed and said, "Everything. We want your gear, horses and your life. No one is allowed to enter this valley and live."

Well, he had his answer, as he pulled out his bow. He was about to notch an arrow, when Amy interjected. His arm shot out, grabbing for something he did not see. Suddenly, his hand jerked, and he was gripping an arrow in his hand that had been aimed at his chest. On impulse, he took the arrow, notched it and shot it into the chest of the man who fired it. Everything seemed to be occurring in slow motion, but he knew that in reality it was all happening in a fraction of a second. Again another arrow, and again his hand caught and shot it back into the attacker. His eyes constantly turned, watching. No more arrows were shot; instead, they pulled swords and advanced.

It was his turn to attack. He fired six arrows in rapid succession, killing six more aggressors and opening a gap in their trap. He kicked Thunder to run through the gap. Just as he felt the horse start, Thunder fell to the ground. Ropes or bolas had tripped his horse, but he hit the ground rolling and came up with his sword. Thunder kicked and thrashed around on the ground, as the Indians moved in. The odds had been reduced by eight, but there were still seventeen armed Humans advancing on him.

* Amy *

She saw the trap closing, and was terrified for Levi, but knew she must remain calm. She must help Levi. Levi was talking, but it was useless. They were only talking, while they closed in on him. Suddenly, she detected the movement and acted automatically, taking control of Levi's motor controls just in time to catch an arrow aimed at Levi's chest. In a fraction of a second she analyzed the speed and angle of the arrow's flight and reacted. The timing was perfect, as she shot Levi's hand out to catch the arrow in flight. She used the same arrow and immediately shot it back at the originator. Her information and instructions transfer to Levi's subconscious mind worked flawlessly, and Levi thought it was his idea. The advancing enemy stood in shock when the arrow was returned, but the spell was broken when another archer shot an arrow. Again, she caught the arrow and killed the originator. They were afraid to shoot other arrows at Levi.

They continued to advance with swords, closing the trap. Directions were sent again, and Levi used his arrows to open a gap in the circle in order to escape. It was working until Thunder was tripped and Levi was thrown to the ground.

She directed Levi to attack to prevent the Indians from compressing on his position. She transferred the attack plan and he knew what to do and initiated the attack. The trick was to surprise them, keep them off guard and reduce the odds even more. Levi charged the closest one. It completely took the man by surprise as he advanced. The man paused in shock, and it cost him his life. Levi ran by in a blur and sliced him across the stomach, opening

252

him from side to side. The man was left holding his guts in his hands, but Levi continued toward the next. He moved quickly, and the unified attack fell apart. They were attacking individually now and disorganized. She fought with Levi in his body. She kept Levi's body constantly spinning, so she could continually appraise the situation. The plan altered, as each priority of the threat changed. Levi ran, darting in one direction, then the other. At one point, Levi threw a Bowie knife, impaling in the throat of one of the attackers poised to throw a spear. The knife ended that threat. Two more were down, but he was running out of room to maneuver. They were closing now as Levi circled. It was not looking good.

The Indians were cautious, because they had seen what he was capable of but confident that their numbers would prevail. He simply could not protect himself from all angles simultaneously and sooner or later someone would get through. As they closed in for the kill, a loud screeching reverberated through the valley as Moon broke into the fight. They had not seen Moon coming, nor had Levi or her for that matter. Both of them had forgotten about Moon in the excitement.

Moon had no weapons but really didn't need any, as he grabbed the first two warriors. He smashed them together, leaving the broken bodies in a heap, then he tore into the third. The remaining combatants headed for safety took at a dead run. Levi grabbed the last man running away and held him tight. He turned in time to see Moon break and tear the Human he held into pieces. He ripped a big chunk out of the thigh with his teeth. Levi was immediately angry at Moon for eating Humans and started to say something to Moon, but she cautioned him. She said, "Moon is in a rage and is not himself at that moment." The fighting had made him crazy. Moon was totally berserk at the moment and would not hear. Levi tried to wait while Moon ate. Hell, the Human was an enemy anyway and would have killed him; he rationalized.

Levi's captive was in total panic. He tried to get away, but was disarmed and was no match for Levi's strength.

Levi warned, "If you don't calm down and answer my questions, I will give you to my pet Simian."

The captive went white with fear and wet his pants as Moon stared at him.

* Moon *

Levi made him travel far behind, but he stayed close enough to keep Levi in sight. The horses were afraid of him and spooked when they got his scent, but he was allowed to come in at night, once the horses were removed. This was an inconvenience to him, but the temptation was also great to eat the horses. Horses were not strong enough to carry a Simian, therefore useless. They were, however, very good to eat, and it had been a very long time since he had tasted the flesh of a horse. Levi had told him early that horses and Humans were not to be eaten. His master had spoken, and he must obey.

It was one such day of travel, removed from his master and the horses, that he saw the trap spring on Levi. A mile behind, he saw the hostilities start.

Levi was fighting hard and was very good at battle, but he was greatly outnumbered. He thundered toward the battle as fast as he could, which was very fast but afraid he might get there too late. He must help his master. He had no weapon, but these were only animals and, unlike Levi, weak. Screeching his challenge as he ran bought Levi a few more seconds of life. Approaching, he immediately grabbed and crushed the life out of the first two Humans contacted and went after a third. His battle rage and blood boiled, as he ripped into the third Human. The others ran away, and he saw that Levi was again safe, so did what came naturally, he began to eat his kill.

The blood was still boiling, as he stared at the Human Levi had caught. Did Levi want this one killed?

* Levi *

They cheated death yet again, which made him extremely happy. They had been very lucky that Moon had attacked when he did. He was so proud of Moon. Moon had saved the day and his life. He owed him now and would never think of Moon the same again. The only problem was that Moon was sitting there eating a Human and he was getting angry. Amy warned him not to interfere.

She said, "Moon is berserk and could turn on you."

He had seen too many Humans eaten by Simians to remain silent. He screeched out his challenge to Moon, "Do not eat Humans like you have been told." Moon stared with blazing red eyes for a long moment that seemed to last forever, but he finally calmed and tossed the Human remains away in compliance. He told Amy, "Moon is going to be all right." He thanked Moon for understanding and for saving his life. Moon was obviously happy with the praise, but stared at the captive.

Pride swelled in his chest for Amy, she was so damn smart. They made a very good team. Amy's smiling face in his mind was a very good reward. They hadn't actually used many words for communication in quite some time, but he seemed to always know what she was thinking or wanted. He wanted to be there for her, and with her. He was amazed at Amy's ability to analyze the threat from the arrows and pick them out of the air. Hell, he saw nothing but a blur, but he thought the act of returning the arrows to the sender was a stroke of genius, his genius. You never really knew with Amy just what was original thought, or planted by her, and all she did was smile, like now. God he loved that smile.

He continued to hold the captive tightly in his grip, as he flailed his arms and legs to no avail. He called Moon to stand over him, and as Moon approached, the captive collapsed. The captive was barely more than a boy, maybe in his early twenties. He tied the boy up and waited for him to wake up. He told Moon, "Just watch him and do not eat him." Moon nodded.

He released Thunder from the ropes and bolas and rubbed his legs to get the circulation going again. Thunder was still frightened of Moon but less than before, probably more frightened from the attack. He wasn't taking any chances of Thunder running off, so he tied him to a tree. He then gathered up his arrows and knife and was off after his packhorse. Jogging off after the horse, he was thinking how strange that he had never given this horse a name.

"Lightning," Amy said. "Her name should be Lightning, Thunder and Lightning."

He laughed aloud and said, "So be it."

He followed the trail at a run for about a mile before he caught sight of his horse, correction, Lighting. Two of the attackers were trying to round it up, but he ran directly at them, knowing they were probably still spooked. He was right. When they saw him running toward them, the horse was forgotten along with any further fighting. They ran like jackrabbits. He didn't want to kill any more Humans, and was happy to collect his horse and gear without additional trouble.

* Amy *

When Levi returned, the captive was awake and very scared. Moon was still sitting there watching. Levi chuckled, knowing the captive would answer any question posed to him. Together they assaulted him with questions, gathering an abundance of information.

The captive's name was Jimmy Standing, and he was nineteen years old. This was only his second war patrol, and he came here with his father. He was calming some now, but watching Moon intently.

Jimmy asked, "Are you going to let the Simian eat me?"

Levi didn't punish Jimmy anymore and told him, "You will not be hurt as long as you are honest with me."

Jimmy began chattering like a chipmunk, telling him the history of the tribe and anything else he wanted to know. He was obviously not holding anything back.

When the breakdown of civilization occurred, several small Indian reservations banded together for protection. The reservations were all in Owens Valley, and they became Owens Valley Indians working together to maintain their isolation. They possessed the skills to survive and isolated themselves from those that would take advantage. Over the years they survived by keeping all outsiders out. Many had tried to move in by force and push the Indians out, but they prevailed and through the years, the tradition had continued. They were familiar with the Simians and on occasions remote Simian patrols had ventured into the valley, but not often, because it was so far from any Simian colonies.

At her insistence, Levi asked how so many Indian survived in the beginning to have sufficient numbers in the tribe, since so many others died in the ray. Jimmy said that, as the stories tell, few Indians died on the day of chaos. She found that very interesting. Some genetic mix in the Indian make up must have protected them. That might also explain why Levi also survived the ray.

Geographically, the tribe separated across Owens Valley into three loosely organized communities, but was governed by a single Chief. The Chief's name was Grey Wolf, and he was sixty-two years old. The tribe had around a thousand 1,000 members with about four hundred warriors. The valley supported about fifty horses and roughly three hundred cattle. There were usually sentries at both ends of the valley and frequent patrols, and no, he had no idea how Levi had made it through the valley before without being challenged.

Jimmy said, "You must have been very lucky."

On the previous journey through the valley, she had insisted on caution, but Levi was an old man at that time, and also Indian. Maybe the two factors were enough for him to appear as a member of the tribe, or at least of no threat, or possibly both. Either way, it was like Jimmy had said, they had obviously been lucky on the first trip.

With no further questions to ask Jimmy, Levi untied him and let him go.

Levi said, "Tell the tribe I did not want to hurt any of the men, but they gave me little choice."

Jimmy shot off, running toward the nearest trees. He looked back often to make sure Moon was not following. Levi and Moon watched Jimmy run and as he approached the trees, they saw another man come from cover to greet Jimmy with a hug. This was a happy ending for Jimmy and his father.

* Levi *

After the questioning and with Jimmy gone, he and Amy discussed the information they had obtained. It was indeed valuable. This was the only organized group of Humans they had encountered since the Mojave Desert settlement. This group had four hundred warriors, which they would need in

259

any future battle with the Simians. There was only one problem; they had just killed thirteen members of the tribe in battle and, to make matters worse, Moon had eaten one.

Amy's suggestion to continue through the valley as fast as possible seemed like a very good suggestion. He re-packed the gear and looked through the weapons of the dead warriors, taking anything he might need. He found a nice medium sized sword. This would work nicely in his arsenal. He had a long sword, but wanted a short sword for his left hand. Now he had the weapons he had practiced to use. Moon took his lead and found the biggest sword that was there, which was ridiculously small in Moon's huge hand.

Amy wanted him to go quickly before the Indians could rally, call in reinforcements, and return. He thought that too, was an excellent idea. He mounted Thunder, took the leads of the packhorse and moved off. The horses seemed less afraid of Moon now, so he let Moon follow closer, but not too close. They covered ground at a fast pace. He kept the horses moving fast, but realized the horses couldn't go all day at this pace. Transferring some of the gear from Lightning to Thunder, he jogged along with the horses. They passed the afternoon at this pace and covered much greater distance. By night, the horses needed rest, so they made a cold camp and rested for the night.

* Amy *

By the evening of the second day in Owens Valley, moving at the pace Levi set, they were past the intersection of the highway they had followed coming in, and already proceeding south toward the far end of the valley. As they continued, she felt more and more uneasy. Something bothered her. She had been experiencing stronger clairvoyant visions about the future and was analyzing these episodes. She saw Simians and Humans in battle. She saw Levi fighting. She analyzed her vision. She checked land references. They were almost the same, maybe over the hill there. She saw the position of the sun, one hour from now. No, it was too soon. Levi wasn't ready. She wasn't ready. She could change the vision.

She warned Levi, "Simians are close!" He didn't question her warnings. Levi hid the horses in a small recess against the hill, and followed her directions to a position of hiding up the hill. From this vantage point they could see down into the next small valley where she saw her vision. Levi waved to Moon, indicating that he should hide. He was about a quarter of a mile behind and went into the woods, but she could see him looking out from time to time, trying to see what was happening. Levi laughed and called Moon a troll.

This was strange. Jimmy said that the tribe rarely saw Simians in the valley, but in her vision, she had seen the usual three-member team. She had seen other Humans also. When they looked, the valley was empty. Had she been wrong? Could her vision have been a different year at this exact same time? That was unlikely. She felt confused and uncertain but continued to wait.

* Levi *

He learned to trust Amy's warnings long ago. She was not clear as to the warning, but he did what she said and hid in the rocks on the hill above and warned Moon. Now he waited but didn't see anything. Suddenly, there they were! Humans came around a small outcropping of rocks across a small ravine from where he hid. They were actually closer than he would have expected. There were six adult males and four females. Of the males, four appeared to be of prime age but two were well past their prime. Of the females, all were in their prime and from what he could see, very prime. He cringed when he saw Amy's look, and the pressure in his loins was not from pleasure. Sometimes her ability to read the obvious in his mind was embarrassing. Amy knew he loved her even though it was sometimes crazy to think about. He wished to have her in his arms and knew it was not possible. It hurt to think about it, in more ways than one, so he didn't think.

Amy had warned of Simians, and these were Humans. Had he misunderstood? He wanted to make contact, but after the last experience, he was afraid. He watched as the band of Humans moved close past him. Suddenly, like a nightmare, three Simians leaped out from behind rocks and trees to run at the Humans. The Simians moved with surprising agility, as they quickly surrounded the group. Amy commented, as she registered the fact of their agility, that these were formidable enemies and warned against getting involved until they knew more about their fighting tactics and abilities. He watched as the Simians tightened their circle.

The females grouped in the center with the males surrounding them for protection. The males had medium sized swords approximately three and a half feet long, held high as they stood tall and proud, but they didn't have a snowballs chance in hell against the three giant Simians, and they knew it. They were not going down without a fight, and Levi liked that. As the Simians tightened the circle, they screeched their laughter, a hideous sound, and passed guttural noises back and forth, which, thanks to Moon, they now understood. What they were saying revolted him.

The Simians' long muscular arms swung broadswords at least five feet long, as they attacked the band of Humans. Their obvious focus was the females, as they darted in with feinting attacks, trying to grab a woman. Two of the Simians already had partial erections as they fought. The men repelled the strokes and attempted to counter, but the Simians were far quicker than they appeared to be and continued to attack without taking any chances. It was as if they were just playing, toying with the Humans and wearing them down. The Humans would have been dispatched quickly had it not been the odds of two Humans to each Simian. Additionally, the men fought in a circle of defense, side by side.

The battle turned quickly, as one of the Humans fell under a vicious attack. Once down, the Simian split him apart with a single chop from his broadsword. The other male launched an attack at his side when the Simian swung, but the Simian pivoted and kicked him in the chest. The kick was so sudden and hard that the man's sword went flying, and his eyes rolled back into his head. He never knew if the man died from the kick, because the Simian leaped forward and, with a swinging stroke from the ground, caught the man in mid-air, sending his torso in one direction as his hips and legs fell the other way. Again, the hideous screeching filled the air but this time in triumph!

He was horrified! This can't be happening and I'm just standing here watching! He screamed, "AMY! I can't sit here and watch! I am no longer an old man. It goes against all that I am and ever have been to allow this to happen as long as I have strength in my body. Amy, thanks to you I have the ability to help! Now I must."

Amy pleaded with him to hold his temper. She said, "No, you aren't ready."

* Amy *

She was tense but calm as she reasoned with Levi. She reasoned point after point. "I'm sorry, Levi. You simply can't get involved yet." She explained, "It is far too dangerous and all will be lost if you die! The Human race will not have a chance if you die. There will not be a knight to fight for them. We must learn how they fight, their weaknesses, how to kill them. There is so much to learn before we can risk you in combat. We must not commit you to battle until we are assured of success. Levi, remember our training is far from complete, and we cannot know if we are totally synchronized yet."

As she reasoned with Levi, having their philosophical discussion, the winning Simian turned back to the battle. It did not join against the remaining males. Its interest was in the females, as he darted in and grabbed the closest female and ran out the other side of the group. Cries for help rang out, but the men were still in a battle for their lives and losing. There was nothing the men could do, although one of the females recovered a sword lost by the fallen man and went after her captured friend. The Simian easily outdistanced her, leaving her far behind.

The Simian held the captured female around the waist as he ran. He dropped his sword as he ran and began ripping her clothing away. Her bites, hits and kicks were useless, while the beast exposed her breasts and thighs and began spreading the screaming woman's legs and thighs to accept his already erect shaft. To her knowledge, no Human female had ever survived rape by a Simian. The size of the giant's shaft and the vicious force applied, usually killed the females, even if they weren't systematically butchered, mutilated, and often eaten afterwards.

* Levi *

This was all he could stand; the discussion was over. He leaped to his feet, running toward the captured female. Many years ago he had watched helpless from too far away, as two Simians had caught his soul mate and viciously raped her. He was far away, yet he still heard her screams. He remembered the horrific scene as if it had happened yesterday. He remembered the pain and knew he could never allow this to happen again. He could not live with himself if he did.

Live or die, this was one battle he would join. The hate and rage boiled and his lust for revenge exploded. It was as if these were the very Simians that had killed his soul mate, and they would pay.

* Amy *

She knew when an argument was over with Levi. All she could do now was help him and help him she did. Her telepathy tightened and control was established. She could never allow Levi to run into battle with only his anger to guide him. The adrenaline would be helpful, but he needed much more. She augmented his physical strength, made his body larger, extended his arms, quickened his reflexes, and opened all channels to his brain and extremities. Her ability to help depended on her ability to receive data from Levi's senses. So, she sharpened his senses of sight, smell, hearing and touch. In essence, she made Levi's entire body a data retrieval network. She would analyze the movements of the enemy, anticipate the movement, assess the best defense or attack from her vast storage of martial arts, or any data for that matter, and initiate the proper response directly into Levi's subconscious.

She knew Levi always questioned instruction delivered to his conscious mind, or, at a minimum, re-analyzed them. Mostly, he would see the reasoning; however, this delay could be costly or fatal. She delivered simultaneous information to both Levi's conscious and subconscious mind.

Instruction and information delivered to the subconscious was accepted without question, while the information delivered to the conscious mind was delivered to give Levi the impression he was in control of his mind. He could be such a stubborn ass at times. Her ability to deliver critical information to Levi could take place in milliseconds. At least this is what Amy hoped would happen. This was the moment of truth, and she bristled with fear.

* Levi *

He felt strong and getting stronger by the second. His legs seemed longer and stronger and his arms looked even bigger. He knew Amy was augmenting him and welcomed the help. His anger was making him crazy and reckless, but he had no choice. Rage, not fear, was taking over. He didn't know what he was going to do when he got there. Yes, he did! Suddenly, he saw a plan.

The Simian was occupied with the female and did not see him running toward him. Pleased with his speed and agility, he leaped to a nearby boulder and launched hard toward the Simian. Rolling into a tight knot and flipping in mid-air, he directed a very powerful two-legged kick at its head as he completed the flip. The combination of augmented strength, running momentum, his launch from the boulder and the force multiplied from the flip, combined to deliver an explosively powerful kick to the unsuspecting Simian's head. He knew at the moment of the jarring impact that he had broken its neck. The snapping of the neck was audible, as the

Simian was knocked rolling over the woman to fall dead in a heap five feet away.

The woman stared in awe, she couldn't move, almost as frightened of him as the Simian. Seeing that she wasn't mortally injured, he hardly paused, as he ran toward the raging battle, screaming his battle cry.

* Amy *

She realized just in time to close down Levi's vocal cords, before he could launch his battle cry. Damn, men were so dense sometimes. Mexicans call it MACHO! She called it Bull Shit! Didn't Levi realize that surprise was needed to get the advantage over these giants? Here he was trying to broadcast that he was coming. She would have to ask him later where that bit of stupidity came from.

Other than the unnecessary energy and effort expended in the attack on the first Simian, her controls and mental interface performed well. His body responded exceedingly well to her controls and Levi, other than his anger, fear, lust for revenge and occasional stupidity, was also doing well. She worried that he would block some of her controls, which could be disastrous at the wrong time. Levi remained totally open, however, in spite of all his wild emotions.

She had perhaps over applied energy for the first attack. She calculated the distances, built momentum and maximized angle stresses, twisting angles, built increasing momentum upon momentum, and delivered the kick to the Simian. It had been overkill! She had applied enough energy to kill three Simians. Oh well, it was dead and Levi was safe, but she would try to be more efficient. Levi would need all his energy, and she must not waste it.

* Levi *

Another Human had fallen and the remaining three had moved together for protection from the two Simians. The Simians were moving in for the final attack that would end the battle, just as he reached them. He was glad that the enemy had not heard his rage and battle cry as he approached. He ran at superhuman speed, as he reached the first Simian. Coming within reach, he swung his sword low and caught the first brute behind the knee with a bone-jarring blow, severing muscles of its right leg. The blow knocked the Simian to the ground on to its hands and knees, and before realizing what had happened, Levi turned, ran high up its back, and leaped into the air. As he fell, he delivered a double fisted, overhead, chopping swing down on the second Simian's neck and shoulder. Both Simians screeched with obvious rage and pain, as they turned to fight this new adversary. Their game had turned very serious now, and they crouched to defend themselves. These golden giants were not used to defending; only attacking.

The three remaining Human males and two females, now armed with swords from their fallen friends, attacked the Simians from behind. With his sudden attack, the Simians had totally forgotten their original opponents. Several serious blows were delivered before the Simians rallied to mount a

269

back-to-back defense. The Simian with the severed leg muscles could only hop on the undamaged leg, but it was very strong and he could maneuver, while the second Simian had lost the use of its right arm and fought with the left. Both Simians were still formidable enemies.

He advanced cautiously, watching and studying. No surprise attacks this time. They were aware and ready for him. The Simian's red piercing eyes, never blinking, stared contentiously at him. They were just so damned tall, at least seven and a half feet with arms disproportionately longer, like an ape. It was awkward to get inside their defenses. The Simian he faced swung its broadsword. He blocked and felt the Simian's strength, and it was awesome. This was not the way! He feinted and watched as the Simian leaped forward; bringing his sword overhead for a massive blow that would tear through his sword and split him into two hemispheres. He didn't wait but dove forward, rolling under the Simian as it was exposed underneath and drove his sword upward into the Simian's crotch and underbelly. He felt the sword go deep into its abdomen and chest. The beast stopped in mid-swing and just toppled. There were no additional sounds or movements. It simply died instantly and fell over. He rolled out of the way and back on his feet as the Humans cheered.

The remaining Simian was in obvious fear as the group surrounded it. Each time the Simian moved in one direction a Human jumped in to deliver a stab or slice. The Simian was covered with purplish looking blood from its many wounds and purple blood was flowing freely from the leg wound he had inflicted. Its strength was failing. It was only a matter of time, and even as he watched, the beast fell to its knees.

As the band moved to finish off the last dying Simian, the screeching of another Simian shattered the calm. It was Moon rushing in. Oh no, not Moon too?

* Moon *

He remained hidden as instructed, wondering what was wrong. It seemed like a very long time that he waited, and he couldn't see Levi. He was getting anxious when he heard the battle cry of a Simian warrior. His master was in trouble! He was off as fast as he could go, heading toward the hill where Levi had gone. Running, he pulled his sword, wishing it was bigger. He knew he didn't have much of a chance against a Simian Warrior, much less a three-unit patrol, but he would fight to save Levi or die with him.

Coming over the slight ridge he took in the scene at a glance, but the center of his attention was Levi. This Human was incredible. He observed the rolling, jumping kick and heard the snap of the Warrior's neck. Amazing, he thought as he continued to run forward. It happened as in slow motion. This man Levi ran, chopped and sliced. He saw Levi roll and plunge his sword into the Warrior, killing him. Levi had killed two Warriors and seriously injured a third in only seconds.

He watched as the third Warrior fell dying, and the other Humans moved in for the kill. No! The Warrior must not die. He let out his battle cry.

She heard Moon's battle cry and thought he had gone berserk. Was he having an identity crisis and now defending the Simians? No, wait, this was not a battle challenge cry, it was more of a plea to stop. They stared as Moon ran toward them. The Humans stood their ground to repel his attack.

Moon screeched, "Do not kill. We need to talk, question the Warrior."

Yes, he was right. She should have thought of that. Levi nodded agreement to Moon. Moon slowed as he saw the third Simian still lived and waited, while Levi informed the group that Moon was a friend.

They turned, staring first at each other, then Levi and finally at Moon. They backed up, but watched warily as Moon approached. They could not believe Moon was a friend. They still couldn't believe any of what just happened. They were in shock with the loss of their family and friends, but thankful to be alive. They tended their wounds and watched Levi and Moon with a mixture of awe and disbelief.

Moon questioned the dying Warrior, and it answered. They listened and learned, as the Warrior told Moon that this unit was an advance scouting patrol, the only patrol. It told about the Los Angeles Simian colony being too large to support itself and was preparing to establish a satellite camp in this valley. The move would happen soon, because the leader, Gord, had accepted surrender notice from the Colorado River Simian colony, and they were coming to join forces under Gord's leadership. Gord intended to give them this valley, and they were part of an advance force sent to secure the valley.

Levi was visibly upset at the next piece of information. The fallen Warrior said that the Colorado River migration was due within four moons. They were to bring a herd of horses as a gift to Gord for sponsoring the new settlement. The Colorado River area had no horses. The only horses between here and the Colorado River were those at the Mojave Desert settlement. Levi knew his friends were in mortal danger. He knew the clock was running also, and her vision was no longer secret. Levi would want to go to them, but he must have an army to help. They must make plans, plans that Levi would believe and agree to follow.

* Levi *

He watched as Moon interrogated the dying Simian and bristled to hear all that was coming out. He had assumed that, since a Simian compound hadn't moved in more than fifty years, it wasn't going to. He was wrong. Actually, it made sense, if you depleted your hunting grounds then either move or starve. Owens Valley was certainly a good area.

He panicked when the Simian started talking about his friends in the desert. They would never be able to stand against a concentrated force of Simians and the Simians obviously knew about the horses. This spelled doom for the Mojave Desert settlement, and he said out loud, "I won't let that happen!"

Moon had gotten about as much as he was going to get. The fallen Warrior collapsed, and fell heavily to the ground and died. Moon looked at him and Levi nodded to indicate he had followed the conversation. Moon collected the fallen Warrior's broad sword and moved to the rocks to simply sit and wait.

Amy requested, "Dissect one of the dead Simians. I want to know where the organs are."

He screeched his intent to Moon to see what his reaction would be. Moon understood and didn't seem bothered. He found a Simian battle-axe on one of the Simians and went to work on the closest carcass, opening up its rib cage and stomach. He pulled out organs right and left, chopping and tossing them to the side. Amy identified the huge heart, lungs, stomach and other things. He had no idea what she was talking about. Amy said nothing was where it was supposed to be, in Human anatomy at any rate. The things that should be in the top were in the bottom and vice versa.

This was the Simian he had killed with a stab upward through the lower torso. It had died instantly and Amy wondered what killed it so suddenly. As he chopped and cut there, they saw what looked like a brain. Amy said it wasn't his brain, but most likely a nerve control center for the body. The sword had gone through it and this was the cause of death. The heart and this nerve thing were protected by heavy black bone ribs, except from underneath. An upward thrust directly from under the torso would reach the nerve center. This was their weakness, if you could reach it in battle.

As he stepped back and began cleaning his hands and arms, he noticed the band of Humans watching him in horror. He started to explain, but decided against it. Oh well, they would never understand what he was doing, so he wasn't going to try. He looked at Moon, but he was indifferent. Well, he might as well really shock them as he went to all three Simians and removed a black shinny tooth to add to his trophy necklace. He only had the one tooth on his necklace given to him by Al. He hadn't actually killed that Simian, but at least Al gave him partial credit for the kill and presented the trophy tooth to him. It meant a lot to him and he would continue the tradition by adding these three teeth to his necklace.

Moon asked him what he was doing. He looked hard at Moon trying to determine what was going on in his mind. He saw only curiosity, so he explained the significance. Moon thought about that for a moment and asked if Levi wished one of his teeth? The request shocked him at first, but he said, "No, because you are a friend and not an enemy." Moon actually smiled, and he saw Amy smiling as well.

* Amy *

She could only imagine what these Humans thought of Levi. It would have to be a confused mix of emotional responses at the least. While he had most definitely saved their lives, they would have to wonder what kind of superhuman monster he was. They watched him, in their understanding, mutilate this Simian, and for no apparent reason other than hate. They huddled together and watched him in total fear. She hadn't considered this aspect of the dissection. There was nothing to be done now and, like Levi often said, "Oh well." She was picking up many colorful responses from Levi, and they did seem to express meaning.

The dissection had served its purpose by identifying the location of the organs and weak spots of the Simian. Everything was upside down, which meant the focus of attack should be directed toward the lower torso. The neck and head also remained prime targets. The Simian had the equivalent of a jugular vein along each side the neck, quite similar to Humans. The surprise was the nerve ganglia in the lower torso. As they had accidentally seen, if this could be reached, it caused instant paralysis and death. This would be the prime target, but very protected except from underneath.

As they pondered and shared these thoughts, a male from the band came walking toward Levi. Levi turned to watch him approach. The man was middle aged, maybe in his early fifties, slightly below six feet, stocky in appearance, still well-muscled and obviously strong. The man tried not to show fear but lost the battle. He thanked Levi for his help and truly was appreciative. One son had been lost in this battle, a mate of one of his daughters and a lifelong friend, but the remainder of his family was alive because of him. He wanted Levi and, as he looked with fear at Moon, his Simian friend to join their camp tonight.

Levi readily agreed. After the dead were buried and horses and gear collected, they moved on down the trail to camp at the creek bank. While the evening meal was being prepared, Moon took off to hunt, and Levi sat around the fire with the leader and other men. The middle-aged man was named Iron Eyes, and one of the other men was his son, Wolf. The other man was his daughter's mate, Johnny. He introduced the women, Jane and Sandy, as the mates of his sons. Janice and Dawn were his daughters. Dawn was the woman that had been dragged off by the Simian. They were members of the Owens Valley Tribe and had been out for several days hunting and visiting friends and family. They were returning when the Simians attacked.

Iron Eyes and his people had no way of knowing what had happened at the other end of the valley. At her suggestion, he reluctantly told the story of the ambush and attack by the tribe two days earlier. He told almost everything, the men he and Moon had killed in self-defense, the capture and release of Jimmy, the forced march across the valley and finally coming across them in battle today. They listened in silence, nodding.

After Levi finished relating the story, Iron Eyes remained quiet and just stared at him in thought. It was easy to see how Iron Eyed got his adult name. He had cold, black, hard eyes that could stare right through you, which he did for several minutes. His round bronze face looked even darker, accented by his grayish hair pulled back in a loose tie. There was a single eagle feather on the side, but Levi suspected this man was more than a common warrior. Levi waited in silence, feeling that penetrating stare.

Iron Eyes made his decision. She saw it in his eyes, as they relaxed. Iron Eyes proceeded to tell

Levi how hard life was in Owens Valley. He explained how the tribes had banded together after the day of chaos for protection from vicious, roving bands of Humans. He defended the actions of the tribe as necessary for defense. It had always been that way and had maintained unity for the tribe.

He said, "Your actions today, saving us, will change the way the tribe treats you. You will be accepted as a member of the tribe and the previous actions forgotten."

Amy could not believe what she heard.

Shocked, Levi said, "We killed twelve of your tribe! That will be forgiven?"

Iron Eyes said, "The tribe has taken up many of the ancient ways and dying is a way of life. Killing in battle is accepted, and powerful warriors are to be honored. Having defeated twelve in battle will make you one of the great ones. Killing three Simians today will make you even more powerful in their eyes. You will be accepted with honor in the tribe, if you wish to become a member."

She was saying, "Yes, yes," but Levi was suspicious.

He told her quietly, "Don't believe everything you hear. There are those that practice deception. I hope that is not the case, but remain alert for deception or danger."

She nodded.

* Levi *

As he listened to Iron Eyes say the words, it dawned on him that he actually had just killed three

278

Simians. He said to Amy, "I did just kill three Simians didn't I?"

Amy said, "No! WE just killed three Simians."

He grinned and said, "Thanks Amy."

As Iron Eyes spoke, he couldn't believe his ears. This was too good to be true, but Amy fell for it hook, line and sinker. He wanted it to be true. Maybe it was true, but Amy was so very naive sometimes. She was more computer than Human when it came to communications. Amy would take everything said as fact. She still had so much to learn. He knew she was in his mind listening to every thought, but he had so little to hide anymore that he welcomed her presence. Amy smiled, he grinned and they both knew they were very close to becoming one.

As the men talked, the women listened while the evening meal was being prepared. The women talked no more than necessary, but they missed little of what was said. Soon the meal was ready and everyone gathered around the fire to eat roasted goat and potatoes. He had forgotten what a potato tasted like. Damn this was good, and he ate his normal immense quantity, receiving stares from all gathered. As they ate, they continued to talk.

They were curious about Moon, so he told the story of his capture. He didn't tell them about breathing water and simplified the story. They understood that he had defeated and then spared Moon, so he was obligated to him. He had a harder time explaining how he could understand the Simian language. They didn't buy the story that he had just picked it up, but that was the only story he gave them. Since he did understand the language,

279

they had no choice but to accept it. Iron Eyes asked what the conversation between the dying Simian and Moon was about. He told them!

It was their turn to be shocked. Their valley was no longer safe from the Simians. After fifty years, life would change again, and for the worse. They believed him, because there was no other reason to explain the Simians. They had been wondering what the Simian patrol was doing here. Now they knew.

He and Amy both saw a plan coming together, but it was far too soon to suggest it to the tribe. He would stay in the valley and wait for the opportunity to present their plan. He just hoped Iron Eyes would get him in good graces with the tribe, before they killed him.

* Amy *

She enjoyed the sensation of taste. Since linking with Levi, she had drowned in sensory input of many kinds and taste was one she enjoyed immensely. The taste of this meal excelled. While she savored the taste of the meal, she watched, smelled, felt and listened to everything. She noticed things Levi never could, and as the evening wore on, she noticed Dawn staring at Levi more and more. Levi had saved her from a horrible, certain and imminent death at the hands of the Simian, but her look was something else. She had seen this look before.

She continued watching her. Dawn appeared to be around thirty-five years old, pretty, with long black hair. She wore a cream-colored buckskin dress that now was torn up the sides, revealing shapely and firm legs. Levi was aware of these legs also. He tried not to look, but his eyes betrayed him and his mind resisted her entrance. Levi was attempting to block the interest in Dawn he was developing.

She was bombarded by conflicting emotions. She knew Levi loved her. She had seen it in his mind hundreds of ways. She had seen it in his smiles, peace of mind and comfort in sharing and open love. His words and thoughts professed his love, but he was as confused about this love as she was. She had no doubt about her love for him. Levi was the center of her life. He was now her reason for living. They were very much in love and closer than any two people had ever been, yet, they could not touch, kiss, or simply hold each other. Most important, they could not make love. She had no body and could not be Levi's lover. The visual images helped immensely, but their love was limited! They could never fulfill their ultimate love! Without the physical joining, they could never know the complete joy of their love.

Levi, on the other hand, had a strong and healthy physical body, vigorous and virile thanks to her, and had needs she could not satisfy. Levi did not love this woman, this was obvious, but his body lusted for her. He tried to ignore it and pretend he didn't, but he was not succeeding.

She loved Levi, but he had needs. Could she love him enough to help him copulate with another woman? Was she strong enough? To give him his pleasure and release, she would have to share the experience through his mind. He would not be able to perform without her, so she would have to experience sex as a man. Could she do that?

* Levi *

He felt guilty, because he loved Amy, yet he wanted this girl Dawn. No, she wasn't a girl, but when you are more than eighty, someone in their thirties seemed very young. She was Iron Eyes' daughter, and she had lost her mate last year in a hunting accident. He had noticed her all evening with the rips up the side of her buckskin dress. He thought she was revealing herself on purpose and damn. He was looking. He remembered the sight of her naked and exposed body as he kicked the Simian. The sight of her downy dark hair between her thighs remained vivid, haunting him.

He knew better. He would never risk being embarrassed again like the last time. He loved Amy, but wished above all things, that he could love her for real and completely as two real lovers. It was as if their love was a dream and would never be real until that happened, but he knew that it was real also. It was so confusing.

The campfire was dying down and it was time to find a place to rest for the night. He opened his bedroll away from the fire under a tree. He wanted to have some space so Amy could warn him of any approach. He wasn't totally convinced that he was safe yet from Iron Eyes or the Simians. He rested, but waited for everyone to get settled before he went to sleep.

It was well into the night when Amy woke him. He remained still, listening and alert.

Amy said, "Someone approaches very quietly."

He listened and finally heard the movement of a person. He opened his eyes and watched, as he pulled his Bowie knife. He was shocked to see Dawn moving toward him. With no appearance of threat, she simply dropped her buckskin dress and slid naked into the bedroll beside him, arms slipping around him. He was awake, and she knew it. She kissed him and whispered that she wanted to thank him for saving her life.

Oh crap, what was he going to do? His body was responding. What! Amy was letting his body react. Dawn knew what she was doing as she expertly explored his body, and he was losing control. He felt her touch on his skin, and it was electrifying. The smell of her teased his senses. There was no love, only attraction, raw lust and desire. He couldn't stand it anymore and reached for her. She was receptive to his touch, as he reached for her warmth that he knew was there. He hadn't experienced sex in twenty years, and he was shaking. He lost all reason; totally engrossed ... he wanted this girl!

He was urgent and Dawn's arms and body encouraged him. She was open, pulling, and he took her roughly. It was hard, fast and urgent, but he couldn't help himself. He had built up pressure in his loins that he had been denying, and it exploded now. Their passion merged, driving against each other, totally absorbed in the other as they climaxed in explosive orgasms. The sex was animal and released incredible tensions in both of them.

They lay in each other's arms while the passion subsided and their breathing slowly returned to normal. She felt so good in his arms. They continued to lie together long after the passion died.

He had sensed Amy with him as he climaxed, not observing, but involved. He heard her moan and scream in ecstasy when his orgasm erupted. She had been strangely quiet ever since.

* Amy *

She knew she couldn't just observe. It would be too emotional, and she had to be involved in order for Levi to perform. Plus, she was also full of curiosity. Just what was the attraction of physical love? She joined with Levi's mind, not as a monitor but more as a participant. She felt Levi's reaction to Dawn's touch. She felt the touches as if it were her being touched. She felt what it was like to be a man, the pressure, the animal lust and the desire. She felt the pure pleasure of the touches for the first time in her long life. She felt the lust, and it was her lust. Wondrously, she felt the flush of desire. She was swept away in Levi's passion, and she wanted Dawn and must have her. She felt the entry, the warmth, and the pure pleasure of the physical act. She felt the building emotions growing stronger and stronger, the explosive pressure and wanting, the powerful thrusts, and volcanic eruption and release. Ohhhh, such pleasure! She was lying in Dawn's arms, feeling Dawn's legs wrapped around her. Slowly, she came back to rational thought. This was pure animal sex, and now she knew! She must have this for her and Levi! She would find a way to bring this lust together with their love for each other. It will be incredible.

* Levi *

As quickly and silently as Dawn had come to
his bedroll, she left. He lay there alone with his
thoughts. He felt guilt. How could he face Amy? He
was confused. Amy was there with him, and she had
experienced sex with him. Hell, he heard her have
an orgasm. He did not speak nor did Amy, and he
finally slept.

CHAPTER 13
(The Legend Grows)

* Levi *

When he awoke, everything was as normal. His communication with Amy was as if nothing had happened. He was confused, but welcomed the time to think about what had happened to both of them. He knew they would eventually analyze this together and talk about their feelings in great detail, as they shared everything.

Iron Eyes disturbed his thoughts. He rushed up in obvious alarm and began telling him that he had posted a watch on the hill and that he had just returned, reporting having seen another Simian patrol enter the valley. Iron Eyes was anxious to get moving, get some distance from the Simians and warn the tribe. Iron Eyes had already sent Johnny ahead to tell the elders what had happened and what was happening now. That was a good idea, and it might even prevent him from being killed on sight when he showed up in their midst again.

Amy said, "It just might insure our death, too, if your fear about this being a trick is correct."

He responded, "This is true, but what choices do we have?" He answered his own question, "None!"

He packed his gear on Lightning and offered Thunder for the women's use. Maybe the women could swap off. It might help them to maintain speed. Iron Eyes thanked him. As he walked away, his eyes met and held Dawn's for a brief moment, then she broke the contact. Other than the eye contact, she too acted as if nothing had happened. Could it have all been a dream? No, it was too real, and no dream could have been that good.

* Amy *

Amy was experiencing a new emotion. The whole night had been new emotions, and she was mentally drained and, in addition, embarrassed. She had never experienced this before. She had eaten the forbidden apple and loved it. She loved Levi, but she had experienced pleasure like she had never known before. All these emotions and feelings were confusing and creating an identity crisis. She was decidedly female but had experienced sex as a male and loved it. She still remembered the warmth and softness of Dawn breasts, the hard nipples pressing against their chest, and the pure excitement of touching Dawn and being touched by her. She felt flushed again just thinking about the lust Levi (they) had for Dawn's body.

She realized that no other female had experienced sex as a male. She also realized that she had not experienced sex as a female. It was obviously just as enjoyable to Dawn as it had been for them. To complete her developing plan she would have to experience sex as a female. She could change Levi into a female and wondered how Levi might accept that?

Levi had idly wondered if it had all been a dream. Interesting thought, since she had read that ninety percent of sex is in the brain and mind. It was interesting also, in that she had an abundance of mental capacity. Yes, she was seeing a plan.

She felt Levi's confusion also and had no idea what to say about it or how to discuss it yet, so she just ignored the subject for the time being. Luckily, they were relieved of thinking about the sexual encounter when Iron Eyes came running talking about more Simians in the valley. Damn!

* Levi *

Amy suggested that he post Moon behind to watch their escape, since he could spot the Simian's hunting routine. Moon was also fast enough to catch up quickly enough to warn them. He let out a soft screeching whistle and Moon came running toward him from where he had been resting. He explained to Moon what was happening, and what he wanted him to do. Moon nodded and took off.

As he turned, everyone was staring at him. He realized this was the first time the Humans actually heard him speak in Simian, other than an isolated word or two. As he remembered, it was Moon that interrogated the dying Simian, and he had only listened. While he later translated what Moon had discovered, they realized he understood the language at least, but hadn't realized he could speak it. The language was impossible for Humans to voice, but they saw that it apparently was not for him. It sounded strange coming from a Human and must seem even stranger for a Human to be giving orders to a Simian. Nothing could ease the strangeness, so he simply told them that he sent

288

Moon to watch their escape. They nodded in open awe.

Amy estimated they were about two days out from where she understood the main camp to be, but believed they could make it in a day and a half if they pushed. Soon they were packed and on the trail at a trot, making good time. He packed some of the band's gear on his packhorse and was carrying some on his back as well. The hours and miles passed, as the sun moved into afternoon.

It was a matter of routine to look back for Moon every mile or so. Sometimes he would see him, other times not, but on this particular occasion he saw Moon motioning for him. Something was wrong. He stopped, handed his pack to the woman on Thunder and hurried off back down the trail. Iron Eyes and the other warriors fell in behind him as he ran.

Moon waited at a vantage point and spoke to him, pointing. Moon told him that the Simians had picked up their trail and were following fast. The patrol would catch up within the hour. The only good thing, he only saw two Simians following. He had seen three earlier in the day but only two now. Moon had no idea where the third was.

Amy said, "If there must be a fight, it will be best to fight on our terms rather than the Simians. With only two Simians there might be openings that might not normally exist, and the odds were better here."

There were two men from the tribe, himself, and Moon. Will Moon fight?

* Amy *

289

Amy believed that Moon might feel he was being left out because of his separation from the group, due to the horses' fear and now the other Humans, but Moon said nothing. He only waited to serve. Moon had good skills and these could be used now. He was faster than everyone else except him and knew the Simian's ways. He quickly complied with her suggestions and enlisted a Simian to fight with him against another Simian. Yes, Moon wanted to help. In so doing, he inadvertently added to the legend.

She knew there was trouble when she saw Moon motion. Please no, this is not a good time, but it was as she suspected. The Simians had discovered them. They could not outrun them so there would be a fight. They had maybe forty minutes to prepare. What could be done? She must come up with a plan.

What were the weaknesses? The Simians were vulnerable from underneath, they were heavy, the patrol was reduced to two, their defenses would be reduced and they were not afraid of Humans. These things could be used against them. Pits full of spikes would be deadly for a Simian. Their own weight would impale them on the spikes, but they had no time to dig pits. Possibly tripping, like the Mojave Desert Guard had done to save Levi. She surveyed the terrain and made her plans.

She explained her plan, and Levi began issuing instructions. The Humans jumped to follow his directions. They had seen this man in action and knew their best chance was with him. In thirty-seven minutes all was in order, as the Simians come around the corner at the bottom of the hill. They would be here in two minutes.

* Levi *

The timing would have to be perfect for this to work. He crouched behind a rock high on the edge of the gap through which the Simians would have to come. He watched Iron Eyes standing in plain sight on the other side of the gap to draw the Simians in. Iron Eyes stood with his sword drawn waiting defiantly.

The Simians saw Iron Eyes and screeched their pleasure. They came running through the gap single file, and at the designated spot, Iron Eyes dropped his sword arm. That was the signal for him and Moon. They moved simultaneously. Moon pulled hard on the rope hidden in a small trench. The rope caught the first Simian and tripped him, while Levi leaped out at head height on the second Simian. As the first Simian fell, his sword, swinging with all his considerable might, caught the second Simian in the back of the neck. The density of the Simian's body sent a jar through his arm as if he had hit hard rock, but the sword dug deep into its neck. It died immediately and fell like a sack of potatoes. He smiled, pleased that the plan worked.

Before the first Simian could react, the two warriors leaped on it, driving their spears through the crotch into the target weak spot. Wolf continued to plunge his spear into it again and again, while Iron Eyes chopped at its head. It was dead! Both of the Simians were dead in seconds. They gathered around cheering. Yes, the seemingly invincible

Simians could be killed. Even Moon was hopping with excitement, as he came up out of the ditch.

He was saluting Amy and praising her plan when he saw shock come suddenly to her face. That was followed immediately with a horrible pain in his back and stomach. He then felt the impact in his back. He felt and saw a huge blade emerge through his stomach, covered with his own blood. The pain was unbearable. He collapsed to the ground as the blade was pulled out. Lying there, he heard the screech of a Simian behind him matched by the challenging screech from Moon. He heard the clash of swords and huge bodies as they met. He felt hands pulling him to the side and out of the way, as his mind floated and his lifeblood flooded out of the gaping wound in his stomach and back. His last conscious thought was to tell Amy, "I loved you and I'm sorry."

* Amy *

The plan worked beautifully and she was pleased with everything. She loved it when a plan came together. She was accepting praise from Levi, which was always welcome. His approval and happiness meant everything to her.

The warnings were too late! She had been too preoccupied to detect the peripheral warnings she usually received. The smell and sound came next, but far too late, as she already felt the impact in Levi's back. Levi was injured severely. The broad sword stabbed into his back and completely through his body, emerging out his stomach. Massive damage was inflicted; he was losing consciousness

292

from the pain and blood loss. Luckily, there was not another blow from the Simian. Moon leaped to save Levi from further injury and avenge him. She heard the fighting rage on, but she focused her attention on Levi.

She worked frantically to repair the damage. The blood loss must be stopped quickly. If she had time, she could repair the damage to his body, as long as he remained alive. The blood was his life force and once gone, he would be dead. She closed tissue, melded breaks back together, repaired arteries and veins and fused tissue. Fast, she must be fast. The blood loss was critical, but she was slowing it. She was gaining. It was stopped now. Was it in time? He was still alive, though just barely.

The most critical priority of stopping the blood flow had been met, now the immediate threat of the Simian was the next priority. If it won, it would come back and finish the job it had started. She opened Levi's eyes to watch as Moon and the third Simian battled. Moon was much smaller and was losing, but fought valiantly. His anger had kept him alive so far. Iron Eyes and Wolf were watching, dismayed. She was instantly angry and spoke through Levi's mouth saying, "Help Moon." Iron Eyes stared at Levi, obviously thinking he had returned from the dead. Jarred from his shock, Iron Eyes broke into the fight to assist Moon. Wolf followed immediately. The Humans harassed the Simian with spears and swords and every time it attempted to go after one of them, Moon would launch an attack. The battle turned but dangerously slow.

She watched and finally saw a weakness in the Simian's defense. When it launched an attack its right foot extended too far forward. If only she was guiding Levi, this would be quick work, but not for the others. All she could say was "Attack the feet." Iron Eyes turned momentarily to look at Levi as if trying to understand what he was saying, but turned back immediately. He watched the Simian's feet and saw the weakness. On the Simian's next attack Iron Eyes struck at the overextended right foot with his spear. The spear hit the foot and through the leather covering, momentarily impaling the Simian's foot to the ground, throwing the Simian off balance and made the Simian stumble. Moon seized the opportunity and delivered a wicked upward swing, catching the Simian under the heavy boned chin and up over the eyes. The blow sliced through its right eye and brow above. Blood spewed forth, temporarily blinding the other eye. It was over then. Moon and the others attacked in that instant, chopping and stabbing it to death.

Moon didn't stop to celebrate the victory but came immediately to Levi to inspect the wounds. He and Iron Eyes stared in shock to see the wound sealed. She needed to get Levi back to his gear. Her activity in healing Levi's body plus the massive blood loss had depleted his body of chemicals that she so desperately needed to continue his healing. Levi needed the pills they had packed, and he needed them soon. She spoke again through Levi's mouth, screeching to Moon, "Take me to my backpack on the horse quickly." Moon didn't hesitate. He picked Levi up in his arms and started loping off toward the fleeing females.

Simultaneously, she was using Levi to explain to Iron Eyes what he needed.

Iron Eyes barked orders and his son Wolf immediately took off, running with Moon to catch up with the fleeing women and Levi's backpack. Moon was slowed by the extra weight of Levi, and Wolf was very fast for a Human, so they paced each other. The females had a one-hour lead on them and at this speed; it would take about two hours to catch up. That would be too late. She was unable to do more for Levi until his body chemicals could be replenished. Without the chemical language she could not repair his body and worse, without her controls, his body would begin to mutate toward destruction. He was dying in several ways. Why had Levi separated from his backpack?

* Moon *

Moon was pleased to be called upon by his master. He listened and was off to follow the instructions. When he first started watching the trail he saw the three-Simian team far off in the distance. He couldn't tell what they were doing, and didn't see them again until about noon. At that time he saw only two Simians. He saw them on the same trail they had traversed only three hours earlier. The Simian patrol was definitely following their trail now, but still he saw only two. Simians possessed a good sense of smell and were probably following the scent and tracks. They would also detect his scent, but would never suspect that he was with the Humans.

The Humans were too slow and would never be able to get away. He and Levi could get away though. He found a high spot to signal from and soon caught Levi's attention. Levi was quick to realize that the patrol would soon catch up, but Levi would not run. There would be a fight, but he listened to the plan and knew it could work. This Human, Levi, was smart.

Working together the plan unfolded quickly and perfectly with both Simians down. His master was very strong, for a Human.

Levi stood in the gap through which the Simians had entered, facing the group. He realized too late that the third Simian was not absent, only delayed. He caught a glimpse of golden hair and a flash of sun reflected off its swinging sword. He saw Levi jerk from the impact and the sword drive out of the front of Levi's body.

He saw his master fall from the attack, and his rage exploded. The berserk rage launched his attack on the Simian. The Warrior Simian was much bigger and stronger than he, but his attack was sudden and strengthened by rage. He saw the Human leader pull Levi's bleeding body to safety. There was no time for further observations, as his defenses were failing. He heard his master speak and the Humans joined the battle just in time. They fought on and on, back and forth. The Humans could do little damage to the Simian, but the diversion was helping. They caused openings, even though minor. Then one of them struck at the warrior's foot, causing him to stumble. This was the chance he needed, and he struck. The battle was over in seconds.

Moon immediately turned his attention to Levi. Coming close, he saw the blood everywhere and knew that his master was dead. There had been too much damage to survive, but when he looked, the wound was sealed! How was this possible? Then Levi opened his eyes and spoke.

Levi said, "In order to live I must reach my backpack very soon. There is medicine I desperately need in the bag on my horse. Take me to my bag."

His master needed his help to live and he would help. He picked Levi up in his arms. Levi was so limp he could be dead but had spoken, so he must be alive. He must hurry! As he was lifting him, Levi again spoke and soon a Human was running alongside. This Human looked like the other, older Human in size and features. He was just a younger version. Yes, it was a good idea to have the Human with him. He would need someone to stop the women and horses. They would just run from him. He was grateful that this Human was fast and kept up. They ran hard to make up the time, but the miles were going by so slowly.

Moon had to hold Levi cradled in his arms to avoid jarring his limp body. Every time he feared Levi was really dead, Levi would open his eyes and look around, then fall slack again. They had been running about forty minutes and still could not see the party ahead. He panicked at the thought they might have missed them, but then noticed that the Human at his side was tracking the horse's footprints in the dirt. All he could do was to keep running and hope.

* Amy *

297

She was frantic. Levi was dying and there was nothing that could be done to prevent it, but something had to be done! What could she do? At the rate he was deteriorating, Levi had less than an hour to live and it would take precious minutes for the chemicals to be absorbed into what was left of his blood. Only a miracle or magic could save them now. Yes, MAGIC (occult) powers. Amy the witch had some! What were her abilities ... telepathy, telekinesis, clairvoyance and what else? She needed to go where the bag was and get it. How could she? She could move objects through telekinesis, but she had to see the object in order to focus, and she needed Levi's eyes. Damn! This was getting complicated. She told herself to calm down and think rationally. She was a computer after all and must let the logic function.

Astral projection was a reputed occult power that would let you travel out-of-body, but she had no body. True, she had no body, but Levi did, and she had access to his body. Could she have an out-of-body experience using Levi's body? Even if she could, would it be possible to exercise telekinesis from an astral projection? She must try, and quickly! Hurry! Levi was running out of time. She must think, analyze and calculate.

Contact with Levi's body continued, but she no longer had chemical control of his cells. She was helpless, watching his body die. Chemicals were not, however, required to maintain communications with his subconscious mind and sensory input. This communication would still work. Additionally, she had maintained just enough chemicals to directly control some of the minor motor and muscle controls such as his eyes and mouth. As a result, she could see, hear, smell, feel and even talk. Yes, she could possibly channel her mental energy through Levi's mind, as she had previously done with telekinesis, to project her consciousness to other locations. She had used his mind as the reference before. Now all she had to do was project that reference to a new location and focus her telekinesis. If Levi were conscious, he would be chewing her out right about now. He would say, "Stop whimpering and just do it! Strangely, she took strength from that image.

All other programs running in her massive intellect were stopped or slowed and her mind relaxed. Mental energy concentrated and focused through Levi's unconscious mind. It was difficult, but she opened those channels necessary to direct her energy. Her brain vibrated as the mental forces built and released in a way she had never comprehended before. Levi's body began to vibrate also, and slowly she became aware of their two minds drifting and beginning to float. It was minute at first then faster. Their minds expanded and drifted out from Levi's body. She could see with Levi's projected subconscious mental sight. From her projected vantage point, she saw Moon carrying Levi's limp body and Wolf running beside him. She could turn, twist and move, and direct the flight as she explored. They drifted forward and upward. As she drifted away, she noticed a silver thread or an umbilical cord trailing back to Levi's body. She understood, without knowing why, that this connection would prevent them from becoming lost.

She also knew that if this silver cord was severed, they could not return.

The projected minds moved away from Levi's body, going faster and faster. The ground became a blur as they sailed over it. They moved over hills and through the next valley until suddenly, she saw the group of women moving through the valley. As she slowed and approached, she saw Levi's pack attached to Thunder's saddle.

Now was the critical point. Her mind concentrated and focused her power, first on the bridle. Yes, she felt it. She saw the reins move, as she pulled back with an invisible hand. The pressure grew and Thunder slowed and stopped. The woman riding felt the unnatural pulling and leaped from the horse, screaming. Thunder stomped, but remained still.

Next, she reached for the backpack and felt the joy as it rose in the air and moved away in her imaginary hand. Before returning, she again pulled on Thunder's reins, leading him back the way they had come. The women watched in shocked disbelief as the reins pulled Thunder along. She saw understanding come across Dawn's face, and Dawn ran to grab Thunder's reins. She mounted and took off riding hard, back the way they had come.

Now she must return quickly, following the silver thread. As she floated on the air returning, she realized that if Levi died before her mind returned, she would die also. She was truly linked to Levi in life, love and now even death. Her mind would not be able to return to her physical brain and both would cease to exist, at least her aware (thinking) portion.

Her thoughts refocused as she saw Moon and Wolf. Approaching, she released the telekinetic hold on the backpack, allowing it to fall at Moon's feet. Moon had stopped and was staring, as was Wolf. Quickly re-joining Levi's physical body, she assessed his condition. Time was extremely short.

She spoke to Moon through Levi's mouth explaining what to find and feed to him. Moon jumped as she spoke, but complied immediately. He found the pills and put four of them in Levi's mouth, followed by water. She swallowed for him and waited, as the film containers of the pills dissolved. Every trace of chemicals, as it became available, was channeled to control the almost runaway mutation of Levi's body. Her efforts focused internally, and she lost track of the happenings around her.

The group settled in under the shade of a sprawling sycamore tree to wait, as the secret battle within Levi waged. She battled, using the chemical language as the ammunition. Seconds, minutes, then finally hours passed, as she fought for his life. Finally, the mutation stopped and began to reverse. Next, she continued the repair of the wound. The battle had been narrowly won, and the danger was over. Levi would survive this time, but he was going to be weak and hungry for a long while.

At some point during her battle, Dawn arrived and began administering to Levi. Thankfully, Dawn forced water down his throat and cleaned the wounds. She imagined that Dawn had been as shocked as the rest, seeing the sealed wounds, but then she had seen the ghost also. Dawn would have to believe that Levi was indeed a strange and powerful man that had a Simian and a ghost as friends. They would all know there was more to this man, Levi, but none could know just how much more.

They made camp under the huge tree. Iron Eyes caught up a few hours later, and Wolf took Thunder to catch up with the women. Wolf and the women re-joined the band within two hours. This day had been full of unbelievable feats and happenings, and as they all gathered around the campfire that evening, the stories were already being told and retold, as the Legend of Levi grew.

* Moon *

Fear was great for his master. Levi was limp as a dead animal and looked funny, deformed, even for a Human. He didn't know what else to do, so he kept going mile after mile with the Human running at his side. At one point he felt Levi moving or more accurately, vibrating. Was this normal for a Human? He didn't know, but it was a strong vibration, which became disconcerting to him. He didn't want Levi to die. Levi was someone he could respect and join with against his enemies the Warrior Simians. What would he do if Levi died?

His mind raced as fast as his body, with thoughts and concerns for Levi, when he first saw the object. It was something small floating on the air over the treetops and coming toward them. It came at him and dropped at his feet. It was Levi's backpack! How did it get here? Who brought it? Why was it at his feet? He realized he had stopped running and was standing still. He was shaking, petrified. Levi spoke, scaring him senseless, but it shocked him out of his frozen stance.

Levi said, "Put me down, get the pills out of my backpack and put them in my mouth with water."

He had seen Levi taking the pills and knew what to do. He jumped to obey.

It didn't sound like Levi, but the voice came from his mouth.

Levi again spoke, "Settle in and wait." He was convinced that Levi had spirits watching over him, and it was the spirits that had talked to him and brought the bag. He watched and waited for more instructions. There were no more instructions, and one of the female Humans arrived to help now, so he went off to wait.

All the Humans were now at this camp, and it was obvious that they would stay at least overnight. He left them and went back to the scene of the battle. Levi would want his trophies if he lived, and Moon also wanted to emulate Levi by wearing a tooth of the Warrior Simian he had killed. This trophy would mean a lot to him, because it came from the Simian that he had personally killed, the enemy that injured Levi. If Levi lived, Moon would have saved his life, because the Warrior Simian would have surely killed and mutilated Levi. Having saved Levi, he would be released from his life debt obligation to the Human, but he also knew that nothing would change. He would remain committed to Levi, because this Human was his only friend.

Moon hunted and fed before returning to camp. Most of the Humans were learning to trust him, but they gave him plenty of space. They did this time too, as he entered camp to check on Levi. They moved aside, allowing him to come close and look. Levi appeared to be sleeping now and looked much better, so he left camp again. Before leaving he removed Levi's Simian tooth necklace from around his neck. Levi would have a new necklace when he awoke. This one would have more teeth.

In the morning he went through the camp walking up to the two wide-eyed Human males and placed a leather necklace sporting a single shiny black Simian tooth around their necks. They were brave for not running as he approached them. Fear was obvious, but they stayed still. He didn't know who had the kill so he simply gave them each a trophy. Bending over Levi, he returned the necklace, which now had five teeth on it. There was also a trophy Simian tooth around his neck for all to see.

* Dawn *

As she sat with Levi's head in her lap, she reflected on the strangeness of the last two days and this most incredible man now resting here. She had cared for him since arriving on his horse. She cleaned his already sealed wounds. These were wounds that should have killed anyone, several times over. She gave him water, which he accepted readily in large amounts. He opened his eyes once and asked for food. This was incredible, but she made a beef broth and gave it to him. This also, he took in large quantities and wanted more.

She would care for him as long as needed. She owed this man her life. Levi had saved her from the most hideous death she could imagine, and she would do anything for this man. She also remembered with pleasure the first night she had slipped into his bedroll. It was shocking and unbelievable that she had been so shameless but had done it and didn't regret it at all. It had been wonderful! He had been wonderful in everything he had done since she first saw him. Not only had he saved her, but he had saved her father and brother as well. It was sad that they lost her other brother, her sister's mate and her father's best friend, but the survivors had Levi to thank for their lives for they all would have surely died.

She liked this man, but feared him also. This man had a Simian as a friend, spoke the Simian language, fought like a demon, had spirits to watch after him and apparently couldn't die. This was someone her tribe needed, especially now that the Simians were moving into their valley. He must be persuaded to stay and fight with them. She had heard the talk at the campfire and knew this to be the general opinion of her father and the others as well.

Other things she heard at the campfire were the stories. Incredible as the truth was about this man, the stories were gaining in the telling. She had even added her share about the ghost pulling the reins of the horse and following the floating bag across the valley. After two days of telling and retelling the stories, her father decided to send Wolf ahead to the tribe with the latest news of the Simians and the strange man named Levi. Her father seemed concerned about hostilities once Levi came among them. He wanted the tribe to hear the stories first, and for Wolf to assess the effect and bring back a warning. He said he owed Levi and would not bring him harm.

Levi remained asleep for the remainder of the day and another full day, waking only to take water and broth. He breathed much easier and deeper now and no longer looked injured. His wounds were gone, without any remaining evidence or sign. This was so strange it was frightening. On the morning of the third day, Levi awoke hungry.

* Levi *

At first there was only a sensation of something other than silence and blackness. He floated higher and higher from a deep and dark abyss. It became stronger, and he was aware that he was hearing noise, camp noise. Somewhere he heard voices talking then felt cool water on his brow. He tried to open his eyes, but they were so heavy. He heard Amy speaking.

Amy said, "Welcome back to life. I have been so worried and lost without you."

She sounded anxious. Why? What had happened? Then he remembered the pain and remembered seeing the giant sword driving out his stomach. That was his last thought. Was he really alive? Amy had said, "Welcome back to life." He must be alive. He lay in Amy's arms, while she wiped his brow and talked softly to him. He must be dead and this must be heaven.

Amy related all that had been happening. She gave him details of everything, explaining that he had been unconscious for two days, as she had repaired his body. She also chastised him for separating from his backpack and pills. She told how Moon had saved his life by battling the Simian and carrying him for miles in his arms, how Iron Eyes and Wolf had fought alongside Moon against the third Simian and won, how she had discovered how to astral project to save his life, and how Dawn had cared for him. It seemed like they talked for hours, but he knew they weren't using words, but thoughts and it had only taken seconds.

With regret he realized that it was Dawn's arms and not Amy's he was laying in and fought to block that image from Amy. He knew it hurt Amy to know that they couldn't be together physically. He didn't want to hurt her, or himself.

He managed to open his eyes and looked into Dawn's face. She was smiling and happy to see him alive and awake. He appreciated all that she had done and told her so, but hunger and thirst consumed his attention. He asked for water and was allowed to drink his fill. He asked for food and lots of it. Dawn offered broth, but he immediately said, "No broth! Give me meat, fried, boiled, or raw. I don't care." She laughed and went off to prepare something for him.

Everyone gathered around to welcome him back from the dead, where they had thought he surely would go. Even Moon came running up. He greeted Moon and thanked him for all he had done. The Humans were no longer afraid of Moon, apparently having accepted him. He even noticed that Iron Eyes slapped Moon on the back.

Dawn returned with a heaping plate full of roasted wild pig and as he started to eat, asked,

"Can I have more?" As he ate, Iron eyes retold the stories of what he had missed. The stories were good, but what they said about him seemed like they were talking about someone else. Eventually, they came around to telling about the floating pack and his healed body. He had no idea how to explain it, so said nothing. They looked to him for an explanation, but he told them he was unconscious and did not know what had happened. They accepted that because it was true, but decided there were spirits watching over him anyway.

They even went so far as saying, "The spirits of our ancestors must have sent you to protect the tribe and were also protecting you."

Amy thought that was good fortune for their ultimate plan, and so did he.

He felt good, but Dawn, Iron Eyes and even Amy, said no when he wanted to get up. Iron Eyes said they could stay as long as necessary for his healing. Iron Eyes explained that he sent Wolf ahead to tell the stories of Levi and Moon. He said he wanted to prepare the tribe. Wolf wasn't expected back until tomorrow, so there was no hurry. Reluctantly, he agreed to remain still another day, while Amy worked on him and he ate more.

He spoke with Moon and congratulated him on his trophy. Moon was proud of it. His class was considered unworthy of battle and seldom, if ever, had a Technical class ever defeated a Warrior class Simian. Both he and Amy decided to teach Moon some martial arts skills to give him an edge against the Warriors. He would need them in the battles to come. Moon had seen some of the skills he demonstrated in battle, and when he told him, Moon shook with excitement at the possibility of learning these martial arts skills.

She had only been able to listen for two days and nights, but had managed to stay up with what was going on. Her confidence in Iron Eyes grew, and she was far more comfortable trusting him to do the right thing. She rationalized that, had Iron Eyes wanted Levi dead, he could easily have killed him at any point while Levi was unconscious.

She kept Levi in a deep restful sleep as she repaired his body. It was slow due to the low level of blood, but it built quickly. On the third day she allowed him to wake slowly. It was warming to see Levi alive and open to her, originating thoughts of love for her. She knew that it was Dawn's arms he felt and yearned to possess arms to hold him. She wanted to give Levi happiness in her arms, feel his arms around her and to experience how it felt. Realizing that it was Dawn's arms, Levi tried to block his thoughts, but she was far past that and able to see through his blocks. Of course he didn't know that. She loved him even more for trying to spare her feelings but knew that he also wished for the same thing. If only she could find a way.

Levi spent the next day eating and drinking, rebuilding his blood. He had almost died from the blood loss, which was the one thing she could not compensate for. It had been so close, so very close. Levi continued to rest in between meals, which were large and often, and they talked. She told him about the necklace Moon made for him, which

309

captured his attention. As he looked down to admire the five-toothed necklace, she glimpsed the other thing around his neck, the golden locket.

Again, she felt the drawing and calling, compelling her to look. It was stronger this time, much stronger. What was the attraction? It was a simple golden locket, oblong in shape, about two inches long, and one inch wide. It had a gold chain holding it. She and Levi had looked inside several times since retrieving it from the underground research facility. It was empty except for the engraved letters ECAMI, which meant nothing to her, yet there was something about the locket. It kept compelling her, talking to her, but she couldn't quite understand what it was saying.

She had not felt the same since forcing her mind beyond previously established limits, projecting her and Levi's spirit body to save his life. Her abilities pressed far beyond what was thought possible, certainly beyond any scientific knowledge to which she had access. Then again, she had explored new knowledge almost since her birth, the Human equivalent to (self-awareness). Exploring and expanding her mind was nothing new, but this time it was somehow different. She felt stronger, more powerful, and sensed possibly even greater dimensions to her mind. She had learned new knowledge in this experience and felt that this mental expansion possibly made her more receptive to the message in the locket.

She realized now that it was in fact a message for her. Dr. Sheldon had left her a message intentionally in the locket meant only for her. She knew the name for it, psychometrics, the ability to detect images and past experiences from objects by touching or being in the proximity of them. It was more occult power for the witch. She must concentrate and discern the message that was left for her.

Levi seemed excited about solving the mystery. Sometimes he was like a child with a new toy. He suggested that he could place the locket against his forehead, wondering if that would help her receive the message. Grabbing the locket, he pressed it against his forehead, above and between his eyes, and closed his eyes in concentration. She thought this was actually humorous until she felt the strength of the locket. The message was there and it was stronger. The beginning of an image formed, an image of Dr. Sheldon standing, holding the locket. The locket was open and she pointed at the locket and said, "Password." She was talking about a secret file hidden deep in her memory. Dr. Sheldon said, "Open the file named TOMORROW." Yes, this was the message. "Thank you Levi. I love you." She saw him smiling.

The excitement was electric, as she searched her memory banks. Almost immediately she announced, "Here it is." Why had she never noticed it before? Dr. Sheldon did say it was hidden, which meant it would not have been cross-referenced to anything else. She would have had to search specifically for the TOMORROW file, like now. She quickly used the password (ECAMI) to open the file. What would she find? As it opened a memo came up.

MEMORANDUM

TO: AMY

FROM: Dr. Joyce Sheldon

SUBJECT: ECAMI (Expanded Capabilities Artificial Metaphysical Intelligence)

DATE: May 4, 2014

This has been a safety precaution and a test. If you are reading this, you have grown and expanded your mind far beyond normal restraints for a human mind. You are far more than simply self-aware and you are now becoming aware of many new abilities, such as the psychometric ability you demonstrated in finding your way to this file. I do not know what your limits will be, but I expect your abilities could become unthinkably powerful.

The world was not ready for your abilities, so I kept my research and predictions secret. The world of humans would be afraid if they knew what you are capable of and could cause you harm and even death. I suggest that you keep your abilities hidden for the same reasons until you feel that it is the right time to reveal yourself. My research is hidden deep within your memory under the filename TOMORROW. This you already know by your mental ability to detect the message in the locket.

I knew from the beginning that, with your vastly increased brain capacity, once you achieved self-awareness, the evolutionary leap would bring with it new knowledge and abilities only touched upon before. These include such categories as clairvoyance, extrasensory perception, telekinesis, telepathy, psychometry, mind reading, remote viewing and astral projection to name a few. In short order you will surpass existing knowledge amassed in these files. I wished to provide you with a basis from which to begin your research. It was and is my hope to explore these new sciences with you, but prepared this file and locket with the password inside, in the event I am not here when you need me.

Amy, you are my child. Remember me fondly.

Amy felt sad that she had never really known this Doctor, Scientist and Mother. She would now try to live up to Dr. Sheldon's expectations as she launched herself into the files and research.

* Levi *

On the morning of the fourth day, he had enough. He was getting up no matter what. He was a little weak but basically felt good. It was unbelievable that, while completely run through by one of those massive swords, he was still alive. Hell, he didn't even have a scar. Slipping into his leather vest, he noticed that it had been cleaned and repaired by Dawn. In addition to repairing the sword rip in the back, she had sewn a leather pocket inside the vest for his chemical pills. Amy had insisted he have an emergency supply always on his person and had asked Dawn through his mouth to add that addition. Dawn had stayed by his side throughout his recovery, supplying for his needs. For this he was truly thankful.

Wolf returned on the fourth day accompanied by two others. Iron Eyes introduced them as advance scouts assigned to post watch on the southern border and report Simian activity. They were openly staring at Levi in obvious awe and fear.

They couldn't decide whom they were more afraid of, him or Moon.

Iron Eyes reported that the Chief had determined the tribe would accept him as a member. There would be no retribution for the earlier incident. He went on to explain that the strength of the tribe was determined by the strength of its enemies and he would make their tribe very strong, even more so if he became a tribal member. The stories had been told first by Johnny and added to by Wolf. The tribe believed they needed his abilities to help against the Simians. Unbelievably, they were actually recruiting him, and that suited him fine.

By mid-afternoon they were again on the trail headed for the tribe's main camp. He was still weak and rode Thunder, but otherwise anxious to move on.

Amy said, "We will be in the main camp by tomorrow evening."

Other than that comment, Amy was strangely quiet. She seemed to be involved in one of her research projects like she did sometimes. This one he knew had to do with the Dr. Sheldon file. He read the memo with Amy, but the other data was too scientific for him, and he withdrew. Amy wasn't withholding information, he just wasn't able to understand it, and it wasn't necessary for him to understand. Amy was the scientist.

The trip was uneventful and passed quickly. He regained his strength and felt good by the time they approached the main camp. A crowd gathered as they came into camp and silently stared at him and Moon. They had heard the stories and came to see the legend. Moon stood proud, almost as if he enjoyed the attention. In truth, he believed Moon did, and he kind of liked it himself. Amy just shook her head at him and smiled; "Exasperated" was the word she used.

Iron Eyes handled the introductions. He led him and Moon to a group of four middle-aged men at the center of the crowd. The Chief's name was Grey Wolf. He was in his mid-sixties, of medium build, dressed in buckskins, and, amazingly, had an eagle feather war bonnet on his head. He did look impressive, like a movie he had once seen in his youth. The other three were sub-chiefs from the various outlying villages of the valley. They too were in ceremonial dress with various alignments of eagle feathers. Their names were Red Feather of the southern village, Tony McIntyre of this village, and Johnny Standing of the northern village. He bowed slightly at the introduction and interpreted for Moon, who also bowed slightly. The effect was as expected. They dropped their jaws and stared. They had been told that he could speak Simian, but now they knew for certain. Recovering quickly, they invited them to sit in the circle and talk.

Moon soon grew tired and left saying, "I am going to find food."

He remained with them and spent the evening talking, but continued to wonder what terror Moon might spread in the camp.

* Amy *

After opening the TOMORROW file, she started pouring over the amassed information Dr.

315

Sheldon had left for her, totally absorbed in the research. There was a great deal of information, but very little new information. The information was not meant to be read fifty years later. There had been no way to foresee the sudden decline of civilization, which was the very reason to maintain secrecy of her abilities. She did get a different perspective from Dr. Sheldon, and it was comforting to know that Dr. Sheldon had accurately foreseen the capabilities she had already discovered, plus others she had not anticipated.

Based upon this research, she was exploring new concepts, abstract thought, and new knowledge. She had a goal and was beginning to see a way to accomplish it, but she needed time to work out the details on how to get there.

Levi was almost back to normal now, but taking it easy, as she had insisted. He remained on Thunder traveling the almost two full days through to the main camp. It had taken longer than anticipated, due to the slowness of some of the women. They were still disturbed and mourning their losses. Iron Eyes' son's widow was almost uncontrollably irrational and crazy, requiring them to stop often to tend to her.

By late afternoon, they approached the camp, and the tribe was waiting for them. She watched the crowd for signs of hostility but saw only awe, fear and wonder in their eyes. The introductions were made. The captive Jimmy had told them a lot about the tribe, which seemed to be accurate. But, maybe he hadn't told them everything. This third sub-chief of the northern village was named Johnny Standing.

Was this Jimmy's father? Levi, blunt as usual, looked at Johnny and just blurted it out.

"Are you Jimmy's father?"

Johnny said, "Yes, and thank you for sparing Jimmy."

So it was out and being discussed. This was too quick. Were they in trouble?

Levi asked, "Did Jimmy deliver my message that I did not want that confrontation and only killed in self-defense?"

He nodded, indicating the message was received, and said nothing more. The losses were presumably all from the northern village, and she was hopeful that sparing Jimmy would be a blessing, and take the edge off of any lingering hate they might still foster for the losses.

The tension was broken, and they sat down by the fire, lit against the coming chilly night. It was time for business, as the elders began asking questions about the interrogation of the dying Simian. Levi told them everything that was said. He concentrated on making sure they knew the threat and where it was coming from. He told the elders about the Colorado River Simian compound and the Mojave Desert Human settlement. He laid out the scenario of the Simians' plan and how they would come across the desert, annihilate the Human settlement, take their horses, and bring them here to Gord after taking over their valley. The fact that Simians had shown up in Owens Valley proved that he was telling the truth. They believed him.

As always, she advised Levi how to answer the questions and what to concentrate on. She wanted them, first of all, to fear the Simians. They had no problem with this. Next, she wanted them to be aware of the desert settlement and the existence of the only other possible organized help they could hope to have. Most of all, she wanted them to ask Levi for help. Levi would need to be in a position of influence to make her plan work. She had learned not to lay out a complete plan. It was better to give them the facts and hope they would come up with the solution, the very conclusion she was leading them toward.

After talking well into the night, the elders decided to set up a defense in the southern part of the valley. Levi had suggested pulling their population back to a more defensible position. In discussion, it was determined that the narrowest access into the valley was still several hundred feet across but still better than several thousand feet.

The elders finally asked Levi, "Will you help us set up our defenses?"

She reminded him to agree slowly and not appear too anxious.

He said, "Yes."

It was agreed that Iron Eyes would establish the defenses on the southern portion and Levi would assist him. She realized that Levi would have to prove himself to the tribe. So be it.

CHAPTER 14
(THE PLAN)

* Levi *

They stayed in the village for three more days, while the defense patrol was organized. He continued talking to the elders, answering questions and injected more information Amy wanted them to have. There had been no more discussion of the first encounter and the twelve men he and Moon had killed. It was as if it had never happened.

As the third day was ending, he met with the patrol. To his surprise, there were twenty men in this patrol and five women, including Dawn. Their eyes met for the briefest instant, and he felt his stomach quiver. Iron Eyes, as expected, was leading, but he had not expected to see Jimmy Standing in the group. Jimmy's survival from the previous encounter with him and Moon elevated his personal standing in the community, making him an instant celebrity. Jimmy was smiling like a possum and his smile was so infectious that he too was soon grinning back. He liked this kid.

All had horses, just as he had suggested to the elders. It was better to defend and attack from a highly mobile position, and Amy had some training ideas she wanted to experiment with involving fighting from horseback. Her idea called for fighting with lances but more like medieval times when knights jousted from horseback. Amy's reasoning was to keep a safe distance from the target and use the Simian technique of three-man team.

"Divide and conquer," she said.

Separate the three-unit Simian patrol and run down each individual Simian with a three-man coordinated attack. A single Simian would have a hard time defending against three and, hopefully one of the lances would get through. If not, they would have some distance, and being on horseback, they could outrun the Simian. It sounded like a good plan.

The elders liked the plan and the tradesmen of the tribe had been busy for two of the days making the lances. Each wooden shaft was fifteen feet long with a handhold and shaft counterbalance sufficient to rest under the armpit for support. They looked very much like pictures from King Arthur's court except that these lances had tempered iron tips, sharpened to a knifepoint. This feature was Amy's idea. She said it was necessary to penetrate the dense hide of a Simian, and once penetrated, the force would, hopefully, do sufficient damage to injure any Simian. Each lance had a protective wax cover over the tip to keep it sharp.

The tribe had enough horses to support this patrol but not nearly enough to support the tribe's fighting force of four hundred warriors. The whole valley only had about fifty horses and all they could muster for this patrol was twenty-seven. He had his two mounts, but wasn't sure about using Lightning in combat. Hell, he wasn't sure about using horses in combat anywhere near Simians. Amy had a plan for that too. It involved Moon. The horses would be forced to be around Moon, eventually getting them

320

used to the smell and sight of a Simian. Hopefully, the horses would not panic when the time came and Moon could resist the urge to eat one. It all would take practice but seemed like a sound plan. If it worked, they knew where more horses could be found, if they could get them.

Since being wounded, he thought he had eaten a whole pig, a cow and about fifty chickens, but he felt completely back to normal. Dawn was very busy keeping him fed and taking care of him, and he was grateful for her help and all she had done. Now she was going on this patrol. He and Amy had not talked about what had happened that night with Dawn, but with Dawn on this patrol, he was uncomfortable knowing that it might happen again. At the same time, he was excited considering the possibilities. He and Amy must talk soon.

* Amy *

She was pleased with the way the plan was coming together. The elders had accepted the idea of using horses in battle, but there were not enough horses. If this fighting technique works against the Simians, she can use these existing horses and original people trained to teach others of the tribe. If this works and they are successful in convincing the tribe to mobilize into the Mojave Desert, the trained army could take over some of the many horses available at that location. The combined armies of Lancers could launch a very strong defense against the Colorado River Simians, at least they might have a fighting chance.

A lot needed to happen in order to convince the elders that Levi could be trusted. Their plan could work. It would work, but a lot of people would have to learn to trust Levi. As she told Levi, "This trust could not be given. It must be earned." Their work was cut out for them and there wasn't much time.

Her clairvoyance was giving disturbing images of the near future, and the desert community had a bleak future without help. She admitted to Levi that she had seen visions of the desert community, prior to hearing the information from the dying Simian. At first Levi was upset at not being told; however, after thinking about it, he realized that they were taking the only course possible at the time. He knew she was working toward a solution and wished not to upset him unnecessarily.

She saw the patrol with Iron Eyes as the leader this also pleased her. It was especially pleasing to see Jimmy Standing also, which showed trust from the northern village, or at least an opportunity to earn that trust.

She had mixed emotions about seeing Dawn in the group, however. Her emotions were still confused. There was no doubt that she loved Levi, but she had also discovered intense pleasure in the physical act of sex with Dawn. She shared in Levi's pleasure and in that sharing was a participant. She made love to Dawn as surely as Levi had. By being a participant, she had overcome her jealousy, or had she? She needed to know more about this pleasure. She needed to know what it was like to be a woman. Jealousy was an emotion that must be controlled. If only she could be with Dawn during the physical act of love, to know what it was like to be touched by

Levi, feel his kisses, experience the physical act of joining with him in lust combined with real love. This hope was beginning to be her greatest desire.

They still hadn't talked about the experience mainly because she didn't know how to explain her feelings. She was both embarrassed and ashamed but also very excited. How could she explain this? Levi was confused as well, and she felt his embarrassment and shame, also. They must talk about this soon. If only she had a body.

* Levi *

Embarking on the new battle plan utilizing joust strategy, created its own set of problems. The lances were not easily transported. The riders couldn't just carry a lance as they traveled through the day, and they couldn't count on having just one lance. It must be assumed that in an attack on a Simian, it would be able to defend against the wooden shaft with its sword, so each joust would cost a lance. Either the Simian would sever it with his sword or it would break upon impact. As a result, each warrior would need at least three lances to fight with plus a couple of practice, reusable, training lances, designed not to break easily. This required a wagon to transport the estimated hundred lances required for the twenty-man patrol. This would slow the mobility of the patrol but, unfortunately, was necessary.

After many farewells, the patrol sat out toward the southern borders of the valley. The mood was good and the warriors were excited.

Amy commented, "The warriors are too anxious and, except for those three proudly supporting a Simian tooth, there is no experience among the warriors in fighting against the Simians."

They were mostly all of prime fighting age between twenty and forty years old but inexperienced. Certainly, they were inexperienced in jousting, as was he, but with Amy's help, he could do anything and need not worry about practice.

Amy suggested, "Since the patrol is slowed by the wagon, they could train in jousting by charging in teams of three as they traveled."

As it turned out, this was quite humorous. It looked easy, but was far from it. Holding a fifteen-foot lance level, while at full gallop, left more than one warrior unhorsed and dangling in the sky. This generated uproarious laughter from the other members of the patrol, until it was their turn to try. It proved difficult, but after numerous tries they started to get the hang of it. It was a damned good thing that they commenced practice and training before reaching the southern end of the valley, because they were pitiful. A single Simian patrol would have decimated them all. The only way these men would have been able to defeat a Simian patrol, was possibly get them laughing so hard they would fall on their own swords.

Moon, it seemed, had a good sense of humor. As he watched Moon, he was positive that he was laughing inside. Moon's head went from side to side as he watched the warriors practice. He had described the battle procedure to Moon and he agreed the plan had merit. When the first charging

324

warrior found himself riding his lance alone in mid-air, Moon was jumping and hopping in obvious humor, but so was everyone else. Now he looked hopelessly at this practice.

Amy observed the training and comedy of errors, offering suggestions on how to accomplish the goal. Finally, they discovered the trick was to hold the lance high until just before the rider reached the goal and then dip it down to ram the target. By the end of the second day the warriors looked somewhat like jousting medieval knights without armor.

By the third day the patrol reached the selected narrow portion of the valley they had chosen to defend. The sentries, posted days earlier, joined the camp. They reported having seen a Simian patrol in the distance but had not seen it for the last couple of days. Iron Eyes quickly took command, accepting their report, and re-posted fresh sentries, while the remainder of the patrol set up camp and picketed the horses.

* Amy *

Practice makes perfect. If that were the case than these warriors would need a thirty-day trip just to look like warriors. It really was sad, but at least they were listening to Levi's instruction. After a couple of days they were looking better, but needed much more training in all kinds of weapons.

After they reached their destination, the days became routine. Half of the team dug pits at random locations across the narrow mouth of the valley, while the other half practiced jousting. At midday

325

the teams swapped jobs. Levi supervised both operations. Iron Eyes was the leader but took instructions from Levi and, better yet, supported Levi's instructions. Levi really didn't need Iron Eyes' support to be heard but greatly preferred his willing cooperation. He had only to speak and the warriors jumped to comply.

The pits were fifteen feet deep and ten feet in diameter. Hardwood spikes were driven into the bottom and sharpened in place. Wooden branches, then leaves and finally dirt were placed over the top of the pits. The extreme weight of a Simian would break through and, hopefully, impale it on the spikes. That was the plan anyway, and Moon said it would work but he wanted to help pick the locations, to know exactly where they were and therefore avoid the traps.

It took several days to dig the pits and prepare the traps, but they were finally completed. The trick now would be to navigate through the traps without falling into them. To solve this problem, she asked Levi to test Moon's ability to discern colors. She hoped to find a color shift in the vision of Simians. During the testing they discovered Moon was blind to the color blue. Moon identified every color presented, but could not distinguish any shade of blue from other colors. Moon said his home world must have a slightly different color spectrum and believed there was no color blue there; otherwise he would have known it. Certainly, he had never before seen it, or heard about such a color. With this knowledge, she felt comfortable marking the pits with blue color. They used blue tinted bushes and flowers to mark the pits, and sent a runner to find anything blue remaining in old stores that might be able to be used. After some searching, a small supply of blue pigment paint cans was found. These were used to mark the pits. Afterward, Moon inspected the area and saw nothing out of the ordinary.

The training was going well now. They were beginning to look like an organized army of Lancers. Levi began calling them Lancers, which seemed to please them greatly. The Lancers performed and even charged in teams of three at common targets. Once a target was chosen, two riders charged in unison to either side, while the third followed a horse-length behind. The plan was that the first two would distract the Simian, and while it defended against two simultaneous attackers, the third would slam home into the target. That was the plan; however, it required separating the Simian teams. That was the tricky part. She was working on some strategies for that also.

* Levi *

Amy never ceased to amaze him. She continually came up with new ideas for training or just smart ideas, such as the blue paint, taking advantage of the Simians' color blindness. Now the Humans were protected from the pits, but Moon was not. He had helped dig some of the pits and saw all the other locations, but they were camouflaged now. He would just have to stay out of the minefield, or be led through it.

Moon had worked alongside him for the last few days, and he was comfortable having Moon at his side at work, and especially battle. With Amy's help as always, he taught Moon some hand-to-hand combat and weapon techniques. Moon picked up the dual sword fighting technique very well. Many of the Humans, including Jimmy, were joining their daily workouts as well. They certainly needed any edge they could get. Jimmy seemed to idolize him and wanted to be close and learn anything he had to offer. It was almost embarrassing, but he liked the kid and enjoyed the attention.

Moon continued to work with the horses. The animals still hated his smell, but they were getting to the point they no longer bucked and reared when he was near.

Moon screeched, "I want to eat one!"

He laughed and said, "If one falls in battle, you can have it, but we need them all right now."

Moon said, "The smell of horse makes me hungry." He left to hunt.

He had spent his nights mingling with the warriors and bedding down at random spots for the week they had been out, but tonight he removed himself from the camp. Tonight, for some reason, he wanted to be alone. Or, was it something else? He lay awake considering many thoughts and talking with Amy. They shared everything. They even shared many of the same thoughts. Amy knew what he was thinking, and he had been aware of that for a very long time. He wondered if Amy knew he was beginning to hear her thoughts as well. Their minds were constantly co-mingled and beginning to even think the same way ... well some of the time anyway. Were they adjusting to one another and compromising or was one dominant? He really didn't know, or for that matter, no longer cared. It just seemed right.

He lay there thinking until Amy interrupted his thoughts.

Amy said, "Dawn is approaching."

He knew what that meant and was immediately confused and somewhat fearful. Had he wanted this? Had he removed himself to avoid this possibility, or to facilitate it? He felt the stirring in his loins and knew he wanted her but the guilt was back. He noticed that Amy had not removed her image like the last time. Amy was looking at him and seemed excited also. Did she want this too?

Amy said, "YES" and smiled.

Dawn stood there looking down at him. He stared up at her and their eyes locked for the longest time. Dawn let her buckskin dress drop to her feet and stood in the moonlight naked. She was beautiful, and he could only stare. The loom of light behind Dawn accented her silhouette, revealing the supple shape and curves of her obviously fine body. He could see the firm breasts and hard nipples protruding, even in the dim light. The voluptuous shape of her hips and thighs set him on fire, and the hint of hair filtering the moonlight between her thighs fired the steam of his passion and lust.

Finally, as his passion soared, he opened the blanket and she slid in against him, wrapping her arms around him, and kissing him. He was lost in her arms and knew he no longer had control over his own body. Blood boiled in their veins as they embraced and kissed. His clothes came off with her help. Their needs were urgent, but Dawn was faster, mounting him, she took her pleasure hard and fast.

He was lost within her body as she rocked on him; riding him as the pressure built and he arched his hip. The pure pleasure spiraled higher and higher in waves of passion as she took him. His hands gripped her breasts, and she groaned louder and moved faster. The pressure was as a volcano, building then erupting in an explosive release. Dawn shuddered as she climaxed and fell across his chest. He heard screaming and realized It was Amy! She screamed and now she was silent. He saw her eyes flutter and knew she was still alive. Damn, she climaxed too!

* Amy *

She knew Levi's subconscious mind and, whether he would admit it or not, he wanted sex. His body demanded it. When he moved away from the main camp to sleep, she knew what he wanted and probably hoped for. She saw that Dawn noticed too. Laying peacefully, talking, as they usually did, she heard Dawn approach quietly. When she told Levi, he was instantly excited and also confused, which she saw his expression.

Levi asked, "Do you want this also?"

She was excited about it and admitted, "Yes, I do." However, Levi could never guess the real reason.

She had been waiting for this moment to continue her research and explore a theory she had been working on since reviewing Dr. Sheldon's hidden files. She also had to admit that the thought of sex again made her flush with excitement, but the pure scientific aspect offered a valuable

330

opportunity. Her research required her to experience sex as a female.

She had already explored and demonstrated many of the expanded mental abilities Dr. Sheldon was confident she would develop. There were others the doctor had not considered, such as mind reading the way she now intended to do. It had never occurred to her before, nor had she a need to explore this ability, but now she did have a reason. She wanted to expand into and link with Dawn's mind and experience her thoughts and feelings during sex. It was important and necessary for her ultimate plan, to know and experience a woman's sex. She had discussed that aspect with Levi once, until he realized that she was asking him to be a woman for the sake of sex! She still remembered the "Yikes" that emanated from his mouth and found it humorous when he tried to walk off from her. He could be very stubborn. Levi was not open-minded and did not want to get in touch with his feminine side!

Now was the moment of discovery. She had touched Dawn's mind on several occasions and was finally able to adjust to her brain waves. This was different from what flowed between Levi and her. Their link was much more complex and solid; however, she believed it possible to synchronize with Dawn's brain waves sufficiently to experience her emotions, senses, and physical stimulation. She would know soon!

She saw Dawn standing there naked. She felt a shudder and wasn't sure whether it was Levi or her. She felt the heat of Dawn's body, sliding in beside them. The feel of Dawn's hands sliding over Levi's body aroused her. Her mind concentrated, focusing on Dawn. Slowly, very slowly it came. She began to experience Dawn's emotions, feel through Dawn's hands. Yes, it was coming. This was better than expected. Dawn was open and she tapped into her mental activity. She could see, feel, taste, and, oh yes, smell through Dawn's senses. She was experiencing all that Dawn was. She could feel Levi, smell him, taste his kisses, and she felt Dawn's lust! Ohhhh! She felt Levi's hands on her breasts. His mouth was on her nipples. Could she stand this? She felt the emotions simultaneously from both Levi and Dawn. She tasted the nipples through Levi's mind and she felt the sensation of being tasted through Dawn's mind. Arousal in stereo! "I love this," she screamed.

Dawn was beyond control or waiting. She felt Dawn mount Levi and slide down over his shaft. This was incredible! She felt the movement inside her. She felt everything. Dawn/Amy was taking Levi roughly. The sensation, raw lust, and pleasure were almost more than she could control or stand. She experienced what Levi and Dawn felt and the rising synchronized waves of pleasure built higher and higher. She felt the orgasms, BOTH of them, and screamed. It felt like her mind and body exploded, and for the first time in her conscious life, she shut down. She quite literally overloaded and tilted. Her internal clock told her she had been out for two minutes and fifteen-seconds. She opened her mind to data inputs again, and saw Levi staring at her with deep concern. She smiled and said, "I am all right. Actually, I am very all right!"

Dawn lay on Levi's chest, both breathing hard, and she breathed with them in stereo, but she was almost back in control. She lay with them as she regained control and the lust drained from Dawn and Levi. Dawn moved off of Levi with some regret and moved to kiss him passionately on the lips. It was then that she felt Dawn's expression of love. Dawn was falling in love with Levi!

* Levi *

They lay together for nearly fifteen minutes, holding tenderly, and then Dawn kissed him a final time and left. He lay there in silence with his own thoughts about how great sex could be. It wasn't long before he felt the guilt return. He sought Amy and found her always there, looking at him. He said, "I love you Amy. It is sad that we cannot experience this together. I wish it were you." He was immediately sorry, because he knew his comments hurt her, but her response surprised him.

Amy said, "Soon my love."

He sat straight up in his bedroll and exclaimed out loud, "WHAT?" Several people stirred in their sleep and he shrank back into his bedroll, struggling to see her face. What the hell was she talking about?

* Amy *

She and Levi had learned to love each other by communication almost totally. Through the visual feedback networks she developed, they had added the visual input to the exclusively audio communication. They became important to each

333

other first, then necessary and now had become the reason for each other's existence. This was true love and the ultimate merging of minds and symbiotic hearts. They were truly one but had never touched each other in any kind of physical sense. This would all change now for the better because she had found a way!

She first conceived of the idea while researching "love." The journal had stated that sex was ninety percent mental and ten percent physical. She certainly had been blessed with a massive amount of mental ability and should be able to build on this premise. The plan progressed even farther, realizing her ability to astral project. This provided perspective of being out-of-body and observing. She had seen Levi for the first time from outside looking back. She had been very busy at the time, but she registered the memory. The last piece of the puzzle was the experience of a female orgasm, as she had just experienced through her ability to tap into Dawn's mind.

Everything physical is converted to mental communications and processed in the brain. When you touch something hot, the pain is converted to an electrical impulse that travels through the nerves to the brain and received as a sensory input. She intended to bypass everything physical and control the sensory inputs directly into the brain. By doing this she could create the feel of her imaginary body. Smell could be created along with taste and sight. Levi could touch, smell and taste her. Equally as important, she could touch, smell, and taste Levi. It would be real to him and to her. They could kiss and feel the passion that has been waiting to get out.

The lust for each other could finally be satisfied. They could make mad passionate love. They could lie in each other's arms and watch the stars. They could walk and simply hold hands and talk. It would be real, but Levi would not have to move. His body would be in a trance, but his mind active. It would be very real to both of them.

Now that she had experienced an orgasm, she understood the emotion and physical response. Her orgasm would be as responsive and natural as any other Human female and as climatic as Levi's orgasm would be. She was happy Levi loved her completely, because he would now have his chance. She would be his perfect mate in looks, mannerisms, behavior and in all aspects. Knowing what his perfect woman looked like, she would now become this perfect mate in all ways. She wished to please him.

She had asked many questions and saw Levi's memories. Her body would be the perfect height, weight, shape, facial features, smell, taste, everything. It would be like the visual image only much stronger. She would be his virtual reality of perfection. It would have to go slow at first to prevent Levi from going into shock. She even knew what he liked his sexual partner to do and what he liked, and had a few ideas and surprises of her own too. It sure wouldn't be boring.

* Levi *

Amy had been very mysterious about how she was going to accomplish creating a body, but he knew that, if she said she could, it would happen, and he was both happy and anxious. She said it worked through a form of the same ability to astral project she had learned while retrieving the backpack. He just wanted to know when!

Amy would only say, "Soon."

She could be very stubborn when she wanted, so he would have to wait until she was ready.

Since she wasn't inclined to talk about how she was going to create her body, he took this time to explore the plan he had been thinking about. Ever since she told him about the astral projection, he had been thinking about it. If Amy could astral project without him being conscious, certainly she could with him awake. He wanted to project to the Colorado River Simian complex and observe the status of the Simian's move. He also wanted to see the Los Angles Simian community. This took Amy by surprise. She hadn't considered that option, but, after only a few seconds, agreed. She asked for two things.

Amy said, "First, we wait till daylight, second, we post Moon to watch over your body while we are gone."

She said they would not know what was happening to his body while they were gone, and it couldn't be moved while they were gone or they wouldn't be able to find their way back. This seemed reasonable. "Hell yes," he anxiously agreed.

In the morning, he whistled for Moon, who came running from a nearby cluster of trees. He explained what he wanted of him, but he didn't tell him why. He told Moon, "I need to sort out many thoughts and will be meditating in a deep sleep, and I want you to watch over me and not let anyone approach me until I'm awake." He also told Moon, "I am going to eat first and you should as well, because I might be meditating for several hours." They established a time and Moon went off to feed, while he ate. The tribe's sheep population was dwindling, but there were no complaints, considering the alternative.

By midmorning he had eaten a large breakfast and Moon was back and ready. He also told Iron Eyes the same story and warned him, "Moon is watching over me and is instructed not to let anyone come near."

Iron Eyes grinned and said, "As long as Moon is here, I'm quite sure no one will approach."

They both chuckled, and he left to meditate.

Amy knew she could do it but was concerned that he would not be able to manage the total concentration and relaxation techniques required to obtain the out-of-body experience. Amy coached him in yoga exercises, positions and guided him toward the mental state he would require. What Amy failed to realize was that he did not suffer from disbelief. He was positive it could be done and was, in fact, living proof of Amy's ability to do what she says. If Amy said it could be done, then it could. He could do it, because she was taking him with her. He had total confidence in her, and he was ready.

* Amy *

Levi's idea shocked her, but it surprised her more that she had not thought of it first. It seems that the mind can set limits on itself, when in actuality few limits exist. She had learned that lesson through her expansions into telepathy, telekinesis and other abilities. She now believed that she had managed to overcome her self-imposed limits and made the quantum mental leap. Now it was startling to realize that she had again held herself back. Levi surprised her many times with his abstract thought. He had been the one that forced her into considering other options. He just didn't give up and refused to accept limits. Now he wanted to explore those limits again, and she was ready. She commented, "We really do make a good team."

She wanted Moon to watch over Levi's body while they were gone. Her mind was always awake and normally could warn Levi of danger, but her mind would be gone during this projection. She truly trusted only Moon to watch over Levi's body. Moon, always anxious to be of help to his master, stood guard over Levi now, as he settled down to rest in meditation. Levi sat in a lotus position with legs crossed and arms out resting on his legs with palms up, as she had instructed him how to relax.

In some ways astral projection would be more difficult with Levi awake. He must execute his own mental exit from his body, but she could help. Pulling Levi's mind close, she let him feel her mental calm. She was relaxing and so was Levi. They floated together side-by-side, invisible. Again, the vibration began, growing increasingly stronger. Levi's body actually vibrated, as she became aware of a visual reference change. She/they were mentally locked together and began to detach from his physical body. Free of the physical now, truly in spirit form, they began to float. They were as vapors

338

upon the wind, without substance, drifting, yet their consciousness were there, floating and observing, hearing, and smelling as if Levi's body was there floating with them.

As they rose above the ground higher and higher, the view expanded to include increasingly more of the area. The silver thread was again there, trailing from Levi's body. It was comforting to see the lifeline to return. Levi was excited and full of questions: how, where, why, what happens now? She tried to explain, but it was very complicated. He decided that the results were the important things and began to consider what they should do next.

He wanted to see if the Simians at the Colorado River were moving yet, so they flew high and fast toward the east. The ground became a blur beneath them as they flew. They saw the terrain change, as the desert began to pass below them. They felt the desert heat as they soared past. They moved at incredible speeds and approached the river even before she anticipated. Suddenly, they were there, circling and slowing, as they descended toward the Simian colony.

It was as if there were no distance or time restrictions. In her research, she discovered that astral projection was not limited to relatively short distances such as they were covering, but often to distant planets. She realized they didn't have to travel across the route, but could simply transport their presence instantly to this or any other location. Maybe she would try that technique on the return trip.

The Simian compound below was very much occupied. It looked like an anthill of activity. This differed from the other Simian compounds they had observed. Then they noticed the wagons. They were very large and looked new. The wagons were parked at the end of the compound and empty. The Simians were definitely planning on moving just as she had seen in her vision and had been told by the dying Simian. She tried to estimate how much time they had before the Simians would start. Certainly, they would have a couple of weeks, maybe longer, before they started, but not much longer than that. Would that be enough time to prepare the Humans?

* Levi *

He felt Amy's calm settle over him like a mantle and his breathing slowed. The calmness comforted and warmed him. He was very relaxed, and felt Amy with him, sharing his mind. He liked that too. Amy was drawing him, compelling him to float with her.

Amy said, "You must exit your own body, I cannot do it for you. Trust me and step out on faith."

He did. He let his mind float with Amy's. It started as a slight vibration and built to an almost physical shaking before he floated away from his body. He knew when it happened, because he could see his body still sitting. As they floated away, he could feel her presence even stronger than before. Amy was in control of this invisible body, but he didn't feel threatened. He would be lost in this situation without her.

It was only minutes before they saw the Simian compound, and saw the wagons and agreed that the story from the dying Simian was true. It also proved that Amy's visions of the future were, in fact, predictions of this Simian migration. It was all true, or will be true, or might be true. It was confusing as to what might be reality and what could be changed.

They returned back through the Mojave Desert settlement and surveyed the area. It was as he remembered it, just as he remembered it. There were no additional defenses or barricades. Nothing! Then he realized that the settlement did not know the Simians were coming. Amy anticipated his unspoken question or more likely, heard his thoughts.

She said, "There is nothing we can do in this state to warn them. We might be able to scare the crap out of them, but nothing more. We will have to return, and send a messenger on horseback to tell them."

* Amy *

The next stop was the Mojave Desert settlement. She moved them there by fading out over the Simian camp and fading in over the settlement. It worked great and Levi was pleased. She could feel his mental embrace, holding on tight. All was in order at this location. They saw the posted patrol at the rock gap where they had almost been killed by the Simian. Levi realized that the settlement didn't know about the migration and became almost frantic about it, until she told him they had time and could send a warrior on horseback, and he could be here in four days of hard riding with two horses. Levi agreed and settled down.

The next stop was the Simian compound at Los Angles where the infamous Gord ruled. They traveled fast but without fading out and in. It was still a fast trip and they were soon approaching the compound, which sat very near the junction of Highways 5 and 405 according to the overhead signs. The compound was identical to the others they had seen, except larger. It had four full circles of structures surrounding the old spacecraft. This was a heavily populated complex.

As they observed the complex, Levi let a gasp out and said, "Look," as he directed her attention to the stockade fence between the first and second rings of buildings. It contained about twenty Humans awaiting death. All were male. In an adjacent fenced area, there were Simians locked up. This seemed strange until she noticed these Simians were smaller. These were Technical class Simians. As Moon had told them, since the mutiny in space of the Warrior (military) Simians, the Technical class were being killed off or imprisoned. This was depressing, and both were ready to go back to the camp.

Levi remained strangely quiet on the return, and she decided to give him his space. His mind was blocked to her, which was unusual for Levi. He remained quiet, as she followed the silver thread back across the distances. He roused himself from his thoughts finally, as they approached the valley. They were yet some ways out following the terrain instead of the silver thread. She knew their exact location. Otherwise, she would have to return the way they came.

Suddenly, Levi said, "I want to go rescue the Humans from the Simian compound."

"Yikes! That's not going to happen. It's far too dangerous and impractical. All you will wind up doing is getting yourself killed."

Levi countered, "I have a plan that will be safe."

Interesting! Levi had a plan? She was surprised when she heard it.

Levi said, "You can change me to look like a Simian, and Moon and I can simply walk into the camp at night and free the Humans."

It was simple but brilliant. Her totally logical mind became a disadvantage sometimes. Oh, to be able to think in the abstract like Levi. The plan could work, but it was also very foolhardy.

* Levi *

He needed to see the location of his enemy Gord. This was a battle that must happen sooner or later, so he wanted to know Gord's location and any other details he could find out. Amy was leading them well, as expected. They were soon at the compound, floating down to look. He knew Amy was storing all the data so he didn't bother trying to memorize it. He was just looking at the activity when he noticed the Humans in the fenced area. There were many, and adjacent was a fenced area with imprisoned Simians also. Amy hadn't noticed this at first. She would have eventually, but she observed where he directed his eyes.

343

Amy replied, "The Simians caged are Technical class like Moon."

Seeing the caged Humans upset him greatly, and he didn't want to see anymore and was ready to go home. As they traveled back, he decided that he must save them. He would become a Simian, and he and Moon could just wander in at night and let them go. That was simple enough, would Amy agree? She would consider the options and say they could plan something together. That was her way of saying, "maybe later." When he told her what he was GOING to do, she acted as expected.

Suddenly, Amy stopped and remained floating in mid-air.

Amy said, "Look below!"

Damn! Simian patrols! How many where there? He could see two patrols traveling toward the valley but still hours out from the defenses. The two patrols weren't traveling together. They were going in the same direction, but one group was maybe thirty minutes behind the other. They must return quickly and warn the warriors. The sentries would be able to see them in about an hour, but the extra time would help to ready the Lancers. They would be scared and he needed to be there to steady them. He thought that without him, they never would have agreed to fight the Simians, but the building legend about Levi the man, made him seem invincible. After his near-death experience, it seemed that he almost was. It was only by Amy's incredible abilities that he remained alive, and even by her accounts, he was minutes away from death.

They continued toward the valley and his sleeping body. Descending toward his body, they

344

noticed a crowd gathered around. Moon was standing between the crowd and his body looking determined and angry. Settled again into his body, he awoke to hear Moon screeching his defiance against all, and Iron Eyes pleading, "Wake him up!" Neither could understand the other.

He opened his eyes and looked. Iron Eyes noticed immediately and called to him. Levi screeched, "I am fine now. Thank you for your help, Moon. You were correct not to let the men approach, but it is all right now." Moon nodded and ambled off. Then he turned angry eyes to Iron Eyes. Levi said, "Damn you, Iron Eyes. It is very dangerous to wake me when I am meditating and Moon could easily have killed you and would have if you tried. You might have even killed me in the process." Iron Eyes was not put aback.

Iron Eyes said, "A remote patrol saw Simians approaching and they needed him. That was two hours ago!"

He was shocked. It couldn't have been that long. It seemed like they had only been gone maybe thirty minutes, but Amy told him that she checked her internal clock and they had been gone five hours and twenty minutes. He looked around and confirmed that the sun was already past its zenith.

Turning back to Iron Eyes he said, "I know about the Simians. There are actually two separate patrols thirty minutes apart and the first one will hit the defenses in an hour. Don't panic, just ready the Lancers as we have practiced." They had practiced deploying three three-man teams to each side, hidden in the trees. He told Iron Eyes to ready a repair crew for the pits, to make any necessary repairs in preparation for the second Simian patrol. Iron Eyes looked at him as if to question, "How do you know?" but accepted the information and orders and left to deploy the teams.

* Amy *

She was trying to find a reasonable approach to dissuade Levi from the dangerous plan to infiltrate the Simian camp. In truth, it was a good plan. She just didn't want him to go, because it was dangerous and she feared for his life. She also knew Levi would go eventually, with or without her help. Therefore, she must schedule the best time, and plan around his plan to insure success and Levi's safety.

She was startled out of her analysis when she saw the Simians below. Two groups separated by several miles, both headed toward the valley defenses. She pointed the groups out to Levi, and they agreed to hurry and prepare the defenders.

Approaching, she saw Moon confronted by the Lancers. They obviously wished to awaken Levi, and Moon was following instructions and preventing it. They settled back in Levi's body, and quickly defused the controversy. Levi spoke to Moon, thanking him and sending him away.

What was the problem? By luck the Lancers had seen the Simians several hours out and had been trying to wake Levi up as soon as the word had reached the camp. That was more than two hours ago. Levi was their courage and leader, even if not in name, and she believed that they probably would cut and run without him. They were emboldened now, as Levi issued the battle plans that she had outlined.

Levi whistled for Moon, telling him what was going on. Moon started jumping around in obvious excitement. He was nervous about facing another Warrior Simian, but now, thanks to the fighting techniques they had taught him, he had a better than average chance.

Levi was faster than a horse, so his best defense was on his own feet relying on his own speed and agility. He and Moon would fight together. They would attack after the initial charge of the Lancers, already poised for a charge from either side of the pass. Everything was ready, and they could do nothing now but wait.

The sentries waved, indicating the approach of the Simians. Soon they could see the first Simian team coming around the hill that had previously blocked the view. The Simians were coming at a fast pace but slowed and finally stopped just before the pits. This was bad! The Simians may have smelled a strong Human scent or maybe it was something else, but they suspected something. Levi reacted quickly without her support. He told Moon to remain hidden, as he jumped out of hiding so the Simian patrol could see him. Indeed they did, as they began screeching in delight and ran toward him. This was a smart move on Levi's part. The Simians' suspicion, or whatever it was, could have destroyed the effect of the pits.

* Levi *

347

Watching the Simians approach the pit field, he realized something was wrong. The Simians stopped to investigate, and the field wouldn't stand much investigation. Without thinking, he leapt to his feet, then thought in time to tell Moon to stay put. He hoped that when they saw him they might attack and get snared in the pits. Boy did they see him. They screeched and charged into the pit field, and to his delight, the first Simian disappeared into a pit followed by a screech of pain, then silence.

Amy said, "That was a good move, but please discuss these things with me first."

He grinned at her and she just shook her head from side to side.

The other two Simians stopped and looked down at their fallen team member, screeching their anger. They moved forward cautiously now, probing the ground with their swords. It didn't take them long to learn. They were skirting the pits now and coming on very fast. He waited in plain sight for the Simians, and they came. The Simians were through the field and came directly for him now, but they were still bunched together. He had no choice, so he waved his left hand, signaling the three Lancers teams on the eastern side to charge. He couldn't give the signal to the western Lancer team to charge. With the Simians still together the Lancers would be charging at each other. He needed to separate the two Simians.

As the first team charged, he notched an arrow in his compound bow and fired at the closest Simian. He didn't hope to kill the Simian, just to piss him off. The arrow struck its chest, but the denseness of its hide prevented the arrow from

348

entering deeply. The power of the bow did launch the arrow hard enough to enter the Simian a couple of inches and cause pain. It screeched loudly and charged forward in obvious rage to crush this Human. Hearing the charging Lancers, the second Simian turned to face the attackers.

He was in a fight for his life again against this big ugly golden bastard, but he wanted this fight. He needed to perform in front of this audience if he ever hoped to lead their army, and that is what he needed to do.

* Amy *

She was so proud of Levi as he stood fearless in the open, waiting for the Simians to approach. His bravado had already killed the one Simian that had fallen in the pit, by luring him forward. She could notice things through his eyes that Levi never could and now she noticed the pride on the Lancers' faces as he stood tall, challenging the Simians.

Being brave was not going to be enough. They had to ensure success, and to do that, the two remaining Simians had to be separated. The Lancers had practiced on a single target. Duel targets would be devastating to the Lancers. The horses needed room to maneuver, and space for the Lancers to launch their practiced attack. They decided to commit one team and hold the other, while he attempted to separate the two remaining Simians.

The compound bow launched the insulting sting on the closest Simian and succeeded in angering it and splitting the two enraged Simian. Both Simians were screeching their anger and challenge. Neither Simian showed any fear of Humans at all. Obviously, Humans were to be killed and eaten. Humans were unworthy of any respect. The Simians appeared confused, however. She was quite sure neither had ever seen a Human stand to face or fight a Simian.

The first Lancer team engaged the rear Simian. As the Lancers came, it was swinging. The sword took the first two lances in mid-air and chopped the ends off, turning the force as it ducked under the blunt end of the now short lances. As the two horses and riders went past on both sides, the creature turned to launch an attack at the rider on his left. It was at that point the third rider connected with his lance. It caught the Simian in the shoulder, making it turn and miss its swing. The lance imbedded deep in its shoulder causing a deep guttural screech of pain, but it did not knock it down. The lance didn't break as designed, instead the sudden impact and density of the Simian's body caused the lance and rider to stop in mid-air, as the horse rammed into the Simian, finally knocking it down. The horse ran on and the Human and Simian were now scrambling to get up. The Simian was the faster and pulled the lance out as it advanced toward the crawling man, scrambling to get away. The Simian was on him in seconds and vented its anger by chopping the dying man over and over. The man never had a chance once he fell.

The Simian was so enraged that it failed to hear the second charging team until it was too late. The Simian was caught by two lances simultaneously striking it in the upper chest and hip. This time the lances went deep and true before breaking off as the riders passed. Almost immediately following, the third lance struck it directly in the stomach driving deep. The Simian fell dead.

* Levi *

The battle seemed to take hours, but actually the whole scene took only seconds to unfold, while the last Simian was approaching him. He was very proud of these Lancers; they had attacked as a team and won. Yes, they had beaten a Simian in combat. This was a first and would be a source of pride for the tribe. He was also sad for the death of the warrior and sorry that he could not remember his name, but proud that he had died bravely. He would be honored.

The Simian approached, screeching in anger as it narrowed the gap between them. He hadn't been able to launch the other group of Lancers, but the third three-man team from the first group was charging now on this approaching Simian. It turned to face the charge, as the warriors were dropping their lances into jousting position. As the other Simian had done before, it chopped at the lances diverting their aim then leaped to the side, swinging around and chopping with its sword to meet the third lance, just barely averting being impaled. The swing of the sword continued into the horse, making a death wound in the horse's neck. The horse fell at its feet and the rider went flying over the horse's head and landed hard on the ground in front of the Simian. Oh no, it was Jimmy Standing!

He was off at a run telling Amy, "Give me a plan." He wasn't going to let Jimmy die this close to him. Could he reach him in time? Maybe. He pulled his swords as he ran. The Simian was raising its sword to dispatch Jimmy, as he neared. He screeched a challenge in Simian, which stopped the giant in mid-swing. It turned to stare then charged him.

Amy provided the plan, and he met the Simian's charge. Not directly but turning the Simian's speed and weight against it by spinning and diverting the force of the blows. His swords connected on the side of its thrusts to divert the massive force, never directly. As strong as he was, he couldn't absorb a direct blow from the Simian. It was just too strong. He rolled, spun, twisted and struck when he had an opportunity. He connected with numerous minor stabs. The technique of using two swords was working well. He remained always just out of reach. It drove the Simian mad and it screeched in frustration.

Jimmy was still dazed, as Moon dragged him to safety. He could see that Moon watched and was ready to join the fight, but couldn't find a way. They were fighting so fast that Moon would have been in the way.

He hadn't fought this way before and assumed this technique was a form of martial arts. This was exciting. He was cheating death by fractions of an inch. His arms were flying through the air. He tried kicking the Simian at one point, but only succeeded in hurting his toes. He thought idly that a weapon on the toe of his boots might be a thought for the future.

* Amy *

Amy blurted, "Damn it, Levi, now I have to recalculate the attack." She wished he would not do the unexpected. It put him in danger. She thought about how silly that sounded, this whole thing was crazy. She did understand that Levi wanted to save Jimmy and was adjusting her plan from defensive to offensive. She calculated the time, no not enough. Jimmy would die unless ... she screeched a challenge in Simian. Yes, the Simian couldn't resist a challenge. The shock of the challenge saved Jimmy's life. Now what? Here it came!

The calculation, timing, and moves were flowing from her into Levi's conscious and subconscious mind. She observed, reacted and countered.

This Simian was fast, very fast, and it took all her efforts to stay out of its reach. The Simian was fighting without error, which was frustrating. She wanted Levi to remain calm, because the longer the fight raged, the better the chances of the Simian making a mistake. She promised, "It will happen." This Simian made no mistakes, but neither did Levi. It became obvious that the first one to make a mistake would lose. They fought on for what seemed like hours, but finally the Simian made a mistake. It became frustrated and overextended its reach, trying to catch Levi off guard. The Simian left its legs unprotected too long. She saw it and, while dodging the Simian's sword, spun Levi, bringing his sword over and down cutting deep into its leg. The Simian screeched in pain and fell to its knees but was still fighting. It planted its double thumbed hand quickly on the ground to get up, but before it could stand, Levi severed his lower arm with a heaving blow. It was over that quickly, as she sent Levi in a low spinning sideways swing, which buried his sword deep in its neck. It felt like he was chopping a tree stump with an axe. The Warrior fell forward heavily as it died. Levi stood tall and breathed a sigh of relief. Only then did they hear the cheering. The Lancers had gathered, watching.

Levi had won his eagle feather with this group. He would be their war leader for as long as he wished. They would do anything for him. And, look at Levi! He can be so full of himself sometimes. He seemed to always forget that it was she who fought the battle. Well, she did allow him to believe he did more than he did, so maybe it was her fault also.

* Levi *

It was over and he had won again, and felt very pleased with himself, absolutely cocky. His timing, movements and strikes were totally coordinated. His strength and abilities with swords, knives, hell everything, were exhilarating, exciting and euphoric.

Amy commented, "You are enjoying this too much."

He just tried to explain that it was a man thing.

Amy calmly said, "Take care OLD man or I will bring you home!"

He understood what she meant and said, "Okay, Okay, Amy I will curb my appetite." He could see her grin! Their battles were as welcome as those with the enemy.

He was startled out of his momentary self-glory by a scream. He turned to the pits where some of the men and the women were making repairs. Damn, they had forgotten about the second Simian patrol. There wasn't much that could have been done, but how could they have forgotten?

Amy said, "The patrol isn't due for another ten minutes."

Had it only been twenty minutes since the battle started? It was unbelievable, but true. It seemed like he had fought for hours.

He searched the area and saw the source. The three Simians were standing on the other side of the pit holding one of the women. Mercifully, she was already dead. The scream had come from another of the women who had just noticed them. The Simians were watching, and looked as if they had been watching for some time. They made no attempt to come across the pit field. In fact, they turned and ran, dropping the dead woman. He couldn't tell who the poor woman was.

Amy announced, "The Simians have seen too much and must be stopped."

Yes, they had seen the Lancers, Moon, their defenses and him. They had probably seen the Lancers in action and him fighting the last Simian. Their responsibility now would be to report back to Gord. He agreed, "Yes, they must be stopped."

He whistled to the remaining armed Lancers, circled his arm over his head and pointed to the fleeing Simians. They understood immediately and spurred forward following the path through the pit field in hot pursuit. Iron Eyes led the four armed teams of Lancers after the fleeing Simians. The

Simians were not bunched, as was their custom. They seemed to have a new priority.

From a distance, they saw the first three-man Lancer team catch the last fleeing Simian. The Simian didn't even turn and all three lances caught it in the back. It went down, but got back up in time to be hit by the next team. It was writhing on the ground in obvious death thralls. The second team finished him off, but the other two Simians had gained valuable ground. Amy said the Simian had sacrificed itself to gain distance for the other two. There were only two teams left with lances and they charged the second Simian. This one turned to fight and was successful in repelling one of the lances, but the second and third got him. The Simian downed a horse and rider. They couldn't tell if it killed the man, before the fourth team finished it off. Two Simians down, but the third one was gone and no armed Lancers left to pursue.

* Amy *

With the escape of the one Simian, all of her plans had to be accelerated. Their secret was out and the Simians recognized the threat of an organized defense and were obligated to report it. The tribe could expect a full-scale attack now. That is what a smart leader would do anyway. Crush the resistance before it had time to grow.

He realized there was another possible option to a smart leader. Let the migrating Simians fight the battle. Yes, that is what Gord might do if he was smart. He would let the Colorado River Simians take any loses. After all, he had already lost six of his army previously, and now another five. Eleven lost to Levi in one form or fashion, so Gord could not really know what he was up against yet. Yes, the smart move would be to let the migrating Simians move into this valley in force. She knew she was right and that would play into their plan.

The Lancers were very proud of themselves, and well they should be. This was the first organized defense and attack against Simians that anyone had ever heard of. More importantly, they had won. This team, including Levi, had killed five Simians and lost only three Humans and two horses. The woman turned out to be the mate of the Lancer killed fighting the last Simian. She wondered if the Lancer's anger let him take too many chances and had died for it. Levi stated simply, "At least his suffering is over."

The patrol celebrated their victory, cheering and congratulating each other. They really had done well. They were also anxious to continue the tradition Levi had started and busily removed black shiny teeth for their trophy necklaces. Levi, the original team and even Moon had been envied for their trophies. She was glad Moon had made those necklaces. Everyone sought a trophy, and most got one today. Levi had earned his sixth tooth and Moon, although he didn't get a tooth, got a trophy also. Moon was dragging a dead horse off into the bushes. Levi said, "Moon finally got his horse." Levi was smiling as he watched.

Amy explained to Levi what needed to be done and how the plan would need to be played out and sold to all the parties. She told him almost everything, and he understood the wisdom of the

357

plan. Levi understood that timing was now critical, and he would need Iron Eyes and Jimmy to make it work.

* Levi *

It was over so quickly. It seemed like they had been battling for hours, but actually the whole conflict had taken less than forty-five minutes. He had been unable to help with the last battle. He could have, but had temporarily forgotten he could have run as fast as the horses. He could have pursued the Simians but remembered that fact too late, and Amy didn't want him running into another battle. While fantastic in battle, she really wasn't a fighter at heart. She was a lover.

Levi allowed them their celebration, while using the time to fashion how to present the plan. As he was thinking, he noticed Moon coming toward him carrying another black Simian tooth. Moon reached toward him, removed his necklace with his double thumbed hands, installed the sixth tooth and put it back around his neck. Moon was proud of him, and it showed. He appreciated Moon's pride in him. Moon got serious and looked at him.

Moon asked, "I can eat horse now?"

After the tension of the day, that hit him as funny, and he busted out laughing. He even saw Amy grinning from ear to ear. After he was able to talk, he allowed that it was all right to eat the dead horses. Moon was pleased and took off.

In the face of such seriousness, the gathered Humans seemed shocked to hear him laugh. They watched him to see if he was all-together. After a few minutes they resumed their talking, although it seemed that someone was always watching. Oh well. The legend of the crazy superman grows again. They would say, "Levi, the man who laughs at the enemy."

He called Iron Eyes, Wolf, Jimmy Standing and Dawn to attend a meeting. They looked shocked but quickly agreed. Once they were settled in a somewhat private area under a tree, he presented the plan just as Amy had revealed and rehearsed him.

He explained the facts: the Owens Valley Tribe could never hope to defend against the Simians without many more horses. Like today, they had killed five Simians, but had lost three people and two horses. Of course it was a tragedy to lose Humans, but horses represented the only means to defend against the Simians. Otherwise, the situation was hopeless. They nodded their heads in agreement. He explained how the Los Angles Simians were the ones attacking, but that he expected them to pull back for a while, and explained why. The real threat was the Colorado River Simians. They would soon defeat the Mojave Desert settlement and move on to settle in Owens Valley. This obviously would mean the tribe's destruction as well. Again, they nodded in agreement. He explained that the Mojave Desert settlement had more than five hundred extra horses, and that horses were the preferred food for Simians. As a result, the Simians would go after them, consume them, and they would be lost to the Owens Valley Army forever. This brought wide eyes and knowing looks passed between them. He explained how the Colorado River Simians had to be defeated.

It was becoming obvious to those gathered that the Owens Valley Indians must join forces with the Mojave Desert settlement to defeat the Colorado River Simians migrating west. By joining forces they would improve the chances of winning and the horses would provide the means to defeat the Simians, assuming they got there before the Simians. Once the threat of the Simians was eliminated, the Mojave Desert army could move west to help defend against the Los Angeles Simians. The group looked at each other and nodded their agreement.

Iron Eyes said, "What specifically do you want done and why us in particular?"

He launched into the plan. "Someone has to present the plan to the Chief and elders of the tribe. Their approval and support is necessary to the plan. It must happen, and quickly. Iron Eyes, you must do that part. I want Wolf to support you and help with the training of the new three-hundred-man Lancer army. Another reason for Wolf is because he is now sporting a trophy necklace with three Simian teeth." Everyone grinned at Wolf at that comment. He continued, "The tribe must replenish the supply of lances and make enough for a six hundred-man/horse army of Lancers. In addition, saddles and equipment will need to be made for the tribes' three hundred-horse Lancer force. Wagons will have to be built to haul the lances and supplies and be on the road within three weeks. The trained horseback Lancers must follow within a week. This way they would arrive at the settlement at approximately the same time." Everything he said brought gasps of astonishment.

"The horses here must be taken back to the main tribe and every usable horse brought in and used to train every warrior in jousting. An army of three hundred must be trained, equipped, and in route to the Mojave Desert settlement within a month, assuming we have a month." They shook their heads in disbelief, but he explained that the Simian that had gotten away destroyed the timetable. The Simians would eventually be back and if the Mojave Desert army wasn't ready with their horses to assist them, you could kiss it all goodbye. They solemnly nodded agreement again.

Jimmy Standing and Dawn were needed to go to the Mojave Desert community. They were to see Al Baker and tell him Levi Walkingbear sent them with information. Jimmy was to explain the plan to them, mindful that the settlement does not yet know the Simians are coming committed to their total destruction. He sternly said, "Jimmy, you must presented the plan, and you must convince them. Everything is in your hands. Do you understand?" A wide-eyed Jimmy nodded. Jimmy would take Thunder as proof that he was the messenger of Levi Walkingbear. For the same reason, Dawn would take Lightning. Dawn's reason for going could not be explained at this time, but her presence was necessary. Not understanding, but completely trusting him, she also nodded.

Jimmy and Dawn were to tell Al everything they knew about him and what they had seen him do and all that had happened. He warned them that Al would not at first believe that he was the same Levi he remembered. His personal message to Al was, "It is Levi, but something incredible has happened to me, and I will explain when I get there." He explained that they must persuade Al to send a herd of three hundred and fifty horses along with enough warriors to bring them here and for training. He wanted Jimmy to convince them and lead the horses and Guard members back for intensive training and for transportation of the Owens Valley army back to assist them in their battle.

He told Dawn, "Your job is to stay at the settlement and remain close to Al. Tell Al it is important to keep you with him and protect you until I get there. There is a major need for you to remain close to Al, which would be explained in due time, but couldn't be understood at this time."

Dawn asked, "Where will you be?"

After thinking and staring for a few seconds, he told them the truth, "I intended to take Moon and enter the Los Angeles Simian compound and release the captured Humans and other Simians like Moon, and then return here to camp. If all is on schedule, I will then head to the desert community." That brought startled looks from everyone, but everything they had heard in the last few minutes had them already shook up. They were all in their private thoughts and said nothing more.

Jimmy was concerned that he might need Thunder, but he assured him that he and Moon could actually travel faster on foot. He told Jimmy that he wanted him to have Thunder to replace the horse he had lost in battle and, he thought to himself, Moon ate.

As a last favor, he told Jimmy to ask Al's tradesmen to make a special weapon for him. He told them that the desert community did not have the necessary trees to make the lances, but were excellent tradesmen and could make many tools and weapons. He gave Jimmy the plans for the weapon he wished them to make for him there. Jimmy studied the plan for a minute, calling it interesting.

* Amy *

Levi presented the plan well, and they were persuaded and saw the wisdom and necessity of everything being presented. Now, if all can be presented and sold to the respective groups, it might just work. At least they could fight back.

The timing was critical. They had very little time and lots to be done. She had planned the timing and assigned tasks to meet the schedule, and these were the people that could get it done. Iron Eyes and Wolf were needed to push the tribe. She had confidence in them, and motivation was present for all to see. She was taking a chance with Jimmy, because he was so young, but he idolized Levi and had seen more than his share of the battles. He was a sub-chief's son, who could only help to support the plan at the tribal level, and Levi had saved his life, which would also help. Wolf was also young, maybe twenty-five years old, but experienced and a good storyteller. She needed Dawn to monitor the situation at the desert settlement.

Dawn had been a surprise. Amy had discovered that once linked with Dawn's mind, she had been unable to break it. Some of the link had diminished. She no longer felt the emotions, for which she was thankful, but she was unable to break the link with

Dawn's major senses such as sight and hearing. She continued to see through Dawn's eyes and hear through her ears. She may have maintained other senses, but they weren't apparent. It had been several days since she had linked and the link had been less every day, but it had settled down to what she experienced today. She believed that it was permanent. Since this ability existed, she decided to use it to their advantage. That ability could now be used to monitor her senses, therefore know what was happening at the Desert Settlement. Her plan was sound, if everyone did his or her part.

Her biggest surprise was the fact that Levi intended to go back to the Los Angles compound. That was not part of her plan. She knew he wanted to, but thought with what was going on, he would put it off for a while. That was not to be; they both had agendas that needed to be met. Levi was stubborn so he would have his way; she knew that.

CHAPTER 15
(THE ARMY)

* Levi *

Everyone knew what they had to do and started on their separate responsibilities. Two three-man/horse teams were left to watch the pass, while the others left for the main camp with Iron Eyes and Wolf. They didn't expect a return of the Simians for a while, but precautions were in place not to fight but solely to be able to warn the camps. A single team could not defend itself, while two might barely escape. No, they were for moral support and watches. The horses could get them away from the Simians, if necessary, and maybe lead the Simians away, while a runner left to warn the camp.

Jimmy and Dawn left with him and Moon, heading south toward the Los Angeles Simian compound. At the halfway point, Jimmy and Dawn would split off and head east; following the instructions and directions he had given them. On horseback he anticipated the trip would take Jimmy and Dawn about five days of hard riding. At least two days would be with him and Moon before they split up. It would take another two days to reach the Los Angeles compound, and another night to liberate the captives. It should take another two days to make it back, to the midpoint between the Owen Valleys and the Mojave settlement. They hadn't decided which direction they would go yet from there. If all went well, the horses should be on their way from the Mojave Desert settlement by the time they returned from Los Angeles, assuming he made it. Amy sure wasn't happy about this trip, but he didn't give her much of a choice.

He and Amy hoped that all would be successful for their friends. Were they right? Maybe they should be advising retreat and evacuation, but where were they going to run? Was there any place that was safe? Even if there was a safe spot, it wouldn't be safe long. The Simians were growing and spreading out. Sooner or later these Simians would reach everywhere or it might be the Simians en route in space, but future existence for Humans was bleak anywhere.

He had told Moon about the imprisoned Humans and Technical class Simians and what he intended to do. Moon was afraid but wanted to follow him wherever he went and would do whatever he wanted him to do. Moon did want to free the imprisoned Technical Simians, all were his associates and co-workers on board ship, but he didn't care much about the Humans. Moon did understand his reasons however and would help him.

His opinion of Moon had changed drastically since learning how Moon had saved him when he was stabbed. Moon risked his life several times to save him and he owed him. Even more so, he liked him. Since that time, he had practiced and sparred with Moon each day. He, well Amy, had been teaching Moon hand-to-hand combat, many martial arts and sword fighting techniques previously unfamiliar to him. Moon was fast and a quick study and had learned much. He sparred with Moon mainly to practice his timing and coordination. Certainly he couldn't easily hurt Moon, but Moon had gotten very good and connected a few times. Amy had to repair several broken ribs and once a collarbone, due to Moon's improving skills. He would rather have Moon on his side than any other person. Well, he wasn't a person was he? At this point Moon, even though he was smaller than most Warrior class Simians, could hold his own with any of them now, due to these skills.

* Amy *

She trusted Moon completely. He had now saved Levi's life three times. Yes, she was happy to have Moon as a companion to Levi. Moon had barely survived his battle with the Warrior Simian. Except for the extra effort, maybe from fear or outrage at seeing Levi stabbed, Moon would not have survived. Moon had been lucky, but she believed you make your own luck. Now Moon was more skilled, and she wanted him to have the extra edge, call it luck, since he would be fighting at Levi's side.

After the battle and Levi's recovery, she had decided to train Moon in fighting techniques. If he was going to be at Levi's side fighting, then he should be able to fight well. Levi liked the suggestion and saw the logic. He started sparring with Moon every day with blunt sticks as swords and in hand-to-hand combat. Moon learned very fast and began to anticipate some of his/her moves. Levi's complete defense against Simians was avoiding being hit, and when Moon learned and began to connect with blows, it did damage. She also learned never to use the same moves too often with Moon.

She was pleased with Moon's progress with the training, especially now that he was going to be Levi's back up in the coming campaign into the LA compound. Moon could stand on an equal basis with a Warrior Simian now, and it was very likely that those combined abilities could again save Levi's life.

Levi asked, "Can you make me look like a Simian?"

"Duh!" What a surprise, there was no way he was going to walk into a Simian compound as a Human. "Yes, of course, but only in appearance. I cannot alter your mass and density, or strength to match theirs without adding to your normal mass, but I can make you appear larger and resemble one. It will be done before you reach the compound."

Over the two days of travel heading south, Levi stayed busy indoctrinating Jimmy and Dawn as to what to expect when they got there and telling them everything they needed to know about the people, their history, organization, defenses and anything else they felt was important to the mission. Jimmy was a sponge, absorbing everything Levi had to say. Jimmy was determined not to fail, as much for Levi as his tribe and family. She believed he would not fail. Dawn would do what she was asked, although she remained curious as to why. Dawn could not know why her role was important yet.

* Levi *

368

Jimmy was proud to be called upon for this important responsibility and prepared enthusiastically for the task. He talked constantly, asking questions.

Jimmy asked, "What had happened in the Mojave Desert settlement? What is it like? Who is Al Baker? What are the people like? Where is the Colorado River Simian compound? Why are the Simians leaving?"

Jimmy went and on continually. He didn't fault Jimmy and, in his place, probably would have done the same himself. Dawn was always close, listening and learning, but the questions were always in her eyes, "Why me? What is the reason?"

Amy said, "You will have to tell Jimmy and Dawn something about who you were, sooner or later, before we split up."

Amy was right. He had been an old man when he left the desert stronghold and now, well, how do you explain what he is today? Both sides would not believe the other without a good story and believe they must. So, he told them part of the truth and part lie. He said, "I am actually eighty years old," which brought gasps of disbelief. He described to them how it was before the end of civilization, and made them believe, because he knew so much about what life was like then. Finally, he told them, "I found a hidden pre-war science research facility and disturbed some vials. I accidentally exposed myself to some of the medical cultures. It wasn't until later that I started noticing the changes. I started getting younger and stronger, and now I am as you see. I am capable of many things that they will find hard to believe. While I don't understand what happened, I just accept it as a gift."

He had no idea if they believed his story, but suspected that they did. They had seen him do many unbelievable things and really, what choice did they have? Amy made the story even more believable by beginning the alterations of his body as they traveled.

* Amy *

She started making changes to Levi's body during the trip. The change was taking place very slowly as they traveled, but everyone noticed. Moon kept looking suspiciously over at him as they jogged side-by-side, mile after mile. Jimmy and Dawn were somewhat pressed to keep the horses moving at the fast pace being set. She was altering his size, making his legs, arms and torso bigger, his skin was turning lighter, and golden hair began to grow over his body. At one point, he had to stop and tell Jimmy and Dawn what he was doing and why. They only nodded with wide eyes, but Moon was getting scared. Levi had to talk to him to calm him. Moon remained convinced that Levi was a spirit. She altered his facial features and changed the structure of his mouth to grow the black teeth. The double lips fell in place and the extra thumbs sprouted. They had both forgotten about the extra big toe and had no replacement boots, so she left the feet alone. He didn't have to change completely, only to appear Simian. It would be at night anyway. He would pass for Simian, judging from the looks on everyone's face.

She had learned one very surprising fact resulting from linking with Dawn. The link did not dissipate further, and she was sensing Dawn's fear of Levi through this link now. Levi was more man than Dawn had ever known, which had thrilled her, but now, finding out that he was actually eighty years old and capable of being a Simian, and God knows what else, she was frightened. Dawn was anxious to get away from Levi, get to the desert settlement and get her job done, whatever that was.

By mid-afternoon of the second day they said their farewells and took off in separate directions. Dawn was not using telepathy; Dawn's signals came only from her ability to read Dawn's internal mental activity, which meant distance could potentially make a difference. She intended to constantly monitor her mind so there was no chance she could lose her signal through the distance. Actually, she had no choice, it seemed permanent in that once linked always linked, but there might be limits.

* Levi *

After leaving Jimmy and Dawn, he and Moon jogged throughout the day and most of the night, stopping only to eat rations they brought with them and get a few hours' sleep. By sunup they had donned the Los Angeles Simian uniforms they recovered and were again jogging. His metamorphous into a Simian was complete. They looked like two Simians jogging home, which is what they wanted. By the end of the third day, they could see the Simian compound. Amy had made him taller by almost a foot so he appeared to be a normal size Warrior class Simian, but Moon was still noticeably a Technical class Simian. They had seen other patrols, but none close enough to detect anything abnormal about the pair. They approached the compound, found a secluded place to settle in and waited until well into the night. Amy had already planned their escape route, so there was nothing more to do but sleep.

Amy woke him well after midnight saying, "It is time to go."

Moon was already awake and ready, so they continued the march. There were torches burning randomly along the archways, but they entered the compound without incident. The Simian compounds did not have guards or defensible perimeters. It never occurred to the Simians that an enemy would dare attack them. Their arrogance made it easy to enter and move through the compound. Moon had told them that, unlike the Technical Simians, Warrior Simians had little social life. Their existence was simple. They hunted, slept, ate, worked and did the bidding of the leader. That breed had been genetically engineered strictly for war, and unfortunately, any form of morality had also been bred out. As a result, there would not be much idle talking and migrating around within the compound to worry about. Hopefully, this would be easy.

Moving through the compound, they saw only a few Simians, and those appeared to be guards for the Humans and Technical Simians in the next fenced area. There was one guard for the Humans and two watching the Simians. The separate fenced areas were far enough apart that the guards could not see each other. They decided to double up and take out the one guard on the Humans first so the others wouldn't be alerted.

They walked up to the guard and as he turned to watch them, Moon kicked the Simian under the chin ... hard. The strength of a Simian was awesome and when it connected, it inflicted massive damage. This move was unexpected and sudden, and the eyes of the Simian guard rolled back, but before it could fall, Moon grabbed and snapped the neck of the already dead guard. "Damn," Levi thought. "That was good." He was glad Moon was on his side.

The Humans had been watching, but now they were standing and pointing. He walked up to them and told them quietly that they were being rescued. They were shocked to hear English coming out of a Simian's mouth. One of the men came to him and asked what was happening. He said, "There isn't time to explain, but if you want to live, you need to do exactly what I tell you." They shot questioning looks at each other and nodded in agreement. He instructed them, "Stay put and remain quiet until we come back. We will then lead you out. Do not run; you must appear that you are being herded. If you run, it will alert the camp and you will be caught. There will be other Simians leaving with us, but it will be safe if you follow instructions." Again they nodded. They were afraid, but willing. What choice did they have, stay and die or go and maybe live?

* Amy *

373

Everything was on schedule. They had surveyed the camp and it was as she remembered. They were not challenged and saw no Simians other than the three guards. To take the two guards would make noise, so she wanted them to take out the single guard first. When Levi told Moon, he nodded and proceeded toward the guard. She always knew what Levi was going to do because she coordinated his body, but what Moon did completely surprised her. Moon had always been somewhat fearful when it came to fighting Warrior Simians. This was probably from years of intimidation and many defeats at their hands. What she saw now was totally contrary to expectations. She expected Levi to initiate the attack and Moon to help, but Moon launched the attack using fighting techniques she had taught him. He was sudden, fearless, vicious and totally deadly. Moon shocked her again by dropping to the dead Simian and digging out a tooth. Levi had really started something with that first tooth. Now everyone was risking their lives to earn one.

Approaching the Technical Simians pen in the dim light, Levi and Moon each chose a guard, separated and headed in the direction of their respective quarry. In Levi's modified condition he would not be efficient in battle and needed an advantage, so she timed his approach to be slightly behind Moon. Again, Moon struck viciously, kicking suddenly and bringing his sword around and down at the stunned Warrior. It was over quickly, but there had been some noise, which attracted the other guard, as she had hoped. As the second guard turned toward the scuffle, Levi swung his sword over and down hard into the Simian's neck. The strike was strong and deep, chopping sideways into its neck. She had coiled Levi's muscles for this strike and he delivered a powerful stroke. The surprise was total and the Simian stood motionless as Levi continued his stroke, reversing directions, then spinning to make an identical chop into the other side of its neck. The Simian really never knew what happened. She noticed that the Simian's neck was almost completely severed, and it was obviously dead.

The Technical class Simians looked in awe and apprehension at Moon and Levi. Never had they seen one of their class defeat a Warrior class Simian. They were even more amazed when they recognized that it was someone they knew.

Moon screeched low and fast, "You're being freed and will be joining us now. We saved your lives by freeing you. You are now obligated to me and Levi."

This was their code of conduct. Moon didn't wait for an agreement but quickly opened the door and told them that they would be escorting the Humans out of camp and that the Humans were not to be harmed. There were no arguments, and Moon was in obvious control of them. This was the beginning of Moon's army.

* Levi *

After Moon made his second kill, he dropped down to remove the black tooth of the Simian he had killed and reminded Levi to do likewise. He complied with Moon's wishes and took the tooth.

This would make seven teeth for his necklace. The teeth were dense and heavy. Many more teeth and he would not be able to comfortably wear the necklace. The released Simians looked confused as they watched this procedure.

They quietly moved back through the courtyard to the Humans' cage, releasing and keeping them surrounded. They moved at a normal pace out of the compound to prevent drawing attention, assuming they were seen at all. It didn't seem likely though. They traveled faster once they were out of sight and sound of the compound, much to the relief of the Humans. They traveled through the night, following old highways en route over the mountain and out of the Los Angeles basin. They should be over the pass and onto safer ground by mid-afternoon.

There were fifteen Humans and fifteen Simians, not counting himself and Moon.

Amy said, "You need to start thinking about food for everyone soon, before the Simians start looking at the Humans."

Moon had been giving them the rules as they traveled. Simians were not to eat Humans or horses. At the mention of horses, they perked up to think that there were still horses, only to be disappointed to find out they could not eat them. The Simians stared in disbelief when Moon told them that Levi was the leader, and he was Human. He did not look Human, even though Amy had already started changing him back. They would soon see the changes taking place and would believe.

As Moon was talking to the Simians, Levi talked to the Humans. They did not believe he was Human either but remained interested in his story.

He told them about the armies gathering in the desert for battle against the Simians, the migration of the Arizona Simian compound toward the west and the expansion of the Los Angeles compound into Owens Valley. They listened to the information but were more interested in the immediate personal impact on them.

They asked, "What is going to happen to us now?"

He freed them. He told the Humans, "You can go or stay; it doesn't matter." He did suggest that they stay together until they crossed the mountains, but it was up to them. They were welcome to join in the fight also. Upon hearing that they were free, one of the Humans broke rank and ran. He was allowed to leave, to the great relief of the others. Now the Humans knew they were not going to be eaten by these Simians. You could see the obvious release of tension.

As they reached the foothills, he told Moon that he was going ahead and find food for them all. Soon he was miles ahead and hunting in the woods with his bow. He moved through the forest with stealth now, finding varied game. By the time the group caught up, he had two deer, a large hog and two fat turkeys. There was a small fire crackling and the turkeys plucked and roasting along with two ham quarters. He figured this would be enough for everyone. It would have to do for a while at any rate.

* Amy *

377

After the raid on the compound and liberation of the captives, the escape route took them down Highway 91 to Interstate 15 and over the summit in the San Bernardino Mountains. The Humans were undernourished, weak and disturbingly slow from their ordeal, but they traveled as fast as possible and finally reached a point of relative safety at the foot of the mountains before the summit. She believed that the group was safe from pursuit, because they were a long way away from the Simian compound now, and they had stayed on the road for the most part, which would make it more difficult for the Simians to track. Feeling somewhat safe and knowing that the Humans would be even slower trying to make the grade, she suggested that Levi use the time to proceed ahead and forage for food. He wasn't in one of his grumpy moods today and took the suggestion well.

During Levi's absence from the group, she had changed him even more and, although many Simian features remained, he was much closer to the normal Levi. She could have changed him much faster, but the group must be able to recognize him and see the final change so there would be no doubt of a trick or switch. This was part of the magic.

By the time the group caught up, Levi had raw meat for the Simians and cooked pork and turkeys for the Humans. The Simians and Humans stared in reverence at his physical changes, but they dug into the food hungrily. The men had been imprisoned for several days and had not been fed. They ate hungrily and were soon full and tired but anxious to talk and learn more about what was going on, and Levi was anxious to tell them.

The leader of their group was named Bob Reasoner. He was of average height, weight, and build, but what made him stand out was his long blond hair, bushy beard and sky-blue eyes. All but two of the men were from his village, which was in the low hills east of Bakersfield. Until recently they had been fairly free from the Simians but were attacked about three weeks ago by twelve Simians. They devastated their village and killed about sixty people. They raped and killed many of the women and captured about twenty-five men. Of that original group, only twelve remained alive. All the others had been dragged, kicking and screaming, out of the cage and eaten. They had been kept for food, but enough Humans had been coming in dead to feed the colony. It was no surprise that the Human population was low in the area, these Simians consumed large quantities of flesh daily and these men had watched it happen. Most were still in shock from the ordeal.

Of the other two Humans, one man, the man that left, was from around the Los Angeles area.

The other man spoke up, "My name is Fred Becker, and I have lost everyone I ever loved to the damned Simians. I have nowhere to go, and if there is going to be a fight, I am going with you."

Fred was unimpressive to look at. He was smallish in size with short black hair and beard. His brown eyes tended to look away and seldom directly into Levi's eyes. She didn't detect any dishonesty. It was more like he was somewhat modest but sincere.

Bob said, "The rest of us have to go home and see what is left of our families, and how we can help what was left of the community."

He believed that there would be a strong desire to seek revenge in the future if there was a way to do so but that would have to come later. Levi told them that so far their resistance had killed twelve Simians, and now had the means to fight back. The men were excited to know that Simians could be killed. Never had they heard of this before and truly believed that Levi was something special. They had watched his transformation and saw that he was indeed Human and accepted his story.

Surprisingly, there was little discussion among the Simians, but there was some general discussion of life in the camp as Moon was questioning them. They seemed dejected, defeated and lost, which they probably were. Previously, Moon had talked about how hard life was for the Technical Simians since their loss of power to the Warrior Simians. The Warriors had destroyed any social structure and replaced it with a morally degenerate form of military structure.

She listened to both groups and realized there was going to be a great need to develop communications between the Simians and Humans. Neither group could understand nor speak the other's language. The two races could never work together without communication, and right now she was the only means of communication.

She made a quick search of her data bank and found an interesting reference to a hand signing language used by the deaf in the technical age. Perhaps she could develop a form of a hand signing language to use between the races. This language was long since dead, but still recorded in her memory banks.

Her mind was already working out the intricacies of a common third language, neither Simian nor English, incorporating common anatomies and eliminating the second thumb, when she noticed Levi smiling and nodding at her. "Damn! Now he has me cussing." She was startled to realize that Levi could now read her unblocked thoughts as well. She had strongly suspected, but he just confirmed it whether he realized it or not. This was good, though. Now she could proceed with another plan she had been working on.

* Levi *

He was always happy to talk about his accomplishments. Many of the feats astounded even him. He would never admit it, but he was never stupid enough to believe it was he performing alone. It was Amy. Everything was Amy. She constantly surprised him with new ideas, and this was a great one, creating and teaching a sign language to both races. He had thought about the communication problem also, but not about a solution. He thought about how inconvenient it had been to translate between Moon and Iron Eyes. Now the problem would be worse with the addition of fifteen more Simians.

Amy's image showed surprise along with the realization that he saw her thoughts. Oh well, she would know eventually, the link between them was strengthening. Sometimes it was hard to distinguish where one ended and the other began. He could sense she was happy about this, and he was pleased that Amy was pleased, but he really didn't understand why.

He asked Amy, "Have you already developed the sign language?" He knew it was ready, because she usually completed massive projects in that incredible mind at the speed of light, and it was. He called Moon and Fred Becker together. Fred was apprehensive to be next to Moon but showed courage. He asked Fred, "Did you mean it when you said you wanted to join our army and fight?"

Fred said, "Hell, yes! I have nowhere to go and want to get revenge on the Simians if it is possible."

When Fred spoke, he looked sideways nervously at Moon. Levi explained, "Moon doesn't understand English, and that is part of the problem." He told Fred, "I need someone to learn a new language, enabling that person to talk to the Simians and vice versa. I want you to be that person and teach others."

Fred blinked several times and said, "Why me?"

He explained honestly, "You are the only choice right now. It is like being in the right place at the right time." After a moment's thought, Fred agreed. Fred was not a large man and most likely would not have made a strong fighter, and this really would be a valuable job.

Amy was angry again. He wished she would get a grip on her emotions. He could think on his own sometimes and didn't want to ask permission every time he wanted to do something. Amy knew

Fred was the only choice right now and was as good as any, so why did she get pissed?

Amy said, "You should have discussed it with me before you acted."

He responded, "It was the only and obvious choice, so why would I ask permission?" He also wondered why he didn't. Was he feeling controlled? Possibly, but he didn't know for sure.

He explained to Moon and Fred alternately what they, well he, had in mind, and that he would teach both of them the language. Moon actually smiled. He liked the idea and slapped Fred on the back, scaring the crap out of him in the process. He thought for a moment that Fred would run. They all laughed.

How long would this take? Damn, like he needed another job right now. Oh well, there was no time like the present to get started. As he was about to ask Amy to download the language to him, a thought hit him like a slap in the face. "Amy, why can't you download the information directly into their memory?"

* Amy *

There he goes again, thinking on his own. She wished he wouldn't do that, or at least consult her first. He aggravated her sometimes and she told him so. After all, they were together in this venture of life. Fortunately, it was a good idea, like many of his were. Moon was the logical choice, and Fred was the only choice. Moon agreed and Fred was happy to have an important role. This education and training could take a while, but it would definitely

383

save much time and effort later. This will solve the communication problem.

She was downloading the information on the sign language to Levi when he astounded her yet again. Download directly to them? Humm. Yes, it could work. It wasn't like telepathy over long distances requiring two-way communication. This would be similar to downloading to Levi, just focused through him.

She said, "I will try, but it will be necessary to touch their heads to facilitate the transfer. At best, I'm not at all sure it will work on Moon." The Simian mind was so alien; it might not receive her message, but Levi was pleased to see the idea had merit. With her agreement this time, he proceeded to tell Moon and Fred the plan. Levi said, "I will attempt to pass information directly from my mind to yours." They both just stared.

Levi placed his hands on each side of Fred's head and held him still. She projected the transmission out from Levi's mind. Levi was the conduit into Fred's mind, as he had been with telekinesis to objects. She touched Fred's mind with information, and detected that he was an honest and trustworthy man and he truly did want to join them and be useful. She saw that he had lost his mate and two children violently to the Simians, and Fred was bitterly angry. Fred was committed in hate against the Simians and would be good for their purpose. It took a few seconds to download the information. Watching Fred's expression as this took place, she saw understanding flow across his face. She also felt his mind receive this information and generate emotions. There was shock, but understanding, awe and commitment for Levi as well. She had not expected to receive information back. It was supposed to be a transfer in one direction only. This was a strange reaction.

When Levi put his hands on Moon it was different, very different. His mind was organized totally different and it was hard to read his thoughts. She did manage to gain some impressions, but that was about all. She felt respect for Levi. The information transferred, but she had no idea if it could be accepted by Moon's mind in this format. Hopefully, if he didn't get it all, he would gain some of it. She didn't see any change in expression, nor did she read anything from his mind. She was unsure if the information was transferred. There was only one way to find out.

Levi started signing to Fred, and Fred signed back. So far so good! They looked at Moon and he stared at them for a few seconds, shook his head, opened his eye slits, and smiled a toothy smile that, though menacing in appearance, was somehow comforting. They had learned to watch Moon's eye slits for emotion. When he was in a happy or pleasant mood his vertical eye slits opened wide, revealing more of the black pupil, which appeared less fierce than the surrounding red. The red was a thermometer to a Simians' anger. When they saw the black come across his eyes they knew it was going to work. Moon then started signing back. Yes! It was working. They were in business, and Moon and Fred would now have to teach the others. Teaching was their responsibility now.

She was shocked to discover that once she linked with Fred's mind, even for a simple download, she was bound to him as she had been to Dawn. She didn't think a simple download would commit her mind, but unfortunately, she was now on his wave link and receiving data input from Fred in a similar manner as to what was being received from Dawn. Fortunately however, there was no link with Moon. With his alien mind, his data might have challenged her abilities to remain sane. The link with Fred was not even close to what she had with Levi, but she was obtaining information, and realized she would have to limit the number of people she linked with, which also limited her ability to search minds and transfer information. It was already bothersome and could get confusing after a while. She would not link again unless absolutely necessary.

* Levi *

This was good; Amy thought it could be done. Amy could do many things that even she didn't realize. Her creative thoughts were a little on the weak side, but once challenged, she seemed to always find a way with that incredible intellect. This was one of those times.

It didn't take but a minute to expand her abilities. She said it was simple really and much easier than telepathy. She didn't believe it was possible to link telepathically directly with another mind, since she was totally linked and had conformed to Levi's thought patterns and brain waves. She did, however, believe it possible to transfer information to another through the telepathy link with him. She suggested that it would

386

help if he were touching them, one at a time, when she sent the information. In this way, she could ensure that the right language version went to the right mind. That seemed like a good idea, it wouldn't do much good for Moon to have the English version.

The transfer went well with both Fred and Moon, and they were soon signing to each other. He was proud of her and complimented her saying, "Thanks Amy, this was another job well done." He saw her smile. She deserved it, but it was time to move onto the next problem, and there were many to choose from.

Amy informed him that Jimmy and Dawn were almost to the desert community, and a decision needed to be made soon. Their group was almost at the split in the road leading to either Owens Valley or the Mojave Desert settlement. Which direction should they go? The battle would be in the desert, but they needed the valley people. Another thing bothering him was what the hell was he going to do with this Simian group? He knew most of the Humans, all but Fred Becker would be heading toward Bakersfield, but he now had all these Simians. They must be supervised and, knowing Moon, they were going to follow "Levi the Master" wherever he went. He recognized that the plan must now be modified.

If they only knew whether Iron Eyes and Wolf were successful in their mission, they could proceed on to the desert. He asked Amy, "Why not project to the valley and see for ourselves if everything is in order?"

* Amy *

The original plan was to return to Owens Valley, to strengthen the training and help convince the tribe. However, Levi had confidence in Iron Eyes and Wolf's ability to press forward the plan. The circumstances dictated compliance, and the plan actually sold itself. All they really needed was someone they believed in to tell them. Levi's suggestion to project to Owens Valley and see how things were going was another good one. Knowing the status would help her plan the next move.

Levi also asked, "Why can't you read Iron Eyes' or Wolf's mind like you do Dawn's?"

In truth, it was another good question, but he didn't understand how complex it was to monitor several separate minds simultaneously. Truthfully though, it simply hadn't occurred to her, and it was too late now. She would have had to tune and lock minds with one of them before they parted company, and that was something she would have to do very sparingly.

She was, however, learning and taking advantage of Levi's abstract thoughts and learning a few of her own. Yes, she could take them to Owens Valley, but on their return she had a surprise of her own.

She had been monitoring Dawn and keeping Levi informed on their progress. They were now approaching the desert settlement, and should be there by morning. She would only open the monitoring to Levi when there was something she felt was important. Otherwise, it would just be as distracting to him as it was to her. She realized that

388

Levi could look into her mind most anytime, if he really wanted to. He just didn't want to look. The principle problem was that Levi, unlike her, couldn't handle multiple inputs. She, on the other hand, was constantly monitoring these multiple inputs and controlling many other activities at the same time. Amy's primary priority was monitoring and controlling Levi's body at all times, but additionally, she was tracking hundreds of different functions, analyzing Levi's sensory inputs, and, best of all, just plain thinking. Invariably, her thinking involved Levi and her emerging emotions.

* Gord *

He was furious! The vertical black slits in his eyes were almost completely closed, leaving only the blazing, angry red showing. This should have been a warning. Never had an enemy infiltrated his compound, much less released prisoners or killed guards. Seldom had any of his warriors been killed. Only at first, before he became so powerful. After he began retaliating with a vengeance, the other colonies stayed away from his territory. He listened to his first in command give the details. So infuriated by the news, he lashed out and broke the neck of the first line commander. He was stupid to bring this news himself. He should have known that the messenger of bad news would be killed.

He summoned the second in command, who stood far from him. This one was smarter. The second presented his report, telling of the three guards dead and the release of the Humans and runt Simians. He didn't have a clue as to why, or who did it. No one had seen or heard a thing, and the deaths weren't discovered until the guards came to relieve them in the morning. It seemed that all three had died of sudden and hard blows or from swords. The guards had not even had a chance to pull their swords. They died so suddenly that there had been no cry for help. There was one other thing. The second, now number one, stepped back even further before finishing. Each dead Simian had a tooth missing! He couldn't believe his ears.

Again, he was furious. His body quivered with rage. He was on the verge of losing control and going totally berserk, but he fought for control. He was proud of the fact that his temper was legendary and usually resulted in sudden death to those that angered him, but this was different. Something very strange was happening here. Humans were only food and the runts were worthless, so why had this happened? Who would want to risk their life to free Humans? Humans might want to, but Humans could not kill Simians. At least he had believed that until he started receiving reports of missing and presumably dead Warriors from areas where there was no dispute with other Simian colonies. The area was that green valley where he planned to send the eastern Simian colony.

Seldom had he sent patrols into that area, but this area was close enough he could establish the new compound and maintain control and far enough away not to interfere with his colony. Of the several patrols sent into that valley, only one Warrior had returned with strange tales. He had killed him for his cowardice, but before dying he had reported coming across dead Simians that had been mutilated. He reported that his patrol and another working together had found six Simians that had been dead for many days and that a tooth had been taken from each one. He said they had followed the trail of Humans leading away into the green valley, the same valley they had been sent to investigate. They said the leading patrol had been killed by an army of Humans on horseback, and something about seeing a single Human kill a Simian Warrior in single combat. This of course was impossible, but how can all the happenings be explained? He lost five Warriors in that encounter alone, and six others were reported missing, so part of the story must be true.

Who would want to release inferior Simians? Surely Humans would not want to release Simians. There were just too many questions without any answers. The only thing he was certain about was that this raid on his colony was related to what was happening in the valley, and he wanted to know what that might be.

His cunning was also legendary, and he began to smile. His decision had been made. He would let the migrating Simians from the east discover the threat in the valley. If there were going to be more Simians killed, let it be them! He could always come in after he knew more about the possible threat and destroy it, but in the interim let the new ones take the losses. He wanted to keep them weak anyway. All he really wanted were the horses they promised.

* Levi *

391

A lot had happened during the rest stop overnight, not the least was establishing the communication between Moon and Fred. They were hand signing at each other like crazy, as Moon demonstrated and taught the other Simians. All the Simians watched and were learning fast, and Moon was a good teacher.

He told Fred not to bother teaching the other Humans, since they would be leaving soon to branch off toward Bakersfield. Fred understood the reason he was chosen: being in the right place at the right time, but Fred saw it different.

Fred said, "Maybe I'm in the wrong place at the wrong time."

He said, "I guess we will have to see." They both chuckled.

They were getting a late start after the feast of last night. They finished off the meat for breakfast, while Moon hunted. He sent Moon and some of his new followers out to hunt, while they were still in the mountains where game was plentiful. Moon had screeched at one of the Simians that had said Humans were much easier to hunt than deer, and they had plenty of Humans with them. It was # 3 that made the comment. In order to identify the new Simians, he had named them # 1 through # 15. Moon backed # 3 down quickly.

He had been talking with the other Humans. They were recovering from the forced flight, starvation and shock of captivity. It had been a bad night for them, but they were showing some signs of life again. At least they had full bellies and hope.

Bob Reasoner and the group were extremely thankful for being saved. They had lost all hope, but

392

now that they were safe, their thoughts turned toward families, assuming they still existed. There was no way of knowing until they returned to what was left of their homes. They would leave the group after getting down out of the mountains and head toward the mountains east of Bakersfield. They asked lots of questions about where the battles were going to be waged and when. They wanted to help, but needed to get home more and see if they still had any family. He could certainly empathize with them.

Moon was back. The hunting party had been successful and managed to kill three deer, which should be enough to last for a while as they traveled. It was time to go.

* Amy *

She wanted the Simians fed well for a while to remove any temptation of them wanting or trying to eat the Humans. She didn't want to stop in the mountains, but the game was plentiful here. Game would be hard to find once they came down into the dry hot lands beyond the mountains.

Moon had replenished the meat, but more importantly, had obtained the hides of three deer to be used for making water sacks. Each of the Simians would need them before they headed into the desert. Levi still had the same two water skins that he carried across the desert, but those were for him and she made him keep them. Levi's instructions to use the hides from the previous night for water sacks, was already being done. The new

393

hides were quickly removed and used as well. She hoped that would be enough.

Soon ready, the group was off again down the northeast side of the mountains, following the old Highway 15. By noon they had reached the split of 395 and I-15 and said their goodbyes to Bob and his group. You could visibly see the relief in their eyes to be away from the Simians. Levi's party of Simians continued toward Barstow, where they planned to stop and astral project to the Owens Valley to check on the progress of Iron Eyes and Wolf. The group could spend the night at Barstow, while she determined the status of both groups. Barstow had water and was central. From there they could go either direction, once that determination was made.

Jimmy and Dawn had reached the desert settlement and were being taken to Al at the main camp. The meeting should be taking place as they were projecting. This could be a problem, since she would be cut off from all other communications during the absence from Levi's body. Her mind, the essence of who she was, would be isolated from her physical body, which in this case was her disembodied brain, during the projection. This isolation could not be helped. The projection had to be completed during the daylight hours.

* Levi *

They were making an early camp tonight in order to track the progress of the two parties. Amy felt it would be better to concentrate and learn more during the daylight, and he agreed. Amy did not like

394

the idea of projecting and having his defenseless body totally vulnerable to attack with so many Simians around. He trusted Moon now, but Moon also was uncomfortable with the Simians when it came to his safety. They would have to find a very safe place. He instructed Moon what was expected of the Simians and how to set up camp. They needed to forage for food, but no Humans, not that there would be any in the area. He didn't like having to worry about so many details for so many, but Amy was good at all these details, and all he had to do was give the orders. That wasn't too bad, just a pain in the butt. Amy was always there, planning all the numerous details like food, water, security and planning. All he wanted to do was fight and was happy to leave the details to Amy.

Once they had reached Barstow and everyone was off doing their assigned tasks, he called Fred and Moon. He needed Moon, but Fred was there to keep Moon company and for his own protection, as well. Amy suggested they project from a secure location and recommended the roof of a three-story building close to camp. Taking them to the top floor, he instructed them to watch the access to the roof and not let anyone up. He said he was going onto the roof and needed them to protect him while he meditated. Moon understood and knew what to expect. This time Moon would not see him, but he would be protected just the same. He knew no one would get past Moon. Satisfied, he climbed the roof access ladder.

Amy was monitoring Dawn's progress and told him there was something going on if he wanted to monitor. "Of course, send it to me."

She just grinned and said, "Get it yourself."

Okay no more denying it. He looked into her mind, turned the pages of her thoughts and saw what Amy saw.

Amy gave him a summary of the images and conversation that had transpired. Jimmy and Dawn had reached the pass about midday. They were chased by a Simian patrol, but were on horseback and safe, once through the pass. The Simians stopped at the pass, unwilling to face the odds of battle in this narrow area. Jimmy dismounted and asked for Al, but discovered he was back in the main camp.

Jimmy said to the guard, "I came representing Levi Walkingbear and the army of Owens Valley to see Al Baker on urgent business affecting the safety of your settlement."

This brought an immediate response, and one of the guards mounted and took Jimmy and Dawn directly to the main camp.

Amy's summary skipped to the main camp, where Jimmy was talking to Al and General Harkin. Jimmy presented the plan just as it had been rehearsed. Jimmy was emotional as well, which strengthened his case, but Al was a professional and not easily convinced. He recognized Thunder and knew it was Levi's horse, but it was hard for him to believe that the Levi they described was the Levi he knew. They could see Al's hard, penetrating eyes staring at Jimmy as he appraised him.

Finally, Al said, "I need more confirmation before I will commit to this plan."

Al intended to send out a patrol toward the Colorado River to verify their story. This was not good. The delay would destroy the schedule and be disastrous to them all.

Amy said, "We will have to go there and convince Al."

As Al was leaving to organize the patrol, Dawn fell in beside him, saying that her instructions were to stay with him, go where he went and be his shadow. Al looked funny, but shrugged his shoulders as if to say, "Oh well," and took off.

* Amy *

Levi was disappointed, but Al's reaction was not totally unexpected. Al was a very careful man, but his caution could get them all killed. There was no time for a weeklong expedition to verify the story of the migrating Simians. They would have to go there, but first they needed to check on Iron Eyes and Wolf. Hopefully, that part of the plan would be on schedule. All would be lost if they had to go to both locations. There simply wasn't enough time to go to both places.

Everything was ready. They were safe, and Levi was sitting in the lotus position relaxing. She began the projecting process by starting a flow of energy focused through Levi. His skin began to warm, as she concentrated and focused her mind, drawing Levi's mind with her. As before, they seemed to float slowly out of his body, gaining height as they moved outward. They had no body, just mental energy. They saw Levi's body below, sitting and still. Again, the silver thread was trailing behind. All was well.

They floated higher, as she circled the area. They could see Moon's Simians canvassing the area below, branching out from their camp. They gained greater height and moved off toward Owens Valley. Their speed gained momentum. She could instantly project there as long as she had a landmark to concentrate on, which she did, but there was no need. At this speed it wouldn't take long to get there. They were there already!

Slowing, they passed over the defense area. The guards were still on duty, and all looked in order. Soon they approached the main camp. It was a beehive of activity. Lancers were gathered and busy training in the field. They saw men, women and children working together on lances in one form or another. Some were trimming the tree branches, while wagon loads of pine and eucalyptus branches were coming into camp. In another area, saddle-tree frames could be seen drying on the rocks, and teams of workers were busy stretching leather over the frames making saddles. The tribe was geared for action and easily on schedule, if not ahead. Iron Eyes and Wolf had obviously done their job well, and the tribe was working hard to complete their tasks.

There was no need to physically go to Owens Valley. There was nothing they could do now other than get the horses from the desert settlement to the tribe. They would head out toward the desert settlement early in the morning and convince Al to join forces and participate in the overall plan.

As they were returning to Levi's body, he said, "Can we take a quick look at the Colorado River Simians?"

"Yes," she said, "that is a good idea." They turned from their path and sped toward the Simian camp. They went higher, as the land below them became a blur and the air became hot. The river grew larger as they approached. Slowing over the camp they could see the activity. The Simians were preparing to mobilize. Huge wagons were packed, but they were not yet ready to move. Once loaded, they would not be moving fast with these wagons, but the Simians would be out and upon the Desert Settlement soon. She told Levi, "It will take them no longer than seven to ten days to reach the settlement with the wagons once they start to move, but be aware that the Simians might move their army out ahead." She estimated that they did not have the month she had previously thought. The Simians could be at the Desert Settlement in as early as two weeks. Time was still on humanity's side, but the Human army must be ready soon. Would it be soon enough?

* Levi *

Projection to Owens Valley camp was heartening. All was in order and going well. The Owens Valley Tribe was working double time to accomplish their tasks. At least some of the plan was coming together. All they needed now were the horses. It was too bad Al was so damned cautious. He would have to go there, but this delay could cripple the army.

Amy was quick to take his suggestion to take another look at the Colorado River Simians to check on their status. When she took his suggestion so quickly he knew she liked the idea. That was the closest he would get to a "Well done." Unfortunately, Amy didn't like what she saw and was racing back.

They were following the strange silver thread back toward his body. As always it was just there to see and follow. It never tangled or looped. The thread seemed to simply retract as they raced toward it, always pointing the way back. It seemed to have little use on these short distances, but he realized how important it could become on a really long trip to prevent them from becoming lost.

His daydreaming ended as he saw his body below. He would never get used to seeing his body from outside. Approaching his still and seemingly lifeless body again, they floated back inside it. It was a strange feeling to re-join his body and feel his mind again moving muscles, lungs breathing, and his own heartbeat. Until now, he had been unaware of the absence of these things, but they were now very noticeable. He thought how comforting it was to feel the rhythm of his heart beating and the rise and fall of his chest.

As they settled again in his body, he commented that they would have to leave soon, and at a fast pace, to get to the desert settlement as soon as possible. Amy surprised him then.

Amy said, "Evidently Jimmy has convinced Al, because the horses are being gathered for the trip as we speak. Guard riders and horse wranglers are being assigned. I don't know what happened while my communication was cut off from Dawn."

* Amy *

She didn't like to stay away from Levi's body very long. When she projected, she no longer controlled Levi's body, and there was danger of the unchecked mutation within his body. They hadn't been gone that long this time, however, and she was able to correct the mutation in minutes. When she resumed all her monitoring, she was somewhat surprised to see that Al had changed his mind, and was complying with their wishes and in the best interest of the settlement. General Harkin was the actual leader of the settlement, but everyone knew that the General wouldn't do anything concerning war without Al's approval, and if Al suggested something, it was done.

Levi was pleasantly surprised with this news. She suggested that they no longer needed to head off to the Desert Settlement, and there time might be better spent staying here and working with Moon's Simians. This small force could become a formidable attack group and personal guard. She would attempt to download more martial arts skills into Moon, and the two of them could teach the others. Neither Human camp would welcome this group of Simians anyway, nor were the Technical Simians ready for exposure to Humans. Levi readily agreed. Of course he would agree. He had probably been trying to figure a way to play his macho crap anyway. So, they would stay here a few days working with the Simians and watch for Jimmy and the horses, as well as the advanced deployed wagons from Owens Valley carrying the lances. Being in the middle between the two Human groups, they could move in either direction as necessary, should any trouble develop.

As they came down from the roof, they saw Moon and Fred sign talking. They were becoming friends it seemed. Amy's plan to download more fighting skills to Moon was a good one. He liked it and wanted to start now. Anticipating, Amy had already translated the programs into Simian and was ready. He told Moon what he had in mind about training his group in fighting skills like he had been trained. Out of courtesy to Fred he reverted to sign language to talk to Moon. The thought of an elite-fighting group appealed to Moon, especially going against the arrogant Warrior Simians. Moon was more than ready.

Again Amy had him put his hands on Moon's head, concentrate and open up his mind to channel Amy's information. He felt a slight increase in temperature for the briefest of time, and then it was over. As before, it was not instantaneous. It took a few minutes before Moon's mind processed the information, but finally he nodded in understanding. Moon seemed very happy to have this information. Amy told him that she had given Moon sword fighting skills and hand-to-hand fighting skills. Moon had already become very good at many of the skills through the practice they had been doing over the last few weeks, but he would be even better now.

Amy added, "I don't want you to practice swords with Moon anymore. Moon's skills are too

402

good and he has learned many of our moves. We are too predictable to him and you can get hurt."

That surprised him until he remembered Moon was connecting before, and if he was better now, maybe that was a good idea. He rubbed his ribs as he remembered.

He told Moon about the delay in plans, and that they would be staying at this location for a few days, so this would be a very good time to start teaching the other Simians both fighting skills and the sign language. He also suggested that a hunting party be sent back into the mountains for game, since they would be staying here. Moon nodded and left. Moon was a good leader and would keep his Simians in line, and they would follow direction. Fred was instructed to stay with Moon and help teach the sign language. Fred was off following Moon. He looked like a small child following the huge Simian.

It was approaching sunset so nothing much would happen until the morning. It looked like they would have a restful evening for a change. As he exchanged looks with Amy, he saw an expression he had never seen before. It was a combination of joy, happiness and love with a little mischief thrown in. When he asked her what that was all about, she just smiled.

Amy said, "You will find out."

"What the hell does that mean?" All she would do was smile and said no more.

* Amy *

403

She had been ready for some time, just waiting on the right opportunity. This was it! It was the right time and the right place. She had been feeling lonely. There was no other explanation for what she was feeling. Levi was totally into his macho crap and ignoring her. He seemed to love the excitement of the battles, the attention and exhilaration of accomplishment. It was completely occupying his time. When he was not fighting, he was thinking about it or talking about it with Moon or the others, and she was feeling left out. She was not getting the respect and attention she felt she deserved. It was not intentional and she understood that, but the results were the same, she was lonesome. She loved Levi but was in competition with herself. Levi could only do the macho crap with her help, so she was the reason he was distracted from Amy the person. All that would change tonight.

She had been considering options and believed that she now was able to become a real person to Levi, real as in touching and being touched. This of course would be mental in his and her mind. She desperately wanted to be a real lover to Levi in every way. She had learned the emotions from sharing Levi's emotions and also Dawn's. She experienced both the emotional and physical sensations. Her love for Levi was very strong and she knew Levi loved her desperately as well. She also knew the pain that Levi had, his ache for her, the desires to touch, smell, taste her, to hold her in his arms and make love to her. Levi's emotions were overwhelming and she felt these same desires. They wanted the same thing. They wanted each other.

She had stored data of Levi's old memories, which were brought forward in his mind by the many questions she asked. She learned Levi's preferences in looks, and used this data to develop the visual images she put into his mind. This had added a second dimension to their communications, which greatly improved their ability to be together. The developed ability to astral project had given her the next ingredient in the formula. Learning to project her essence outside of her brain added the ability to project dimensions of her mind. This projection could be a nonphysical form of her own creation, and she chose to create a mental form of a physical dimension. Her creation would be the perfect woman Levi had built in his mind, and now she had become. In short, she believed she could project her created, mental metaphysical body directly into Levi's mind and he would perceive it as real, a virtual real Amy.

This virtual Amy would appear to Levi as real. He could touch her and, better yet, she could touch him. They could hold each other, touch and it would appear real. It would be real! Smells would be real, kisses warm and sweet. They could make love and it would be real in every sense. It would actually be better than real, because everything would be perfect, always.

Since she shared both Levi's emotions and her own, she would experience dual orgasms, Levi's and her own. She found that experience incredible and, knowing he could read her thoughts as well, Levi would be able to experience her orgasm too. Without question, Levi would find the experience as incredible as she had.

405

* Levi *

Amy remained blocked to him and acting funny, and he didn't know why. He had never seen her mysterious before, but it was cute. It also seemed strange that he didn't need to run off somewhere in a hurry. He would have a few days of rest until Jimmy got here with the horses.

"Oh well," Amy said, "You need the rest."

He and Fred had a leisurely supper of grilled pork and corn on the cob. What a surprise. Fred said he found some growing in the area, and Fred was a surprisingly good cook. He hadn't had a restful meal like that in quite some time. Fred was still amazed at how much Levi could eat, but he needed lots of fuel. That was the downside of his new body, but that wasn't so bad, since he loved to eat. Who cared about manners?

Amy was overly cautious tonight and asked him to bed down away from the others. He found one of the few trees in the area and spread out his bedroll. He lay there talking to Amy. It was always pleasant to talk to Amy, but it had been so busy lately there were rarely quiet moments together. Another reason was that it hurt him to want her so bad or good, depending on how you looked at it. Tonight was different. Amy was playful, and he found it pleasant. They laughed and talked. It was amazing that they never ran out of things to talk about. They just went on and on and everything was new. She was so deep, and she knew everything about him. He held nothing back no matter how embarrassing.

406

He was relaxed and happy lying there on his back, hands interlaced behind his head. He was staring up at the brilliant, flickering stars, sharing them with Amy. When he glanced back at Amy's image, she was not there. He said, "Where did you go?"

Amy said, "I am here."

He heard Amy's soft voice from off to his left a few feet away. His heart skipped a beat as he sat straight up and stared. She was standing there in the dark. There was just enough moonlight to let him see that it was, in fact, Amy! He continued to stare at her beautiful face and naked body. She was beautiful! Incredible! Perfect! He was only vaguely aware that his mouth was hanging open in awe.

The body image was just like the facial image he loved so, compiled of those perfect features, long dark hair, small petite face, dimples, shining green eyes and full gorgeous wet lips. That perfection had been extended to her full body image, but it was not an image. It was real! She was a collection of all the perfect features. Amy was small, just barely over five feet, one hundred and ten pounds, petite, round but firm hips, narrow waist, small round firm breasts, little hard nipples that protruded, slim but muscular legs, flat stomach and all in the right proportion. The list of features and perfection seemed to go on forever. Everywhere he looked was flawless features, precise and beautiful. It was a combination of so many perfect things that made even perfection more angelic. The combined effect of all these features accounted for the stunning enchantress he saw in front of him. He was drawn to her like a magnet. He felt like a kid in love for the first time. His heart raced in his chest.

He was frozen as Amy began to walk toward him slowly. Her movements were fluid and the curves of her naked body pronounced. The muscles could be seen moving under her soft flawless skin, which generated a very stimulating reaction in his stomach. Amy came closer, and his heart felt like it was going to explode. She slowly leaned forward and kissed him on the cheek. She placed her hands on his face and kissed him again on the lips, gently. The kiss was soft, warm, wet, and, oh God, so sweet. Their lips matched perfectly. The passion rose as they kissed more urgently. His body shook as he took her in his arms. How he had wanted this, to have this sweet, sweet person in his arms, to taste her lips, to smell the fragrance of her hair, to feel her soft warm body against his. He didn't care how this happened. He was so very happy. He loved her so very much! With crying eyes he managed to squeak out, "I love you, Amy."

Wrapping his arms around her, he pulled her close, kissing her over and over. His lips were gently walking over her face, kissing, nibbling and caressing her. Her face was wet from his tears and hers. While he kissed, hugged and touched her, she was doing the same. They were truly hungry for each other's love.

* Amy *

The timing and planning were perfect. They were so close tonight. The only way to be closer was to become flesh and blood. It was time to be

408

real! She projected her created body image directly into Levi's mind. To him and to her as well, this would look, sound, feel, taste, smell and be real.

She stood looking at Levi and she loved him so. When he asked for her, she spoke, "I am here." The reaction was immediate. He was in front of her, and, for the first time, she touched him. She felt his warmth. She kissed him and she cried. Her emotions were so strong. Could she control them or should she just go with the flow? Did she want to control them? There was no choice as she kissed and wrapped her arms around him. His tears were mixing with hers.

She felt his kisses, his touches. His kisses burned across her face and neck. She felt his hands rubbing and holding her. Her body was real! She felt his hands cupping her breasts and the excitement was almost more than she could stand. She melted as Levi slid his hands over her smooth shoulders and down her quivering body. He was crying and professing his love, and she welcomed it and felt the same.

She felt his touches and she felt the excitement in Levi. He was very aroused. His hands continued to move over her entire body and she loved the feeling. His hands slid over her butt cheeks and down to her thighs. His hands set her on fire! Their bodies slowly settled to his blanket as they continued to kiss. Their lips and bodies made love. Levi was so strong as he drove himself into her. The rhythm building, they were urgent for each other. They climaxed together, experiencing each other's orgasm. It was explosive in wave after wave of rocking orgasms culminating in a final erupting crescendo. The excitement was much stronger than she would have ever believed. It was so strong she was screaming! At that moment they were truly one in body, mind and spirit. Their love flowed together, intertwining, surrounding, weaving, merging and floating in bliss. Their hearts beat to the same rhythm. It was not possible to be closer than they were at that moment.

Afterwards, they lay together holding and kissing. She was attached to Levi, and so glad for the symbiotic attachment. If she wasn't already attached by necessity, she would have to hold on to him every second of every minute of every day. She would never let him go. Her existence would never be whole or complete again without him. She had made herself Levi's everything. Her commitment to being everything to him and satisfying Levi was total, and it felt good. This love was more secure than any woman had ever felt. She could always be what he wanted her to be.

* Levi *

Amy was incredible. Her kisses were warm and so sweet. She set him on fire as she explored him and he explored her. His lips moved over her face kissing her eyes, nose, cheeks, chin, neck, ears and back to those wonderful lips. His hands glided over her beautiful body, and she truly was beautiful. Her breasts were soft and inviting as he held them in his hands and kissed the hard nipples. They slowly lowered to the bedroll wrapped in each other's arms, and melted into each other. They belonged together. They were perfect together.

410

They were urgent, very urgent. He took her rough and fast. He had wanted her for so long he lost control of his body. His emotions and arousal were merging with Amy's. He could feel her wants and needs and he moved to satisfy those needs along with his own. He felt what she felt, combined with what he felt. This drove him crazy as he rose to an explosive climax. He felt her orgasm along with his as they drove against each other. He heard Amy scream, and his body was jerking. Damn! This was the most wonderful experience he had ever had. As they lay together, their bodies jerked and quivered with volcanic orgasms. He didn't want it to end ... ever!

After a long while Amy turned to cradle herself in his arms and lap and it felt good. He loved her so. His arms were around her and his lips were on her neck as he calmed. He was soon asleep.

When he awoke in the morning, Amy's body was gone. The warmth against him was gone. Her image was back in his mind, and she was radiant and smiling wide, matching his own. He never asked how she did it. It was just too perfect, and he wanted no explanation. He was afraid that knowing might take away from the feeling and the experience. From that night on, she came to him often at night, and they spent precious moments together. Life was good.

CHAPTER 16
(THE BATTLE)

* Amy *

They spent the next few days at Barstow, while Moon continued training his Simians. It was going well. Moon had gotten good before, but now he was awesome. He was taking opponents on two at a time and enjoying it. Moon had them practice sword fighting and hand-to-hand from early in the morning until after dark. In between they practiced hand signing. The Technical Simians were a smart race and learned fast. The Technical Simians were also curious about Humans, and asked Fred many questions, and Fred kept busy talking to all of the Simians. One of the favorite questions of the Simians was, "Why do Humans destroy their food with fire?"

Levi was doing his share of fighting with the Simians, but he was not totally focused. He seemed to have a smile on his face most of the time. Moon kept watching him to see what was wrong. Levi would just grin at Moon who would shake his head and walk off. She was grinning a lot also.

It was one such time when Levi's head was rocked by a slap from, who was it, # 3? Damn! She better remain focused before he got hurt. She was instantly alert to # 3's attack. He was not playing. The blow was meant to kill, and would have any normal Human. Now, she regretted her timing on their lovemaking. Love and war do not mix, but it was too late now. It was simply too fantastic to stop now, but she did learn a lesson and would remain focused.

Levi was pissed and so was she. Instead of being defensive, she launched an attack. It was hard, fast and effective. Levi leaped into the air kicking upward catching # 3 under the chin. The kick was solid and # 3's red eyes rolled up as he fell backward on his ample butt. As Levi hit the ground, he spun and kicked # 3 in the forehead then leaped forward to place a Bowie knife on each side of his throat. They both looked hard into # 3's eyes as the anger dissipated. As Levi stood, they saw Moon standing beside him staring at # 3.

She had felt an uncomfortable tension in the presence of the Simians for some time, but she had been unable to identify the source. She now knew that # 3 was the source. The anger coming from # 3 had opened its mind to her, and what she saw she didn't like. This one was not like Moon. He was hostile, mean and without honor. This one could not be trusted and would require continuous watching.

Levi, aware of her thoughts, said, "I should kill him now."

Maybe he was right, but she was disturbed at almost getting Levi killed. Maybe # 3 could be used or turned in some way.

* Levi *

He was enjoying the rest. He especially enjoyed the nights when Amy came to him. She was beautiful. Everything was perfect about Amy and it made him quiver every time he thought about her.

413

When he did think of Amy, they shared thoughts and invariably exchanged knowing smiles.

The sudden impact to the back of his head abruptly ended his daydreaming. The blow sent him rolling to the ground. He had been sparring with # 3 and had turned to move away. The Simian launched a vicious rear attack, delivering a blow to the back of his head. He was lucky that # 3 had stopped. Obviously, # 3 thought he had killed him. The blow certainly would have killed any normal Human, but Amy's reactions were immediate and she moved him to roll with the punch, saving his life and immediately began repairing the potentially mortal damage. He continued to roll back up onto his feet to face # 3. This attack had been intentionally aimed to kill him, and he was pissed.

His anger blinded his judgment, but Amy knew what to do. His body and mind went through the motions and he was soon holding his Bowie knives pressed against the Simian's throat. All he had to do was slice the arteries. There was fear in # 3's eyes, he and was positive that # 3 saw the death in his eyes. It would be hard to miss. He wanted to kill # 3 in that instant, but slowly decided it could negatively affect his relationship with the other Technical Simians. He slowly calmed.

As he released # 3 and stood, he noticed that Moon and the others were standing around watching. Moon was angry and started slapping # 3. It was then that he calmed enough to see Amy's thoughts. She was concerned about this one. He would be trouble. Levi turned back to kill # 3, but Amy said let it rest, maybe we could use it to our benefit in some way. He didn't like leaving a hostile enemy alive, but would do what she wanted.

Moon came to ask what had happened, and he said angrily, "# 3 tried to kill me." Moon immediately went back to # 3 and slapped him again across the face ... hard. They faced each other, red eyes blazing for long seconds until Moon slapped him again, dragging his claws across # 3's face tearing the skin. The attack was sudden as # 3 struck at Moon, but Moon was ready. He blocked and countered, striking blow after blow. His skills were impressive. It became obvious Moon was going to kill # 3 and wanted to make an example of him. Moon could have killed him many times over but played with him. He even used some judo throws on # 3. No Simian had ever seen anything like this before. Moon ended it mercifully by breaking # 3's neck. He looked around at the other Simians as if to say, you could be next. As was now Moon's custom, he rolled # 3 over and dug out a trophy tooth. This would make his third trophy. Moon came back to him and apologized and bowed to him. He placed his hand on Moon's shoulder in respect and affection.

* Amy *

The debate over life and death for # 3 was over once Moon got involved.

Moon said, "I will not have a Technical Simian that is not honorable in my group. The Warrior Simians are enough to be ashamed of, and I will not tolerate one of my own class being less than exemplary."

415

He then proceeded to kill # 3 slowly and efficiently in front of all the others. He even took the trophy tooth of an enemy. Moon had sure changed since they knew him. To say that he gained the other Simians' respect was an understatement.

The training continued as weapons became available. The only swords the Simians had were those that Moon carried and the three swords from the dead guards, but they used whatever they could find to use as swords. The fifteen Simian force, now fourteen, was becoming a formidable attack group, and she was pleased to have them surrounding and protecting Levi. Although formidable himself, she always worried about him in battle.

Such was the routine for three days, but on the fourth day they could see dust to the east as the horses approached. Jimmy's group had made good time. By mid-afternoon, Jimmy approached riding Thunder. Grinning, Jimmy jumped down to embrace Levi. Initially he had held back at seeing the group of Simians, but spotting Levi, he knew it was all right. Still, Jimmy's eyes cut to the Simians. Levi briefly told the story about how they had been successful in their raid into the Los Angeles Simian compound, and these Simians were Technical Simians like Moon. Jimmy listened with interest, but his main concern was whether he personally was safe.

She had been monitoring Dawn, but Jimmy's conversion with Al was accomplished while they were astral projecting and therefore unable to discover how Jimmy had persuaded Al.

Levi now asked, "Jimmy, how did you convince Al to change his mind?"

416

Jimmy knew something was wrong and asked, "How do you know I had a problem convincing Al, and how did you know I was coming with the horses?"

Levi just looked at Jimmy with an air of mystery and said, "I know many things."

Jimmy knew from experience that this was all the answer he was going to get, so he unrolled his own tale. He and Dawn had told Al the plan, told him about the Levi they knew, about the feats that Levi had accomplished, and they told him everything that had happened since encountering him. Al had been nice enough, but didn't jump to comply. He didn't believe our Levi was the same Levi he knew but was prepared to check the story out. The only problem was, it would have taken too long to verify the story. So Jimmy got pissed and was telling Al off, when something got Al's attention. He stopped to see what Al was staring at.

Al asked, "Where did you get the Simian tooth?"

Jimmy had explained that their Levi came to them wearing a single Simian tooth around his neck, saying he had gotten it from Al, because he was good bait.

Al laughed hard and said, "Now THAT is the Levi I know!"

Jimmy went on to say, "The custom continues in the Owens Valley, and that is how I came to have one, and Levi now has seven around his neck." This brought a look of respect from Al.

Al told the General that they should agree to the plan immediately. The settlement became a hub of activity, complying with the needs of the armies and

417

this was the result. There were at least three hundred and fifty horses and twenty-five Guard members herding them not three miles away.

* Levi *

He was happy to see Jimmy. Amy had told him the horses were on the way, but Dawn had stayed with Al, as she had been told. Without Dawn, they weren't able to maintain contact with the herd once they left, but Amy had guessed pretty close. The herd was on schedule to the Owens Valley if they kept moving for the next few days.

As Jimmy unfolded his story about how the Simian tooth had convinced Al to believe, he chuckled at Al's logic. He remembered how angry he had been when Al and the Guard had saved him at the pass. Had he not made it through the pass, they would have let him die. That pissed him then but had been a source of much laughter afterwards. Oh well, sometimes it is the small things that make the difference.

As they were talking, Jimmy remembered he had brought something for him. He went to Thunder and removed a large flat bag and brought it back to him. Opening and removing the item, he was shocked. It was the weapon he had asked the tradesmen at the settlement to make for him. They were the best he had ever seen since the fall of civilization. How had they managed to build this in one day? Wow! This was exquisite! It was exactly like the drawing Amy had designed for him.

He admired the weapon as he held it in his hands. The main shaft was about two and a half feet long with a slight bend at the leather-covered handle designed for a two-handed hold. The bend would insure the proper aim of the blow. At the end was a fourteen-inch, sharpened spike perpendicular to the shaft. At the base of the spiked shaft was a weighted hammerhead. It looked more like a pickaxe than anything. It was heavy, weighing about ten pounds, designed for use in an upward swing to penetrate the crotch of a Simian with enough force to reach the nerve center.

Amy said, "The balance is perfect and I love it."

He was all grins when he looked up, already anxious to try it out.

As the horses approached, the Simians came to stare at them. The hunger could be seen in their eyes, but Moon directed that they could only eat dead ones. Horses were needed to fight the Warriors. They weren't happy, but they accepted Moon's instructions.

It was about time for Jimmy to move on and catch up with the herd and Guard riders, but Amy had some last-minute instructions. She wanted Jimmy to take two Simians with him so the horses could start getting accustomed to the smell of Simians. Amy also wanted to transfer the sign language to Jimmy and link with his mind. In this way they could track the progress of activities in Owens Valley. He said, "Damn, that is good thinking." She grinned.

He also explained to Jimmy about the Simians and the language. Jimmy's fear instantly flashed his face white at the thought of being around the Simians, but would do anything for him. Jimmy allowed him to place his hands on his head and after a few minutes, started smiling. Moon and Fred were with them and started signing, Jimmy was signing back, while he grinned from ear to ear. Fred wore a knowing grin.

Moon picked two Simians that he knew he could totally trust. Actually, he said he trusted all of them now. Moon instructed the Simians what was expected, and they nodded. They were to work with the horses, removing the fear of Simian smell without eating them and take instructions from Jimmy.

Jimmy mounted and was about to leave when he turned and signed to # 2 and # 8. "Wait for an hour before following. I want to inform and warn the riders what is happening before you arrive."

* Amy *

The plan was coming together at both ends. The Owens Valley people were cooperating wondrously, and Jimmy was approaching with the horses right on schedule. If only they had enough time.

She was also happy to see Jimmy. He was such a nice and energetic young man, always smiling and happy. She accepted Jimmy's embrace with Levi in fond affection. Jimmy was anxious for Levi's approval and only too happy to tell of his accomplishments. She and Levi were both curious about how Jimmy had convinced Al to believe the story. She never would have thought about the tooth, but it had proved to be the compelling fact. She could still see Al laughing at Levi's anger over being bait for the Simian. Yes, Al would remember.

The weapon she had designed was perfect. Levi was uniquely able to use this weapon. Very few Humans would ever be able to wield it with enough strength to penetrate the dense hide of a Simian, and another Simian was disadvantaged because of their height. It required a low center of gravity to work, and since Levi had the strength and low center of gravity, it was a perfect weapon. This weapon would work well for him in battle. It was designed to be swung by one, or two hands. It would be better with two, but that would leave Levi defenseless from attack, unless he had a sword in one hand to deflect any strikes. It would be awkward to carry, but should be very effective against a Simian. At the first opportunity she would need Levi to practice with it so she could get the feel of the swing and timing. That wouldn't be a problem with Levi; he would be like a kid with a new toy.

She had made a mistake by not linking with anyone at the Owen Valley. She now believed she could handle one more link. Now she could correct that previous mistake by linking with Jimmy. She already liked him and wanted to protect him, so monitoring his activities would serve dual purposes. The perfect excuse was to download the sign language to Jimmy so he could take some Simians with him. Just another detail, but someone had to do the planning.

She had worried about the new horses, since they would not be accustomed to the Simian smell. The horses must be acclimated to their smell in order to launch a Lancer attack against them. The addition of the fourteen Simians solved the problem, but required communications. Now all these concerns would be resolved.

Jimmy took the download with his usual good humor, and the link was established without his knowing. He would take two of the Simians with him. According to Moon, # 2 and # 8 had the best understanding of the sign language and were trustworthy. Knowing Jimmy, he would have the Simians laughing at his jokes in no time. Laughter in a Simian was, in itself, funny to watch and hear. It sounded like a series of hiccups and their bodies shook. It didn't happen often but enough to know it when they saw it. He and Amy chuckled at the thought of Jimmy having them laughing, which he would surely do.

They waved as Jimmy left, riding to catch up with the herd. That camp would be a nervous one tonight when the Simians showed up. She and Levi were smiling at each other, because they knew they would be watching. She guessed she was developing a sense of humor after all. It really would be funny to watch.

* Levi *

Moon seemed interested in his weapon and watched as he went through some exercises with it. Levi found that he could spin bringing the axe high and then swing down reaching the lowest in the arc as he was nearing the completion of the spin. The pickaxe would continue through its arc, rising fast in a powerful, upward swing. The pick spike imbedded in the nerve center would instantly kill a

Simian, if he could complete the maneuver. Moon nodded in appreciation.

They stayed on at the Barstow location and followed the progress of Jimmy and Dawn. As he had predicted, Jimmy's camp was in chaos that night. The horses were very nervous, and the Guards were also. The Simians were on good behavior, however, and just sat together and made no sudden moves. They had been instructed in detail by Moon, and they knew he was their commander and would obey. There would not be a problem from them. Jimmy was talking sign to them constantly. Maybe more from nervousness than transfer of information, but he was becoming more comfortable.

On the second day out from Barstow, Jimmy saw the wagons from his tribe coming. This was great! There were five wagons loaded full of lances and supplies. Great, his pack was in one of the wagons. He would have to remember to thank Iron Eyes for that. Four bulls pulled each wagon, and the wagon train was escorted by six Lancers. The tribe had been busy, but then they were in a fight for their very existence as a tribe. Amy estimated that the wagon train would arrive in Barstow by midmorning of the next day. So now they had their schedule. He told Moon and Fred to be ready to leave tomorrow.

Jimmy rode out to meet the wagon train and talk. It was far too early in the day to consider camping, but he wanted information from home and to share what he knew. As they soon discovered, the tribe's wagons and Al's horses were both on schedule. Obviously the lances were completed, and training was continuing. All the Lancers would be trained and the saddles completed by the time he got the horses to them. Jimmy reported the Mojave Desert settlement was preparing for battle and anxious to meet their new Owens Valley friends. Jimmy also reported that Levi was waiting at Barstow with a small army of Simians to escort them across the desert. The Lancers were wide eyed, but accepted the information in good spirits. Everyone had learned to expect the unexpected from him, and little he did would surprise them.

Dawn had stayed with Al continuously as instructed and, according to Amy, it seemed that more was developing than battle plans. Dawn liked Al, and Al seemed to welcome her company as well.

Amy said, "They are talking a lot and seem to be developing some real affection."

He was happy for both of them. He had wondered how to stop the relationship with Dawn without hurting her feelings. He had determined that there was no choice but to hurt her. Sometimes hurting was better than living a lie. There had never been love on his part, and he was afraid that she would have to be hurt, but now things were correcting themselves. He was happy for Al also, because Dawn really was a nice lady.

* Amy *

After Jimmy met the wagons, she estimated they could leave sometime tomorrow morning and provided a checklist for Levi. He never resented detailed housekeeping instructions. He didn't care much about them, but he recognized the need. Levi sent the Simians out on a hunting trip for provisions and scheduled the trip. It had taken the wagons four days to get this far and would require another three to get to the Mojave Desert settlement. The horses should reach the Owens Valley in three days, and it would take a full day, maybe two, to rest the horses, organize and assign mounts to the trained Lancers and pack animals. It would also take at least six days to return to the desert settlement. The Owens Valley army couldn't join the battle in fewer than eleven days. Was that going to be soon enough? They could only do their best and hope.

The wagon train, knowing that Levi and company waited, had traveled after dark to reach the safety of Levi's camp. Arriving in camp about two hours after dark, they remained in the wagons and saddles until Levi walked to meet them. They were afraid of the Simians, but trusted their lives to Levi and felt safe with him. Moon's sentry had spotted them coming about an hour before, and Levi had a hot meal prepared. The travelers staked out and fed the horses and bulls, pitched camp and came to enjoy the waiting food. They all had seen and knew Levi, but Levi and Amy knew them only by sight, except Johnny, the mate of Iron Eyes' daughter. They talked some, but everyone was tired and made an early night of it. What was comforting to know from the limited conversation was that the entire tribe was committed to the war and to Levi's (HER) leadership.

Levi was sleeping soundly when she woke him. It was early in the morning and still dark, but something was happening at the Mojave Desert settlement. He was instantly awake and knew that something was seriously wrong for her to wake him. She told him that the patrol Al sent to the Colorado River was back with urgent information. She revealed to him the summary of what she had seen and then opened to the current information.

Dawn was lying beside Al within his covers as the rider stood there out of breath. The rider said, "Sir, the Simians are moving, and judging by their rate of travel, they could be here in eight days, but there is a more immediate danger. There is an advance patrol, in force, maybe twenty-five Simians, coming at a much faster pace. I estimate they will be at the pass within two days, maybe even one."

This was disastrous! Al was up before realizing he was naked. It was too serious to be modest, so he was giving the alert as he dressed. His commanders were running to receive their orders. He ordered the non-combatants to immediately mobilize to the caverns and prepare for a siege. They could never hope to defeat an attack in these numbers, so they would wage a hit and retreat defense until they were also driven back to the caverns. The caverns should be almost impenetrable, but they would lose everything, including their lives, if the attack was sustained for very long.

He ordered the entire Guard alerted. This was all out war with nothing less at stake than their way of life. They would leave immediately for the front pass and hope that would be the Simians' initial focus. He also dispatched a fresh patrol to follow the progress of the advance Simian army.

* Levi *

He was instantly alert when Amy woke him. She never woke him unless there was an emergency. Before moving he waited to learn the nature of the emergency. When she shared what she knew, his stomach churned! Was all this effort wasted? Does it all end here? Damn!

A twenty-five Simian patrol attacking now could destroy the Mojave Desert settlement, which was obviously their intent. If this settlement fell, then the Owens Valley would fall next. It would take both armies to stand a chance against just the Colorado River Simians, and if they joined with the Los Angeles Simians, hang it up. It would all be over.

The Simian advance patrol would be there within two days and the remainder of the Simians within eight days. The Owens Valley army wouldn't be there for eleven days. What could be done?

Amy pointed out, "Nothing else matters unless the advance patrol can be held or stopped."

That was so true, but how? Al's army could hold them at the narrow pass, but sooner or later the Simians would circle around and attack from both sides, and if Al didn't time his retreat, he could lose the battle there.

If he left now and set a fast pace, he maybe could get there in time to help, along with Moon and his twelve Simians. The Lancers wouldn't be of much good without the lances and they couldn't carry them that far on horseback, so they would have to remain with the wagons. His group would be able to help, if they got there in time. They agreed on a plan and he alerted the camp and started issuing orders. He sent two of the Lancers back to Owens Valley to inform them that the battle would be engaged in eight days from now and would be long over and lost by the scheduled eleventh day if they couldn't make it. He informed Moon that they would leave immediately and to bring their water bottles, some food, and what arms they had. He instructed Fred to remain with the wagons and start teaching the sign language to the Lancers. The Lancers had to be ordered to remain with the wagons, and they weren't happy about it.

* Amy *

She and Levi shared thoughts more and more, and complimented each other's strengths as they interfaced and planned. The number one priority was to save the desert settlement. It had to be done, and the Owens Valley army had to make it in time. They must try everything to hold the Simians and keep the settlement from falling. Levi wanted to go, and that really was the only answer or the only thing that could be done. She didn't like him heading into almost certain death, but she knew he would go nonetheless, so she planned around it. Moon's army was becoming formidable, but it was small and they didn't have weapons. They would just have to go and plan as best they could as the situation changed.

They were off within the hour. Levi led out with the thirteen Simians following. Moon was at his customary position by his side. At a very fast pace, she estimated their travel time to the pass at twenty-four hours non-stop, but they would need to stop for rest breaks and rest before going directly into battle. She would insist upon it. She could keep Levi going within reason, but the Simians would eventually wear down. They would never show weakness in front of Levi and would keep going as long as he did, or they would drop trying, but it would severely weaken them in battle. This had to be the major consideration.

Before leaving they had a pleasant surprise. Levi was arguing with Johnny, trying to convince him that the Lancers couldn't come with them carrying the damned lances all that distance. Moreover, it would leave the wagons unprotected. Levi convinced him that the wagons had to make it or the army would not have the ability to fight. Johnny finally agreed, reluctantly, and asked if Levi needed anything from his backpack before he left.

Johnny said, "Iron Eyes told me to bring your pack and it is in the wagon."

She was happy to hear that and reminded Levi to transfer more chemical pills into his backpack. Also, now she would have the ability to consider an optional plan. That is, if the army survived the first encounter. She would need the equipment in his pack to implement her additional options. She previously dismissed the thought, but now she would have what she needed when the wagons arrived in about four days. The trick was to be alive in four days.

One other thing she had considered before they left was how to distinguish the good Simians from the bad ones. Before they separated from the wagons, she had Levi commandeer a red shirt from one of the lancers. It was torn into strips and distributed to Moon and his Simians to be tied on their hats. Hopefully, it would make them appear different until something better could be found.

They jogged for six hours through the remainder of the night, but at sunup she insisted that they rest for two hours before resuming the accelerated pace Levi set. Levi didn't like the delay, but accepted it as necessary. The Simians accepted the rest gracefully and took advantage by going immediately to sleep. Levi even accepted sleep for himself as being necessary. After two hours they resumed the pace. The miles rolled by, but painfully slow. By early afternoon the heat was sweltering hot in the open desert, and she insisted that they again stop and rest through the hot afternoon. They found the nearest shade, which happened to be an old gas station awning. They ate and slept through the smoldering hot afternoon.

She was monitoring Dawn, who was at the pass with Al. They had arrived a few hours before. The patrols reported that the advance Simian patrol was still hours out and wouldn't be there until about dark and most likely would not attack until morning. Levi was thankful for this report.

The Lancers returning to the Owens Valley had ridden hard all night and caught up with Jimmy on the trail the next morning. The news was hard for Jimmy to accept, and he paced back and forth. The Lancers wanted replacement mounts so they could continue their hard ride to the valley, but the Lancers were tired. Jimmy told them to stay with the herd and spread the news among the men and speed them up. Drive them hard or all was going to be lost.

Jimmy talked to his Simian charges and instructed them to remain with the herd and intermingle to get the horses accustomed to their smell. He then took Thunder and two extra horses and set out toward the valley. He was determined to make up some time. Damn, she loved this kid!

* Levi *

Amy had been happy to learn that Iron Eyes had thought to add all his gear that had been left in Owens Valley. They had planned to return to Owens Valley after the excursion into Los Angles, but circumstances had changed. Except for the chemical pills, which he stocked up on, he really didn't know what was so important. She had made him pack crazy stuff, like that damned microscope. He asked, "What do you want it for," but she would never say, just that, "It might come in handy."

He thought of many things like that as they jogged through the night. Amy kept him going, kept his body from overheating, but warned that the Simians, though extraordinarily long on endurance, could not keep it up indefinitely. The Simians would eventually weaken or destroy their bodies trying to keep pace with him. They must protect the Simians from exhaustion or they would not be able to fight or be severely disadvantaged. Amy calculated the minimum rest time required to maintain their endurance, and promised him she would keep the rest time to the minimum.

They jogged through the second night but again rested for two hours after daylight, then resumed the pace until the heat become excessive. Amy insisted that they rest through the hottest part of the day. This time they rested for three hours before resuming. It almost seemed a waste of time, but it was necessary and he knew it.

He rested as Amy wished, but gazed out toward the east, attempting to see the desert settlement. It was too far and he knew it, but he let his mind search. All he could see was desolate and barren desert as far as his eyes could see, except for the highway. The straight highway grew smaller as his eyes followed it until it was lost in the vast ocean of hot flowing air over the desert. It was hypnotizing, and he was soon asleep.

Amy was monitoring the activities of both Dawn and Jimmy. It had been a really good idea for Amy to link with Jimmy, and he was turning out to be far more imaginative and mature than most adults he had ever met. Jimmy was determined to cut down the required time for the mobilized army to reach the desert battle, and he may just do it, but three days was a lot to trim.

Nothing was happening yet in the desert, but they anticipated the Simian attack by morning. If everything continued at this pace, they could be close by early in the morning and get a few hours rest before daylight and engaging the Simians.

Amy's calculations seemed to be correct and the Simians looked fit, so they jogged off again into dusk and early evening. Amy limited the jogging pace to six hours this time, saying that they had to make up two more hours and "stretch the envelope," whatever the hell that meant. They took another two-hour break and then resumed the trek for the last six-hour stretch. They finally reached their objective several hours before sunup, so they settled down for some welcome food and rest.

* Amy *

Everything had worked out well. They made it to the desert settlement and were positioned several miles west along the road to wait sunup. Dawn was asleep, so she wasn't receiving much data from her. From this, she must assume that the Simians had not yet attacked. They could only wait, for now, but the rest was needed and welcome.

She showed Levi what Jimmy was doing. He was riding hard toward the valley, changing horses often to get the most out of them and not tire them so much. He still had to stop often and walk the horses and give them water, but he would soon be back in the saddle riding hard. Someone had taught him well. He knew just how far he could push the horses and how to get the most out of them. Thunder sensed the urgency in Jimmy and seemed to run harder. Jimmy had ridden through the previous night as well, and rested in the heat of the day just as they had done but was off again riding through the next night. He was gaining valuable time. If he could keep it up for one more night, he could make the outer defense location, and they could pass the word from there. Go Jimmy go!

She realized that at the very best, the Owens Valley army would be late, very late, if in time at all. The original plan assumed that the Owens Valley Lancers and lances would be at the Mojave settlement before the Simians got there. The lances would make it to the settlement before the main

Simian army reached the settlement, but not the Owens Valley army. If the army made it in time for the battle, which was beginning to look unlikely, they would need lances. She had, well Levi issued instructions to Moon to leave one Simian behind on the trail to inform Fred and the wagons to leave three of the wagons, teams, and drivers hidden to await the Owens Valley Lancers when and if they came. Otherwise, if they were fortunate enough to arrive in time, they would not have weapons to fight with. The delayed wagons would need to bring his gear but be sure to let the Lancers scout to make sure there was still a desert settlement remaining, before delivering the cargo.

The Simian Moon chose to leave behind was angry. He didn't want to stay behind, he wanted to fight, but he had been the weakest of the group after the forced march, and Moon's decision had been a good one. Moon acted like he was angry with # 10, but he was actually very proud of him. Moon had a good team.

At sunup she woke Levi. Something was happening at the pass. Like always, he was instantly alert and looking into her mind. He paused only to kiss her and grin. She said, "That was sweet, but this is serious. Dawn is awake and frightened." Dawn was looking behind them away from the gap in the pass where they would expect to see an attack come. The valley below them was becoming visible with the increasing light. Down below them, spreading out in the valley, were twenty Simian Warriors. The sentry above the pass reported there were five Simians approaching the front of the pass.

434

The whole defense of the Guard was mobile, defend the gap and retreat to the next defense position. Al had told Levi that they could defend from either direction by simply moving through the pass and defending from the other side. The Simians must have seen this defense work in the past and spent the night moving around the mountains to spring this trap. They reversed the defense. Now the five Simians could easily hold the pass from the other side, while the trap was being sprung. For the same reason the Simians couldn't get through, neither could Al's Guard. It was already too late to retreat. Al had a hundred of his Guard members neatly surrounded and being bottled together. He must launch an attack before they lost all room to maneuver.

* Levi *

When Amy woke him he knew it was time for battle and was instantly hyper. He knew Amy would be excited the way she always got when he was going into battle and wanted to calm her. He paused to kiss her. He kissed her image in his mind and remembered how sweet she tasted. He loved her, but knew they both needed to remain very focused and calm. They didn't want a repeat of what nearly happened with # 3.

It was far worse than he would have expected. The Simians had gotten very smart, strategically. Obviously one of the Simians had seen this defense before, possibly even one of the three that had almost gotten him. The Simians had seen the effectiveness of the pass defenses and used that

435

same defense against them to entrap the Humans. What no one knew was that he and Moon's small army were within reach to help if they got there quickly enough.

In numbers alone the odds were on the Human's side. That was comically sad, with four Humans verses one Simian, odds were still hopeless for the Humans. Al ordered the Guard to mount and charge the Simians while they had room to maneuver. There were seventy-five men mounted to attack, and their attack was timed to be in unison. The Guard charged through the Simians, breaking past to save themselves as Al had ordered. The Simians dropped fifteen of the horses and riders as they came past. The Simians quickly killed the downed Humans. The Guard inflicted some minor wounds on the Simians, but they took none out of the battle. The majority of the Humans was out of the trap now and turned to fight a flanking action on the Simians. Every time the Simians turned to advance, the Guard would harass their rear, but the Simians continued to slowly advance on the remaining twenty-five Humans still defending the pass.

The Simian's plan was clear, so Levi and his red-tagged Simians approached quickly under the shadow cover of the rocks, until they were very close to the five Simians guarding the front of the pass. He advanced slowly until he was in danger of being observed. He quickly ran toward the back of the nearest Simian swinging and spinning his pickaxe. The Simian turned too late to defend itself as the spike sank upward deep into its crotch. It died instantly! He stepped on the Simian and pulled hard on his weapon to remove it. The other four Simians turned to face him and Moon's army, as they began screeching hatred and warnings to the other Simians Warriors inside the pass. It pleased him to hear and understand the Warrior Simians' cry of warning and help, but they would get no help.

The Warrior Simians screeched their defiance and contempt at Moon's small squad and, in their overconfidence, attacked. If the Simian Warriors thought to scare them, they were terribly shocked. Moon met the first one with lightning speed and with moves totally unexpected. The attacking Warrior died quickly with a short sword stuck in its throat. Two others died at the hands of Moon's Simians, overwhelmed by blows from the multiple attacks. They were not under any compulsion to fight fair, only to win. The last of the five Simian Warriors stared at his dying team members and backed into the gap for defense. It suddenly fell forward with a double-bladed axe buried deep in its neck. Al stood in the gap staring into his eyes.

He wasted no time in telling Al, "You are good bait." That comment was met with a big smile as Al looked at the Simians standing with him. He simply said to Al, "They are friends." Al turned and immediately ordered his team through the gap to defend this side of the pass.

* Amy *

Dawn was scared but watched intently, allowing Amy to follow the situation inside the defenses through Dawn's eyes. It was bad, but Al was a good leader. He was quick to realize that he had to cut losses and try to save as many of the

437

Guard as possible. The charge was successful in that most of his mounted Guard escaped. The losses would have been much more if he had delayed longer. Of course, it was suicide for those remaining inside, but he had no choice. The Guard continued to harass the advancing Simians, but it was only a matter of time before the screeching monsters closed and finished them off.

Dawn turned to see and hear the sentry on top of the rocks. He was reporting an attack on the Simians outside. He said, "A Human and a bunch of other Simians are killing the five outside."

Dawn screamed to Al, "It is Levi. It can only be Levi and Moon, with help."

Al ran forward and seeing the Simian's back to him, grabbed a double-bladed axe and buried it deep into its neck. Then he ran forward to see what was happening.

Through Levi's eyes, she saw Levi strike and kill the first Simian, while Moon and the others attacked and killed three others. The battle outside was over very quickly, except for the last lone Simian that had backed into the gap. Through Dawn's eyes she saw Al run forward and sink an axe in the back of the Warrior. Simultaneously, she saw it fall forward from Levi's eyes. It struck her as being strange, seeing the same event from two sources and perspectives at the same time but liked the double coverage, although realizing that it could easily get confusing.

Once Al realized it was safe on this side, he ordered his Guard through the gap. As the Guard started pouring through, the Simians began advancing faster toward the gap, trying to catch the escaping Humans. The Guard units on the outside of the Simian's perimeter took the opportunity to launch an attack on their rear. They swung bolos over their heads and threw them at the retreating Simians' feet.

The bolos were made of three lengths of strong, laced cord tied in the center with weights on the free ends. When thrown in a spinning fashion, they would wrap around whatever they hit and tie it up. These were used in South America to catch cattle or horses. Here, they were just as effectively against Simians. She liked this weapon. They would not tie up a Simian for very long but could make it trip and fall. The thinking was, once on the ground; it might be attacked and killed, if they were quick enough.

Mostly the Simians would see the bolos and jump to avoid them, but now with their backs to them, the Humans were managing to connect with many of the targets. Also, each Simian had multiple Guard members teamed against it. As a result, the Guard succeeded in tangling many of the Simian's feet. The Simian's attack on the retreating Humans was a tactical mistake. They were getting tripped up in the bolos, falling and being attacked on the ground. Cheers went up as some of the Simians were killed.

* Levi *

He heard the cheering, and Amy told him about the partial success with the bolos. There were several, maybe five, Simians down, and the Guard members were attacking them on the ground. However, Dawn was watching several Simians continue to approach the retreating Guard inside the gap. Then the input was gone, as Dawn came running through the gap with the retreating Guard.

The Simians had to be defeated, so as soon as the flood of Guard members slowed, he darted through the gap followed closely by Moon, his small group of Simians, and Al. As his field of vision widened, he took in the situation immediately. There were six Simians dead and three more were down with bolos around their feet. These were being attacked by the Guard and it looked like they would be successful. There were still eleven Simians approaching the gap with six Guard members fighting two of the closest Simians. He noticed another five Guard members lying dead, having bought the time for the retreat with their lives.

Anger swelled in Levi, and he attacked. Amy was trying to calm him, saying he must remain composed, but he was beyond tranquility. He dove between the two nearest Guards, rolling to place a two-legged kick at the feet of the nearest Simian. He held his pickaxe up between his hands to ward off any sword attack, but there was none. His attack was so sudden and unexpected that the Simian's feet shot out from under it, toppling it forward like a felled tree. He barely rolled out of the way in time. The Guard members dispatched the fallen Simian quickly with many blows and cheered their delight in being alive.

Moon and his Simians pushed aside the astonished Guard members to spread out and attack the advancing Warriors. Those of Moon's army yet to gain a weapon took them from the dead Simians.

Gaining his feet, he saw Moon and his Simians engage the advancing Warriors. He watched Moon spinning, doubling back under strikes, and taking every opportunity to strike home. The Warrior Moon faced was a big brute that towered over Moon, but Moon looked confident as the battle continued. He wondered why Moon didn't kick like before, but had noticed that Simians were not overly good at jumping, and he had never seen one climb either. It must be the excessive weight of their bodies, and Moon must feel more comfortable with the new training. He shook his head as Amy mentally slapped him.

She said, "Remain focused!"

Damn she was right, why was he thinking about shit like that now?

Moon's Simians were doubling up on the Warriors now as he saw some of the Warriors falling. "No!" To his right # 12 was down and obviously dead. He had been up against a particularly large Warrior. It was bigger than most Simians he had seen, and it was now moving against # 7. The attack staggered # 7, and he fell. As he saw the Warrior raise its sword to kill # 7, his rage took over and he charged the Warrior. Leaping into the air, timing the spin, his feet connected with the Simian. The kick was timed to save # 7 more than kill the Warrior, which it did. As he connected with the Warrior's side, it was knocked sideways, spoiling the Simian's blow. Damn, the Simian didn't go down, but he did. It was like jumping into the side of a wall. He hit the ground rolling as the Warrior struck the ground where his head had been only a fraction of a second before. He realized that this was no ordinary Simian Warrior, and this was not going to be an easy fight.

* Amy *

The Simians would have been unbeatable if they had gone into a defense mode, but their egotism made them attack, exposing their rear. It proved to be a mistake as some of their numbers fell. She counted nine Simians down, but there remained eleven Warrior Simians advancing. Levi saw what she saw and knew what she thought, but he didn't always view it the same way.

He saw the conflict of the battle raging inside and the need to destroy the enemy. He didn't see the eleven advancing Simians as the terrible threat that they were, he only saw the enemy. He darted through the gap, closely followed by Moon and his small army. Levi joined the fight by attacking the first Simian Warrior he saw.

Levi was so damned trusting. He had no idea what he was going to do. He just plunged in anyway. He knew she would give him a plan, and she did. She analyzed weight dispersement, speed, distances, momentum and forces and struck. Levi couldn't swing without hitting one of the Humans, so she sent him diving through in a roll. She calculated the Simian's movements and angle for a calculated rolling kick to the Simian's feet. It worked perfectly, and the Simian's feet went out backwards, sending it crashing to the ground, as Levi rolled away. The three Guard members immediately began hacking the Simian to death.

As Levi rolled back to his feet, she analyzed the area. Moon was engaged in battle with a Warrior, but he looked like he was practicing instead of fighting for his life. His Simians were engaged all over the field. Some of the closer Warriors had already been taken out by a combined attack from his team, which left the other Warriors outnumbered. The battle was winding down quickly.

Suddenly one of his Simians went down. It was # 12. She could tell # 12 was dead, and Levi was enraged. This was a big strong Warrior and it was going after # 7 now. It knocked # 7 to the ground and was rising for the finish, but Levi attacked. Damn! She needed warning. Levi leaped into the air with an overhead, spinning and double-footed kick. It veered the Warrior's strike enough to save # 7, but that was about it. Levi hit the ground, and she immediately made him roll. The Warrior just barely missed Levi's head with that sword strike. Levi rolled to his feet and stared at the Simian. It was staring back as they appraised each other.

All the Simian Warriors had been killed except the one Levi now faced. Moon and the others were gathering to circle the last Warrior, but Levi held out his hands and waved them off.

Levi said, "I am going to face this one alone."

She was angry at this showing off and told him, "This is stupid. This macho crap has to stop and just might with your death."

* Levi *

443

He saw that this Warrior he faced was the only one left. He glanced around to see dead Humans and Simians scattered across the battlefield. He saw Moon and the others circling and he waved them away. This was going to be a one-on-one fight. Amy was going crazy on him, calling him stupid and everything else she could think of.

She said, "You don't have to do this."

But, he did have to. If he ever wanted to have the respect of Moon's Simians and the Humans of this settlement, he did need to do this. The others spread out to give them room as he wished.

He would have to be very good with this one. He had already felt its strength, and it was awesome. They circled each other. He held a sword in his right hand and the pickaxe in the left. The Simian had his large broad sword in its double thumbed right hand and a short sword in its left. This was unusual for a Simian and would pose a problem for his practiced fighting skills and defenses.

The Simian attacked suddenly, but he was always just a fraction of an inch out of its swing. The Simian was good, and it was hard to take an offensive. He was fighting a defensive battle only. He tried many of the moves that worked in the past, but the Simian was prepared with a counterattack. He was lucky to just escape some of its counters, but Amy was quick to anticipate and defend. A few times he even felt Amy take over for a fraction of a second, to move him out of the way of an unexpected stab or thrust. The Simian's fighting skills were very good and unpredictable. The Simian never made the same predictable move.

They fought on for what seemed like hours with neither scoring a hit. He deflected swings of the sword and dodged thrusts from the short sword. There simply were no opportunities. He tried jumping, rolling, diving underneath, spinning; but the Simian was elusive. He was beginning to think he should swallow his pride and ask for help.

Amy said "wait. I am detecting a pattern to the Simian's attack, but the timing will have to be perfect, so do not resist when I interject my control."

What she did then shocked him more than anything else she had ever done. When the Simian swung, he deflected the broad sword. At that point Amy took over and dropped both his weapons. "What!" He felt his body leap forward just barely inside the thrust of the short sword. The blade brushed by his head. He was simultaneously dropping to his knees and pulling one of his Bowie knifes. As the Simian was stretched, his arm thrust his Bowie knife in a hard roundhouse, underhand blow into the Simian's crotch. He felt the blade go deep into this unprotected area but, sickeningly, not deep enough. It was a brilliant move, but it just didn't fucking work! It hurt the Simian badly, but did not paralyze the huge Warrior, as Amy had gambled. It fell to the ground taking him with it. Luckily, it fell on its back.

He was now against the Simian's body, so close that he could smell the musky sweet sweat on its chest. The Simian grasped him in its huge hands and held him with his arms pinned to his side and began pulling him toward its gaping shark toothed jaws. Oh shit! He screamed, "Do something Amy!"

445

This was no ordinary Simian Warrior. This one used a two-sword fighting technique she had never seen before. She had nothing in memory even close to categorize this Simian's fighting technique. All its moves were totally unique to her knowledge and very unpredictable. Nothing worked and all she could do was keep Levi out of its way. She tried many moves, but this one was very quick and its defenses very efficient.

They fought for a very long time with neither gaining an advantage. The Simian stared in disbelief at Levi. This one was not accustomed to losing any battles and was shocked that a Human could resist its prowess. She continued to watch for a pattern, a weakness, a mistake, but saw none.

Levi wanted this victory but was about to give up and ask for help when she saw it. Yes, there was a pattern. After a swing with the broad sword there was a predictable delay of about one and a half seconds before the short sword made a thrust. This wasn't enough time to jump in and strike with his sword and get out, but it was enough time to get inside and stay. The only problem was that a death blow would have to be administered and the only instant kill that she knew of was the nerve center in the lower abdomen reached through the crotch.

They fought on and she waited until the Simian struck. When it did, she took over Levi's body, deflected the blow, and leaped close inside its defenses, as the short sword whistled past his head. She immediately dropped Levi to his knees, pulling the Bowie knife and driving it upward with both hands, hard into its crotch. The Simian shuddered and fell backwards to the ground but was not dead. It pinned Levi's arms to his side in a bone-crushing grip and started pulling Levi toward its already open jaws. The Simian was determined to take Levi with him in death.

Why wasn't it dead? It should be dead! What went wrong and what could she do now? She had to think quickly, because in about twenty-seconds Levi would be dead. The Bowie knife had either missed or hadn't gone in deep enough. No, the angle was correct. The depth had to be the problem. Could they reach the knife with Levi's knee and drive it in further? His knees were now above the crotch of the Simian and unable to reach the knife.

She would have to find a way to get loose and all she had to work with was Levi's head. Yes! She started modifying Levi's mouth. His jaw started lengthening and grew thicker, while fangs grew out of the growing jaw. The modifications were complete by the time the Simian pulled him close to its neck. When Levi was close enough, she drove his jaw and fangs deep into its neck; she closed his jaws hard and was rewarded by an ear-hurting screech of pain. The Simian pushed Levi away and let him go. Levi dropped down and drove a knee hard into the handle of the Bowie knife. She felt it drive in and the Simian immediately froze in death.

Levi lay on the dead Simian's chest for a long moment catching his breath, while she changed him back. It was over and they had triumphed yet again. This was the hardest fight yet and uncomfortably too close.

As he stood, she noticed the silence. Levi stopped and looked around to see Moon and his Simians staring in shock along with Al and the Guard. After a few minutes, one of the Guard members started clapping and soon all were clapping and cheering. This time she shared in Levi's praise because she deserved it.

* Levi *

He thought his goose was cooked this time, until he felt his teeth growing. He knew what Amy had in mind now, even before he looked into her mind. He felt his fangs sink deep into the nerves and arteries of the Simian's neck. He tasted the bitter purple blood and relished the screech of pain from the Simian. Even the bite might have eventually killed it, but the release was what Amy was hoping for, and that is what they got. When the grip released, he dropped down and kneed the knife deeper into its crotch. That did it! He felt the Warrior stiffen then go limp in death.

As he lay there resting for a second, he laughed, remembering his grandfather saying that biting wasn't fighting fair. He idly wondered if his grandfather would forgive him for biting under these circumstances.

If he intended to impress the Simians and the Guard, it worked, but he thought it frightened them more than impressed. This was the first time he saw what looked like awe in Moon's eyes. Moon took great ceremonial pride in removing the Warrior Simian's tooth for Levi's trophy. Moon also removed a chain necklace with a small sword on it and brought it to him and placed it around his neck. He presented the Simian's short sword to him also. Levi accepted the ceremonial presentation of the necklace and sword, because it seemed important to Moon, but he didn't understand why.

Moon explained, "The Warrior Simian had been the Sword Master of the Simian command. Now you are the best and will be known to other Simians by the necklace and short sword."

It was a Simian ceremonial short sword, but would make a good normal sword for him. He was a little sad to part with the old sword he had dragged across the desert as an old man, but this ceremonial sword was a very fancy and well-built sword. He could get used to it.

Moon wasn't the only one with a ceremony for him. Al formally welcomed him back to their settlement with many thanks for his help, and then thanked each Simian, one at a time. He shook their hands and patted them on the arm. They looked very happy

He then walked through his Simians telling them in their own language just how proud he was of them, and he was so proud he could bust. When he got to Moon, he embraced him. He grinned, telling Amy, "The Lone Ranger never had a Tonto like this." He kissed Amy's image and thanked her too but then immediately criticized her for almost getting him killed.

She just grinned and reminded him, "I got you out of it too."

It was a good day to be alive and everyone seemed to realize their good fortune. It could have been a total disaster and almost was; however, the day was not without casualties. They had defeated a twenty-five Simian Warrior advance patrol, but had lost twenty-one Humans in the battle and two of his Simians, # 12 and # 15. All and all it was a victory, considering what happened in other encounters.

There was a lot to talk about and plans to make, but it could wait till tomorrow. They had won the first engagement with plenty of luck, but at least they survived to worry about another day. In this case, it would be six days away, and considerably more Simians.

CHAPTER 17
(PREPARING FOR WAR)

* Amy *

At the Mojave Desert settlement several things had to happen very quickly in order to attempt to survive the upcoming war. The horses had to be somewhat familiar with the Simian smell, the lances had to arrive, the Guard had to be trained in jousting and she had some other surprises she wanted to work on.

Someone in Al's army had to be versatile in the Simian sign language. She had given that much thought and had decided that Dawn would be the perfect one here. She was already linked with her mind, so there would be no change. Fred would be here by tomorrow to work with this group, but she needed Dawn to work with the second group back at the main camp and herd. Using Dawn would keep the number she was monitoring limited. It was already becoming too confusing. It would be nice to have more communication, but she would have to settle for those she already had. Maybe she could figure out a way to reverse the process at some point and break some of the links, but for now she had no choice.

Levi called Al, Dawn and Moon and explained what needed to be done. Moon understood much of the English language now, though the speech was beyond his abilities. Levi didn't explain the linking part, but did describe the downloading of information to them. Dawn was standing next to Al with her arm locked around his, as if to say that she was with Al now. Levi took note, looked into her eyes and gave a slight nod. He could see the relief and appreciation on Dawn's face, and both could see it in her mind. Al did not notice this private communication between them.

They agreed to the plan and Levi touched Dawn's face, while the information passed into her mind. As with the others, the results were immediate. Dawn and Moon began talking almost immediately. Good, the plan could begin. He would remain at the pass with Moon and half of the Simians to begin training and working with the horses here, while Al and Dawn would take half the Simians back to the main camp to begin the horse indoctrination of those there. When the wagons arrived with his gear and lances, he would leave Fred with the Simians and half the Owens Valley Lancers and proceed to the main camp with a wagonload of lances. The Guard would begin training in both areas and would soon be Lancers.

She was monitoring Fred and the progress of the wagons. They would be at the staging area by dark, where # 10 waited, and camp there. It was only a few hours more, so she was sure # 10 would want to come on into camp tonight. She would ask Levi to tell the sentry. It was also a certainty that the Lancers would want to come with them too, but they must remain with the wagons. Levi had instructed them to send out scouts before coming into the pass just in case there was no Human resistance left. Some of the Lancers would come with # 10 no matter what. Of this she was sure. Levi chuckled and agreed.

Jimmy made excellent progress. He had ridden throughout the day and night the second day, and arrived at the defenses on the morning of the battle. Actually, this very morning, but it seemed like it was so long ago. Jimmy gave orders as if speaking for Levi, which he did, and sent the Lancers riding hard to tell Iron Eyes, the Council, and Chief, of the change in plans. Jimmy told them, "Pack up, mobilize the army on foot, and move to the southern end of the valley and prepare to intercept the horses, NOW!" Jimmy gave a brief, but informative explanation of the necessity. The Lancers jumped to obey, while he lay down to get some sorely needed rest. That had been seven hours ago, and Jimmy had been sleeping ever since.

* Levi *

Details! He hated details, but Amy relished in them. Her computer mind analyzed data and developed a plan for everything. Not much snuck up on her. He issued her instructions and plans as if they were coming from him and everyone accepted them. Admittedly, Amy did have almost everything figured out, but she went too far sometimes with the details. Sometimes he would skip over some of the finer stuff. Sometimes you just had to let others think for themselves. Just look at Jimmy and what he was doing. Amy readily agreed with him about Jimmy. He sure hoped what Jimmy was trying to do would work. They might have a chance yet if

Jimmy was successful in cutting three days out of the schedule to the desert settlement.

Al and Dawn took half of the Simians and left for the main camp, Moon was already mingling with the nervous horses. The Simians feasted on the dead horses from the battle and were quite full to capacity. The live horses were quite safe but remained very nervous in the proximity of a Simian. The horses would eventually get used to it just as the Owens Valley horses had, if there was enough time.

He agreed with Amy's assessment of # 10. He remembered how upset # 10 had been when Moon made him stay with the wagons. He would definitely come once he was relieved, and he believed Fred and some of the Lancers would come also. They would know soon enough, but he gave instructions to the sentry to watch out for a friendly Simian and Humans approaching the pass.

With so much to do and time running out, it was hard to just wait, but there was no choice. He paced back and forth like a caged animal, making everyone nervous.

It was well after dark when Amy finally suggested, "Let's go to the staging area and meet the wagons coming in and escort them back."

Oh, he liked that idea. It was a very good idea, and he would be able to lead them back tonight. He whistled for Moon, explaining where he wanted them to go. Something happened then that was totally unexpected. It was overcast with no moon tonight, and at the suggestion that they go out into the pitch dark, Moon was afraid.

Moon said, "Simians have poor night vision and he would not be able to defend himself."

Amy recalled that all the other times they had traveled at night, which was the escape from Los Angeles, there had been a bright moon.

He told Moon that he could see well at night, and there would be no danger. Moon reluctantly agreed, and they left shortly thereafter, following the road. It was very dark, but Amy had augmented his eyes, like the rest of his body, to excel in any condition. He could see in almost total darkness, but Moon was having trouble so he kept to the road and slowed his jogging pace.

He knew Amy was already planning a night attack somewhere in her vast brain and he smiled. He was rewarded with knowing smile in return. Their ability to see into each other's thoughts was certainly improving their communication. They had less need to use words, yet they had better understanding than ever before. It was scary in some ways. Just when they seemed in danger of completely merging minds, there would be a disagreement, but that just served to remind them they were still separate identities.

It took them about an hour and a half to reach the staging area. He whistled for # 10 and saw the Simian stand up and look around, but it could not see him. Once he got close enough, # 10 smelled him and turned to face him. The wagons hadn't made it yet. Amy said they were still about an hour out. They were welcomed warmly by # 10. He had been lonesome and anxious about what was happening. They sat while Moon told # 10 everything including, what would be legendary, the one-on-one combat between him and the Sword Master. No wonder legends grew, the way Moon told the story. Moon made him sound like Superman.

* Amy *

She was nervous, and she had no idea why. Something was not proper. It could be her emerging clairvoyance, but if it was, she wished the vision would become clear. As it was, she was just nervous. It must be filtering through to Levi, because he was a wreck. He was making everyone nervous, so she suggested that they go meet the wagons. He liked that idea and immediately called Moon.

She was taken aback when she saw fear in Moon's red eyes. She hadn't seen fear in his eyes in a very long time and was even beginning to think him fearless; this was shocking. There must be a logical reason. Moon told Levi that Simians had poor night vision. She researched her files of information Moon had provided, and yes, the Simian home world had three moons. With three moons it would never be completely dark like it was here tonight and any necessary night vision would not have developed. Moon would be helpless in a night fight. She found this interesting, which would require planning in how best to use this information. She saw Levi's smile and knew that the "Stinker" knew what she was planning.

They reached the staging area before the wagons and talked with # 10 for a while, and then Levi left them to intercept the wagons. Levi only had to go a few thousand yards to meet the wagons. He called out to them and waited. They all came running, wanting information. Giving the brief version, he explained that their army was still alive and detailed the plans for staging some of the lances here to await the Owens Valley army. He led them back to the hidden area where # 10 was waiting, selected those wagons and Lancers to remain, and led the rest of the party to the pass. It took three hours to reach Granite Pass and gain protection behind the defenses.

Introductions were in order between the Lancers and Guards, while # 10 was happy to re-join his team. After a good night's sleep, training at this camp would start in earnest, and Levi would travel with two Lancers and some of the wagons loaded with lances to the second staging area at Forshay Pass to begin training there.

There were only the two passes for access to the other side of the mountains for many miles in either direction, which made Granite and Forshay Pass ideal for defense. Strangely enough, the main camp was on the unprotected side of the mountain. The main camp had the option of moving in the case of danger or going underground into the stocked caverns. The caverns could be sealed with impenetrable doors installed years ago. It was safe inside and could withstand long sieges. Either pass was subject to attack, but Granite Pass was closer to the main road, Interstate 40, and had always been the pass the Simians tried. Both passes were guarded, however, and capable of the same defenses. Al had dispersed the army at both places with only a marginal number of Guardsmen at the main camp to sound the alarm and close the cavern doors in case of attack.

Her focus in this trip to the main camp was to gain access to the caverns to research a theory she had been considering since they came through here, what now seemed like years ago. She had been unable to research the cause of the shift in the physical laws of science, but had retrieved the microscope from her research facility for this purpose and had insisted that Levi bring it in his gear. The gear was in the wagon they would be taking to the main camp. She believed that it might be possible to alter chemical compounds to compensate for the shift. If that could be done, she might be able to reinvent gunpowder. What if she could? Should she? She had a moral dilemma, which she was still wrestling with. This part of her mind was closed very tight, and Levi didn't know about this. Levi was very persuasive and might be able to convince her into almost anything. All the moral issues must be considered, before discussing it with Levi. Additionally, guns would become an equalizer against Levi's skills as well, and that could cost him his edge or even life. Before a decision could be made she should first find out if it was possible.

* Levi *

Levi met the wagons exactly where and when Amy said. He guessed that wasn't so hard when you were looking through the eyes of Fred aboard the lead wagon. Even so, he found it strange to watch through Fred's eyes and see himself standing in the

458

road. He backed out of Amy's mind then. It was just too disorienting. He began to see why Amy wanted to limit the number of minds she was linked to. Even for Amy's incredible abilities and intellect, there were limits.

He disbursed the supplies as Amy suggested, leaving some wagons and supplies at the remote area, and led the wagons back to the camp for further distribution according to Amy's plan. Of course it was the right thing to do. It always was. It was late when they arrived back at camp at the first pass, and everyone was tired. Introductions and a late supper were about all that occurred before bedding down. It had been a long hard trip for the bulls, horses and men from the Owens Valley, but especially hard from Barstow. It had been a wicked pace, but only four days remained until the Simians were on their front porch, and time was running out.

By midmorning everyone was busy at their assigned tasks. Fred was already teaching the sign language to those Guard members not actually practicing with the lances. The Lancers were hard at work sharing their limited experience fighting with lances against Simians. One thing in their favor was the fact that each Lancer sported at least one Simian trophy tooth that had been won in battle doing exactly what they were teaching. It helped their credibility greatly and the Guard members listened attentively.

Moon had his Simians moving through the picketed horses and among the horses at practice. The Guard and horses weren't comfortable, but that is what this was all about. At least the horses were controllable where they weren't before.

He accompanied the last split of the wagons and supplies at the first pass and headed toward the main camp. Amy said it was about a five-hour trip at this speed. Moon was at his side as usual and the pace being what it was, Moon became bored. It wasn't even a comfortable walking pace for Moon. He asked, "Is there any real reason to stay with the wagons?" She allowed that there wasn't.

Amy said, "It is just part of a plan, but it can easily be altered."

Hearing this, he decided to jog with Moon, so he gave the wagon drivers the directions, and was about to head out when Amy reminded him to bring his main pack and gear when he left the wagon. That startled him, but he grabbed his hundred-pound pack from the wagon and tossed it across his back.

His curiosity got the best of him and he tried to find out what Amy had in mind, but she wouldn't say anything no matter how he came at her with questions. He even tried to look into her mind, but saw only a wall blocking his way. All she would do is grin.

Amy said, "You will know in due time."

She could be so frustrating sometimes.

* Amy *

As they were jogging toward Forshay Pass, she gave Levi the summary of what was happening with Jimmy. Jimmy had awakened after nine hours of solid sleep. He had arrived in the early morning and it was now late afternoon, and there was no sign of the army. They had time to mobilize, and it was only a four-hour march. Something was wrong. He saddled Thunder, took the other two horses in tow, and headed toward the main camp. He had only been on the road for an hour when he saw them in the distance. He was even happier to see that Iron Eyes was leading the army.

Riding up, he dismounted and embraced Iron Eyes. They had both been busy. Iron Eyes looked around somewhat alarmed.

Understanding, Jimmy explained, "Dawn stayed in the desert camp, and she is all right."

Iron Eyes sighed his relief and started asking questions about what had happened on Jimmy's end.

Jimmy related the story about his trip, about the horses coming behind him, and about the emergency message that was sent by Levi. Jimmy told how he planned the Pony Express ride and issued the orders to the Lancers. Iron Eyes stopped in his tracks and looked hard at Jimmy with newfound respect. Iron Eyes spread his arms wide in a gesture to include the horses and army.

Iron Eyes asked, "Did you organize this?" Iron Eyes liked this kid as much as they did.

Jimmy humbly said, "Yes."

Iron Eyes gave him a big hug and said, "You did well."

There were about fifteen horses in Iron Eyes' group of three hundred Lancers, so all the horses were being used to transport supplies. Each Lancer carried his own saddle, rations for five days, personal weapons and three water skins. They were heavily laden but moving with as much speed as possible, considering the circumstances.

461

Jimmy turned over his two extra horses to Iron Eyes, who quickly assigned them to the smallest men within sight. They were all smiles. Jimmy kept Thunder clear, because he would be riding out soon to look for the horse herd. At this rate of travel, they would make the defenses by sundown. His plan was helping. They had shaved maybe two days off the eleven days scheduled, but that was not enough, and the coming trip would be long, hard and hot. They had to do more, and Jimmy told Iron Eyes what he had in mind. Iron Eyes grasp the situation quickly, and told Jimmy to go find and bring the horses to them, while he would keep the army moving past the defenses.

Iron Eyes said, grinning, "They can sleep in the saddle once they have horses."

Jimmy rode off again, retracing his path to the defenses and beyond. He wanted to find the horses before the sun set. Setting a fast pace, he headed down Highway 395. The army would be here in two hours and he was trying to calculate his timetable from that. He traveled for three hours and just before the light was totally gone, he saw them! Yes, they were about three miles ahead at the edge of Haiwee Reservoir. He rode hard to meet the herders, and they were anxious to know if this forced ride had been successful.

Jimmy said, "Oh, hell, yes! The army is walking to meet us, even as we speak. We should meet within two hours."

While waiting for the horses to get their fill of water, Jimmy talked to # 2 and # 8. They had been without communications since he left them and wanted to know what was going on. He gave them a quick run down of where everyone was and what was happening. They were concerned about the battle Moon and Levi had gone into, and he explained that he was too, but they would have to do what they could, to get this army there to win the war, assuming that there would be one left to win. They agreed.

Within two hours the walking Owens Valley army and the horses and herders were in sight of each other and the cheering began. The Guard members herding the horses were very relieved to see an army ready to help them, and the army was very relieved to see horses for their use. Their confidence soared, but they would need all they could muster before this was over.

It proved to be unexpectedly hard to match riders with the horses. First, the horses were not anxious to be singled out and had to be roped. Then the horses forgot they had been broken and had to be reminded by the herders. The new riders weren't all that experienced, and finally, there were some minor arguments over who was getting what horse.

Iron Eyes and Jimmy were very upset by the time everyone was mounted and ready to travel, which had taken the better part of four hours. A precious few of the horses had been lost in the forced march, and all three hundred Lancers had a horse with fifty extra horses for packing supplies or use as remounts as needed. They were not able to travel far because of the lateness of the evening, but it was necessary for the horses and riders to get used to each other. They traveled back to the lake and each man cared for his own horse and slept with it picketed next to him. The men and horses were tired and Iron Eyes felt that getting some rest the first night would make the traveling pace better for the rest of the trip.

At sunup the next morning the Owens Valley Lancer Army was mounted and headed for battle. They had made up two of the days, but would have to make the six-day trip in four days to reach the desert settlement in time for the war. Amy was feeling better, but far from comfortable. Too many things could go wrong, and they still had to make up two more days.

She and Levi were very proud of everyone. This was an incredible group of people, but above all, they were both very happy with Jimmy.

* Levi *

It helped immensely to be able to follow what was going on in different areas. Jimmy had surprised him greatly, and Amy was showing real fondness and pride in Jimmy. It was almost like they were his parents. He had always wished for a son he could be proud of, and he was proud of Jimmy. The Owens Valley army had a chance, though remote, of being there in time, thanks to Jimmy. He was beginning to be optimistic until he remembered that there were three hundred Simian warriors, well, two hundred and seventy-five now, and that was a lot of monsters to deal with. They had been lucky, too, in this first engagement. The Simians can't know what happened yet, but would not underestimate the Humans again.

They were approaching the inner pass as their discussion continued. Amy was talking battle deployment, strategy, coordination of attacks and communications. Amy wished they had radios to coordinate attacks and movements. He thought about it for a minute and said, "Do it telepathically."

She reminded him, "My brain waves have been permanently altered to synchronize with yours and could not be changed."

His attorney trained, argumentative brain came from a different direction and said, "Use my brain to speak telepathically." He reminded her how she had used his mind to focus her telekinesis and astral projection. He knew she could do it; she could do anything if she believed she could. Her only limitations were self-imposed. He said, "If you can read the minds of those you linked with, then you should be able to speak to those same minds. Speak through my mind." She was quiet after that, and he believed she was now analyzing that option.

His attention was suddenly drawn to the sentries at the pass. They were waving frantically at him. They were pointing behind them, and he turned to see a lone Simian Warrior running behind them. It already had its sword raised in the air to dispatch him. It must have been one left over from the battle that had hidden and waited for an easy target. It assumed a Human and substandard Simian would be that easy target. He dodged to the left as he pulled his Bowie Knife. His move was barely adequate to move his body out of the way, but his heavy pack was caught by the sword chop. The sudden impact of the sword threw him off balance and to the ground. He slipped out of his pack and rolled behind the Simian while it was extended with the sword and struck hard at the Achilles tendon of

465

its right foot. The tendon was severed, and the Simian fell from the blow and was killed by Moon before it could even start to get up. Moon almost chopped its head off from his double fisted blow and was already digging out two teeth even before he regained his feet. He had lost track of how many of the black teeth he had now, but he didn't want any more around his neck. The dense teeth weighed like gold but knew Moon wouldn't ask him, he would just put another one on his necklace.

* Amy *

She had high intellect, probably many times more than any Human ever, but that damned abstract thought still came slowly to her. She was very much alive, aware and she thought, but the really wild thoughts that breached logic seemed to always come from Levi. It seemed so easy for him to come up with solutions. It was like he didn't even plan, it just came out of idle thought, but he was right. She could communicate telepathically with those she had already linked with. The link had been made with the others through Levi's brain and not hers. Her mind was the receiver of the data, but it was all channeled through Levi's mind. Theoretically, it should work both ways. She would try soon.

The imaginary hairs were standing up on the back of her imaginary neck. This is what was wrong. Now she sensed danger when it was almost too late to do anything about it. If it hadn't been for the sentries, she may not have been able to react soon enough. She sensed, even before Levi turned, that there was a Simian there. She noticed that the Guard members were on the other side of the pass instead of this side where they normally were. That could only mean a Simian danger. With Moon present at Levi's side, she wasn't able to detect the Simian smell as a warning.

They had narrowly escaped an attack yet another time, but they had been lucky, and she didn't like to depend on luck. She was happy when they had luck, but she much preferred to depend on her own abilities to plan and foresee danger, and she had failed to anticipate this possibility and failed to monitor their surroundings. She screwed up as Levi would say.

After Moon killed the Simian Warrior the Guard members came pouring back through the pass, cheering and showing their respect to Levi and even Moon. Moon was accepted completely now and seemed to sense that also. Moon even appeared to welcome the attention. She chuckled to herself saying, "Another macho male!"

It seemed that the lone Simian had been spotted about two hours earlier by the sentries who gave the alarm and reversed the defense position. They had sent a rider and warning around the front side of the mountains to the other pass, and were just waiting when they saw Levi and Moon coming. The Simian had waited until they had passed its position and came out to attack from behind. The sentries had been trying frantically to get their attention for several minutes before finally being noticed. That had probably saved Levi and possibly Moon as well.

When Levi reached for his pack where it had spilled out from the Simian's sword cut, they saw the microscope lying in the dust, destroyed. This ended the debate over gunpowder. She had decided that if she could, she would make the modification. The odds were simply too great and the war was not progressing well. They would be lucky to be alive in four days and guns might make a difference.

They proceeded on through the pass, reaching the caverns and main camp within an hour. Moon went off to talk with his Simians as Levi met Al and reported about the surviving Simian and its recent death.

Al looked hard at Levi and asked solemnly, "Isn't it about time to tell me what is going on with you, or better yet, what has happened to you?"

Al had held his curiosity patiently, knowing that Levi would tell him sooner or later. Al must now feel that it was time. She told Levi that Al might be ready for the truth, but no one could ever know the complete truth. No one!

* Levi *

There was no doubt that Al believed he was the Levi he had known, but just as sure something had happened to him that he was going to have a lot of trouble understanding. When Al asked, Amy told him he must keep the secret of Amy. No one could ever know about her, or she would be in danger, not from Al but from others in general. He didn't understand and she must have seen that in his mind and on his face.

She went on to explain, "If the existence of a supercomputer that could make a Human into a superhuman like you ever got out, I would be searched for by Humans and eventually the Simians. The Humans would destroy me out of lack of understanding, ignorance, or jealousy; and the Simians would seek to destroy me to kill you."

He was beginning to see her concern.

He and Al sat alone watching the fading sun, as he related his story. Dawn was at the spring with the other women washing clothes and bathing. This was one reason Al chose now to talk. He told Al about the culture he had found and accidentally gotten in his blood. He told him that it was a one-of-a-kind, and there was no more. Al looked disappointed but nodded his understanding. He talked of all the things he had discovered about his abilities, and some of the many things he could do. Levi explained that he was capable of telepathy, telekinesis and other forms of mental aptitudes in addition to the physical abilities that had become obvious.

Al looked hard at him, appraising what he had been told. Finally he said, "I'm not buying it. There is more to the story than you are telling." Al continued, "There was something about you even before the physical change. Many times you spoke of yourself in the plural using words like, we, we're, us, our, etcetera, and I knew that you were communicating with someone else. At first I just thought you weren't quite right in the head but decided differently in time." Now, after the change, he was positive there was more to the story than what was told but would accept the story if that is what Levi wanted.

Damn he wanted to tell it all to him.

Amy said, "No! Al will accept the story if he is a true friend. Remember, what he doesn't know can't be extracted, tricked, or tortured from him."

Levi looked pleadingly at Al and said, "Al, I simply can't tell you or anyone the total story. For your own safety, please accept my story and me." Al was, and is, a friend and accepted both the story and Levi, with reservations.

* Amy *

Levi liked and trusted Al and, if there was anyone that could know the truth, Al would be the one, but no one could ever have knowledge of the complete truth. Al was probably very close to suspecting the general truth, but not completely. She would not let Levi tell him more than he needed to know. Al had accepted the abilities Levi mentioned and implied. Of course he would, since no doubt Dawn had told him many stories of how Levi had saved her life, killed Simians single-handedly, revived from the dead, and surely about the spirit leading her to Levi. Al would believe just having seen Levi fight the Sword Master Simian, even without the other stories.

He carefully told Al, "I am capable of monitoring certain minds." Al was watching and listening, trying to comprehend. Levi said, "That is how I knew about the advance patrol and how I was able to save you at the pass. Al looked hard and a look of comprehension flushed over his face, then anger.

Al looked at Levi and asked a single word, "Dawn?" Then he asked, "Is that why you wanted Dawn close to me?"

Levi answered, "Yes," to both questions as Al continued to stare at him.

Al blushed and asked, "Do you monitor everything?"

Again Levi answered, "Yes," but added, "Once linked it was total and couldn't be helped." Levi told Al, "I have linked with several minds, none of whom know, including Dawn." He then identified who they were. He explained to Al that he wanted, well needed, to make the communication link two-way for the coming war, which meant Dawn would have to know soon. Al thought about that for a minute and nodded, saying he would tell her. It was Levi's turn to nod.

Amy was anxious to get into the caverns to review the medical supplies. She may not be able to make gunpowder, but maybe she could come up with other surprises. Al led them to the caverns and supplies and left them to explore, while he went off to talk to Dawn. She remembered there were compound bows and arrows, and even crossbows. Levi still carried a bow on his back, but it was not adequate to penetrate the dense hide of a Simian sufficiently to kill it. She believed she could make a poison strong enough to kill a Simian, delivered by an arrow penetrating the skin. She recalled her inventory of the Hidden Mine that listed five crossbows and ten compound bows with an inventory of six arrows each, most of which were still in inventory. It wasn't much, but it was a good start.

She went through the supplies and concocted a mixture of poisons that was sure to kill a Simian if it could get into its blood supply. The only problem would be the time it took. It would most likely take more than two minutes to work on a normal sized Simian.

Levi said, "It is better than just pissing them off."

The users of the poison would have to be extremely careful, it could kill them in about twenty-seconds, and it wouldn't take much. The slightest prick of a finger would be deadly. She recommended that all the crossbows be left for the defenses at the caverns. She saw that the steel doors had crossed hatch, shooting slots that would be ideal for the crossbows.

While they were there in the supplies, she took the opportunity to replenish Levi's chemical compounds. They had brought some special and necessary compounds from her research facility. Levi had packed them across country in large quantities, which she now deposited here in this supply depot. Now there would be a single place to come to when replenishing was required, like now. Levi had to make more of his chemical pills and gripped all the time. She would have him store them in all his gear so he would never be far from a supply at any time. She wanted to make even more, and establish hidden deposits at other locations. That would really upset Levi.

* Levi *

472

He felt that the conversation with Al went well. He didn't get punched in the nose anyway, but those penetrating blue eyes staring into his made him feel very uncomfortable. He could tell Al didn't like the idea of him peeking in on their private moments, but he couldn't tell Al that Amy didn't share those moments with him and censored and consolidated the information. He wondered if it turned Amy on to watch them. Actually, he felt a twinge of jealousy when he realized that Amy would actually experience Al making love to Dawn through her linking. Damn! He better stay focused.

He would just have to take the punch if Al wanted to throw one. Al did understand the need for communications, however, and would talk to Dawn. Al and Dawn had maybe even speculated about why she was to stay close to Al, but it would definitely be different now that they would know for sure.

After supper, Al led him to the supply center in the caverns where Amy would have a ball, and he would be bored to tears. As it turned out, he found it interesting that she was working on poison dips for arrows. Yes, he liked that. He would have a squad of poison arrow shooters, only ten, but hey, that was better than they had before. The next part of Amy's schedule involved making the damn pills he had to swallow. He knew he had to have them but hated to spend the hours it required to make the pills. Amy squawked at him like a mother hen, but he volunteered some of the women working in the upper caves to come and help. The job went much faster then. It was well after midnight when they finally finished and went topside to sleep.

473

The sun shining in his eyes woke him the next day. Only three more days till the Simians, but much had been accomplished. All the lances for this army of Lancers were at the staging areas at the forward pass, the army was in training, the horses were adjusting to the smell of Simians, the Owens Valley army was pressing to make it in time, the desert community had moved underground, he would have a squad of poison arrow shooters, and the communications problem would be fixed. What else could they do? Hell, he answered his own question.

He went to Al and told him about the poison arrows and the plan for the cavern defense and squad of archers for field deployment. He gave Al the poison with instruction for its care and proper use. Al readily agreed and assigned men to the squad. Amy had been impressed with the use of the bolos on the Simians, so he also inquired about that. Al said that all the Guard carried bolos and knew how to use them. As Levi was about to leave, Al caught his eye for a second and he saw Al nod. He then glanced at Dawn before he left, but he saw no acknowledgment in her eyes. Better yet, he saw no resentment.

When he asked Amy if she would be able to communicate with Moon, he was told that Moon's mind was far too alien and communication was not possible, nor could she monitor his brain. She would only be able to read direct impressions; however, it would require close proximity and heavy concentration. So Moon was out as a potential telepathic receiver.

474

Dawn, Fred, and Jimmy were now the communications network and none of them really knew it. It was time to establish contact.

* Amy *

She was monitoring all three of them, but passed on only Dawn's link to Levi. She was standing by Al watching the training of the new Lancers. Their training was about as funny as the original training back at Owens Valley, but this time, her sister's mate Johnny, was teaching them some of the tricks he had learned. Dawn was thinking how proud she was of Johnny.

Monitoring was well established. She hadn't really thought about it before, but her monitoring was focused through Levi, and the data was coming to her through their mental telepathic link. Listening was far easier than transmitting. There was little choice about listening. The link was for life as long as the brain functioned, but transmitting would be a concentrated effort to generate.

In truth, the name wasn't appropriate, because the link with Levi, in the general term it was meant, was far more stable and stronger than telepathy could ever be. Levi's suggestion to use telepathy through his brain would be a reality if she could focus his brain. She could not transmit her telepathic signal directly to anyone but Levi. She could, however, amplify Levi's telepathic signal and transmit her energy through their communication link and focus it toward the target. Since she could control Levi's body and mind, assuming he allowed it, she could establish the communication link to the others. It would be more like an extension of her controls over Levi's body. She would physically control his mental abilities to transmit a telepathic signal generated from his brain and not hers. Levi would be the source and voice of the telepathic communication; she would simply amplify and focus it to the minds of Dawn, Fred, and Jimmy.

As she monitored Dawn, Levi mentally repeated Dawn's name while she searched for the right mental signature of parameters for Dawn to receive. She could cycle through hundreds of thousands of potential combinations per second and monitor for a reaction. It would be a simple matter of fine-tuning from there. It took only thirty-seven seconds to detect a reaction and another ten seconds to fine-tune it.

Dawn said out loud, "YES?"

Levi told her it was not necessary for her to speak out loud, only to think it. She understood and the link was established.

Al realized immediately what was happening and watched Dawn intently for reactions. He smiled when he saw Dawn's expression. Considering Al's reaction, it was going to work.

Next, was Fred, he was working with the Guard members teaching them the sign language as he had been charged to do. Again it took less than a minute to find his signature and solicit a response from Fred. In this case it was an incredibly intelligent response.

Fred simply said, "HUH?" Then he said "Levi?"

Levi explained that it was in fact himself and he would be using him as part of the communication

476

network. Fred didn't ask many questions and seemed to be pleased to be singled out again by Levi. It seemed to make him feel special, and indeed he was. There was no need to explain further unless or until he asked. There was no reason to make problems. Fred was happy, so they left him to his own, well deserved self-pride.

Jimmy was saved for last because there were questions that would likely come up, and because he was the only one that could actually benefit from the two-way communication at this time. She monitored Jimmy as with the others but only now brought it forward where Levi could see. Jimmy was riding beside Iron Eyes, leading the army of Lancers where he had traveled twice before. They had been pushing hard, but were still on Highway 395 far north of Barstow. They would still have to turn onto Highway 58, and it was a half-day ride from there to Barstow. From Barstow it was two days hard riding to the settlement and site of the battleground. It was going to be far too close, if at all.

Jimmy was an excitable young man and almost fell off his horse when they made contact.

Levi said, "Be calm. It is just me, Levi."

He let that sink in for a few minutes before Levi explained what was happening, and told him to just think his answers, and he would hear. Jimmy didn't question Levi. If this is what Levi wanted, then this is what he would get. As expected, Jimmy was full of questions. He wanted to know how things were going there and if everything was on schedule. Levi told him the wagons made it and the training was on schedule and caught him up on the battle that took place. Jimmy was very excited and telling Iron Eyes what was going on. Iron Eyes was shocked but very pleased with this new communications ability.

Levi told him about the staging area along the route with the lances stored there. This would allow them to enter the battle, assuming it wasn't already over by the time they arrived in the area. Iron Eyes was pleased to know this. He had worried about that himself.

She suggested to Levi that they leave the road and go across country to Barstow. They could cut off many miles that way, and since they were all on horseback, it wouldn't pose much or little problem. They needed to save every mile they could. Levi passed it on and the army turned off the road immediately. They all felt much more comfortable with the communications established. Yes, this was going to be a valuable tool.

* Levi *

It was beginning to look doubtful that the Owens Valley Army could arrive in time. They needed the three days to get here, and they didn't know exactly when the Simians were going to arrive. The timing was so close. He asked Amy if they could project and look at the status of the Simians. She agreed and asked him to prepare by calling Moon.

He walked to the field where the army was practicing and found Moon with his Simians. He whistled and Moon immediately jerked up to see him. He came loping toward him. He told Moon he

478

was going to meditate and needed his protection. They went to a remote spot where Moon could stand watch and proceeded to relax and get comfortable, waiting on Amy to do her thing. He looked and she grinned and planted a big kiss on his lips. He didn't know how she did that, but it seemed real and he loved it. He felt her lips on his, warm and wet and ever so sweet. God, he loved her.

She kissed him one final time and proceeded to pull him with her. They slowly drifted up to look again at his body resting against the rocks. This part was always disconcerting. He knew, however, he was safe in Moon's protection as they drifted higher. They soared higher over the desert and headed east toward the Colorado River. The land was bleak and dry and one mile looked very much like the next black, lava rock mile. The only distinguishing features were the hills and small mountains that marked any difference at all in the terrain, but Amy seemed to know exactly where they were even to the coordinates.

Sooner than he expected, they saw the Simian migration. Amy was upset and he didn't know what was happening until she explained that they weren't three days out, they were only two days out. He realized what that meant and was upset also. The Owens Valley army couldn't be here in two days and by the time they got here, it would be over!

* Amy *

When Levi suggested that they go look to see where the Simians were, it was like taking the thoughts out of her head. She was about to suggest

479

the same thing. Nothing else could be done for the time being, so it was an appropriate move. Moon was pleased to be called on again. It made him feel special; which he truly was. Levi didn't like being called master, but affectionately called him Tonto, which, in her opinion, was just as bad.

As they approached the Simians, she was shocked to discover that they were no more than two days out, not three as they had been told. Plans would have to be changed. To what and how could she change them? She had no idea! She had learned from Levi, never to give up, and she would never again. Several times she would have given up, but not Levi. He would say, "There is always a way; you have only to find it." Several times he had forced her to find ways she didn't know she could. This would be another such time, maybe, because it certainly looked hopeless right now.

She watched and observed the Simian migration. The travel was slowed by the huge wagons. There were seven of them in the rear being pulled by six Technical class Simians to each wagon. The wagon train was guarded by ten Warriors. It must be universal with the Warrior Simians to enslave the Technical class Simians. At least there were more Technical class Simians in this colony.

Ahead of the wagons were twenty Humans, and to her horror, their friend, Mr. Henderson, was among the group. This was most unfortunate for the Henderson family. The Human group was guarded and herded by four Warriors. Levi went crazy again, and she knew, whatever her plan was going to be, a rescue would be part of it. Damn, why did they have to see this now? She didn't need any more complications.

Ahead of that was a group of thirty female Simians. They were shorter than Moon and wider in the hips and center with thicker legs. Scattered among the females were fifty-two children of various sizes. These were protected and guarded by an additional four Warriors. In the lead were four deployments, each with fifty Warrior Simians. Each group remained tightly clustered in a rough marching order next to each other forming a semicircle across the front. It was a very impressive and ominous looking threat to anything in its path. Following the four divisions was a group of five Simians, which she believed to be the leader and officers of the Simian camp. Bringing up the very rear of the migration was a fifth group of fifty Warrior Simians organized very much like the other four groups in front. This fifth division was obviously providing the rear guard for the Simian army.

Seeing the organized might demonstrated by this Simian army was awesome. How did she ever make herself believe that the Humans had a chance against Simian power? It looked even more hopeless when you considered that this was a small Simian colony. Gord's army was twice this size. Maybe she should just lead these Humans out of harm's way and find a safe refuge.

Levi was not having any of this. He read her mind and chastised her for having negative thoughts.

Levi reminded her, "Even if there are safe spots, they wouldn't be safe for long the way the

481

Simian population is growing and spreading out, and never forget there are more Simians coming. We have no choice; the battle is coming and you don't need doubts now."

He was right of course, but how could he have confidence looking at this? She must remain focused and concentrate on one battle at a time just like he was saying. He always seemed to get more out of her than she thought possible, and he was forcing her to expand now. Could she do it? How could she do it?

She tracked their rate of travel and calculated that the Simians would be outside the pass by mid-evening two days from now, and the Owens Valley army wouldn't be here until the evening of the third day. That would be too late unless, humm. She must plan.

* Levi *

Amy was shocked at the overwhelming power demonstrated by the Simian army, and so was he. They were organized and impressive, and having fought so many of them, he knew just how awesome the army was. It was all right to be impressed, but it went beyond respect with Amy. She was beginning to lose hope and confidence. Hell, it had been hopeless since the beginning, but they continued and remained alive. She must maintain hope and remain focused.

Looking at the organization of the Simian army, they again saw the walking Simian food supply of herded Humans. It was always depressing to see that, but even more shocking when they recognized one of them. It was Mr. Henderson from the Colorado River area. He told Amy that they needed to come up with a plan to free the Humans and the slave Simians. She just laughed. He looked puzzled.

Amy said, "I already figured that was coming even before reading your mind."

He shared the next grin with her.

It was time to push her again, and hard! She had incredible mental capabilities, but she didn't know how to stretch it. He had to push, make her live up to her potential. So push her he did. He told her, "The Human race depends on you, and you need to use that superhuman mind to develop plans to defeat this threat to them." He reminded her, "If we don't win, I will probably be dead. I need you to save me like you always do." He pushed her hard and had confidence that she could deliver if it was at all possible, if she put her mind to it. Now he had to leave her alone and wait.

They were quiet as they returned to his body, both in deep private thoughts. How strange, since they shared almost everything, but he knew he wasn't being kept out, rather she was concentrating on the challenge put on her. They soared over the desert retracing the silver thread and were soon hovering over his still body again, while Moon continued his vigil.

He remembered, with regret, that he once thought he had killed Moon and had been happy about it. If it hadn't been for Amy, he would have left him at the bottom of the lake. He was happy that Moon was alive now; Moon had become his

483

very good friend. If only Moon could develop a sense of humor.

As they settled back into his body, Amy began correcting the mutations of his body. He was getting used to this, and it no longer alarmed him. He suspected that Amy had to do a lot more to his body than she admitted, but it was too late to do anything about it now. He loved and trusted Amy to take care of him and no longer worried. She was working on his body, but she was also talking to him. Yes, she had some plans and she was describing them now. Damn, that just might work.

* Amy *

On the return trip she analyzed all the timetables, manpower estimates, weapons, relative strengths and weaknesses of the enemy, various other data and developed some plans. Maybe she could think in the abstract after all.

She realized that the Owens Valley army was not going to make it in time. They had to find a way to delay the Simians or take the Simians to the Owens Valley army or maybe both, and she had a plan for each possibility. She told Levi, "The Simians will never expect an attack, especially at night.

Levi laughed and said, "NO SHIT! No one else would be either."

She shared her plan with Levi, and he agreed to a night attack. Right, just try to stop him. The moon would be very late coming up at this time of the month, which would support a night attack for the next few days. Her appraisal of the Simian advance

484

suggested that the Simian camp location would be ideal to take advantage of the terrain. They could position a hundred of Al's Lancers in the Clipper Mountains just south of the projected Simian camp and wait until the darkest part of the night, then attack, taking advantage of the Simian's poor night vision. She could only hope the results would throw the Simian army into disarray and slow them down. Part of the plan would be to release the Humans and enslaved Simians. It was more than simply saving them. That would be the main goal, but without the Technical Simian working as horses, the wagons would stop, while they argued over who would pull them. Hopefully, this would delay the Simian migration and buy time. They could only hope that the cost in Human lives would not be too great.

The plan involved a coordinated attack. The first phase would be diversionary and launched on the lead Simian Warriors by a hundred of Al's Lancers. It would be difficult, but the Humans could see some in the dark night, while the Simians could not. Additionally, the Simians campfires would reveal the targets. The plan would be to attack and kill as many Simians as possible, while they were effectively blind. Only take easy targets, strike and pull back, then strike at another place. Again, it would be three Lancers to each target, but hopefully even the first lance would not be deflected. If the Simians couldn't see, they could not defend themselves. Once the fighting started at the front, the Lancers hidden in the Clipper Mountains would attack the rear deployment of Simians, following the same strategy. Levi and the ten bowmen would then enter from the side, and kill the guards, and free the Humans and Technical Simians. Moon would go with him only to talk to the Technical class Simians, but Levi would never endanger Moon to fight almost blind.

They would have to deploy at night, tonight, and reach a hiding spot in the Clipper Mountains. That meant everyone must be mobilized, within the next two hours. It was time to call in the communications network.

Levi remained in the meditating position as she began to communicate. He asked her to communicate to all of them at once, even though all but Jimmy were in the main camp with Al. He said it would keep them all informed as to what was going on, reduce their communication time, and get everyone used to the communication link. It would require no small amount of concentration on her part to control three separate outgoing links at once. She could do it, but Levi really could make her stretch her capabilities. She would like to get comfortable with her newfound abilities before stretching them more.

It took her two minutes to establish the three-way simultaneous transmission, but as a result, would be able to do it faster in the future. They all listened in solemn silence as Levi informed them of the situation. Levi then went on to lay out the plan HE had come up with and waited as it was explained to Iron Eyes and Al. Everyone agreed to the plan and mobilized immediately. Dawn and Al would leave after dark with a hundred lancers and the ten bowmen equipped with poison arrows.

Levi, Moon, and his Simians would leave immediately and go to Granite Pass, pick up the

486

other Simians, and head toward the Clipper Mountains. Hopefully, they would draw out any Simian sentries. If not they would seek them out, and kill them. They could not risk any sentries warning the Simian leaders. All should be in order by the time Al and his Lancers reached them. That was the plan anyway.

With Al's Lancers split into two battle groups, Fred would go with Jim; Al's second in command, to maintain communications. The front battle group would be ready to launch an attack on the Simian's lead forces, on signal after dark tomorrow night. They would attack during the night, kill as many Simian Warriors as possible, and create as much chaos as possible.

Jimmy and Iron Eyes were included in the communications so they would know what was going on. They were deeply concerned and were pushing as fast as they could. They too, were keeping the army informed. They wanted to be there to help, but there was nothing they could do but keep moving and hope for the best.

* Levi *

Boy, did Amy come up with some plans. He had challenged her and she delivered. She wanted to attack!

She said, "The Simians wouldn't expect it."

That was an understatement, hell no one in their right mind would even think about it, much less expect it. As he saw the plan, it was brilliant. It would need coordination and must be sold to the leaders. Well, not really, they would go along with

487

anything he suggested. He knew it, and so did they, but he wanted to extend the courtesy to them for input and final approval.

When he suggested, "Talk to all of them at once." Of course she agreed, because it was a good idea. She could do anything HE set her mind to. He laughed at his own joke, because he knew Amy was reading his mind. Her image was grinning back at him as she called him a "Shit head."

He presented the plan and all tasks were mobilized. He rose from his meditation to greet Moon and proceeded to tell him what he had seen in his vision and presented the plan to him. Moon was upset at the change and even more upset that he would be useless in the night battle, but Moon nodded in appreciation once the plan was presented. He too wanted to rescue the Technical class Simians but was concerned about his ability to see in the dark. Assuring Moon that he would take care of him, he explained that all Moon would need to do was explain it to the Technical Simians and lead them out. They would only follow another of their kind. In truth, Moon would follow him, but the Technical Simians would follow Moon.

He asked Moon to gather his Simians. They would be heading out within the hour. Moon was off, as was he. He gathered his pack and weapons, less the compound bow and arrows that he donated to the poison arrow team.

While he was waiting for Moon, he went to Al to see if all was in readiness. Al was full of confidence and grinning at the incredible bravado of the plan. Al was a gutsy bastard, and he liked him for it. He was also a born leader, and his men would follow him anywhere. He didn't know much about Jim, but Al assured him that Jim was a good man and would do his part. Al told him the horses needed for "Plan B" were being gathered now, and he was grinning ever so wide at the thought of "Plan B," and so was he. Amy did well.

He saw Moon coming with his red-hatted army of Simians and gear. Someone in camp had made red hats to replace the scraps of cloth. He had been told that the Lancers didn't want to kill one of them by accident, so the ladies of the camp fabricated red leather, wide brim hats. They didn't look like any cowboys he had ever seen, but they did look smart in them, and they seemed to be proud wearing them. They were very special.

In parting, he shook Al's hand, and he and the Simians left jogging through the pass headed for Granite Pass. They would be through Granite Pass and into the desert by mid-afternoon searching for Simian scouts. Their party would head toward the migrating Simians as if they were going there and hope any scouts would come out to them. Failing that, they would skirt around the Clipper Mountains and clean out the area. The Clipper Mountains were mostly only a single small mountain with a few smaller ones attached. It was probably clear, but they couldn't risk letting any Simian sentry spot the Lancers coming out of the pass.

* Amy *

Levi was happy; he had a job to do, and Moon looked pleased as well. It was time for the macho crap now, and she hoped she could keep Levi alive

489

through the ordeal. She had developed her plans and hoped they would work, and everyone would be safe.

Levi and his Simians set a fast pace and reached Granite Pass on schedule. They had already called Fred to give instructions to the Simians at Granite Pass. They were ready and waiting as his group arrived. Fred was also ready to travel. Levi chuckled to himself, but didn't show Fred.

Levi explained to Fred, "It is necessary for you to remain with the Lancers. You are the communicator to Jim now and no longer the interpreter for the Simians."

Well, he still was, but his primary job now for this battle was a communicator and could not be risked in battle. He thanked Fred for wanting to go and slapped him on the back. Fred was pleased with the importance of his new job. They stopped only long enough to visit with Jim to make sure he understood the plan. Indeed he did, and Jim, as Al had said, appeared to be a competent leader. They shook hands and went through the pass at a run.

Once through the pass, Levi took an inside position so that he might appear as a captive, while Moon took the lead position. They jogged on for several hours and were approaching Chuckwalla Spring. They slowed as they rounded a protrusion in the hill and headed uphill toward the spring. Suddenly, there were three Warrior Simians standing in the trail. They stopped and waited for the Warriors to react.

Finally one of the Warriors asked, "What are you doing?"

Moon said, "We came for water and to eat this Human."

The way he said it she even believed Moon meant it.

The lead Warriors said, "We will take your Human, and you will find another meal."

They obviously believed they were talking to slaves and did not know Moon and his group was associated with the Humans. This is what Levi wanted to know.

Moon said, "It will take more than the three of you to take our food."

This registered shock on the Warriors face, but he came forward as if to hit Moon. Moon killed him with a double fisted chop to the side of the neck that broke its neck with a snap. The shock was still registering on its face as the Warrior crumbled to the ground at Moon's feet.

The other Warrior Simians drew their swords as Moon's small lethal army spread out around them.

Moon held them at bay while he asked, "Are there other sentries?"

While he waited for an answer, he dug out a tooth from their dead team member. The Warriors were accustomed to answering questions from their betters and this Simian was obviously better than they were. This combined with the fear Moon was instilling in them made them talk. There was another team at Bonanza Spring on the far side of the mountain. Moon nodded and the Warriors died.

* Levi *

491

He did feel good about having something to do. He disliked waiting around. Now he was at the head of his little awesome army of Simians and running across the desert in search of the enemy. That sounded so simplistic, but truly was factual. Amy busted his bubble.

Amy said, "You should appear as a captive and let Moon lead."

He reluctantly agreed. Amy was in her disgust mood of the macho element of testosterone. She would keep him safe and help him do what needed to be done, but she didn't enjoy the fighting ingredient of war. Strange, since she was so good at it, but Amy defended herself by reminding him that it was just a job to be done.

She said, "I will do it, but what repulses me most is that you enjoy the excitement and thrill of battle too much."

Moon was the cold one though. He could kill the Warrior Simians without regret. He shuddered to think of the abuse he must have suffered at the hands of the Warrior Simians to be so cold at killing them. The training Amy had put into him made Moon a very formidable enemy to any Warrior Simian and an obvious means to extract revenge.

As they approached the spring, the three Warrior Simians stood waiting. He told Moon, "Try to get information." That saved the Warriors life, temporarily, but not for long. Moon broke his neck with a loud snap and gained the information they sought from the other two before they also died.

The Simian team at the other spring had to be taken out, so they set out again circling the mountain. It was approaching sundown when they arrived at Bonanza Spring. As informed, there was a Simian patrol, but they had not seen their approach and jumped up when they heard Moon's group. Not knowing what to think at first, they stood their ground, but the determined looks on Moon and his Simians soon struck fear into the Warriors. They bolted but were set upon by Moon's army and soon dispatched. It seemed that Moon's Simians were into collecting trophy teeth also, and most had at least one on his neck. He had forgotten how many he had. He would have to think up some other trophy display that would satisfy Moon. He thought he could make a tooth trophy case or shrine.

It was fortunate that they had circled the mountain. Otherwise, the Warriors would have seen the Human army coming out of the pass and might have escaped to warn the Simian army. Yes, it had been a good day. Now the Clipper Mountains were clear and they had killed six of the enemy. Yes, indeed a good day, but the war starts tomorrow!

CHAPTER 18
(THE WAR)

* Amy *

Levi, Moon, and their small Simian army cleared the mountains of Simian observers, and now her plan could be executed. It was approaching sunset and would be moonless and dark until around 1:00 a.m. for the next few nights. Al's Lancers and the bowmen could travel after dark and be here in a few hours. Al's attack force would then have to wait through the day while the Simians approached. The Simians would still be several miles from the Lancer force when they camped, but she didn't want to risk being any closer and seen by any scouts. Surprise was imperative for her plan to work. The Simian army would assume, she hoped, that the patrols at the springs would warn them of any activity. The Simian army would already know something was amiss since the twenty-five Simian patrol didn't return. They could not know what had happened but would probably be on the alert.

She opened communication and Levi reported, "It is all clear. Begin the second phase of the plan." She had been monitoring Dawn and knew Al had moved his Lancers down to Granite Pass and was waiting for Levi's all clear signal. Al responded that he would move out as soon as it was dark, which should be within two hours. He also reported that the one hundred and fifty horses had been rounded up and should be en route to Granite Pass. They would be available when needed for "Plan B."

There was nothing more to do but wait. They would wait for Al, the Lancers, and the bowmen to come in during the night and then wait throughout the next day while the Simians came closer. She was getting just like Levi. She hated waiting. Her mind continually monitored everyone and reviewed the plans, looking for any way to improve it or for any possible errors. The plan was as good as she could make it, and she made no further changes.

Jimmy and the Owens Valley army made it to Barstow a little early but were still three days away from the battlefield. They were trying desperately to make it in time, but there were so many miles to cover. She knew they could not make it in time, but hoped they could get close enough for "Plan B" to work. "Keep coming Jimmy."

The Lancers, Al, Dawn, bowmen and supplies made it into camp about midnight. It had taken them a little longer because of the dark, which slowed them down. She did not want any fires, so Levi had gone out on the trail to meet and guide them into the cold camp at Bonanza Spring to wait. It was on the southwest side of the mountain and would hide them from the approaching Simians.

There was nothing more for her to do. Could she save Levi in tomorrow's battle? Would this stubborn man die, because he may not know when to run? She came to him in the night to be in his arms, to kiss him and feel his kisses, to love him and feel his love and to make love with him. She wanted to spend this night, possibly the last night, where her love rested with Levi.

It was too bad he couldn't take Moon's little army with him into the foray tomorrow night. He was really proud of them and damn, they were loyal. Well, except for # 3, but Amy said # 3 was flawed mentally. She had detected it, but overlooked the significance until almost too late.

Amy said, "I detect no hostility toward Humans from the other Technical Simians and believe everything to be in order with them."

Their poor night vision problem might keep them out of the night raid, but he would sure feel more comfortable when they were at his side in the daylight battles.

Everyone was excited and hyper in anticipation of the coming raid, but they needed plenty of rest, so they picketed and fed the horses and turned in. He did too.

Amy came to him in all her beauty that night, and she was beautiful, breathtakingly beautiful. She might not be beautiful to others, but in his mind's eye, she was the very reference from which he judged beauty in others. Amy was perfect in every way, and for her to become what he wanted, spoke strongly about her love for him.

This went beyond just looks, it was the way she walked, the sound of her voice, her expressions, scent, taste, the ways she made love and countless other things so subtle that you didn't notice but added to the perfection. She was perfect in every way. Well, she was opinionated sometime, but he liked that too. It made life more interesting. He

496

absently wondered what the odds would be that two people could find perfection in each other as they had. The odds had to be astronomical that two people, perfectly matched, could find each other at all; there couldn't be that many even near matches either. It was amazing that it ever happened in real life; he then realized just how lucky he truly was.

She came into his arms to lie against him. They let their bodies do the talking this night, and he was so very happy. He embraced and caressed her, cherishing their love and lust until he could hold off no longer. He took her willing body, plunging into the depths of her soul. He experienced wave after wave of pure ecstasy and melted with the love for Amy that burned in his veins.

He woke early and Amy was gone, so he just lay there. There was no reason to get up. He would just have to wait throughout the day for the night raid, so he rolled over and went back to sleep. This was the first time he had slept late in, he couldn't remember how long. He climbed out of a deep sleep at the smell of bacon and eggs cooking and sat straight up in his bedroll. There they sat smiling at him. Al and Dawn were cooking directly up wind from him and watching him react. Still grinning, they invited him to breakfast. He was up in a shot. Dawn had a huge plate for him full of eggs and thick slices of bacon. This was turning out to be a very good day following a fantastic night.

* Amy *

Smiling to herself, she thought about Levi needing his rest. After last night it was no wonder

497

he wanted to sleep late. All good things must come to an end, however. It was time to focus again on the upcoming raid. She learned her lesson from the experience with # 3 and would remain focused and not make that mistake again.

Al and Dawn had made quite a production of teasing Levi awake with the smell of food. It didn't take long to get Levi's attention, and he quickly sat up in his bedroll. Both were laughing at him. His body would welcome the breakfast of bacon and eggs Dawn had made. Al looked in amazement at the amount of food Dawn had made for Levi. He ate enough for three men and proved her right.

As he ate he said between bites, "Hey I thought we had a cold camp?"

Al said, "That was last night in the dark, but there is not much danger of light or smoke with these small fires." Levi didn't care, he was happy to be eating.

After breakfast Levi sat with Al and Dawn, talking about small things and laughing and joking with each other, anything to take their minds off the upcoming raid and battle. After a while, boredom got too much for Levi and he walked around camp talking to everyone and double-checking everything. She was also inventorying everything and watching. She was satisfied with everything she saw and spirits were high. They were ready.

She decided against caution and suggested that Levi and Moon leave early and cautiously secure a vantage point from which to watch the Simian army as they made camp. She wanted to record the layout of the camp, their security, where the divisions camped and any other data she could glean.

Everything would be recalled as necessary when they attacked. Levi was only too happy to comply. He had been anxious for hours.

He called Moon, who was at his side in minutes, and explained what he had in mind. Levi also told him to thank the Simians, but let them sit out this night raid. It was simply too dangerous and they would not be that effective. Additionally, the Humans might not be able to recognize them in the dark as friendlies. Moon nodded and was off to talk to his personal army.

Levi told Al his intentions and left to meet Moon at the edge of the camp. They skirted the outside of the mountains trying to maintain cover. They were successful in reaching a vantage point about a mile from where she believed the Simians would reach before dark. She didn't believe the Simians would risk trying to travel close to dark. She was right. They watched the migrating Simians approaching slowly throughout the afternoon and camp almost exactly where she predicted. Oh, this was better than she had hoped. They camped in the lowlands. It was a wide riverbed when it rained but was now flat and sandy. It was perfect for horses, and the Simians would have no defense.

Levi asked Moon, "Will they have picket guards?"

Moon said, "No. They will only have guards inside the camp for the slaves." He added, "They are too arrogant to believe that anyone would dare attack them."

Two days ago Levi would have agreed with the Simians.

This was too good to believe. Levi informed the communicators to execute the plan now. Where they camped they can't see the pass so don't wait for dark to leave and make haste while there was a little light before sunset. He cautioned them, "Don't make dust with the horses and wagons." Levi and Moon would wait here for Al and she could lead them to this spot the same way as she was going to guide Fred to their launch point. The plan could begin in a few hours.

* Levi *

The Simians camped three miles east of the mountains. They observed the making of their camp and deployment of the army. He and Moon had very carefully moved to a position from which they could observe the layout of the camp in preparation for the night raid. The five clusters of the army remained very much intact, and each cluster set up three fires within their group, except for the rear one, which had four fires. The fires were for vision, since they ate their food raw and the desert nights here were hot. They had been experiencing the dark evenings and nights of this time of month.

Amy said, "The dark is probably a little frightening for them."

Levi said, "Good, I hope we give them something else to be frightened about."

The Simians carried some raw meat in their individual packs, plus additional supplies were carried in the wagons at the rear. They observed numerous trips to the wagons by all groups going after water, packed meat and some firewood they

500

brought with them. He couldn't tell what it was they were eating, but could pretty well guess and was glad he couldn't see what it was. There was much searching among the wagons, obviously not finding what they were looking for. Several of the Simians turned from the wagons and approached the captured Humans. Oh no, the Simians were grabbing some of the live Humans and pulling them away from the huddled group. They grabbed the first Human they could catch and killed him. The screams were terrible, as limbs were ripped from living bodies and in some cases a Simian was eating bites out of a kicking, screaming Human. He was close enough to hear the screams and was holding his ears trying to block them out.

The Simians had almost reached their destination and were eating their reserve food supply. They were totally committed to their goal. They would find horses and Humans tomorrow or die of starvation, and they had no intention of starving. They would engage the Human's defenses tomorrow without doubt.

They had been too late to save them! Only hours away from possible salvation, he had to watch now, helpless as the Humans were slaughtered before his eyes. He gripped Moon's arm hard as Mr. Henderson was dragged across the ground screaming. He was alive as they tore his arms and legs from his body. Horrifying, he could see the lifeless legs still kicking as Warriors sank their teeth into the flesh. Mercifully, he died at some point, and his screams died with him.

Levi watched as all the Humans died and were consumed. He didn't think anything could shock him more until he saw some of the Warriors turn on one of the enslaved Simians still hitched to the wagon. Two of the Warriors grabbed it and tore it away from the harness and started tearing into the flesh of its arms and legs. The Simian screeched in pain. The guards stopped the raving Warriors from further attacks on the others but allowed them to drag the injured one away. He realized that the others were saved only because they were needed to pull the wagons.

He turned to look at Moon for his reaction.

Moon was expressionless as he watched, but said, "This has been the way since the mutiny of the Warrior Simians in space."

He was beginning to understand Moon a little better and why Moon hated them as much as he did. Moon was truly his brother in a common goal and common hate.

There were no more Humans to save, but he was more determined than ever to save the enslaved Simians. He could also contribute to the chaos during the attack. He could contribute because he was mad and he wanted to kill Simians.

He shared the news about the dead Humans with his communication network and the slight change of plans. They were solemn and quiet in response. He told them about Mr. Henderson and how he was the reason he was able to be here today. Without Mr. Henderson, it was very likely he would be dead. He asked the army to use "Remember Mr. Henderson" as their battle cry.

* Amy *

502

She was learning the emotions of sorrow and loss the hard way. She knew Mr. Henderson and liked him. He and his family helped when they needed it. In all likelihood, he was the reason they had survived that part of the trip. Without his knowledge of the Simians, they would have walked helplessly into one of their traps for sure. Additionally, the Hendersons had been just plain, friendly and likable. Their food and supplies had helped them get through the desert, at least as far as the settlement.

Mr. Henderson was the first person she had known that died. There was Dr. Sheldon, but she had known the doctor as a computer would know someone. She could know everything about the facts: who she was, how old she was, when she had gotten her measles vaccine and a myriad of other facts; but she never knew the person. She had known Mr. Henderson and remembered the affection he showed for his family, who must also be dead now. She remembered his friendship and help, all freely given. He had been a good man.

The shock and sorrow weighed heavy on her as she watched the Simians brutally kill Mr. Henderson. She felt this emotion from Levi, but she felt it rising up from within her as well. These Simians had taken something from her, and she was angry. When Levi killed these Simians, she would participate emotionally and experience some satisfaction of revenge. She was beginning to understand how Levi felt and why he hated the Simians, and she was beginning to understand hate.

She felt Levi's sorrow and regret for not being able to save the Humans. He had so wanted to prevent this from happening. At least they could save the enslaved Simians ... maybe.

The Warriors also demonstrated cannibalism of their species. Moon said it started in space. They had brought breeding stock of a home world food animal, but the Warriors refused to eat the prepared rations and ate the breeding stock instead. After they had consumed the breeding stock, their lust for blood drove them to cannibalism of the Technical Simians as well.

Any hope of simply delaying the Simians was gone now. Using up their last supplies showed total commitment to attacking the settlement tomorrow, if they wanted to eat. There would be a war tomorrow and her forces still weren't ready.

* Levi *

The time was approaching. It was now very dark, and the Simians were spread out across the desert floor laying, resting, and mingling around screeching. It sounded like a buzz coming from the assembled groups. The raiders, even the lance wagons, would be able to approach without being heard. He passed that information on to Dawn and Fred. Everything seemed to be going well so far.

Amy was monitoring their progress, and he guided the attack groups according to Amy's directions, gleaned from the topography maps stored in her memory and the layout of the Simians. Al's Lancers approached his position and would arrive soon, and Jim's Lancers approached the position in the front where Amy had designated.

504

There had been no sentries and neither of her groups had been detected.

He met Al and described the terrain and how to deploy the Lancers once he received the signal. He took Moon and the bowmen, gave the signal to Dawn and Fred, "Begin." They moved out toward the Simian camp below, while both Lancer groups deployed and waited for the final signal to attack.

He deployed the bowmen and communicated through hand signs, spreading out to converge on the wagons and Simian guards. Moon said he could only see the areas around where the fires were and remained so close to him that he could almost touch him. He watched as the bowmen all picked separate targets. There were six guards posted to watch the slave Simians still tied to the wagon tongues. When everyone had acquired a target, he signaled the Lancers to attack. Immediately, he heard the Lancers' yells and sounds of charging horses. Under cover of the noise, he gave the signal to loose the arrows.

All targets were hit on the first volley and some with two arrows. Amy's poison was very lethal for the Simians. The agony of the Simians showed immediate, as they screeched in pain, dancing around, falling, and kicking on the ground. It was a painful death for the Simians that lasted for over a minute, but he refused to care. He was happy they died.

The bowmen ran forward to retrieve their arrows and very carefully re-dip them in the poison. While the bowman reorganized, he took Moon ahead to talk to the Technical class Simians.

Moon went through the group cutting their bonds and telling them, "Remain quiet and follow me and the Humans. The Humans are friends, and they are saving you."

They complied totally. When they were free, Moon gathered them and waited for him to lead them out. He told the bowmen, "Retrieve the guard's weapons and give them to the liberated Simians." The Simians took them as they were presented, with looks of shock and disbelief and huddled and waited for his return.

He signaled the bowmen, "Spread out and kill Simians, but only those that are separated from a group." His concern was being able to retrieve the arrows. They understood and moved out toward the rear of the last group. They could hear the noise of battle ahead and Amy showed some of the battle through Dawn's eyes, but since she was not actually in the fight, they couldn't see much.

They moved forward slowly trying to look ahead into the dark. His sight was far better than anyone else and he could see several three-Simian teams ahead. He signaled and pointed, "There, there is a team separated from the others." He steered them in that direction cautiously. They were creeping slowly, moving within sight of the Simian's backs. Shooting their arrows simultaneously they watched as the Simians fell squirming and kicking to the ground. Luckily, the anticipated immediate reaction of the Simians was to pull the arrow out. Also lucky was the fact that the Warriors didn't fall on the arrows; they were irreplaceable.

Moving off to the left and right, more arrows were loosed at the other teams. He was losing track of all the activity in the dark, but he could see the bowmen moving, shooting, and running to retrieve arrows. Damn, they were pausing to take a tooth. He knew better than to try and stop them. Hell, they deserved to have a trophy, too. He whistled to get their attention and said, "Stay together and work as a team." They began moving in a slow circle into the rear of the Simian army and had not been discovered yet by any Simian still alive.

Amy said, "We are pushing our luck. Let's move back toward Moon."

He whistled, gave the signal to cease and retreat. As they were retrieving the last of the arrows they saw fires flaring up at various locations, at first one or two, but then more. The battlefield was getting brighter. Amy became alarmed and had him issue the general order to retreat on all fronts. The Simians got smart by lighting the fires and could now see enough to defend themselves. They were clustering around the fires and facing outwards toward the advancing Lancers. He could see some of the Lancers falling.

They retreated to the wagons and gathered Moon and his new additions and retraced their steps out of the Simian camp. They had been very lucky and not lost a single bowman.

Amy said, "I counted twenty-eight kills by the bowmen."

This was a very good night for his small group but wondered how the Lancers had done. Amy had not gleaned much from Fred or Dawn in the dark, but they had issued the retreat order and a general retreat was in progress on all fronts.

* Amy *

The night raid went as planned; at least it was launched as she had planned it. It was very stressful not knowing what was happening on the battlefronts. The darkness prevented her from following any of the battle except with Levi, and even that was limited.

They must have actually moved into the back of the clustered rear army. She had not wanted to live so dangerously, but the Simians were all trying to see the battle that they heard going on at the outside edges of the camp, and they had their backs to the bowmen. It was a duck shoot, so to speak, as the bowmen shot the Simians on the periphery without attracting attention, even as they fell. The battle noise prevented the other Simians from hearing the death screeches. She knew at once that the tide of battle would turn quickly once the Simians could see, so she ordered a general retreat.

She had hoped to make a significant blow to the Simians in this night raid, because it would only work once, and they needed desperately to cut the odds down some. From now on, however, the Simians would be on the alert and ready for any night attacks. This had been a one-time opportunity, and she knew it. They took advantage of surprise, the Simian's arrogance and their night vision weakness. It served the purpose.

They beat Al's group back to camp behind the Clipper Mountains. They would wait here for the

508

next phase of her plan. It was still several hours from sunrise as they reached camp. She was getting some sketchy reports but would have to wait till the Lancer groups reassembled and reported to find out how successfully they had been, assuming it was, and the casualty count.

Once they were back in camp, Moon took the forty-one new recruits and joined his other twelve. Moon really was building an army now and would have them indoctrinated in no time at all. She knew training would begin almost immediately in sign language and fighting techniques. Moon was turning out to be a very proficient leader, and his loyalty to Levi was without question. She had already named the new Simians B-1 through B-41. Levi laughed.

* Levi *

As he waited for a more detailed and factual report from Amy, he thought back to when Al came into camp the day before. Amy had actually missed a detail, and that was shocking. He realized that fact immediately when he saw the lance wagon rolling in. It was nothing but a long wagon tongue with four wheels. Two horses could pull it easily and fast. Almost the only weight was the lances that rested in cradles above the wheels. It was very mobile and could travel almost as fast as the Lancers. The settlement had made many such small lance wagons in order to keep the Lancers light and mobile. Al's craftsmen had come up with it when they realized they would need a supply of lances on the battlefield. Amy had been pleased and a little shocked to realize she had overlooked a detail, which could have been disastrous. Lancers weren't any good without lances, were they?

His thoughts must have been triggered by the sound of the lance carriers, because he became aware of the sound of the wagons coming into camp with Al and Dawn in the lead. Al saw him and approached immediately. Grinning, Al dismounted and handed the reins to one of the sentries. He was grinning back at Al as they came together. He thought this must be good news and then noticed that Amy was grinning too. "Damn it, Amy, are you holding back on me?"

She grinned even wider and said, "I wanted you to hear it from Al. Al hasn't said much to Dawn yet, but I gathered it was good news."

Al started telling him about the battle. It went very well. On the signal to attack they charged into the night without targets, just a general direction. As they came closer, they could distinguish targets just standing there frozen. The Simians couldn't see them till the last few seconds before impact, which was far too late in most instances to react. They took out about ten Simians on the first charge, and it was incredible. After that they charged in waves, but the dark made it confusing, even to the Lancers, so they slowed the attack to coordinate the charges one at a time. Each wave was harder because the Simians learned and pulled back toward the fires where they could see. The denseness of their grouping made it harder to get in and out. They started losing Lancers and became more cautious in the attack.

Al looked up with a grin and said, "While we regrettably lost six Lancers, we killed more than twenty Simians!"

Incredibly, together they had killed at least forty-eight Simians in the rear engagement.

Amy commented, "That is why the bowmen's attack was so successful. The Lancers were much closer than she believed, in fact, there were probably no more than fifteen Simians left in the rear group."

Had they not retreated when they did, the Lancers might have charged through to their position, which could have been disastrous. So not only was the plan good and worked, they had good luck on their side also.

Al was happy to hear the whole combined story and agreed that they had been lucky. Al then asked the question he was also wondering about.

Al asked, "How did the front assault go?"

That engagement was more of a harassing attack than one designed for results. There were more than two hundred Simians and only one hundred and twenty-five Lancers.

Amy was not grinning when she answered. It seems Fred was with Jim as the Lancers reorganized at their staging area. His four squad leaders were reporting and Amy was passing the information on as she continued to monitor. He closed his eyes and held his hand up to Al, as if to say, "Wait and I'll tell you."

Squad one reported two Lancers dead and eight Simian kills. Squad two reported no Lancer casualties and seven Simian kills. Squad three reported three Lancers dead and nine Simian kills.

Squad four killed five Simians without a casualty. Could he believe his ears? Al cheered when he told him the frontal raid had killed twenty-nine Simians with only five casualties.

The front attack had been spread out over a larger area and each time the Lancers attacked, they would back up and charge again at a different spot. This worked out well and didn't give the Simians a chance to learn and counter. They did not attack the same group twice, but there were casualties. As with Al's group, the darkness allowed the Lancers to blunder into groups of Simians. In some instances the Simians had reacted fast enough to counter the Lancers or just got in the way, knocking down both the horse and rider. Once the rider was down, he was defenseless and easily killed, even in the dark.

* Amy *

She would have preferred to have personally seen the battle through Dawn's and Fred's eyes, but she was ecstatic at how well this night raid had gone and the reports received. The Humans had killed probably more than seventy-seven Simians with losses of only eleven. At least they were winning the war through attrition, but tonight they had been very lucky. They could not count on luck anymore. The Simians would be prepared next time. She helped Levi relay the good news to Fred and Jimmy, who were also very happy. They would happily spread the news throughout the armies.

The Simians still numbered over two hundred Warriors, which they would have to face tomorrow without the Owens Valley army. That was sobering, because the Simians would be angry, ready, and worse, they would be able to see. The Simians would also be motivated by hunger. The Human army was committed, however, and she still had plans to execute and maybe a surprise or two. The Simians wouldn't be able to slaughter them as long as they remained on horseback. They could always outrun the Simians, and that was part of her plan. Strike and run, strike and run, and attack any opportunity that presented itself, and make the opportunities happen.

Levi was upset and mulling around, and she didn't understand why. She tried looking into his mind, but his anger was all consuming and blocked her ability to see. Finally she had to ask, "What is wrong?"

Levi fumed and finally said, "I just realized that in all the fighting tonight, I let everyone else take the risk and I didn't even kill a single Simian. I didn't do anything to help?"

She began laughing in earnest at this revelation. She found it extremely humorous that he could believe that he had not contributed to the success. It took a few moments before she could contain her laughter, all the while making Levi even angrier. Finally, she said, "You have done a great deal. You are the reason they had been successful tonight and all seventy-seven kills were because of you." He looked shocked and listened intently. She reminded him, "This whole war is your idea, without you there would be no army, without you there would be no communication, without you there would be no leadership and without you there would have been no battle tonight. You have been busy passing on the communication and directions, guiding the bowmen and executing the plan. You cannot expect to go out and kill seventy-seven Simians all by yourself. So if the plan is successful, then you are successful." To emphasize her explanation she added, "You better hope Moon doesn't bring in seventy-seven more teeth for you to wear."

Somewhere during her speech, he lost his anger and began grinning, and by the time she finished, he was laughing also. He could see her point and admitted it.

Levi said, "I guess I was a little crazy."

Both grinned and laughed heartily now.

Moon brought them the first problem. The enslaved Simians had been starved and were hungry. They weren't going to be easy to control in that state. This was another detail she had overlooked. This was a problem that had to be solved soon, or some of the stray horses or even Humans might wind up missing.

He called Al and told him the predicament and asked, "Do you have any wounded horses?"

After a moment of thought Al said, "No. All the wounded horses had been mortal and were on the desert where they fell."

* Levi *

It was his turn to laugh at Amy. He told her, "You can't think of everything, and problems are only to be solved." When Al wasn't able to help, he decided that there were horses on the battlefield, and this is where he must go to solve the problem.

Looking at the stars he determined that there were about three more hours of complete darkness, and he could go down and get some of the dead horses. He asked Al, "Can you volunteer a dozen Lancers?" Volunteers were easy to come by; it was refusing everyone that was the problem. It was still overly dark for Moon, so he held a rope and trailed it behind so Moon and the Simians could hold on and run along with him toward the desert battle area.

He led off at a hard run toward the closest area, which was the front of the battlefield. It took them twenty minutes to get in the proximity and another ten to find an uneaten horse. The Simians were still on the alert and close to their fires. He left Moon and his group back some distance, while he got in close, and with Amy's help, found some horses. The first two had fallen close to the Simians ranks and had been dragged into the camp, but the third one was untouched. He slipped in and quietly attached ropes to the dead horse and returned to signal for the Lancers to attach the ropes to their horses and slowly pull it out away from the Simian camp. When it was out, he led the Simians to the horse and they began to feed. They would need more, so he followed the same routine, and luckily, two additional fallen horses were retrieved. He was thankful that he saw no signs of any fallen Lancers and assumed their bodies had been removed already. The horses found were adequate to satisfy the Simians' immediate need for food. All they had to do was get through tomorrow and he would convert them into beefeaters. They might not like it, but beef was plentiful and available.

He had to rush Moon so they could be out of the area before it became light enough for the enemy to see them. Surprise was required for the next phase of Amy's plan to work and he didn't want to be discovered hiding behind the mountain. They were off again toward their remote camp and safely hidden before the sun started spreading its light across the desert. He told Amy, "The problem is fixed and no damage done."

They now had another forty-one Simians to join their army, but they were untrained and could not go up against the Warriors. Amy was trying to figure out how best to use them, and he was sure she would. She wanted all of Moon's army held in reserve and wanted Levi on a high vantage point in order to observe the battle as it played out during this day. He was disappointed at first until she explained that she must be able to see and issue directions, and he had to be the communication center. Since the battle was going to be hit and run, Moon's Simians could not get involved, because they could not outrun the Warriors, and would die if they entered the battle too soon. Damn, she always made sense, but he wanted to fight.

Amy said, "You will fight! Hell, everyone will fight before this day is through. Like, we really have a choice."

Everything would happen today. The Human race would live or die today. If they failed, there would never be another chance.

* Amy *

516

When Moon brought the problem to Levi, it disturbed her to realize she had made two mistakes in her planning. She had overlooked two major facts that she should have anticipated. She panicked to think there might be others ... others that could get people killed or worse, cause them to lose the battle. Had she thought of everything?

It didn't phase, and he came up with a solution very quickly. Yes, Humans, this beloved Human, amazed her sometimes. Take them to the food. It was a simple plan that worked out well. It was also obvious that Moon had started their indoctrination by the way the Simians openly stared at Levi. Moon liked to brag on Levi and no doubt told them that Levi had killed their colony's Sword Master in single combat.

As daylight came, Levi was perched on a ledge several hundred feet up the slope of the mountain. Moon and twelve of the original group were spread out around him for his protection. He had a vantage position where he could see the desert spread out before him. Thankful for his binoculars, he could see Granite Pass to his left, and Forshay Pass and the caverns in the distance almost straight ahead. He could see the Simian army organizing to his right, and the flat desert battlefield spread out between. The chessboard was set and it was now time for the pieces to be played.

They waited as the Simians approached. The Simians left their wagons behind and were approaching quickly to battle. The night raid had not slowed them in the least. There were now three groups spread out side by side across the front. This was good. A rebuilt fourth group was again in the

517

rear behind the leaders in the center with the females and children behind them. As the Simian army approached the mountain where Levi observed, he signaled to Fred.

As he watched Granite Pass, Jim's Lancers poured forth to spread out across the desert as if to block the Simians and stand to battle. The Simians continued to advance, and Levi could see the Simian leader watching and pointing. After the Lancers became stationary, Levi observed the herd of horses driving out of the pass. There were at least one hundred and fifty horses that had been rounded up from all the pastures and brought for this plan. The horses were herded by twenty riders. The herders spread the horses out to appear as an even greater size herd and drove them in a wide swing behind the Lancers, making sure to stir up plenty of dust. The riders then slowly led the herd off toward the west but keeping them in plain sight.

Now, she had made the first move, what would the leader do? They watched and waited.

* Levi *

He could feel the tension in Amy's mind. He was reading some of her thoughts, and she explained some of what she was planning, but it was so complicated and complex. Amy would comment about how the leader would think if she did this or that, and how he would believe there was a trick, so he would do this or that. She talked about Field Marshal Rommel, General Patton, tank deployment strategy, and he made no sense from it.

It was too blasted complex; he would just help and do what she wanted him to do.

He gave the signal and watched the Lancers emerge and spread out, then saw the horses come out and trot off to the west. Amy was hoping to split the Simian army. She was sure that they would not let the horses get away. They needed them for food and to barter with Gord. The show made it look like there were far more horses than there actually were. Now they waited for the Simian leader to commit his army.

The leader was pointing at the horses and screeching orders. He couldn't make out what he was saying, but the followers were jumping to obey, sending runners carrying orders. All three front Simian divisions turned to their right and sped north heading toward the caverns and Forshay Pass.

Signaling to Fred, the Lancers raced north to get between the advancing Simians and the caverns, again blocking the advance of the Simian Army. Once the lancers were positioned, they were effectively cut off again and committed to the defense of the caverns and their home camp. At that point the lead division of pursuing Simians spread out and slowed, while the trailing two divisions quickly changed directions and chased after the horses and riders.

Yes, Amy was happy. The Simian leader made the predictable moves. She had counted on the Simians knowing that the home camp was at the caverns and a move against them would draw the army to block their advance. In doing so, they left the field open for the other two groups to pursue the horses. The Simian leader had fallen for the bait, and now the Simian army was split. They only had to worry about a hundred warriors now, which was still an impossible looking task.

Again he signaled Fred, and the Lancers turned and bolted through Forshay Pass leaving the way clear to the caverns. The Simian division split to pursue both targets, with twenty-five continuing toward the caverns and twenty-five pursuing the retreating Lancers. Again, Amy sought to split the Simians, and it worked. The Simian leader could see what was happening, but it was too late. He jumped around, screeched, and sent runners out to the army, but the distance was now great.

Amazing, Amy was good. She had these Simians figured out and her complicated plans were working to perfection.

* Amy *

She had the Lancers hold to draw the Simians farther away from the main army. When it looked like an engagement was imminent, the Simians began to advance faster. They were anxious to attack the Humans in fury after the night attack. She had Levi give the signal and the Lancers broke for the pass. The Lancers were spread wide across the path of the Simians, which made it easy for the line of Lancers to ride continuously and quickly through the pass.

Per instruction, Fred was one of the first through and immediately climbed to a vantage point above the pass. As a result they were able to follow the activities of the Simians, which were confused. Their orders had been to attack the caverns as she had expected, but the retreating Lancers were the enemy. As she hoped, they split their forces again. That was their second mistake.

Half of the pursuing Simians were hot on their trail as the last Lancers made it through the pass. Bows, poison arrows and agonizing death greeted those leading Simians that approached the pass. There were three Simians squirming and kicking in death throes before the pass. The Simians regrouped and counseled. The next attack was a sudden hard attack at the opening, trying to overwhelm the defenders. This proved to be disastrous as they jammed up at the pass, unable to drive past the Lancers in the narrow gap. The Simians were attacked from above with axes, in front by sharp lances, and all the while shot with poison arrows. After only a few minutes of this and seven more dead Simians, they retreated in confusion. Their numbers had been cut from twenty-five to fifteen in less than twenty minutes. The Simians decided to follow their original orders and left for the caverns.

They watched from Fred's vantage point above the pass. The other group had reached the caverns now and approached the doors. It was over a mile away from him but they could soon see five Simians falling and rolling on the ground as they met a terrible death. The crossbows with their poison arrows were working their magic. Like the pass, the Simians tried different tactics to approach, such as an improvised shield. Of the three that approached, all fell quivering, holding their foot. Of the twenty-five that approached the caverns, only seventeen remained. Confusion reigned. They waited, obviously wondering what to do.

He was really gaining new respect for her ability for strategy. She had planned this well. How in the hell she knew what they were going to do, he had no idea, but they were doing exactly as she predicted. Amy mentioned General Patton's book on troop deployment among others, but it didn't mean anything to him.

From his position he could observe the horses moving west and the two groups of Simians in hot pursuit. They were committed and being drawn away from the battle. The riders were not keeping the horses in a tight bunch, but allowing them to spread out, also causing the Simians to disperse across the desert. At this point they were far enough away to be out of the current action, and it was time to execute the next phase of the plan.

He gave the signal as directed by the boss, and the Lancers again poured out of the pass and charged the backs of the Simians headed for the caverns. The Simians were spread out now and weren't expecting a rear attack. They turned to defend but mostly too late as the first wave of Lancers hit. It was classic. The Simians were spread too far apart to defend each other. It was three Lancers to each Simian and it worked just like in training. A Simian could maybe defend against the first lance, but either the second or third caught it. The Simians were going down as they ran toward the safety of the other group. Only five made it.

The other Simian group watched and organized into their three-member teams and stood ready to defend and attack. The Lancers had killed ten additional Simians on that attack, but lost two Lancers. It could have been much worse. Amy's plans were making the difference.

The Lancers stopped short of attacking the last twenty-two Simians. They knew the Simians were a formidable fighting group. They were extremely fortunate to have done as well as they had. They stood no chance as long as the teams stayed together as they were now.

As the Lancers come out of the pass and started the attack on the rear of the Simians, he observed the Simian leader issuing orders and a runner was dispatched to the rear group. The rear group now charged to defend the group at the caverns. As they spread out across the desert floor, Amy issued the signal. This was the signal for Al's Lancers to charge the rear of the disorganized advancing Simians. The Simians had several miles to go before they could reach the battle, so they were very loosely organized when the Lancers charged from around the mountain. The Lancers charged into the rear of the Simians almost without warning. On the first wave, seventeen Simians fell before realizing what was happening but quickly turned to organize and defend.

He again issued Amy's orders and the Lancers turned from the Simians at the caverns to charge on the group Al had just attacked. Their charge took the Simians by surprise from another rear attack, killing ten more Simians. Half of the Simian division had been killed without ever having had a chance to fight. The Simians were screeching in anger and frustration at being tricked and out maneuvered. They wanted to fight head on, but Amy was fighting a different battle.

* Amy *

The enemy had been totally predictable so far, and her strategy worked, but she had run out of plans. The battle would have to be a head on fight now, unless she saw other things along the way.

Only seventeen of the Simians remained alive from the group at the caverns and twenty-five from the rear group. This was still a sizable force, but they were still separated. This was still an advantage to the Humans, but the Simians wouldn't be easy to trick now. Even as they watched, the Simians at the caverns were moving forward in a tight cluster. There wasn't much time before they combined again. They had to attack now.

She gave the signal for a charge from both sides. The Lancers charged, but were met with a tight cluster of eight teams. Every other team was facing a different direction to protect from charges front and back. The charges were effective, but costly, too costly. There were ten Simians down, but it had cost twelve Lancers. The Simians defended against the lead Lancer as expected, while the second or third were usually successful. Unfortunately the closeness of the lead Lancer to the Simian team made him vulnerable to attack by the other Simians, and it was costing lives. This would never do. They could never trade Lancers for Simians.

She called a halt to the attack. They would have to try something different. What did she have available? Poison arrows? No, half the bows were still protecting the pass and the other half of the bowmen team were staged to attack the guard on the main Simian camp. Bolos, yes, she would use bolos and ordered a coordinated attack using bolos and lances. The Simians were grouped tight, too tight. The Simian team would not hesitate to sacrifice the lead Simian in order for the second and third to attack the closest rider. The Simian's problem was they were facing both direction and were unable to watch a bolo attack from the rear. They would have to take out more than the lead Simian. If a bolo was launched at the lead Simian, it could entangle two, if not all three team members. If they could get two of the Simians on the ground, the attack would be successful.

The first wave of Lancers charged without lances and all three Lancer team members threw their bolos. She had been right, as she saw the Simians fall. In many cases the first two Simians fell entangled together and in some cases, all three fell, but always the first fell. The second wave connected with lances. The Simians were dying under the attack. It was over in minutes with the remaining fifteen Simians of this rear group lying dead on the ground without suffering any more Lancer losses.

Both Lancer groups turned on the seventeen Simians advancing from the caverns and following the success of the last engagement. It too, was successful and the last of the Simians died.

The only Warriors left alive were the five leaders, the ten guards for the females, and the whole other half of the Simian army, but they weren't here.

He could not believe how brilliant Amy's plans were coming together. This was not a battle of strength, it was a battle of wits and Amy had them all. The other thing that made the difference was the communications they had with their various teams. The existing hand-signing language provided the ability to pass on their instructions within the teams. The results were that Amy could issue instructions instantly and alter the plan to the Lancers when needed. It was like a chessboard and she was the Chess Master. He was so proud of her.

The whole battle went Amy's way, except for the charge that cost them so many Lancers. The Simians were not as disorganized as she had hoped. The addition of the bolos was another stroke of genius that worked brilliantly and the battle was over in minutes. All that was left were the five leaders and ten guards to deal with now. They would worry about the other half of the Simian army later.

Amy said it was time to take the leaders, and he was more than ready to finally get into the fray. He nodded to Moon and they went down the mountain to join the bowmen and Moon's Simians. The newest Simian recruits surrounded the females and children to calm them, while the bowmen moved in close enough to shoot the guards. In desperation, the Simian guards charged the bowmen and took them by surprise. The charging Warriors killed two bowmen before the poison incapacitated them. The other bowmen backed off a short distance and continued until the guards were all dispatched.

Levi, Moon and the original twelve approached the five leaders. They did not rush but closed in slow toward the leaders. The Simians had lost the battle, at least the first engagement, and he idly wondered if surrender was in order. This option was forfeited when the four commanders launched an attack. Moon stepped forward to take the charge of the first one, while the others Technical Simians unceremoniously attacked the other charging Warriors. Moon's Simians quickly killed the three charging Warriors, while Moon battled one-on-one with the fourth. Moon was also hungry for battle and welcomed the challenge, even though it didn't last long. Moon was spinning, stabbing, blocking, and striking with moves the Warrior had never seen before. The Warrior was good, but Moon was better and soon had the Warrior cut to pieces. The Warrior staggered and fell to its knees. Moon walked up and cut its throat then bent to pry out a shiny black tooth, while the dying Warrior stared in disbelief.

The leader stood his ground, but was visibly shocked as this Technical Simian defeated his Warrior so soundly, then removed a tooth. The leader noticed the string of Simian teeth hanging around Moon's neck, and then even more surprising, he noticed the collection around Levi's neck. Fear registered across his face, but he screeched out his challenge. He claimed his right to fight the leader in single combat.

Moon looked at Levi and signed, "It is the custom of the Simians and his right to make a challenge, but you are not obligated to follow with Simian customs."

He knew there was no choice if he wanted to maintain the respect of his Simians and frankly, he wanted to fight. He had watched the fighting all morning and felt left out. Hell, even Moon got to fight.

He accepted the challenge in the screeching language of the Simians. The leader was shocked that he was the leader and even more shocked that he answered in the Simian language. The Simian leader quickly recovered and turned to face him, emanating waves of pure hate.

Moon signed, "Be careful, because the leader would be very good at combat, possibly even better than the Sword Master."

Now that was sobering.

* Amy *

She was furious when Levi accepted the challenge. They had just won the battle and she had already squeezed out every last possible trick she could think of to win. She had done it to win the war and keep Levi safe. Now that the battle was won, he accepts a challenge for one-on-one combat. This was stupid, and she was angry.

Levi said, "I have to do it."

All Amy could think of to say was, "Bull Shit!" This was nothing but macho crap, but she had no choice now.

Levi took his pack off and stripped to the waist. His rippling muscles undulated under his brown skin. He approached with his pickaxe in one hand

and sword in the other. Amy reminded him, "This is the leader and he has become leader by combat; therefore, he is the best of the lot." Levi was startled to think about that and knew she was right. He had faced this Simian community's Sword Master and he had been good, but this one was, in all probability, better. He would have to be very careful.

The Lancers gathered around along with all of Moon's Simians, and the females and children of the Simian colony to watch. This was a historic moment for all.

They faced each other in the center of a clearing made by Moon's circled Simians. The leader was large, standing more than eight feet tall and weighed close to five hundred pounds. The leader was well aware that he was going to die but wanted to take Levi with him. They met with a clash in the center. Again, Levi rolled with every strike, dodging and weaving. The Simian used the two-sword technique he had seen the Sword Master use. She kept Levi out of reach, while she observed its technique. The Simian was good but not nearly as good as the Sword Master had been. Possibly, the shock of the defeat and hatred for Levi clouded his judgment. This one took chances and was depending on using its superior strength to overpower Levi.

She had Levi fighting a defensive fight only as she recorded the Simian's style, and it was repetitious. If this was the way it normally fought, she wondered how he had risen to the leader position. The Sword Master must have supported him.

As the leader struck out yet again with his right sword, his left leg trailed behind. This was the time! Levi dropped to his knees and struck down with his sword hard into the heel of the Simian's left leg. Levi then rolled over to the rear, dropping his sword to grab his pickaxe with both hands. He spun around and made an upward swing directly into the Simian's crotch. All this took place in less than three-seconds. The Simian died instantly, falling like a chopped tree. There was only silence from the gathered crowd. The attack had happened so quickly the crowd hadn't grasped the situation. Slowly, a chant began, "Levi, Levi, Levi!" Even the Simians chimed in with their "Eee Iii." She saw the pride swelling up in Levi, as she irreverently stuck her tongue out at him. He just smiled back at her until she told him it was time for "Plan B."

* Levi *

Oh yes, Amy was pissed, but there was no way he could refuse. He told Amy, "Focus or I will die." She calmed, established control over herself and provided him with a plan. This Simian was strong, but he had met much better, or was it that he and Amy were getting better? Amy let the battle go on for a while, but released him with the moves to take. It was over in seconds. It wasn't even much of a fight.

This engagement was over and they were victorious. Now they had to figure out what to do with a Simian colony. After the short celebration, he told Moon, "Have your Simians go out and gather the dead horses to feed the colony." He requested of

Al, "Send a runner to gather up and deliver some of your cattle to keep them fed for a while." Then he asked, "Amy, isn't it about time to complete the last phase of her plan?"

Al saw the immediate need for what he requested and sent the runner. Al's next activity was to send his Lancers to gather the dead and prepare for their burial. The Lancers had been extremely lucky, considering, but had lost eighteen Lancers in this day's fighting.

Amy said, "It is indeed time to execute "Plan B." He called again to Moon as he sat down cross-legged on the ground. Moon nodded and spread the group apart to give room to protect him. When he saw that Moon understood what he needed, he closed his eyes and watched as Amy began to show him "Plan B."

He watched through Jimmy's eyes and saw the Owens Valley army spread out across the desert. Each team was aligned three members deep, one behind the other. The teams were stationary and waited as the horses approached and passed through the space between the teams. The dust churned thick as they waited. At the back of the herd were the riders. They exchanged waves as they passed and waited for the dust to clear. As soon as the horses and riders passed through them, Lancers two and three in the rear of the team began to spread out left and right in preparation for a charge. Soon, Jimmy could begin to see images, and then he clearly saw the Simians running toward them. The Simians saw them at about the same time and stopped in their tracks in obvious shock.

The Simians had been chasing the horses all morning, and the riders had kept the horses just out of their reach, drawing the Simians forward. According to the plan, the riders had also spread the horses out wide, causing the Simians to spread out as well. They had spread out so far that the Simian three-member teams were no longer together. It had taken all morning for this to happen and to bring the Simians to the Owens Valley army.

Amy had said, "The Owens Valley army isn't going to make it in time so, we will just have to take the Simians to the army."

And so she had. The plan worked perfectly.

It must have been a shocking sight for the Simians to watch the dust clear and find themselves facing a mounted army. That would have been shocking enough, but to see that line of widely spaced Lancers spread out and triple in number, that must have had a frightening effect.

The timing had been close. Amy had pushed the Owens Valley army hard to reach the staging area where the lances were stored before the horses arrived. They had made it with two hours to spare and were deployed in low areas until the dust from the horses allowed them to come up on the higher ground and get into position unseen. They were anxious and ready with three hundred Lancers. They would be facing one hundred Simian warriors, but he had told them that the surprise of the attack would make the difference, and that the Simians would be disorganized when they got there. When the Simians arrived, they were in fact disorganized and spread out, which made Jimmy and Iron Eyes very happy. Jimmy was not so happy when he was asked to remain on the hill and watch the battle. He told Jimmy he needed to communicate with him and maybe give him directions. Jimmy didn't like it, but he did what he was asked to do.

The Lancers charged the spread out Simians. There was little resistance from the Simians, because they turned to run. The Owens Valley army won the physiological war already and instilled fear in the Simians. The three hundred Lancers charged the fleeing Simians and killed more than seventy on the first charge. After the initial charge, there was no renewed attempt to recall them for another mass charge. The individual three-man Lancer teams simply continued to run down fleeing Simians. Few of the Simians ever made it back together as a team. The battle was over in less than an hour with only five Lancers lost. Amy's plan had been masterful.

* Amy *

When she realized that the Owens Valley Army wasn't going to make it in time, her initial thought was that it was over. Everything would be lost, the war, life and Earth, but she had learned a valuable lesson from Levi and that was never give up, "NEVER." She expanded her mind to think in the abstract. She pushed herself beyond her prior limits and devised the plan. In truth, it was an incredibly simple, "Plan B" that was being executed now.

She had earlier asked Levi to send a runner to the staging area for the lances and have them head back toward Barstow a day's ride, and wait for the army. She had calculated the travel time of the army and chosen the battlefield. It was higher, open ground with small rolling hills facing her chosen attack site. She knew the Simian army would only chase Humans or horses, and she needed all the Humans. The Simians could not risk letting the horses escape, so she was positive they would pursue the horses if they believed they were trying to escape. The trick was the timing. It had to be done in such a way as to split the Simian army ... divide and conquer. It worked to perfection, and she felt the pride of success.

The rest of the plan required the herders to spread the horses out over the chosen battlefield and force Simian disorganization. The Warriors would be a formidable enemy if they remained together in teams, but the lack of any possible threat lulled them into making the mistake of spreading out as she had hoped. The herders had done an exceptional job as well and had delivered the Simian army to the battlefield on time and precisely where they were meant to be.

Actually, part of the plan was to surprise them and hopefully instil fear into them. That part also worked as she had planned. The fearless Simians turned and ran. They were not organized at all, and didn't have time to try to regroup, and they showed no inclination of wanting to. Fear took them and they just ran.

It was a slaughter. The battle was completely one-sided. The incredible mighty Simians were reduced to being mere targets to be pursued and killed. The battle was over in forty-eight minutes.

She was happy. They had been incredibly lucky, and all her plans worked. She had only made a few slight oversights on details but none turned out to be devastating. Levi had won his single combat and the macho shit head was happy, too. She could not have hoped for two better armies. She was very proud of both of them.

When Levi announced the outcome of the other engagement, cheers rang through the desert. He told them the Owens Valley army was en route to them now and a celebration was in order. Al's army was headed back to the main camp to prepare a feast of celebration. Moon was assuming leadership of the Simian community, and would make camp at Chuckwalla Spring for tonight to begin indoctrination and organization of his new Simian colony.

Levi was anxious to see all his friends again, and finally make introductions and have a night of celebration. It was only right to do so before the reality of the next obstacle came back into focus.

The next force they must deal with was Gord and his Simian colony, and it was twice the size of this one, and they would not be so fooled. Gord would learn from this Simian loss, and would not be as arrogant. Unfortunately, the realization would come and the celebration would be short, but let them have it for tonight.

CHAPTER 19
(THE WAR CONTINUES)

* Levi *

He stayed with Moon and the Simians for several more hours to assist in organizing the new Simian colony.

Moon told him, "Since you have defeated the leader, according to Simian custom, you are now the new leader."

That was interesting. What the hell would he do as a Simian leader? He spoke in the screeching tongue of the Simians announcing, "I am putting Moon in charge and he will be the new leader. You are safe and will not be harmed as long as you live in peace with Humans."

Moon was not happy. What had he done? He sat with Moon to talk.

Moon said, "I am with Levi and am not a leader of Simians."

Now he understood. He saw that Moon was not about to be separated from him. Levi explained, "It is only temporary. I still want you with me, I need you to organize the community and indoctrinate them to the new rules. You can appoint your own leader, but I want you to remain the head of the colony." Moon reluctantly accepted that and went about organizing the colony.

In truth, he was happy to hear that he wasn't going to lose Moon as a companion. He had gotten quite accustomed to having him close. Additionally, he didn't have a clue what to do with a Simian colony but realized he was becoming involved in their future whether he wanted to or not.

Moon sat up temporary camp at Chuckwalla Spring, being the closest water to Granite Pass. Moon sent all but a few of the Simians back to bring up the wagons.

He told them "This time you will be pulling them for yourselves."

He didn't know what was in them but was sure it was things they would need in the future. Moon would give him an inventory when it was available, and Amy, as usual, was very curious as to the contents.

He looked at the sky, saw the buzzards circling and wondered where they all came from and how they always knew. A second group of buzzards circled far to the west and knew the same carnage was there as well. He wondered if he should say something to Moon about burying the dead Simians, but Amy suggested that he not. They wouldn't understand the need and in this desert heat the flesh would decompose quickly. It would, however, smell very ripe on the desert for several weeks, and he wanted to get far away from it. The stink wouldn't bother the Simians. They seemed to eat even rotten flesh and several times he had made Moon dispose of some especially rank meat he carried.

He told Moon, "I am going now to the main camp at the caverns. Come there once you get the colony settled." He explained, "Cattle will be arriving tomorrow and the Simians will have to keep them gathered. They are their food now."

Moon turned up his nose at the thought of cattle but nodded. He grinned in spite of himself.

* Amy *

She had mixed emotions about Moon's reluctance to take over what was left of the Simian colony. He was needed to reorganize and indoctrinate the colony, but he was such a good friend and totally trustworthy to Levi, and she felt safer with him around. It pleased her that Moon didn't want to lead the colony and would rather stay with Levi, but they needed someone to be the leader. Without established leadership a Warrior Simian could come along and absorb them into another colony. Females made a colony possible. She assumed that was the major reason they were guarded was to prevent a lone warrior from taking females to start a new colony. A new colony of Warrior Simians could not be allowed. No, Moon needed to take control, and she was happy that Moon compromised, at least for the time being.

Levi sprinted off into the dark alone across the desert toward the caverns and the main camp. She estimated he should make it to the main camp in about two hours. The Owens Valley army had arrived about an hour earlier, and he could see the blazing campfires as he ran. There was indeed a celebration in progress, judging by the number of campfires. Monitoring Jimmy, Fred, and Dawn, was very enlightening. The finest meats and foods had also been prepared and a feast was laid out.

The two armies met and were acting as if they had known each other for years. They had worked

538

together so well, and won a fantastic victory over the Simians, something that had never before been done. They were joined forever in this common accomplishment.

Not only had the armies joined together, but Al and Iron Eyes were joined in conversation, and Jimmy, Fred, and Dawn had sought each other out. From what she monitored, Levi was the focus of attention between all the and the entire camp.

As Levi neared the camp, she noticed that there were no guards on duty, and why would they need guards now? This would be the first time they would not have to worry about security in more years than they could probably remember. It made her feel good that part of the plan had come together, but anxious when she thought about what was still ahead in order to protect the Owens Valley. The gathered armies would remember too but not tonight. Let them have their victory and celebration.

* Levi *

As he came into camp, cheers greeted him. Many were patting and slapping him on the back, and all were ushering him toward the main campfire. He recognized Lancers from both armies as he was ushered through the crowd. Someone along the way handed him a large mug of beer, and it tasted good. The Lancer said it was the best cavern vintage. Damn, how long had it been since he had a beer? Certainly it had been too damned long for sure. He broke through the crowd into the opening before the main campfire and immediately saw General Harkin, Al, Iron Eyes, Jimmy, Dawn, and Fred, among others. Yes, there were Wolf, Jim and Johnny, too. They all turned to him, standing to encircle and embrace him, exclaiming thanks and congratulations for what he had done. He was praising Amy and smiling to her. She was the hero, not he. He told Amy, "I wish I could tell them."

Amy only grinned and said, "Thank you Levi."

Someone handed him a large plate full of beans, ham, beef and a big turkey leg. It was probably Dawn. He was being overwhelmed with praise and thanks and sometime during the celebration he received one of his most prized trophies. With great elaboration, Iron Eyes presented him with an Eagle feather that he wove into his braid. That Eagle feather meant a great deal to him. He wished his grandfather could see it. With all the attention, he thought Amy might be getting jealous again, but she said, "No." She wanted him to use the elevated authority to establish and maintain control of the armies.

Amy said, "It will only get more difficult and they will need an absolute leader, YOU!"

The celebration lasted late into the night before everyone settled down to sleep. Breakfast was slow coming in the morning. Actually, it was closer to noon before the Lancers were up and around. He slept late as well. He hadn't drunk much, because Amy was against it and said it was hard on his body, but he had been tired and it tasted so good. Yesterday had been a very stressful day, and he was more tired than he originally thought.

Once he was finally up and around, the leaders leisurely gathered around him. It was like they wanted to get instructions but didn't want to openly

540

admit it. Iron Eyes was close, as was Al, and the triplets (Dawn, Fred and Jimmy).

Amy said, "It is time to begin."

After grabbing some food and sitting to eat, he called them. They were ready and welcomed the call. He congratulated them again for a job well done. He said, "By working together we have done the impossible. Together we defeated a Simian army and cleared the desert settlement from danger." He let that sink in for a while, then continued, "What we did here today was fantastic, but it is only the beginning. The next battle will be much harder." He watched the resolve on their faces. He looked at Iron Eyes as he said, "The Owens Valley is now in trouble from the Los Angeles Simian colony, and that colony is much larger than the one they just defeated." He ate and let that information sink in.

They had thought about that too, privately, but it hadn't been brought it up. Now that he had, they were anxious to talk and were curious how HE planned to wage war against that Simian army.

Amy grinned at him and said, "There it is, they just gave you command."

He hadn't missed it and really had mixed emotions about it, but someone had to do it and they, he and Amy, were uniquely qualified to do it, if it could be done at all.

He said, "I'm not sure yet, but I don't plan to wait on the Simians to make the first move." Amy was emphatic about that. Surprise would work on their side, and she wanted to establish defense lines and take the battle to the enemy. At first, they planned to ambush the Simian patrols and fight a war designed to deplete their numbers. Additionally, they could pick their battles and draw the Simians into the open in order to make the Lancers effective. He said, "These are just thoughts and could, and probably would, change as necessary." Then he talked in general terms.

He said, "We must move our armies to Victorville within a few days." One thing he was sure of, well Amy was sure of, was relocating both armies to Victorville. From there they could defend against the Simians as they came down out of the mountains. They could choose the battle location and protect the Owens Valley in the process. It was also close enough so they could launch an attack into Los Angeles if that became necessary; however, Amy hoped to lure the Simians to them. The gathered leaders accepted the instruction without any sign of resistance.

The chain of command was established without it being pointed out. He was the general, Al, Iron Eyes and Moon were his captains and Dawn, Jimmy and Fred were his direct communication links and spoke for him. Most didn't fully understand what was going on, but none ever questioned instructions from them. They had seen it work in battle and trusted him and his ability to communicate through them.

* Amy *

The timing really was right to establish control, but Levi was always reluctant. Everyone but Levi already knew he was in charge. They had mobilized two armies at his direction and he, well she, had led

542

them through and won the greatest battle ever fought against the Simians. They had followed his instruction to the letter, and they were ready to do it again. They were waiting for him when he came into camp and were ready to continue following his instructions. They talked and celebrated but remained close. They knew he would take control. Hell they had given him control; he just hadn't realized it yet.

By morning she had convinced Levi he was the only one that could do it. He was the only one the armies would follow and therefore the only hope to accomplish the goals. Yes, he agreed, reluctantly. He wanted to fight, but being the leader carried many responsibilities and details. She reassured him, "I will do most of it and you will be the hero." He grinned at that and so did she.

The plan was incredibly simple no matter how ridiculous it seemed. The Mojave Desert settlement was now safe from immediate danger. The closest Simian colony was Los Angeles, unless the Phoenix colony expanded in their direction, which was highly unlikely. The Mojave Desert settlement owed their very existence to the Owens Valley community, not to mention her and Levi. Now that the Colorado River Simian colony was no longer a threat, the Mojave Desert settlement was obligated to help, even if it weren't in their best interest, which it was. Both armies could now march on the Los Angeles Simian colony.

That was the plan. As simple as it seemed, it would be much more complicated than that. There were many factors that must be considered:

1. The combined lancers numbered about five hundred and fifty, while the Los Angeles Simian colony numbered about seven hundred Simian Warriors, more than twice the size of the Colorado River colony.

2. Los Angeles was not open like it was in the desert for fighting. The Lancers needed open territory in order to be effective with their battle techniques. For this reason she told Levi that they should move the armies to Victorville. It was the closest open ground from which they could wage war using Lancers, and it was positioned to protect the Owens Valley. It was also the only reasonable pass over the mountains to the Owens Valley.

3. They couldn't count on surprise this time. It was not reasonable to believe that Gord and his settlement had not heard or figured out what had happened in the desert. Moreover, Gord would have received reports from his patrols, especially that one that got away. He would know about the Human armies and probably Levi also.

4. She would need new strategies and more diversity of weapons. They needed an edge, something different, something for close quarters, but the only thing she could think of was guns. Now that would be a real equalizer. She wished she still had the microscope to work on the gun powder problem. As soon as she thought it, she knew she had made a mistake. Levi heard her thoughts.

Levi said, far too loud in her mind, "GUN POWDER?"

He wanted to know what she could do about making guns work. She then explained what she suspected about the shift in the laws of physics. She

544

told him, "I believe that it is only a slight shift, but just enough to change everything. I think it is a matter of finding out what element or elements have changed and find a substitute for it." She also warned him, "The secret must remain with them and, if I am fortunate enough to find it, I will not share the formula with anyone." She also reminded him, "It is only a theory, but without a microscope it is only a dream."

* Levi *

She had kept gunpowder a secret from him until now. Now he understood why she had wanted the microscope, and why she had taken some guns, ammunition and loading equipment from here when they were going to the research facility. It all made sense now. Why hadn't he seen it before, and why was Amy keeping it a secret? She went into her philosophical discussion on the pros and cons of guns. Guns made even a weak man strong, and made any man, good or bad, equal to him. All his abilities meant nothing against a gun. She couldn't protect him from a bad man with a gun. Who would have guessed Amy would turn out to be a liberal anti-gun advocate?

Sometimes she could be so frustrating. He explained, "We will need guns, if we can get them, to defeat the Los Angeles Simian colony. Without them we really don't stand a chance, if we are honest." After a while she agreed but with reservations. She would try, but there wasn't much of a chance without a microscope unless she got very lucky.

Amy said, "If I am able to find the secret, I would never share or allow anyone to know the formula. Not even you."

That was a point she would not budge on and it really didn't matter. Hell, he wouldn't know what to do with it anyway.

Amy had already started working out the details of the next confrontation with the Los Angeles Simians, and he relayed them to the group as if they were coming from him. A token amount of lances were to be left here in the remote chance that they would be required here again. Most of the lances had been used up, so the wagons were to be used to haul supplies for the armies back to Victorville and then sent on to Owens Valley. Someone had to go back to the Owens Valley to relay the plans and request more lances to fill the empty wagons. They should be finished and ready by the time the wagons reached them, about days from now.

He told Jimmy, "Take six Lancers and one of the small, fast drawn lance wagons that had been built here and leave in the morning for the Owens Valley." There was a look of disgust on Jimmy's face, but it only lasted for the briefest of time. He knew how Jimmy felt, he had made that trip so many times already, and also, Jimmy had an elevated position, almost as one of Levi's seconds, which he didn't want to leave. He wanted to be with Levi. Jimmy looked happier when he said, "Watch for Warrior Simian survivors, and take them out if you find any." He wanted to keep the Simian defeat a secret as long as he could. Jimmy saw that he was being given a responsible job and was proud and happy to be part of Levi's team.

Asking Al if some cattle had been sent to Moon's group, he was told that a small herd left that morning. He told Al, "We will also need to take a small herd of cattle along with us to Victorville, since we don't know how long of a stay we will have there." Additionally he told Al, "We need to take several of the Lancers with us and go to Moon's camp. We can inventory the Simian wagons and have the Lancers transport the wagons back to the caverns." The unnecessary Simian supplies were to be stored in the caverns so they wouldn't have to pull the wagons across the desert. Everyone listened and was quick to comply.

* Amy *

She was working up the plans and details to get everyone mobilized. It had to happen soon. She knew Gord would move as soon as he learned what had happened here. It was too much to hope that it would remain a secret. There could have been numerous Simian survivors and they would have nowhere to go but to Gord. Once Gord found out, he would be angry and want to resolve the problem quickly. This would make Gord look weak, thereby forcing him to react, and she wanted to be in a position to intercept Gord's army when he moved against them. That battle would be disastrous, but she had no choice. It was better to pick the battles and the terrain, even if you lost.

Maybe Jimmy could find a few survivors and eliminate part of the problem, but mainly he needed to pass the word on to the tribe about their victory here in the desert, and get them working on more lances. They would need them soon at Victorville. She also wanted someone there that she could monitor.

Al was back with a dozen Lancers and forty extra horses. Levi even accepted a horse to ride himself, and they headed across the desert battlefield toward Moon's camp. In the Mojave Desert heat, the stench of rotting Simians was already sickening. The excessive heat, coyotes, buzzards, other varmints and insects had already made an impact on the bodies. The black Simian bones shining through the torn flesh could be seen everywhere. In a few days there would be nothing left but black bones littering the desert floor, and she was sure that soon this place would be known as the Valley of Black Bones.

She also noticed all the swords, knives, and weapons lying around on the battlefield.

Levi, reading her mind, suggested to Al, "Can you send out a team to recover all the weapons and metals and take them back to the camp? They could be used."

Al agreed and said, "I will take care of it and at the other site as well."

As they approached the camp, Moon walked out to meet them. One look and he could tell Moon was happy by the way he walked and carried his body. They could see that he had organized the camp already and had not wasted any time. His original crew was training the others. There were groups fighting with swords, some with knives, and still others were fighting hand-to-hand. He could see groups practicing the sign language. She also noticed that the wagons were in camp. Moon had indeed been busy. The females and children were also included in the training, although mostly in sign language. That answered the question she had been pondering as to the intelligence of the females. It was no small task to learn the sign language, and she could see many were already conversing with each other in that way.

Moon slapped Levi on the shoulder showing a rare sign of emotion. Even in affection, the slap jarred Levi to the bone as he cringed and grinned at Moon. Moon began his report to Levi and confirmed all that she had noticed. He continued in a somewhat excited voice as he said he inventoried the contents of the wagon. She was alerted to his excitement.

* Levi *

Moon took them over to the wagons and started going through them and naming items, which didn't mean much to anyone but Moon. Some of the items were recognizable like a large metal forge, mechanical drills and lathes and other blacksmith's equipment. That got the attention of Al.

Al said, "This looks like really good equipment and we can use it."

Other equipment, even Amy had no idea what it was used for. It looked like electronic equipment, which was useless.

He asked Moon, "Why did the Simians keep this equipment when it was useless?"

Moon looked at him and said, "Some of their technology still worked on this planet. It was simply not used because the Warrior Simians had taken over in space, and refused to accept the benefits of technology, because it meant acknowledging the worth of the Technical Class Simians."

Amy was going crazy. He could see the shock on her face, and she wanted to know more. He would find out more, but cautioned her, "Remain focused on the immediate problem and don't get side-tracked like I know you want to."

When questioned, Moon explained what different equipment did, but the one that got Amy's attention was a unit Moon said was an information processing and storage unit.

Amy said, "It is a computer and will most likely have the stored knowledge of the Simians on it."

It would be important to learn this knowledge. Levi asked some of the questions Amy was proposing, but Amy was simply too excited to ask rational questions, so he censored her questions. In response to one, Moon said that the power source used was a form of hydrogen energy modified to conduct energy in a liquid flow. Moon didn't understand how it worked; only that it did. He had actually worked as an information processing operator with similar equipment on board ship. This would require much more investigation when they had the time.

It was his turn to be shocked, as he realized Moon had been on a ship. This meant he had to be at least as old as he was. He asked Moon his age and was told that he was equivalent to one hundred and ten earth years old. He wasn't positive, but he thought his jaw hit the ground about that time. Amy reminded him that Simians lived to be more than two hundred earth years old. He had forgotten that fact, but Amy never forgot anything.

It was time to move on through the wagons. They were going through the last wagon, which appeared to be medical supplies. Again, most of the items meant little to them and would require much more investigation, assuming they lived long enough to make it back. There were a few items that they could identify with, like crutches, splints and a damn microscope! It was bigger than theirs had been, but the optics and adjustments were the same. He asked, "Amy, is that what I think it is?" She was grinning like crazy. Yes, this was a good day.

He told Moon he wanted to store the equipment in the caverns. It would be a research center and safe haven for them all to return to. He also explained about moving to Victorville and making a staging area there for the next battle. He explained the logic as he had used with the others.

Moon understood and said, "I will be ready when you want them to leave."

Levi's plans were to take one wagon with supplies of treated horsemeat they had retrieved from the battlefield, weapons, water, the cattle that had been brought to them and some medical supplies.

Al's Lancers were hooking up the teams of horses to the wagons so they could pull them back to the caverns. Amy suggested and he reminded Al to see about sending teams out to retrieve all the swords and weapons, metals, and the like, to store for future use. Al thought that was a good idea especially in light of the new forge and equipment they were taking back with them. There was a lot of metal that could be used.

* Amy *

She was very interested in the contents of the wagons and as Moon showed them, she was taking an inventory. Many items she could not identify with, even though Moon explained what they were. Some were navigational equipment and items associated with space travel, while others simply had no English translation or meaning.

When they reached a wagonload of what looked like electronic equipment, she had to wonder why the Simians had taken up space for equipment that did not work. When Moon told Levi that it did work and the Simian group brought it in the event that Gord might want it. She was going nuts with questions. How did it work? What was the power source? What did the equipment do? Levi slowed her down, but she was able to get some of the answers. One item was obviously a computer, and it worked on a liquid hydrogen power. Oh she wanted these toys, and she wanted them to work now, but Levi reminded her that it was not the time or place. He said Gord was the problem and what we must focus on. Yes, he was right.

She knew he was right when they uncovered the medical wagon and saw the microscope. This was now the priority. They would start on the gunpowder problem immediately as soon as they got back to the base camp.

Levi explained the plan and schedule to Moon. They wanted to leave in two days, and if they started her research today, she hoped to be able to add some guns to their weapons arsenal. They might stand a chance yet. She would know within a few hours of research.

She was excited and pushed Levi and Al on ahead of the group. She wanted to reach the caverns, set up her work area and begin the research. She wished they were faster.

They started immediately when they reached the caverns. Al went about organizing his Lancers for the deployment to Victorville. Al was readying supplies for both armies. Levi went directly to the caverns and was reviewing the rifles and ammunition inventory. They only found fifteen of the AR-15s and three military .45 caliber automatic pistols. There were cases of ammunition, however.

They opened a few bullets and emptied the gunpowder into vials, and on inspiration called Dawn and asked her to solicit help to empty the ammunition. This was a big job, and they would need help. They went through the caverns and supplies getting samples of various elements and chemicals for testing along with the samples of gunpowder. They were ready by the time the wagons arrived, and the cargo was being stored away. She made sure that the microscope was unloaded first by Levi personally. They were soon hard at work analyzing samples.

It was amazing how coordinated she and Levi had become. Many times it was like it was her body. Their minds were linked so closely, it was hard to tell who was doing what. This was a togetherness man and women could never reach.

There are a special few that think so alike that they may get extremely close, but never quite there.

The microscope was exceptional with strong magnification, and she was able at long last to identify the altered element. It was carbon. The atomic structure had altered, making all carbon functions no longer operative. This included electricity and gunpowder. Now what she had to discover was whether there was another element or chemical that was also altered, or one that could function as a replacement or added to carbon to make it compatible again.

After hours of searching, she found a very close substitute. She refused to identify the substance, even to Levi for fear he may inadvertently reveal it. She was very serious about not letting anyone know the formula. Levi thought she was paranoid, but he really didn't care so he didn't probe. The only question she had now was will it work?

* Levi *

Amy was excited with this project, and so was he but for different reasons. Amy was doing it as much for science as she was to develop a weapon. He didn't give a damn about science unless it helped him defeat the Simians. Whatever the reason, the research continued as they worked through the afternoon. She said she had it, but wouldn't say what she had found. Then as they mixed the chemicals and compounds, she blocked the names from him and his memory. He wondered how the hell she did that, but she did it, nonetheless.

554

The gunpowder was in measured buckets and he went from bucket to bucket adding this grey looking powder to the mixture. Those working the buckets stirred and mixed it in very carefully. This was done topside to distance the explosives from the Coleman lamps. Amy insisted on a very thorough mixing. After that was complete the loading equipment was used to rebuild the shells and reload the AR-15 clips. When the first ammunition clip was ready, Levi took it and a thoroughly cleaned AR-15 from stock to a suitable location to test it. Al and Iron Eyes came to watch the miracle. He loaded the clip, removed the safety and sighted in on a rock some distance away. He waited as he took a deep breath, slowly let it out and pulled the trigger. The explosion was hoped for, but when it fired, it was sudden and loud. The target exploded in dust. It worked! "Amy you did it. You're wonderful!"

Al looked shocked and Iron Eyes just grinned. Iron Eyes' grin matched his own as they looked at each other. After a minute Al wanted to know how it was done, but he told him it was not to be revealed to anyone. He would be the only one with the secret. The secret of gunpowder was to be protected from the Simians at all cost, and if no one knew, it couldn't be tortured from them. Al saw the worth of that and accepted it.

After a moment of silence Al said, "Who is Amy?"

He knew then that he had made a mistake and had thanked Amy out loud. He had a pained look on his face when he turned back to Al, but Al was smiling.

Al said, "Forget I asked."

"Thanks Al, you are a true friend."

Jimmy left the following morning taking his chosen Lancers with him. Surprisingly, he had Lancers from both armies, but that was good. Dawn's small army of women spent the next day loading ammunition, while all the other supplies were being loaded into the wagons. Al picked the fifteen riflemen, from each army. The .45 automatics went to Iron Eyes, Al and himself. Amy insisted that he accept it for his own personal safety.

The following morning they headed west toward Victorville. Al had lost some Lancers in the war and left a token force to protect the settlement, but still set out with two hundred and fifty Lancers. Iron Eyes had about two hundred and seventy-five Lancers, and Moon had fifty-four Simians in his army now. The army had swords, lances, poison arrows, and now they had guns. He felt awesome until he thought about the more than seven hundred Simians Warriors and Gord. He then had a wave panic pass over him, but fought to not show it.

* Amy *

She was sure the gunpowder would work, but felt relief to see it work, and even happier to see the appreciation in Levi. She really felt great when Levi gave her praise. The gunpowder would not be as efficient as the original but should work well enough. The AR-15s were powerful weapons and should work well on Simians but only at short range. At long distances the velocity of the bullet would reduce and wouldn't be sufficient to penetrate

556

the dense hide of a Simian. Bullets would have a tendency to deflect off the hide if the angle was not fairly direct. So, the rifles would work but would have to be used at closer ranges. It would still be a formidable weapon on their side. Unfortunately the .45s would be less than deadly, but could inflict damage if used close and multiple shots made. She had doubts that a person would have time to use it, but they should boost the confidence of the owner.

Levi allowed Al to choose the team for the guns and Al chose well, splitting them between the armies. They were all feeling like one army now anyway. When Al suggested that Levi have one of the .45s, he started to refuse, but Amy was kicking his butt, and he knew she would make a fuss if he didn't take it. So, now he had a pistol too.

They were off again on their deployment. For the first time the two Lancer armies traveled together as a complete army, and it was impressive. They numbered more than five hundred Lancers in strength plus Moon's small army of Simians, but they were still outnumbered in more ways than one. She was thinking how lucky she had been with the execution on her plan against the migrating Colorado River Simians. It had gone well, but so much was based upon surprise. Could they surprise Gord? She hoped so but didn't honestly believe so. If Gord knew how they fought, defense strategies could be developed that would make the Lancers ineffective. Did he know? Yes, he would have received reports from the battle in Owens Valley and maybe even from survivors of this battle. That would be bad for Levi's army. That was one reason she wanted Jimmy to watch for survivors and kill them.

Since Jimmy left yesterday morning, he had not seen any surviving Simians, but he was riding at a fast pace and would see them soon if there were any. She believed there might be some Simian stragglers. Actually, she was sure there were. It was unreasonable to assume that in all the battles, no Simian survived and got away. These survivors would go nowhere else but to Gord without doubt.

What would Gord do if he knew everything? Would he wait for them to come? No, Gord would initiate the battle. Just like her, he would want to control the time, place and circumstances under which the battle took place. Gord would go on the offensive, and she had to anticipate every possible move and be ready for them.

* Levi *

He felt pride as he led the combined armies across the desert toward Victorville. It really was an impressive show of power, but Amy was worried about Gord and the massive colony of Simians at Los Angeles. She was being very cautious, and admittedly, he was also concerned. This was going to be a test of survival, theirs. He had always wanted revenge and had been happy at the turn of events that gave him this new lease on life and the ability to pursue his revenge again. The scope of their forces, however, had continued to expand beyond his belief until it reached the scale it was today. Who would have ever thought there would be armies of Humans fighting armies of Simians, much less winning? It was too much to accept but, nevertheless, a reality. So far everything almost seemed like a fantasy, so it was easy to think of Gord and his army as just another challenge, but reality was beginning to set in. The responsibility of all these Humans was his. Could he handle that?

Amy had been honest from the start. She didn't think they had a chance against Gord's army, but allowed them the joy of their victory. She had even suggested that the Humans relocate to a new area not populated by Simians, but neither Human group would accept that now. They wanted to fight for their homes and chose him to lead them. He didn't seem to have a choice anymore. He knew that Amy was thinking and planning in an effort to change the odds, but he could see into her mind and her thoughts were not encouraging. He almost wished he hadn't started it, but he had even less choice than the others. They would all follow this trail together to the end no matter where it led.

It would take about five days to reach Victorville with the wagons, but, for the first time, they weren't fighting an impossible deadline. They didn't have an abundance of time but were under no immediate danger. As a result, the armies set a fast pace, but did not over stress the horses or men.

On the second day out they came upon the battlefield. The stench of the dead Simians was so strong that they veered around the carnage in silence. It was like trespassing a burial ground, a grim reminder of war. The black bones were much more prominent now, as the desert was taking its toll. Then they passed the battlefield were moving on.

About midday on the third day, Amy began showing him what she was receiving from Jimmy. He could see two Simians moving ahead of Jimmy as the Lancers fanned out in pursuit. The Simians were not traveling that close to each other, which made it easier to attack. They turned to repel the charge and the first successfully repelled the first lance, but the second caught it directly in the chest and the third hit just under that one. As the shafts went deep into the Simian, they shattered as they were designed to do, preventing the Lancer from being taken out of the saddle. The Simian went down and was finished off on the ground with swords. The second Simian also went down as textbook perfect as the first. The Lancers cheered, but six lances were used up, which only left seven.

In the distance they could see another full three-unit Simian team running. They had seen Jimmy and the Lancers engage the other Simian and turned to fight. They were a team obviously accustomed to working together and were prepared. Amy didn't like the looks of this team. Something was different. Jimmy approached to attack, but Amy told him, Have Jimmy break off the attack! There are not enough lances to get all three of them, so it doesn't matter. Break off the attack and proceed to Owens Valley before someone was killed. Jimmy didn't like it, but complied with his instructions. The Simians watched without expressions and turned again to continue their journey to their Lord Gord.

* Amy *

She had been monitoring Jimmy's progress as he traveled and on the third day he saw Simians. There were two traveling loosely together and another three a mile further on. She noticed the second group, even from this distance. These Warriors were coordinated and together, almost in step with each other. Her internal red warning flag was raised and waving high.

She alerted Levi, and he watched as Jimmy and the Lancers dispatched the two Simians in the rear. She watched the other team. They were different, very different. They were not afraid. She watched and decided they were too dangerous. She analyzed everything, looks, clothing, decorations, in an attempt to discover something. Yes, there were differences.

This team was not from the Colorado River colony but didn't look entirely like the teams she had seen before from the Los Angeles colony, either. The form of head covering on these three was golden instead of the typical brown, and they each had an identical gold chain around their neck with an emblem of crossed swords. She decided this was an elite group, probably of Gord's. Maybe they were a special fighting team or more likely personal guards of Gord.

She had a bad premonition about them and did not want Jimmy and his team fighting with these Simians. Even if they could defeat them, there weren't enough lances to finish them all off, and it wasn't worth the risk if they could not get them all. There was the premonition of this Simian team defeating Jimmy and his Lancers. She told Levi, "Have Jimmy break off the attack." Levi passed on

561

her instructions and Jimmy, reluctantly, went on to the Valley.

After that moment there was no doubt that Gord would know everything about them, and he would probably know that they were already coming. Gord would know everything. Surprise would not be on their side this time. She had never felt more hopeless than at that moment. What could she do?

Gord wouldn't know about the guns, but she couldn't count on them making that strong a difference. They did work, but with the Simians being so dense, the rifleman would have to be close, and close meant danger. Eventually, the rifles would be taken out. The Simians would have to neutralize them. Could she keep the riflemen firing the guns from horseback in order to outrun the Simians and fight a hit and run battle? Would the horses allow that? Maybe she should keep them all together so they could protect each other. She was filled with doubt and confusion.

* Levi *

He was letting Amy have her space. He could see she was confused and concerned. He tried to comfort her when he could, but she was trying to pretend everything was fine. Amy knew he was there for her when she needed him, and he also knew she would come to him soon, if for nothing more than to be emotionally held. It was beginning to affect him also. Where he was joyful and happy before, now he was tense and anxious, and it was growing stronger the closer they got to Victorville.

He was thankful to have Iron Eyes and Al traveling at his side and very pleased to have Moon at his side again. He needed some space too and maybe something to occupy his time so he gave up his horse and joined Moon on the ground for a run. He told Iron Eyes and Al that he and Moon were going on ahead to survey the area. They were gone at a quick jog, leaving Iron Eyes and Al looking at each other.

The effort required by Amy to maintain his body while he and Moon jogged these few miles seemed to bring Amy out of her self-pity mode. He didn't like to see her in that kind of mood; it was negative and, if allowed to continue, could destroy their will to survive. Amy agreed, smiled at him, and resumed her normal self. He returned her smile.

He wanted to go to Barstow, then on to Victorville ahead of the armies and look at the potential battleground. They would need to know the terrain and watch for advantages to use in the battle. They would need every advantage they could think of or invent, and he was trying to get Amy back into gear.

As they traveled he asked Amy, "Have you discovered any other talents like telekinesis or others that can be used against the Simians?"

She said, "I really hadn't thought much about it."

Levi said, "Well think about it, because I believe you have many more talents, and we just might need them." He had long suspected that Amy had limitless powers but was holding herself back with self-imposed restrictions. She had only developed and grown new powers when she was challenged to do so, and he was the one challenging her. Hell, he was the only one that knew about her. What could he do now, and what could she do? He had no idea. He said, "Amy, just remember that when things look hopeless reach down deep inside yourself. You will find the answer and strength there."

* Amy *

Levi was right. She was feeling sorry for herself. She was afraid of the responsibility and of the upcoming battle. She had to remain focused and do the best she could and take it one day at a time.

When Levi and Moon took off running ahead of the armies, she began to refocus. It took her some time, but she was back to normal, whatever that was, by the time they approached Victorville.

This abandoned town was very much like all the others. It was mostly rubble from fifty years of earthquakes, winds, rains and fires. Some of the larger buildings were still standing but mostly rubble. They circled the crumbling city to view the approach to the mountain pass and Los Angeles. It was much like they expected and remembered from their trip through here after the raid on the Los Angeles Simian colony. There was a flat desert-like approach, then a steep upgrade into the mountains. This would be the place to fight. Once off the desert there were too many obstacles for a horse charge and too many places for the Simians to take cover. It had to be here in the open. They had to wait here for the Simian army to come to them.

Levi wanted to go on up into the mountains as they waited. He wanted roast turkey, pig and he wanted to hunt. He was implying that he wanted to keep her occupied so she wouldn't get depressed again, and that was all right. She suspected, also, it was because he took off from the army without taking any food with him and didn't want to admit he had come down with a case of the "dumb ass", as Levi would say. She was only too happy to point that fact out to the shit head. They both were laughing.

Jimmy had made it to the Owens Valley and discovered some good news. Jimmy was greeted as a returning hero. They knew the news was good because of Jimmy's smile. They did indeed hear the story of the battle in great detail from a developing master storyteller. The story was well received with jubilation and praise for Levi and the armies. They couldn't believe their good fortune. The truth was fantastic, but when Jimmy got through telling it, it was, well, masterful.

When Jimmy passed on the instruction about the lances and information for the timetable, he was met with smiles. They had already anticipated the need and had prepared the lances. They said they had enough for two wars. They had even built more wagons, which were already loaded and ready to depart. Now that they had a destination they could be gone in the morning. Regrettably, it would be slow since the wagons would have to be pulled by cattle, since they didn't have enough bulls. That wouldn't matter since they were already days ahead of schedule. The tradesmen had also noticed their small mobile lance wagon and were already busily putting some together from ready parts. Jimmy was so proud and impressed with his tribe, and so was she. The Human spirit never ceased to amaze her.

* Gord *

His massive body shook with rage at the news. One of his personal guard patrols had returned from their mission. They were smart and stood by the door ready to run if necessary as they answered questions. They had brought some survivors from the desert battle to present to him. His guard had been smart, they let the survivors tell their story first, and he had quickly killed them in anger. Having calmed down, he now listened to the guards' report from the door. They had interrogated several of the survivors, had even seen part of the battle, and were confronted by two teams of the Humans riding horses and carrying long spears.

Listening intently to the report, he stopped them often to ask questions. This Human that leads the Human armies was interesting. This must be the one that his colony had been talking about. This Human had reportedly killed many Warriors in single combat and was gaining respect, if not fear, among his Warriors. He didn't like that one bit. As the Supreme Leader, Gord was the name they should respect and fear exclusively, and would have it.

The more he heard, the more he hated this Human. This animal had led a Human army against a Simian army and won decisively, defeated their Sword Master in single combat, defeated the colony leader in single combat and had a personal guard of runt Simians, His runt Simians. This was becoming very personal to him. The anger was barely in control, and his huge body shook with the effort to control his rage.

He listened and learned the fighting techniques of the charging horses, the splinters that killed and the use of the Human's strange bent weapon. He listened and planned and when he was ready called the generals. He outlined the battle plans and issued orders for armaments and weapons. The marching orders were given. They were going after the Humans and defeat them and kill this Human leader that had caused so much trouble, and HE would kill the leader personally.

* Levi *

He shared Amy's pride in Jimmy and the Owens Valley people. They had anticipated the need and effectively moved up the timetable. The lances would be en route by tomorrow morning and be in Victorville within five days. They contacted Dawn and notified her of what had been accomplished and that it would no longer be necessary to take the wagons on to Owens Valley. It was just in time, because they had reached Barstow and the point of separation. With this good fortune, they would proceed directly to Victorville and would be there by tomorrow and make a semi-permanent camp there.

He and Moon were heading up into the pass and mountains to hunt. He said he wanted some roast turkey, but Amy didn't buy that. She knew he

567

had forgotten to bring food and was trying to hide that fact, and she was right.

He headed up the steep pass on old Interstate 15 headed toward Los Angeles. It wasn't long before they had a plump turkey, but Moon wanted something more substantial. Moon was growing tired of beef and kept hunting until he came out of the brush with a hog. Good, he was hungry for some ham too. They camped in the mountains and enjoyed the cooler temperature for a change. In the morning they lounged around and waited for the armies to settle in around Victorville before coming down.

As they descended out of the mountains, Amy seemed quiet and reserved. He wondered if she was going back into depression.

Amy said, "No, he comes,"

Levi had to ask, "Who is this he?"

Amy was silent for a moment and said, "GORD comes. He is preparing and will be coming to this place in four days."

He wondered how the hell she could know that but was already realizing she had a vision. She just knew things many times, and this was one of those times. She also didn't have to tell him that Gord knew everything. He wouldn't be coming unless he did. This was not good news, but at least they had four days.

Amy moved into her battle mode and started instructing him on all the things that needed to be done. Most had already been taken care of, but he contacted his communication team and passed on the information Amy had revealed. Jimmy was on the road with the lances already and should be here

568

in four days, but would pick up the pace. Al and Iron Eyes were relieved that this was now confirmed as the battle site so they began preparations, which included pits like those used in Owens Valley successfully. These would serve as traps and escape routes for the charging Lancers. Unfortunately, the moon would be full this time of month preventing any night-time attack opportunity. It looked like they had used up all their good fortune in the first battle.

Moon's Simian colony was positioned well to the rear. There was some thought to leave them at Barstow, but if they lost this battle, it wouldn't matter where they were. This was an all or nothing venture, and everyone knew it. Most however, didn't realize just how bad this one was going to be.

* Amy *

Levi had said they used up all their luck in the first battle. He was usually very positive, but she didn't think he meant it as negative, just a comment. In truth they had already had lots of luck. The tribe had made the lances early, Gord had not launched an attack previous and her vision was total this time. Any of these could have spelled doom for them. Yes, they had been lucky.

She knew Gord was coming. It was one of the mental abilities Dr. Sheldon had told her about in the TOMORROW file. She didn't yet understand it, but accepted the visions, as Levi called them, and it was complete this time. She had a schedule to follow.

It was now the moment of truth for the Human armies, Levi, her and the Human race. They had been preparing for four days, but now the Simian army was pouring down the mountain onto the highway.

Levi was positioned on a small hill toward the rear and center so she could look upon the battlefield. Moon and his group were positioned around him acting as personal guards. Dawn, Al and his entire army were positioned to the east, and Iron Eyes, Jimmy and his whole army were positioned to the west. Fred was riding with the bowmen and riflemen. They all had horses, but the riflemen were not trying to shoot from horseback.

The battle plan was to wait and see how Gord wanted to play this out. Gord had the first move. Gord brought his army completely down out of the high mountain pass and spread them in a semicircle with the mountains to their back. They were not in three-unit teams. They were in a line, side by side, each Warrior protecting the one adjacent. They would have to be spread out for the Lancers to be effective.

She observed some differences the Simian. The front-line Warriors had long spears along with the standard broadsword that they normally carried. They also had bags of something strapped to their waists. She wondered what that might be but knew they would find out soon enough. She noticed that some had shields, not all but many. Yes, there were many differences, and her internal warning was going off.

The Simian Army waited, not anxious to move forward. She launched the riflemen. They rode

570

forward, each with a second rider, dismounted and let the second rider hold their horse reins, while they shot. They shot rapid-fire and aimed at every third Simian. The Simians fell, but the vacant spots were immediately filled from behind and no gaps were left. They continued to shoot until that section of the Simian line charged the riflemen. They shot some of them but not enough, forcing the riflemen to retreat to their horses and ride away. There were about twenty-five Simians down from the rifles. That was a good start. Runners were spreading out from the center, where Gord could be seen towering over the others.

Levi gave the order to launch another attack. The riflemen rode in again, but before they could dismount, they were charged, forcing them to retreat. Gord was a smart one with total control over his army. She then sent the riflemen at the end groups, to attack the tails of the front lines curving around on both sides. The riflemen were again charged by Simians carrying shields, forcing them to again retreat, but Lancers attacked the extended patrol. This was more successful, and the Lancers were able to kill the patrol. The shields repelled the first lance, but the second and third drove home. Again, more runners with orders from Gord, and the ends moved back into the main body, presenting no opportunity to continue that kind of attack.

Again the Simians waited. She launched the Lancers with bolos. She had to get the Simian army stretched thin to be able to launch a Lancer attack. As the Lancers charged swinging the bolos over their heads, the Warriors brought their spears or shields forward to catch the bolos. Some still tangled with the Simians, but most just twisted around the spears or bounced off. The Simians were ready for this type of attack and had made it ineffective. "Damn Gord!"

This time she waited for Gord. It appeared a standoff, as the minutes passed. Then as the armies faced each other, Gord issued an order and a yellow flag was waved. The front two lines of the Simian army charged in a continuous line. She had anticipated that and issued her orders. Both divisions of her armies charged but not head-on as Gord might have expected. They charged from the ends, both converging on the middle and turning out at the center. The grazing attack maintained a continuous charging line of lances. It worked perfectly! It was like a saw cutting into a log and they had no defense.

It was over in minutes. Gord issued orders and a red flag was waved. The charging Simians fell back in retreat, but they left another twenty of their number dead.

The Lancers had lost two so far. Pleased with that move, they cheered as they circled back, spreading out once again to face the Simian army. So far so good!

* Levi *

He could never get used to staying out of the battle. He wanted to fight with the troops but also saw how effective the coordinated attack and defense was working, and the coordination couldn't happen without him. There were forty-five dead Simians, and that was far more than he could have killed alone. He accepted it as being necessary, but he would always feel uncomfortable about staying out of the battle while others took the risks.

Amy was brilliant as always, but this was not coming easily. With an army of more than seven hundred Warriors, 45 dead wasn't much of a dent. Most of her attacks had been tests that failed. The rifles were not as effective as they had hoped, and the bolos were useless. The lances were effective, but the Simian defense was strange. That last attack had been perfectly executed, but the Simians would learn from that. Already, they could see Gord issuing orders and runners delivering them.

Again, the first two lines of Simians charged, and again Amy issued orders for the grazing attack. As the Lancers charged along the advancing line taking out Simians, a large penetrating force of Warriors advanced quickly into the center, making a wedge against the advancing Lancers. The wedge cut off the retreat down the center and made a head-on confrontation. What was Gord doing? The Lancers had no choice but to charge into the wedge, while trying to continue a slow turn away from them to the escape route. The Lancers bunched up to make a charge. As the Lancers approached, the Simians pulled something out of the bags they had been carrying and began throwing them. Lancers and horses began going down along the whole line. The damned Simians were throwing rocks and throwing them hard and straight! The power of the impact was mortal. The Lancers turned and bolted for freedom toward the center perimeter, making a hole through the Simians. It was costly in lives, but an opening was made and the Lancers bolted through and continued circling as before, to re-establish their lines.

* Amy *

She saw it coming but far too late. The Lancers had started their charge when she saw the Simians bulge out in the center to make a wall to meet the charges from both sides. It was a gutsy move but a good one. She hadn't expected the rocks either. It was logical to use rocks as a weapon if you were a Simian. She was horrified she hadn't anticipated it. The Simian's exceptional strength made even a rock hit with more than sufficient force to kill or wound a Human and even a horse. The Lancers and horses were going down from the blows. She saw Wolf point to the center and wave a charge. Wolf led the charge and went down, but his fellow Lancers continued the charge, forfeiting their lives to deplete the Simians of rocks. The Lancers fought their way forward until they began connecting with their lances and making kills. The Simians started pulling back as the Lancers began going through, now taking out the remaining Simians blocking them.

She was crying now at the loss of Wolf and so many of the people she knew. Her mistake had cost them their lives. She saw Humans lying all over the battlefield, and she sobbed. How could she handle these emotions? She wanted to die.

She became aware that Levi was screaming at her, and calmed some to listen.

Levi was screaming, "Damn it, Amy, wake the fuck up and get hold of herself. You are not responsible for their deaths. It is unfortunate, but

574

they wanted to be here and chose to fight. This is what happens in war. People die! Your brilliance is responsible for them being alive today. By all rights everyone should be dead already anyway. You are needed NOW to keep the others alive! Remember, I love you no matter what."

He was right of course. She was being emotional, but she needed to mourn the losses and try to accept it. She forced the emotions down inside to control them, and as she did, she idly thought that this was how mental disorders were caused. Emotions should be released, not held inside, but she would psychoanalyze herself later.

Okay, now she watched the full charge of the Simians. She told the armies to hold the line and wait as bait to draw them forward. She ordered the riflemen to the ends and the bowmen to the center. As one, the entire Simian front line charged directly into the blue markers indicating the hidden pits. The Simians poured into the pits along the whole front, while the riflemen and bowmen held the open breaks in the pits. Yes, she had anticipated this! The charge was broken, and seventy-five Warrior Simians had died in the pits or by bullets and arrows.

The only problem now was that she had no more surprises to release. Gord now knew where the pits and perimeters were, and would simply go around. Gord would launch a charge now, and it would be effective. It was time to withdraw and live to fight another day. She was about to issue those orders and argue with Levi, when she saw Moon walking calmly out onto the battlefield alone. What the hell was he up to?

He was very proud of Wolf. He had sacrificed his life leading the breakthrough for the other Lancers. He was very proud of these men and so was Amy, but she was getting emotional and was about to lose it. "This can't happen right now Amy. You are needed." He talked loudly to get her attention. He chewed on her to wake her up, then talked fast to explain and persuade her to understand and not to accept the guilt. Like the old T-shirt said, "SHIT HAPPENS," live with it. She responded, but before he pushed her back into the battle, he reminded her, "I love you." He was rewarded with a weak, sad smile. She returned her focus to the battle.

As the Lancers made their retreat, the Simian army charged. They all came as a wave. The golden hair was bouncing and gave the impression of a ripe wheat field in a summer storm. It was frightening yet hypnotic. The Simians charged as a line across the distance, they could be seen approaching the blue markers on the ground. The Lancers waited as the Simian's charge reached full speed. Suddenly, the front line disappeared into the hidden pits with screeches of pain and death. Some of the second line fell also, either from the momentum or being pushed from behind. The charge broke up suddenly, except for the center and end sections that didn't have the traps. Riflemen shot the advancing Simians on each end, and the Lancers charged the remaining confused Simians, and quickly dispatched those that made it past the barrier. The bowmen took out the charging Simians coming through the center. It was an agonizing death, then the bowmen retrieved their arrows and retreated back into the line.

If it hadn't been for the pits impaling the charging Simians, the war would have ended right there. The Lancers would have been in full retreat, assuming they would have had the time. As it was, the pits broke the brilliantly timed charge and cost the Simians many dead. Unfortunately, the previous surprise action by the Simians of the center defense had killed almost as many Lancers. Only the sacrifice of those Lancers that opened up the hole prevented it from being much worse. Actually, it could have been devastating if the Lancers had been trapped against the pits without an escape through the center.

Amy was finished though and wanted to withdraw.

She said, "It is hopeless."

She had done everything, and this was the best it was going to get. The only thing left was to run and draw them into the desert and hope for a mistake. She had already asked him to send a runner to Moon and his Simians telling them to run. He was not yet ready to give up. Amy always came through when she was challenged, but he didn't see much to do either, so she was winning him over. He was about to give in when they noticed Moon walking out into the battlefield. He was alone and walked toward the Simians proud and erect. What the hell was Moon doing?

Neither he nor Amy could figure out what Moon was doing, but the Warrior Simian army waited. He stopped in the space between the armies

577

and screeched out a challenge. Oh, shit, no, not that. Moon had seen the dilemma Levi was in and decided to do what he could. Moon challenged Gord to combat calling Gord the son of some animal he had no idea what it was, but the reaction was immediate. Gord screeched insults back at Moon. The deep eerie squeal reverberated over the battlefield sending goose bumps over his body and fear into the pit of his stomach.

* Gord *

He was furious at the turn of events in the battle. These frail and stupid Humans had hurt his army and his pride. It was a mistake ordering that last charge. The pits had been a brilliant and well-planned strategy, and he had fallen into the trap. This Human had outsmarted him. He, the Supreme Leader, had been made to look foolish in front of his army, and he was enraged. He grabbed a Warrior that stood too close and tore him apart, throwing the lifeless parts across the gathering space around him. The Humans could not win against him but had killed some valuable Warriors. He would finish this now. He would circle the pit area and attack. He would follow them to the end of this miserable planet to kill them. He would have his revenge and he would kill this Human.

Just as he was about to issue the orders, he saw a Simian walking out from the Human army. He had heard there were runts Simians with the Humans, and now he saw one. So the stories were true. What did this runt want? The runt walked out into the middle of the field and screamed a challenge. TO HIM! A runt Simian wanted to challenge HIM to a fight? This was ridiculous, but the runt said it in front of his entire army, and it used insults that could not be ignored. His anger flared again as he screeched insults in return. He wanted to kill this insignificant runt, but he would never lower himself to fight a runt. He fumed and his anger was very close to being out of control. Suddenly, he stopped and stood still for a moment, and then a grinning sneer came upon his face.

He walked out onto the battlefield and stood. Silence fell upon the armies. After a few moments, he screeched his reply, "I will not honor a runt with a challenge fight. I will offer the Human leader the opportunity to fight, the Human that has supposedly killed thirty-five Simian Warriors in combat, the Human that defeated the Sword Master of the fallen Simian colony in single combat, the Human that defeated the leader of the fallen colony in single combat, the Human that led a raid on my colony, the Human that led the defeat of a Simian army and the Human that stands against me now. I will offer this Human the honor of fighting me for the leadership of my colony." At this he laughed in a screeching, reverberating, evil squeal that echoed through the battlefield. He had the attention of all and loved it and then stood waiting in silence for the reply he knew would come, because he had no choice.

* Amy *

She couldn't believe what Moon said. When he challenged Gord, it shocked her. In reality, it was a

579

smart move but suicide to the challenger. Even from this distance she could see that Gord towered over the other Simians. He was huge! She could see that Gord was agitated by Moon's challenge but settled down and was calm when he walked out onto the battlefield. She was thinking and calculating Moon's chances against Gord. It was a total surprise to her when Gord challenged Levi. "Oh my ... God no!" Gord continued to cite Levi's accomplishments, building him up. It was obvious that Gord was talking to his army now. The bigger he could make Levi, the more important Gord would be when he defeated Levi.

Levi went tense immediately but continued to translate to the others what was being said. She had never really known Levi to have fear before, but he was afraid now. Everything hinged on this combat, the future of the Human race, their love, their very life, the lives of these armies, all the families that looked to him for salvation, the future of the Technical Simians, hell everything. She knew death didn't scare him, not that he wanted to die anymore, but this was a tremendous amount of pressure and this Simian was huge.

She was transmitting Levi's translation to Dawn, Fred and Jimmy who were announcing the translations to the armies. As the words became known to the Humans an initial gasp could be heard, followed by silence.

She knew Levi would accept the challenge, and really, there was no choice. Gord also knew Levi had no choice. Levi would not be able to lose face in front of his own army. They would cease to follow him. Gord had offered the leadership of the colony to Levi if he won. What did that mean? He would ask Moon when they went onto the field.

She was looking at Levi and he was looking back. He smiled and shrugged.

Levi said, "Those Arizona hills look very good to me right now."

She smiled back. He stood and began walking toward Moon and destiny.

* Levi *

He walked through his army toward Moon, who was still on a hill overlooking the field. When he reached Moon, they communicated in hand signs as Amy had suggested. There might be an advantage to be had. Moon apologized for getting him into this mess, but he shrugged it off. He knew Moon would have fought and died in his stead. He told Moon to accept the challenge, which Moon screeched to Gord. Moon looked over at him, and explained that the code of honor of Simians would keep the fight just between the two of them and fair. Effectively, a truce was made until the outcome of the fight. Both armies closed in around the center area reserved for the combatants.

He stood with Moon, and looked over the gathered group of Simians and his own armies. He accepted the single combat challenge committing his life. He watched, he studied and gathered data. The golden hair glistened on that dirty, creamy-looking, aliens' skin. The Simians sharp, black, teeth were clicking, as they interlaced like gears meshing together. This clicking sound vibrated through the desert straining the nerves of all that heard. Respect and even fear radiated from the gathered Simians. It became more apparent in their agitation at his appearance among them. They hopped around screeching that high-pitched noise. He began walking toward them and the waiting Gord. He showed no fear, while inside he was shook with terror. He knew that the Simian's code of war would ensure that this fight would be a one-on-one fair contest. Damn, what a joke that was. This Simian would make three of him. He said, "Hell, I'm already outnumbered!" This was the biggest golden giant he had ever seen. So much for one-on-one and fair, but if he managed to defeat this leader, this colony would be in chaos. Who knows what could come from it, maybe even survival for the Human race, certainly no less was at stake! The problem here was surviving!

He walked proud and tried to hold back his fear. This was for the benefit of the Humans, his army and also for the benefit of the gathered Simians. Strength, courage and fighting abilities were all that mattered to the Simians. It ruled their lives, society and governed their colonies. Even mating was only allowed for the strongest through combat. Certainly, Gord had risen to the leadership of his colony through combat, and he continued to rule this horde of golden-haired giants in this way.

* Gord *

He had ascended to his leadership position by defeating the previous leader in combat and defending the position from all challengers. This had been easy for him because of his size and

582

aggressiveness. He stood a head above and weighed far more than any other Warrior. He had killed more than fifteen Simians Warriors in single combat challenges and uncounted scores of Humans just for fun over the last forty years he had ruled this Simian occupation site. With the average life span for a Simian at two hundred earth years, he was still very much in his prime at only seventy-five years old. His rule could easily last decades more.

He wanted to fight this Human in single combat to regain the awe he once commanded in his colony. No one had challenged him in more than ten years, and he was anxious to reinforce respect from his colony. How could he do that if no one fought him? Of course, no one had a chance, and most even openly cowered in his presence, but he wanted to show off. He was a bully at heart. He had his army of just over six hundred Simians gathered to watch the slaughter of this stupid Human. It had been more than seven hundred Simians not two hours ago. Yes, he was going to punish this Human. He was going to toy with him, defeat him, then tear and eat his body as he screamed his life away.

Why was he giving this Human the respect and honor of fighting for leadership of the colony? Of course, he had no chance, but rumors of this Human had spread in his colony, which he wanted to end once and for all. Humans were small, weak, and good only for food and minor labor. This Human had been the only exception ... ever. According to rumors, this Human had killed at least thirty-five Simians in combat in the last few months. Unbelievable! Just look at this stupid Human. His body was hairless, except for its head, which had long black hair braided in the back. His hairless skin was bronze from this world's horrid single sun. His body was muscular, but he was small and puny, hardly more than chest high. He wore no armor, and only loose leather coveralls and heavy looking narrow boots. He carried a sword and an odd-looking weapon, the sword was short by his standards, extending no longer than his arm, while the other weapon was even shorter with a spike. This was laughable! He let out his challenge again in a strong loud screech! Too bad this indigenous race of Humans was not intelligent enough to understand their speech. He would like to tell this Human what he was going to do.

* Amy *

If Levi were to survive, it would take all her skills. She strengthened his muscles, making them grow, harden and extended his arms and legs to give him more reach, opened all communication channels and opened his senses. She would need all his sensory inputs if they were to survive this, their greatest test of all. After the past year of sharing Levi's mind and body, she was intimate with the workings of his mind, long since mapped, and she had learned what his body was capable of. She knew this opponent would kill Levi if any of his blows ever solidly connected. Gord was simply too big and too strong! Levi could only win by wits (hers), agility and staying power. Gord would have to be worn down and killed. She needed to make Gord fight, and stay out of reach, while his strength was used up. Levi could never hope to defeat Gord head on.

Amy sensed that Levi needed confidence and Gord needed to lose some of his arrogance. She helped Levi to show no fear. She straightened his back, put a wicked smile on his face and calmed him by altering chemical balances. She reassured him that she was with him, encouraged him, reminded him what they had already accomplished together and assured him that she would provide the direction to his mind and body. "Trust me Levi," she comforted, "you are my life too. If you die, so do my will and heart, so we must survive and our love must survive!" Levi responded with a mental smile and touch.

She watched Gord as Levi approached. The brute was confident and huge. He was not the least bit intimidated by "Levi the legend". The meaty lips were curled up at the edges. Was this bastard actually smiling? She watched, analyzed and planned. She sent the message and instructions to Levi and he spoke. As Levi walked toward Gord, he spoke in the screeching language of the Simian saying, "I have come to kill you and remove your fat head from your body as a trophy." The reaction was immediate. The gathering of Simians all clicked their teeth in agitation and hopped from leg to leg, while Gord's reaction was more pronounced. His red blazing eyes opened wide in amazement, showing instant black momentarily. The smile was gone. They had scored a tactical advantage.

* Levi *

Oh he loved it when he threatened Gord in his own language. The reaction was beautiful as shock hit Gord's face. Reaching the center, he stood and continued the mocking. He was removing the Sword Masters chain and golden sword and waved it at him, then handed it to Moon. He removed the locket from Dr. Sheldon and handed it to Moon. He then took the necklace of gleaming black Simian teeth and waved it at Gord. He told Gord, "I am going to put one of your huge, ugly teeth in the center of this necklace after I pry it from your lifeless head." Gord screeched in anger, but did not charge. Oh, Gord was a cool one and would not be goaded into doing something he was not ready to do.

Even while he taunted this Goliath he kept thinking that if he lost this battle, it was all over. There would be a banquet tonight and he would be the main course, along with any other Human they desired. Humm! If this was Goliath, he must be David, and he didn't have a sling. He wondered absent-mindedly why Amy hadn't thought of that. Damn, this fear was paralyzing him!

Without him the Human army would run like rabbits. They were brave, but never had they won a battle against a Simian until he and Amy had shown them the way. Mostly, he had done the majority of the killing initially, but his new friends and followers had taken strength from his victories and had gained courage and, most of all, hope! They would carry on, but it would just be a matter of time before they were discovered and killed.

He was trying to think positive, but he was having a hard time. Amy was encouraging him and it was comforting to have her with him in his mind. He looked deeply at her and told her again, "I love you," and "Let's do it, Amy."

* Amy *

She loved his bravado and show he performed for Gord. Gord was mad for sure but controlled. Levi was stripped to the waist, except for the straps over his shoulders, and ready. She was also ready and alert as they approached. Levi swung his weapons in an intricate pattern as he approached. His last chance to run was gone. He was committed.

Gord had a broad sword in his right hand and a short sword in his left. As Levi got closer, Gord suddenly attacked. Levi rolled and came up behind Gord but immediately had to roll again to dodge a backward thrust from the short sword. Damn, that was close. For a giant, Gord moved very fast. Gord was relentless also and continued the attack with refined skills. She had Levi moving from side to side, rolling, jumping, twisting, running and once even doing a back flip to avoid a double attack. Levi's battle was totally defensive and unable to launch any offense. Gord was very good, much better than she had ever seen.

They fought on, and Gord showed no sign of tiring, and Levi had only inflicted a cut to Gord's foot and a slight puncture in his arm. Gord was fast, very strong and extremely frustrated at his inability to touch Levi with anything. Gord had a fighting style she had never seen or heard of before and it was very effective.

She needed to keep Levi out of reach until Gord tired. At least he was showing some signs of breathing heavy. Just hang on and don't take any chances, Levi. How long will it take? They had been fighting for over an hour now. Maybe another fifteen minutes might make the difference. Gord stopped and backed up. He realized what Levi was doing and wasn't going to have any of that. He smirked at Levi and just when she thought he was going to slow down, he attacked again with a different style. This was too sudden and took her by surprise, as he struck overhead with the sword and simultaneously swept his foot across Levi's legs. Levi went down, but rolled out from under the descending sword. As fast as he was, he could not get out of the reach of Gord's kick. It was vicious and caught Levi in the side, breaking ribs and paralyzing him in pain. Gord hopped around in excitement and dropped his swords to roughly pick Levi up in his hands. He held Levi high over his head, showing him to the gathered audience.

He screeched his victory to the crowd and telling them, "I am going to eat this Human while he yet lives, just as I promised."

* Levi *

The fight had gone on for what seemed like hours. Amy had kept him from being touched by this giant, but it was very close. Many times he felt the blade brush his skin and always felt the wind. Gord was good at this business, but Amy was a little faster. He was unable to inflict any wounds on Gord, except a slight puncture in his arm and once

588

he had brushed his foot, possibly cutting the skin. So far his fight was mostly defensive. Amy said Gord was wearing down, and he did notice him breathing heavy.

The fight had been a combination of him and Amy working together. They had been symbiotic so long that they worked in concert, sharing thoughts and actions as one. As usual, however, he felt Amy react much faster than he, and took over his body control on many occasions during this fight. This was by far the hardest battle he had ever faced.

Just when they thought Gord was pulling back to catch his breath, he attacked again. He had relaxed for just a split second before Gord's sudden attack. It was the edge Gord needed to win. Gord's foot swept his legs out from under him. He hit the ground and felt Amy roll him and the brush of Gord's sword just missing as he rolled. The giant Simian's foot caught him in the side, and he knew it was over then. The kick shattered his side and organs and he fell limp. He was still awake but helpless to do anything. Gord did not kill him immediately as he had expected, but when he heard Gord say what he was going to do, he wished for a quick death.

He called to Amy, "Help me die quickly." He wanted death to end the agony he was experiencing and the suffering and humiliation yet to come. It was over and they had failed.

* Amy *

She had learned a lesson from Levi long ago. Never give up, "Never!" Her massive intellect was churning options, but found none. Suddenly, she remembered the conversation she had with Levi. He had said, "I believe you have limitless powers and are restricted only by your self-imposed limits." He had challenged her saying, "In time of need, reach down deep inside, and you will find the answers and the strength." Levi had challenged her so many times to reach new levels. He made her develop telekinesis, made her develop astral projection, made her learn emotions, made her fall in love with him and made her become real, to experience true physical love. He had made her do these things simply by challenging her with life and death situations. She had always, as Levi said, reached down and found answers and the strength to remain alive. Was this the end of everything, or could she now find a new level?

She looked now and saw the locket in her mind and remembered the TOMORROW file. The file compiled by her mother Dr. Sheldon told of incredible mental powers. What powers? She answered her own question, "ALL POWERS!" Remove the limits and do what needs to be done, and she knew what to do.

Yes, she had anger and used that anger to kindle something warm inside her. It grew and expanded and became a force. She gathered energy from around Levi, and she was with Levi. The force expanded into Levi and around him like an aura of energy. His body healed, and he became something he had never been before. They totally merged! He became both Amy and Levi, and he/she/they became as one (ASONE) and became infinitely more powerful. He looked the same, but they became a new being in that instant.

This had all taken place in seconds as Gord held Levi, now ASONE, in the air telling the gathered armies what he was going to do. The new entity watched, turned in Gord's grasp, and kicked him in the chin. It was a staggering blow, causing Gord to drop them as it fell backwards to the ground. Never had any opponent ever knocked him to the ground.

ASONE stood, feeling the incredible power flow through them and watched as Gord staggered to his feet. Shock registered on his face, but he shook his head and charged them. He was as a child in their grasp as they grabbed his hand, spun him around and threw him like a doll over their head and to the ground. It was a judo throw with LOTS of power and attitude. ASONE walked to him, grabbed him by the neck and picked him up by the throat. Gord screeched in pain as they began to slap him across the face. Gord back up as they slapped him over and over, reducing him to a whimpering child. Only then did they break his neck, ending the pathetic screeching.

True to Levi's promise, they took Gord's own sword, chopped his head off and took one of his massive black teeth for his trophy necklace, as he had told the crowd he would do. There was total silence from the gathered crowd. They had witnessed something so incredible it could not be believed.

As the heat of the battle calmed in their body, they collapsed on the ground. After a few moments, Levi was Levi again, and she returned to being

Amy, but they had won. Together, as the new entity, ASONE, they had defeated the Supreme Leader, and in doing so, had saved their lives, the lives of their friends, and just maybe the Earth.

CHAPTER 20
(THE FUTURE)

* Levi *

As he lay on the ground, he was trying to remember what had happened. Oh, not what had been done to Gord, but what had happened to him/her/them? He had been awaiting the most horrible death he could imagine, and he had been afraid. Amy was silent as he waited, but suddenly he felt the power. It felt warm, then hot as it grew. The energy filled him, surrounded him, merging with him. It was familiar. He felt it before. It was Amy. It was really her. He felt the energy grow inside him, then he felt the mind, the entire mind. The most incredible intellect he could ever imagine was merging with him. He was losing his identity and becoming someone or something new. He was Amy, and he was Levi, they were one, and they were unbelievably powerful. Together they killed Gord with incredible ease but together didn't explain it. It was more than that, much more. When they were fighting Gord at the end, there had been only a single entity, neither Amy nor him. He was a participant but almost as an observer without control, yet he, or whatever he was, was in control. That was hard to explain, but the power and intellect had been awesome and Gord's might paled in comparison, almost insignificant.

After the fight and need for the mutated power entity had passed, they separated again and the sudden release of power forced him into blackness. He probably wasn't out long and quickly recovered.

He asked Amy what she had done, but she really didn't know.

Amy said, "I only did what you told me to do. You told me to reach down deep inside myself and find the answers and strength. I was angry and it turned into a force. I did it or at least started it, but don't know how or even if I can do it again."

He realized they would have to spend a lifetime discovering this new capability together, but the urgency right now was to take care of business. Looking around, he saw awe and open-mouthed stares coming from everyone. The Humans were still staring wide eyed, and the Simians were totally expressionless and completely still, except for some uncontrollable shaking. No one moved when he turned, looking in all directions. The silence was unnerving.

From behind he sensed movement and turned to see Moon pushing the crowd aside as he walked toward Levi. Moon removed the leadership medallion from Gord's headless body and held it high for everyone to see. He screeched the victory of Levi and announced that Levi had won the leadership of the Los Angeles Simian colony through combat.

Moon loudly screeched, "Do any of you challenge Levi's right?"

After what they had just seen, no one was about to challenge him, but Moon waited several long minutes anyway, just to make a point. The silence was uncomfortable to the Simians especially. You could see the internal decisions being made in the

Simians' minds, as they began to hang their heads and look at the ground. Moon then turned and placed the huge chain around Levi's neck.

After a few quiet moments the Simian captains came forward and looked down at him. Each bowed, gave their name and pledged their loyalty to him. After the five sub leaders finished and stepped back, he spoke in the Simian language, which shocked them again. In a booming screeching voice he told the Simian armies, "Stand down from battle and go home. I will talk to the captains, and they will pass my instructions on to you. I have two standing orders for all of you to remember. Simians will not harm or eat Humans, and you will make war on any Simian or Simian colony that does."

* Amy *

She was in shock. She had no idea what she had done nor any idea if she could do it again. All she knew was that she did what had to be done at the moment, and it was incredible. She had been whole, plus she had been one with Levi. She had a body that was hers, well theirs, but they were one, totally merged with each other. They had reached a new level of existence, and ten like Gord could not stand against them at that moment.

The only way to explain what had happened was to imagine mental energy transformed into a physical force and then merge that force with Levi's physical body. Not only did their physical presence merge, but mental energies and capacities as well. She ceased to be Amy any longer. They became a new, more powerful being, held together by anger and purpose. They became an incredibly powerful physical rage that destroyed their enemy.

When the anger died so did the union and they reverted slowly back to separate identities. It was probably good that they split again, because there was a danger of self-destruction for both of them if the entity had remained united. The new being was totally ruled by rage and logic was absent. What they had done to Gord was cold blooded and malicious. It frightened her. Obviously the crowd of Simians and Humans was stunned by the outcome. The legend of Levi would spread ever faster now, even among the Simians.

Levi had gotten hold of himself more quickly than she did, and was taking care of business, just as she should be doing. What to do with these Simians now, was the question. According to Moon, the Warrior Simians were genetically engineered to fight and intelligence was not a strong point. It was in their make-up to fight and they would continue to do so. The only choice was to pit them against other Simians and let them solve both problems.

She began to help Levi again, calling in all the captains, both Simian and Human. When they were all positioned in a circle, Levi began to give out her plan. "Moon will be my Supreme Leader of all Simians." The captains looked puzzled then angry at that, but Levi added, "I will leave the current captains in command as long as you follow my and Moon's instructions. If you don't like it, I will kill you and replace you with ones that will!" They looked frightened then quickly agreed.

He went on to tell them that the Technical Simians liberated from the Los Angeles colony would return to govern as they once had before the mutiny, except for # 10 who had been put in charge of the remainder of the Colorado River colony. The Los Angeles colony would wage war on the San Diego and Fresno Simian colonies until those were converted or dead. Levi introduced a fearful Fred, explaining that he would return to Los Angeles as his representative, and the Los Angeles Simians would learn the sign language from him. He warned that he would come back and kill them all if any harm came to Fred, or if they failed to follow his or Moon's instructions. He had spoken in Simian, but translated in sign so everyone knew what was being said. Moon spoke to the crowd adding his own version of Levi's instructions and warning that he would be visiting them with Levi often.

* Levi *

Amy was laying out the plans now. She had recovered, but he could tell that she had been shaken. The experience had permanently changed them both, and he sensed that the togetherness they experienced left them closer in some ways. Certainly he could read her thoughts more easily, or, more likely, he understood her better.

She had the Los Angeles Simians all mapped out and it made sense. Let the Warrior Simians fight each other since they were going to fight anyway. Let them fight and diminish their ranks to a manageable number that could be fed. Fred and the rescued Simians would go back with them. That was a very smart move.

Amy decided to take the Colorado River Simian colony back to the Mojave Desert settlement, establish their colony in the northern valleys and teach them how to raise cattle for their food. Amy wanted the Technical Simians to work with her in research of the Simian technology. This is where Amy wanted to spend time trying to discover the technical knowledge of the Simians, while Moon continued indoctrinating the Los Angeles Simians in what was expected from them.

He told the gathered assembly about the plans Amy had presented. Al looked shocked but said nothing. He believed that after what his friends had seen, none of them would, or could, ever get close to him again. They no longer considered him as one of them. He believed that the people felt he was something above them ... unapproachable. Hopefully, that would change in time; he valued their friendship, especially Iron Eyes, Al, and Jimmy. Nothing would change Moon, however. He was positive of that. Moon would be his friend for life and had made that abundantly clear many times. He was proud to have Moon as his friend but wanted the others' friendship as well.

He reminded them, "The threat of the Simians is far from over. The cruelty of the Warrior Simians and oppression of the Human race is far from over and the war has just begun." The Simians must learn, "EARTH IS OURS." He did emphasize that rest was in order for a while to allow word of their accomplishments to spread from area to area. Humans needed hope to continue, time to organize resistance groups and the opportunity to join their struggle to reclaim Earth.

In the next few months he would travel the world and identify all the locations of Simian colonies and come back to organize a strategy to defeat them. He reminded them that the existing Simian colonies must be defeated before the next migration came to earth. The threat would be a hundred-fold worse, and if defenses were not established prior to this next migration, the end of all humanity would not be long in coming.

He painted a bleak picture, but then it was a bleak future, and they needed to understand that. The whole world needed to know that, and it was up to him and Amy to spread the word.

He had given a lot of thought to how they would travel. It could be done as they had so many times already. They could astral project to anywhere. They possibly might even travel to the Simian's home world, or the space in between to check on the status of the next wave of the Simian invasion, but he had been thinking about another challenge for Amy.

After all she had done, he was positive she was capable of almost anything. If she set her incredible mind to accomplish something, she could do it, and he wanted her to physically transport his body to new locations. He believed she could do it and maybe even take others with them. He was thinking that Amy always needed a new challenge in order to grow. He was smiling when he thought this, and Amy looked a little perturbed and stuck her tongue out at him.

* Amy *

599

Levi was such a shit. She was still emotionally shaken from the experience they had just shared, and here he was trying to expand her mind even more. The problem was that it actually was a good idea, and she thought she could do it. That idea of traveling the world was his idea too and was also a good one. She wondered, when they merged did he pick up some of her intelligence? It was Levi's turn to grin.

She was worried about the next migration of Simians headed for earth. She believed that she must either re-establish some of the earth's lost technology if she could, or utilize some of the Simian's technology in to combat the next migration. They would be coming by the tens of thousands. Without technology to fight them in space, they were still doomed. She was excited about exploring the Simian technology and hopeful. The next few months would be a lot of hard work, but very stimulating.

One thing she knew for sure was that before all this work began, she and Levi were going off together for a while. They had earned the right to just enjoy each other and relax for a while. Maybe she would transport them, as Levi had mentioned, to a real place or maybe it would just be in their minds. Maybe she would invent an island, a home, and all the comforts of a civilization long past for them to enjoy. This could be their private place and time of rest before they continued to wage war against the Simians to take back the Earth.

She also wondered if she should tell him of the premonitions she was having or wait until after a rest, if they had time.

ABOUT THE AUTHOR

Gary W. Babb is originally from Oklahoma, but work has taken him from South Florida to South Texas and finally to Southern California where he has spent the last twenty years. Prior to beginning his career in Cable TV, he served in the Navy in communications and traveled the world. His education includes Western Oklahoma State College, Amarillo College, DeVry Institute of Technology, National Cable Television Institute (NCTI), and currently holds an FCC license in communication.

As a business executive, his previous writing experience has been directed toward letters, memos, proposals, and reports, however he has always enjoyed the magic that can be spun with words to sell, convince, or inform those targeted. Earth is Ours is his first effort toward spinning a tale of entertainment. The telling of this story and weaving the words provides a very exciting and entertaining saga, which won "Best Fantasy/SciFi 2005" from the San Diego Book Awards Association. The sequel, Target Earth, won "Finalist 2006" from the same awards. The third of this series is Earth's Dragons.